your
PERFECT
year

# your PERFECT Year

*a novel*

## CHARLOTTE LUCAS

TRANSLATED BY ALISON LAYLAND

**amazon** crossing

Text copyright © 2016 by Charlotte Lucas
Translation copyright © 2019 by Alison Layland
All rights reserved.

Previously published as *Dein perfektes Jahr* by Bastei Lübbe AG, Köln, in Germany in 2016. Translated from German by Alison Layland. First published in English by AmazonCrossing in 2019.

Published by AmazonCrossing, Seattle

www.apub.com

Amazon, the Amazon logo, and AmazonCrossing are trademarks of Amazon.com, Inc., or its affiliates.

ISBN-13: 9781542004619
ISBN-10: 1542004616

Cover design by Kimberly Glyder

Printed in the United States of America

*For my mother, Dagmar Helga Lorenz*
*(March 8, 1945–October 20, 2015),*
*and for my father, Volker Lorenz.*

*You can't give your life more days,*
*but you can give your days more life.*

—Anonymous

*Rather a trite proverb.*

—Jonathan N. Grief

Editor, *Hamburg News*
Hamburg, December 31
By email

Dear Editorial Team,

Before offering you my season's greetings and wishing you a successful start to the new year, I would briefly like to draw your attention to a few errors in your current edition.

On page 18, your review of the new movie *Glacial Age* refers to: "Henning Fuhrmann (33), who became a household name in recent years as the star of a number of popular TV shows . . ."

I feel I should point out that, according to Wikipedia, Henning Fuhrmann's birthday is today—that is, December 31. This means that he is no longer 33 but is now 34, which appears to have escaped your attention. Moreover, the way you have formulated the phrase could relegate his acting career to the past; correctly, it should state: ". . . who has become a household name in recent years as the star of a number of popular TV shows . . ."

Also, on the last page, an article about our beloved Elbphilharmonie concert hall has been given the title: "Now their really going for it!" Whether this is a typo or a grammatical error, there really is no excuse.

If I may refer you to your own style guide:

> "Their" is the possessive form of the third-person plural pronoun "they." Beware of the commonly misused homophones "there" (which means "in that place" or "in that way") and "they're" (which means "they are").

As ever, I trust you will take these observations in the helpful spirit in which they are intended.

Yours sincerely,
Jonathan N. Grief

# 1

*Jonathan*

**Monday, January 1, 7:12 a.m.**

Jonathan N. Grief was not a happy man. His morning routine had begun as it always did: at precisely six thirty, he had donned his track-suit, defied the freezing temperature, and ridden his mountain bike to the starting point of his daily run around the Outer Alster Lake.

And like every year on the first of January, he was plagued by numerous minor irritations. He shook his head at the remains of fire-crackers and rockets that littered the gray slush and turned every side-walk, cycle track, and footpath into a slippery, ugly mess. He tutted over the sooty, smashed prosecco and beer bottles that must have served as launchpads in the night, with no one apparently deeming it necessary to put them in the recycling afterward. He tried in vain to ignore the thick, murky air that the partying (and, in Jonathan Grief's eyes, irresponsible) citizens of Hamburg had, with their brainless pyrotechnics, transformed into a nightmare of fine-particle pollution that now hovered in a blan-ket of smog over the city, making it hard for him to breathe.

(Now, of course, the New Year's Eve corpses would all be lying, hungover and comatose, in their beds, having written down their resolutions to drink less and stop smoking and shot them into space on noisy rockets at one minute past midnight, before rampaging and running riot into the early hours of the morning, not caring that enough money to put the national economy to rights had gone up in flames.)

But these were not the only things bothering Jonathan Grief.

What outraged him most was that his ex-wife, Tina, had this year, as ever, seen fit to leave a chocolate chimney sweep—that cloying symbol of good luck—on his doorstep sometime in the night, along with a card in which she wished him, as ever, "a happy and successful new year!"

*A happy and successful new year!* As he pounded over the Krugkoppel Bridge, to where the path led down past the Red Dog Café into Alster Park, he increased his speed to fourteen kilometers per hour, every step slapping down onto the sandy surface with a heavy crunch.

*A happy and successful new year!* Jonathan's fitness band now showed a speed of sixteen kilometers per hour and a heart rate of 156 beats a minute. It seemed he was on course to complete his 7.4-kilometer run in record time today. His fastest time to date was 33.29 minutes, and if he continued at this pace, he would top it.

But as he drew near the Anglo-German Club, his pace slowed again. *Crazy.* Why should he get so upset about Tina's thoughtless "attention" that he'd endanger his health and put himself at risk of a pulled muscle? They'd been separated for five years, so there was no reason that a stupid chocolate figurine should get him into such a state.

Yes, he had loved Tina. Very much, even. And yes, after more than seven years of marriage, she had left him for his (former) best friend, Thomas Burg, and filed for divorce. Jonathan had always thought they were happy together. It seemed Tina had viewed things differently.

She had protested that the problem had nothing to do with Jonathan—but anyone with half a brain knows that the problem always *does* have something to do with oneself.

Jonathan still wondered exactly what it could be. He had done all he could to give Tina heaven on earth. He'd bought her a beautiful urban villa right by Innocentia Park in the upscale Harvestehude district and had it renovated to her taste; she even had her own sanctuary, including bathroom and dressing room! He'd enabled her to give up her hated job as graphic designer in an advertising agency and live the life of leisure she had always wished for.

He had satisfied her every wish almost before she'd thought of it. A pretty dress, a stylish handbag, jewelry, or a new car—Tina only had to hint that she liked something, and it was hers.

It had been a carefree life without any responsibilities. Grief & Son Books—the publishing house Jonathan had taken over from his father, Wolfgang—was excellently run by a CEO, so all he had to do was put in the occasional appearance as figurehead and make his presence felt at the launches of the more prestigious publications. Jonathan and Tina had enjoyed the most expensive vacations in the most exclusive places, and they'd been sought-after guests at every worthwhile society event in Hamburg, all without the worry that their private lives could fall victim to the popular press.

Tina had fully enjoyed her life with Jonathan, had suggested ever more exotic travel destinations, worn ever more elegant designer clothes, and regularly redecorated every room in their villa.

On occasion he had wondered whether she might be getting a little bored—especially with material things. She constantly repeated the same old refrain: for a long time, she had been looking for "something more," a something she was unable to put her finger on, to express, at least to Jonathan. She had tried running groups (at his recommendation) and also language courses, guitar lessons, qigong, tennis, and a range of other activities, without keeping any of them up for long. He had gone so far as to tackle the subject of children more emphatically (not only in word, but also in deed), despite Tina's protestations that things were perfect for them as a couple.

And then she had seen a therapist.

Even now, Jonathan had no idea what they discussed at her weekly sessions, since she had not deemed it necessary to tell him about it. But whatever it was, clearly Tina had finally found her indefinable "something more" with Thomas, whom Jonathan had known since their school days and who was responsible for marketing at Grief & Son Books.

Had been responsible. After their separation, Thomas had chosen to give his notice, send Tina back to her job at the agency, and set up home with her in a three-room apartment in that hipsters' paradise, the Schanze quarter.

Thinking about the two of them now, Jonathan shook his head in disbelief, his eyes fixed on his neon-yellow Nike sneakers. Wrecking their lives like that in the name of love! And now Tina, of all people, was wishing him "a happy and successful new year"? Oh, the irony!

Jonathan snorted loudly, sending breath from his mouth in a steaming cloud. He *was* successful, and he was also—damn it—happy!

He quickened his pace again, so that by the time he approached the dog park, he almost stumbled and only just managed to avoid one of the little parcels left behind by the unruly mutts unleashed on the unsuspecting population by their nice masters and mistresses.

He stopped, gasping for breath, and rummaged in his sports armband which, alongside his iPhone and key, also held a supply of rustling plastic bags. He took one out, slid it over his hand, gingerly picked up a dog turd, and carried it at arm's length to the nearest garbage can. Not his favorite occupation, but someone had to do it.

Yet another of the myriad concerns that plagued Jonathan Grief on a daily basis. All those "animal lovers" who kept a mastiff or a trendy Weimaraner in the most undignified conditions in their chic old-town apartments, but who couldn't even be bothered to clean up the little heaps of shit left behind when the poor critters were dragged around the district for their obligatory five minutes.

He was already composing another email in his mind to the editor of the *Hamburg News*: Something would really have to be done in the new year about this deplorable state of affairs! The legislators ought to stir themselves and impose harsher fines so that every single citizen understood that their own freedom ended where it affected someone else's life. Dog waste on the sole of a shoe—to Jonathan, that was the ultimate nuisance. Some things really stank.

As he set off again, gradually building up speed, he threw a quick glance at the Run app on his smartphone, and his next irritation was discovering that this brief pause had ruined his statistics. He wished he could get his hands on the dog-mess miscreants and their damned curs—he'd have a thing or two to say to them!

His thoughts drifted back to Tina and Thomas. Tina and Thomas, who probably called each other "Tini" and "Tommy," or maybe even "Bunnykins" and "Honey Bear." Who knew?

He imagined them sitting together in the evenings over a bottle of red wine from the discount store in their cramped Ikea living room, while their daughter, Tabea, slept peacefully in her crib crafted from hand-stained organic larch wood—indeed, life as a couple had clearly not been the peak of perfection after all, since barely more than thirty seconds after announcing her relationship with Thomas, Tina had brought a baby into the world.

Tini, Tommy, and Tabbi, then—as corny as Huey, Dewey, and Louie.

Huey, Dewey, and Louie in their cheap digs. And Huey and Dewey saw fit to worry about Jonathan and wonder how he was doing, so much so that Huey said she simply had to pop down to the nearest Aldi, they had such cute chocolate chimney sweeps there, she could buy one and place it on her ex's doorstep with a card, since she'd left him in such a mean-spirited way and broken his heart.

"Good idea, Huey!" Dewey exclaimed. "While you're there, please could you get a bottle of Chateau de Clochard? It's on sale—we're celebrating this evening!"

7

Jonathan's fitness band showed a heart rate of 172 beats per minute. He had to slow down if he didn't want to risk his health. He had no idea what was wrong with him that morning, until he gritted his teeth and admitted that he still found it impossible to stay calm when he thought of Tina and her new life.

And that was despite twenty hours with a life coach who had assured him that the problem could be rooted out after just two or three sessions. Another incompetent for Jonathan to let off steam thinking about. The fellow had even had the nerve to accuse him of failing to cooperate when Jonathan pointed out shortcomings in his coaching methods.

It was amazing, Jonathan thought as he jogged past "Bodo's Boat's" (could no one get apostrophes right?), how Tina hadn't asked for anything when they'd split up. No settlement, no alimony, no share of the house, nothing.

According to Jonathan's lawyers, she could have demanded all those and a whole lot more. But she had simply left just as she had arrived almost eight years before then—with nothing to her name and an underpaying job as a graphic designer. Despite his protests, she'd even left behind the Mini and all the jewelry he had given her.

Jonathan's life coach had been of the opinion that Tina had shown manners and a sense of decency, since she'd been the one who wanted the divorce. He had consulted the coach in order to put the whole sorry business behind him as quickly as possible, not to listen to an unsolicited opinion on his ex's behavior—and besides, Jonathan saw things a little differently: Tina's refusal to accept everything she was legally entitled to was not some dignified farewell, but merely a small-minded, insidious dig to let him know that she didn't need him. Him or his money. Especially not that.

Twenty minutes later, Jonathan reached the fitness court by the lakeside, sweating and panting uncharacteristically hard. He finished his circuit here every morning with a thirty-minute workout on the small course, which at this hour was rarely occupied. Especially not on New Year's morning, when he seemed to be the only person left on earth.

First he did fifty push-ups, then fifty sit-ups, followed by fifty chin-ups. He repeated the whole procedure three times. Now he felt ready to face the day. As usual, when he surveyed his body after the final cooldown, he was happy to note that his daily exercise program was truly paying off.

He was in outstanding shape for his forty-two years. He could easily compete with any man in his midtwenties when it came to fitness—and, weighing in at 175 pounds at a height of just under six foot three, he was slimmer than most men his age. Not like Thomas, who even back in their school days had suffered a definite tendency toward love handles.

Also unlike the love of Tina's life, Jonathan had thick black hair, with just a few gray strands at the temples. An interesting contrast with his blue eyes, as Tina had always said. A contrast that no longer seemed to interest her, since Thomas, poor guy, had in his twenties developed a shiny, greasy bald pate which only the most loving gaze could see as a receding hairline. And his eyes were some color between muddy brown and glassy green.

Jonathan allowed himself a brief smile as he thought of the many times he had buoyed his former best friend's confidence when Thomas complained of his failures with women.

It made the present situation all the more unfair. He thought of Thomas's words of wisdom at the time: "Don't take it so badly, buddy—you have to let the best man win!" *The best man—ha!* Since handing in his notice, Thomas had gone into business as a "freelance marketing consultant," a polite way of saying *unemployed*; he could hardly be called successful.

*Enough!* Before Jonathan could yet again lose himself in the mire of wondering why on earth Tina had left him for this guy, whom any objective observer would call worse, he set his shoulders and marched over to his mountain bike, locked in its usual place at the fitness-court entrance.

He stopped short when he saw a black bag dangling from the handlebar of his bike. How did that get there? Had someone forgotten it? Why was it on his mountain bike? *Weird.* Or was this another of Tina's little "attentions"? Had she decided to start lying in wait for him during his morning training sessions?

He unhitched the bag from his handlebar. It was relatively light and, when he looked closer, was little more than a zipped nylon shopping bag, the kind that could be bought packed down into a tiny bundle at any supermarket checkout.

Jonathan wondered whether to open it. It didn't belong to him. But he didn't pause for long. Someone had hung it on his bicycle, so he tugged the zipper open and looked inside.

He saw a thick book bound in dark-blue leather. Jonathan took it into his hand and turned it one way, then the other. The book was new, and the leather looked high quality, with white stitching at the seams and a tab with a snap fastener to hold it closed.

It was a Filofax, something very few people—at least, few people under the age of fifty—used in this age of iPhones, smart watches, and the rest.

Why would someone hang a bag containing an old-fashioned organizer on the handlebar of his bike?

# 2

*Hannah*

*Two months before:*
*Sunday, October 29, 8:21 a.m.*

Hannah Marx woke and knew she was in love.

But she had no idea with whom.

One thing she did know, which confused her even more, was that it definitely was not her boyfriend, Simon Klamm, whose longed-for marriage proposal had not yet materialized. Granted, her longing remained secret; she had not so much as hinted. But since they'd been a couple for more than four years now, Hannah thought it was high time he asked.

She pushed the duvet back, sat up, and rubbed her eyes in bewilderment. What a strange dream! She could still feel the pleasant tingling running through her whole body, and a quick look in her bedside mirror showed that her cheeks were flushed. Her red hair was sticking out wildly as though she had spent the whole night tossing her head from side to side on the pillow, and even her lips glowed red and full, as though she'd been smooching for hours.

There was no doubt about it—Hannah had fallen in love in her sleep. No, it wasn't an erotic dream about some stranger; not at all. Nor was it a dream involving someone she knew—no former coworker, neighbor, or any of her friends.

In fact, she couldn't recall a man featuring in her dream at all. Only a feeling. That unequivocal feeling of being in love. Of warmth and security, of butterflies in the stomach, of an excess of joy and high spirits, laughter and craziness. And of happiness. Yes, happiness.

With a sigh, she swung her legs over the side of the bed and sat for a moment. She shook her head in the hope it might bring her thoughts to order and exorcise the nebulous dream. However pleasant the feeling might have been, she needed a clear head this morning. This was going to be an important day.

She and her best friend and business partner, Lisa, had spent the last six months renovating a run-down store on Eppendorfer Weg. They'd drawn up business plans for their new enterprise, filled out endless forms, created a website, and even put together a considerable amount of start-up capital through crowdfunding (with a little help from Hannah's and Lisa's parents). They'd considered the marketing and advertising, had flyers printed, decorated Lisa's old VW microbus with their self-designed logo, and, and, and . . .

And now the time had come: at two o'clock they would be opening Little Rascals Events—"The Entertainment Agency for Kids"—with a massive children's party.

Hannah had been mulling over the idea for ages, if only in the back of her mind. It had been her dream for almost ten years—since the day she and Lisa had begun working at a daycare center together after training as assistants in the same class.

They had both been disillusioned by the low pay and terrible working hours, but Hannah had been even more troubled by the conditions affecting the center—never enough money for suitable toys and craft materials, trips, or additional activities like gymnastics or music lessons; a sandpit in the playground that was usually empty; and a ramshackle swing that was a veritable safety hazard.

Her little charges' parents had always been willing to make financial contributions, but for reasons that were a mystery to Hannah and Lisa, the center's management had refused point-blank to countenance such measures.

Three moves to different daycare facilities proved to be no more satisfactory; the two women found similar deplorable circumstances everywhere. And so Hannah had for a long time harbored the dream of starting up a business of her own. She wanted to achieve something independent of managers and committees, something that would bring true happiness into children's lives. Parents would be willing to pay for the privilege of knowing that their little ones were in good, caring hands.

And so, about six months ago, after turning the idea over and over in her mind, Hannah had brought Lisa in on her plans. She had convinced her they had to try it—they should hand in their notice and make a go of the Little Rascals project. Otherwise, they'd never know if it would have been a success. As those well-known words of wisdom put it: At the ends of their lives, they would regret not the things they'd done, but the things they *hadn't* done.

When Hannah told Simon about their project, he had called it "utter madness," something "the world doesn't need," adding that to leave a secure job because of "some silly notion" was a "kamikaze mission." And in his eyes, adding insult to injury by "dragging your friend into it" was "the height of irresponsibility."

At times he had come close to convincing her to give in. Maybe when she'd been feeling particularly stressed as she battled with the business plan after a demanding day's work, or when she was suddenly beset by the fear that, should things go wrong, she was putting not only her own future in the balance, but Lisa's as well.

Over time, Hannah had managed to convince both herself and her doomsayer of a boyfriend that although the country might be stricken by a crisis in the media industry—which directly affected Simon, who'd recently been laid off from his job as an editor with the *Hamburg News*—her idea for a children's events agency was nevertheless a brilliant one.

Before handing in their notices, she and Lisa had circulated a skillfully drafted questionnaire among more than two hundred parents. With the results, they had determined exactly what the moms and dads were looking for and how much they were prepared to pay for a service that enabled them to continue to work or improve their golf handicap free of the responsibility of childcare.

The information obtained from this exercise—and the sensational success of the crowdfunding venture—had ultimately impressed even Simon. He had to admit to Hannah that even if her idea only half fulfilled her expectations, it would easily cover the pittance she'd earned as a daycare assistant.

The basic plan was simple: she and Lisa would offer their program of events in the afternoons, early evenings, and especially on weekends, appealing to families who needed or wanted care for their little ones outside the normal daycare business hours. At an unbeatable hourly rate of six euros per child—substantially less than minimum wage—they were cheaper than any babysitter but would be offering so much more than paid TV watching or the kind of basic childcare that was deemed a success if none of the children met their end.

Little Rascals was going to be different, offering all kinds of fun and activities. They even intended to host a sleepover party once a month, giving parents the opportunity for a night on the town followed by a longed-for good night's sleep. If demand proved high, they'd hold these events more often.

They figured that with a group of no more than sixteen children between three and six years old, making eight for each of them—a veritable luxury compared with their previous jobs, where they had often been called on to look after twenty or more little scamps between the two of them—they could do some fantastic things. They could take the little ones on outings to adventure playgrounds and to see the deer in the Niendorfer Gehege woods, to visit the fire department or the police, to the Hamburg bookshops, to the banks of the Elbe with a trip on the ferry (which was free for kids), to the educational playground at the university, and, in summer, to the large public wading pool in the city park. The possibilities were endless.

And on the inevitable rainy days for which Hamburg was renowned, they had plenty of space for indoor activities at their premises on Eppendorfer Weg. Past the front of the building with its reception area, coatroom, kitchenette, and bathroom with changing table, the heart of Little Rascals was the large play area covering more than four hundred square feet. Over recent weeks, Lisa and Hannah had spent many long hours transforming this space into a children's paradise, complete with wall bars and thick gym mats; play shop and kitchen; a knights' castle with a slide (bought on eBay for a song); a cozy corner with cushions, rugs, music CDs, and picture books; a play tent; dress-up box; pedal cars; building blocks; craft materials; face paints; and so much more.

In the little courtyard out back of the unit were the requisite sand-box with cover and a brand-new swing (also from eBay, for two songs), a hammock donated by Hannah's parents, a few miniature pieces of garden furniture, and all kinds of sand utensils from Lisa's parents.

The ultimate achievement—Hannah was particularly proud of herself here—was that she had been taking guitar lessons for two months so she could make music with the kids. Meanwhile, Lisa had been busy with a "mini-disco," choreographing simple routines to children's favorites that their charges would know and love.

In short, they had thought of absolutely everything a child's heart could desire. And they firmly believed in the success of Little Rascals—no, they were *convinced* of it.

Neither of them saw a problem with the evening and weekend working hours. Lisa had been single for more than three years—even though she was a real beauty, and not only in Hannah's opinion. She was five foot five and blessed with womanly curves, and her short, tousled black hair simply cried out to be ruffled. Her eyes were a warm amber color, and she had a beautiful natural pout that many a cosmetic surgeon would kill to reproduce. Despite all this, no suitable men had shown up in Lisa's life for a long time, which she insisted didn't bother her in the slightest. Hannah wasn't sure she believed her, but at least Lisa's independence was ideal for the Little Rascals venture.

As far as Hannah was concerned, she had until recently thought she was free to work evenings and weekends, because Simon usually sat long into the night at his editor's desk. It would therefore have fit in perfectly and might even have benefited their relationship. Sadly, that was no longer the case, although she hoped things would change soon. And in the meantime, he had assured Hannah that he saw no problem with her devoting her energy entirely to her project. She wasn't sure whether his declaration pleased or worried her, but she had ultimately opted for being pleased, because she believed optimism was generally the best attitude.

"You can even join in!" Hannah had suggested to Simon. "At least you have the time now. And if things go well, sooner or later we'll need more people."

"So what would I do?" he had asked. "Should I be perfecting my face-painting skills? Or throwing on a clown costume when I get up in the mornings?"

"Hardly." Hannah laughed. "You'd be more like some kind of Pennywise, sending the kids running off, screaming." She shuddered at the very thought of the clown out of Stephen King's *It*.

"What's your problem?" Simon put on a pained expression. "I *love* children!"

"Yes. Especially when they're asleep. Or when you can just about make them out on the far horizon with a pair of binoculars."

"Huh!" He flung both arms around her and hugged her to him. "Wait till we have our own children. You'll see what an amazing dad I'll be!"

"You think so?" Hannah giggled as his embrace tickled her.

But his words made her heart leap. *Our own children.* Had he really meant it? Until that moment she'd assumed that he never gave a thought to marriage or even living together—she merely had the key to Simon's apartment in the Hohenfelde district, which he had ceremoniously handed to her six months ago.

"Yes"—Simon placed a kiss on the tip of her nose—"I'm certain."

"I can't wait to see that."

"Well, as for Little Rascals," he said, disappointing her with the change of subject, "I'll be happy to support you with any advice I can give, and of course I'll take charge of your publicity. But beyond that, I think I'd rather look for a new job in journalism."

"Or maybe you can get around to writing that bestseller of yours."

"I'm really not in the right frame of mind for that at the moment."

"Why not? Surely it's the perfect time for it?"

"Perfect?"

"Well, you're not doing anything else, and you're on paid leave for six months. Together with your severance pay, the money will last you at least a year. You're a lucky devil, if you ask me!"

"Lucky?" Simon stared at her in stupefaction.

"Sitting around the house on full pay with the opportunity to write your masterpiece? It's the stuff of dreams!"

"You know, sometimes your Pollyanna attitude really gets on my nerves. You don't know what it means to have a crisis-ridden profession like mine."

Hannah considered it wise to say no more, even if she felt it was a little unjust of Simon to forget so completely how often she had been shattered by the conditions at the daycare centers. And how he himself had until recently liked to tell her how much more responsibility her job had than his, and how unfair it was that she earned so little from it.

She bit down on the remark that maybe it was time for Simon to consider an alternative profession if the situation in the media industry was oh-so-terrible. Because he had a point: she had no idea what it meant to lose one's perspective on life as well as a job that was supposed to be secure. She was "only" a daycare assistant and had chosen on-the-job training rather than getting a degree—but in its place she did possess an unshakable optimism.

This was evidenced by, among other things, Hannah's firm conviction that for every door that shut another one opened—often an even better one. But she didn't say that to Simon, as the most she could expect would be a snarled "Spare me your calendar mottoes."

No, she was better off leaving Simon to drag himself up from his bad patch by himself. And until he did, he would have to stew in his own juices—or maybe invest in a clown outfit as a precautionary measure . . .

Getting a new job with a newspaper, a magazine, or even an online publication had so far proved difficult. Although he'd applied to them all, including the tiniest outfits, he had received nothing but rejections for weeks. It was hardly morale boosting for him, and it was a cause of quite some tension between him and Hannah.

While she was working away enthusiastically on setting up her new business, Simon's mood deteriorated with every day he was stuck at home without a job. Secretly, she longed for a return to the early days of their relationship, when Simon had swept her off her feet with his sense of humor, his charm, and his loving manner.

Hannah had met him when he turned up at the daycare center one day to collect his godson. They'd both immediately sensed the chemistry between them, and in the following weeks Simon had turned up rather often to pick up the boy. By chance or intentionally? Probably the latter, as after two months or so, he had asked her if she could maybe see her way to meeting him outside work.

"If I have to wait until I have my own children to see you more often, it could take a while," he had said. "And that would mean the ideal time had passed us by." Hannah still broke into a dreamy smile when she thought of the way Simon had asked her out.

She recalled their first date, when Simon had invited her for a picnic on the banks of the Elbe. What a grand affair! The sun had pulled out all the stops on that wonderful day in May, and they had sat at the waterside on his picnic blanket from morning until late into the evening, watching the ships go by and sampling the delicacies Simon had brought in two oversized bags—ice-cold white wine and champagne, fruit juices and water, fruit and cheese, ciabatta, a selection of salads, homemade schnitzel (yes, homemade!), prosciutto, prawns, a range of antipasti—Simon had gone all out to impress Hannah.

He even had the correct glasses, cutlery, crockery, and linen napkins in his bag, and as twilight descended he'd lit two flaming torches. Hannah had felt as if she were at a gala dinner. Well, a gala dinner on the riverbank.

Then there was Simon's first kiss . . . So shy and sweet, so nervous and trembly; his heart was beating so wildly that she could feel it.

And when they weren't kissing, he'd talked. He spoke without pause, telling her about his exciting job with the newspaper, about his plans for a round-the-world trip he wanted to embark on one day, and about the great novel he wanted to write as soon as he found the time. He had laughed and joked and told stories, putting Hannah fully under his spell. Such zest for life, such passion, such enthusiasm!

But not long after that day, Simon's mother, Hilde, had died of cancer, as had his father some ten years before her, and just as he was recovering from the shock, trouble had begun to brew in the media industry.

When his editorial colleagues began having to clear their desks, Simon became ever more uncertain, despondent, and pessimistic, until in the end his greatest fear—that he, too, would be laid off—became reality. Sometimes Hannah couldn't help thinking he might have talked his layoff into being, so often had he wrung his hands over the possibility.

And ever since then, he'd been at odds with his fate, with his life, and with himself. Hannah could understand it to a point, but at times it got on her nerves, however reluctant she was to admit it. She was convinced that Simon's attitude was making things worse. He might well have thought it nonsense, but Hannah was sure that a person's fortune was colored by their attitude: optimists experienced good things, pessimists bad, and the universe would give those who expected the worst what they deserved.

In Hannah's opinion, viewed objectively, Simon had no real grounds for complaint. He was young and healthy, and he had a roof over his head, enough to eat, and a loving partner by his side—a lot of people in the world were much worse off than that! She really hoped he'd return to his old self as soon as he found a new job.

Hannah's telephone rang, chasing away her thoughts of Simon. She jumped up from the bed and raced to the phone on its little table in the hall of her small two-room apartment in Lokstedt.

"Morning!" Lisa yelled into her ear as soon as Hannah picked up.

"Morning." Hannah suppressed a yawn.

"Oh, I'm sorry, did I wake you?"

"Don't be ridiculous! I've been awake for hours," she fibbed.

"Glad to hear it. I was beginning to worry—"

"No, everything's fine."

"So? Are you ready?"

"Am I ready? I can't wait!"

"Shall we meet there at ten?"

"Let's say nine thirty. I'm just about ready."

"Good, then I'll get a move on," Lisa said. "Do you want me to pick anything up on my way?"

"If you're there before me, could you collect the doughnuts and cookies we ordered from Wernicke's?" The bakery was conveniently located across the street from Little Rascals.

"I certainly will," Lisa said. "Anything else?"

Hannah thought for a moment. "No, I think we've got everything. Simon still has the crates of drinks, the helium tank for the balloons, and the paper plates in his car."

"When's he coming?"

"He said he'd be there around eleven."

"Okay," Lisa said. "See you soon!"

"See you."

No sooner had Hannah hung up than she felt the return of that strange tingling from her dream. She smiled with relief as at last she knew what it was. Yes, she'd fallen in love during the night; that much was clear.

In love with the idea that from now on she was no longer a menial, underpaid employee, but Hannah Marx, proud co-owner of Little Rascals Events!

# 3

*Jonathan*

**Monday, January 1, 8:18 a.m.**

Jonathan looked around surreptitiously, his conscience nagging him. It was madness, of course, but he felt a strange prickling at the back of his neck as though someone were watching him.

But no one was there. Not a soul was out walking the banks of the Alster; only a few cars made their way slowly along the nearby street.

Jonathan was about to take another look at the diary when he caught sight of a movement out of the corner of his eye. Someone *was* there! Down by the river, half-hidden behind the Alsterperle restaurant, he could just make out a shadowy figure. Without thinking, Jonathan sprinted toward it, the Filofax and the bag tucked securely under his arm.

He had not been mistaken—someone was standing right by the water's edge, their back turned.

"Hello!" Jonathan called, slightly breathless.

Nothing happened. The figure remained motionless, looking out over the river, apparently deep in thought.

"Hey!" Jonathan called, louder this time, but there was still no reaction. He slowed his pace, near enough now to see that it was a tall, slim man.

To his astonishment, Jonathan saw that he was wearing nothing but jeans, sneakers, and a red-and-white-striped T-shirt. Not exactly appropriate clothing for a New Year's walk by the river in below-freezing temperatures.

"Hello?" Jonathan said once more, approaching the stranger and gently tapping him on the shoulder.

The man jumped and turned. He was young—Jonathan estimated in his early or mid thirties—and stared at Jonathan in wide-eyed shock. The metal-framed glasses on his nose made his green eyes look slightly larger than life. "Are you talking to me?"

"Yes," Jonathan panted.

"What do you want?"

"Is this yours?" Jonathan held the bag and the diary out under the man's nose. He suddenly felt stupid. What must he look like to this guy? A breathless jogger races up to him and shoves a mystery item at him—it must seem pretty bizarre.

As he expected, the man shook his head, slowly at first and then more decisively. "No," he said, "it's not mine."

"Um, that's a pity," Jonathan replied. He felt obliged to explain. "I found it on my bike. I mean, the bag was hanging on the handlebar of my bike, and this diary was in it." As if to prove it, he indicated the Filofax again. "And because there was no one in sight except you, I thought I'd ask if you'd maybe . . ." He ran out of words.

"Left it on the handlebar of your bicycle?" The young man finished Jonathan's sentence with a smile.

"Um, yes, that."

Another shake of the head, this time with visible amusement. "Sorry. I didn't leave anything on your bike." His smile spread to a broad grin.

Jonathan was suddenly reminded of Harry Potter. The glasses and the slightly tousled brown hair, combined with the man's youthful face, made the comparison inevitable.

For a fraction of a second, Jonathan had a mental image of his father, Wolfgang. Until dementia had laid him low and sent him into a nursing home, he had never stopped talking about the biggest humiliation of his life—the time when, toward the end of the 1990s, he had contemptuously turned down publication of the German version of the adventures of the young Hogwarts pupil, despite all his editorial staff advocating strongly for the book. Wolfgang Grief had called the millionfold sales of Harry Potter "a sign of the cultural decline of the West!" and "a stain on civilized literature."

He would still sometimes refer to it even now, in the more lucid moments during his son's every-other-week visits to his luxury care home on the Elbe. Jonathan secretly thought it was rather strange that even in his present condition, his father had nothing better to do than get worked up about a harmless children's book. He hoped that, if it came to it, things would be different in his case—in terms of both dementia and bemoaning missed opportunities.

During those moments of painful recall, Jonathan would soothe his father with the news that Grief & Son Books' young adult titles were doing excellently, thank you, without Harry Potter—a barefaced lie, since Jonathan had shut down the Children's-and-YA program three years ago on the advice of his CEO, Markus Bode, as it was diluting their brand too much, blurring the characteristics that made it unique. They would be better off, the CEO said, concentrating on their core specialty: ambitious literature and quality nonfiction, so popular with bookshops and the wealthier target readers.

Bode stressed again and again how much "concentrating on what really matters" had paid off, and Jonathan could only agree. The money rolled in and profits were good. And it had made them the darlings of the press critics.

"Are you all right?" The young man's voice snapped Jonathan back to reality. A pretty cold reality now, since he'd been standing motionless on the windy bank of the Alster for some time.

"Yes, yes," he hastened to assure the man. "I, uh, so . . . I'm just finding it strange that someone hung this bag on my bicycle."

The man smiled again and shrugged indifferently. "You think it could be a New Year's gift?"

"Could be," Jonathan replied without great conviction. "Maybe. So, well . . ." He stood there indecisively for a moment longer before nodding to the young man. "Well, it was worth asking. Happy New Year to you."

"You too!" Before the man finished speaking, he had turned back to the Alster and resumed his previous activity—looking out in silence over the smooth surface of the water.

Jonathan fidgeted before finally starting back toward his bike.

"It's a pity."

It was said so quietly that Jonathan wasn't sure if he'd misheard. He stopped and turned. The man on the bank was now looking at him again.

"I'm sorry?" Jonathan asked.

"It's a pity, isn't it?" said Harry Potter's double.

"What's a pity?" Jonathan retraced his steps toward the man.

He nodded in the direction of the Alster. "That the swans have gone."

"The swans?"

"They've all been taken to spend the winter on the Mühlenteich lake and won't be brought back until spring." He sighed. "A real shame."

"Hmm." Jonathan had no idea what to say. Because the young man was looking at him so expectantly, he added a dutiful "Yes, such a shame."

"I love watching the swans."

"Yes." Jonathan nodded, though without real understanding. "They're beautiful birds."

"Spiritual creatures," Harry Potter said, so quietly that once again Jonathan hardly caught his words. "They symbolize light, purity, and perfection; they represent transcendence."

"Hmm," Jonathan said again, "fascinating." He was about to ask how the young man knew this, when he realized why he was standing around in the cold on this New Year's morning in such light clothing.

Drugs!

Harry Potter must have rung in the New Year in rather a lively fashion and was now in a world of his own. Jonathan wondered if it was his duty as a good citizen to call an ambulance or the police, so that someone could take care of the fellow before he fell prey to hypothermia or did anything stupid. But he pushed the thought aside. The man seemed to be thinking clearly. Even if he said some strange things and looked a bit pale, he didn't seem completely out of it.

"You could go walk on the banks of the Mühlenteich," Jonathan suggested. "I mean, if you're so eager to see the swans. It's not far."

The man nodded, his smile never fading. "Yes. Yes, that's an excellent idea." He turned and trudged away, without saying whether or not he was heading for the Mühlenteich.

Jonathan stood for a moment more and stared after the oddball. Whatever substance Harry Potter had taken, it seemed to be having quite an effect.

Jonathan walked back to his bike, deep in thought. *Swans. Spiritual creatures. Transcendence. Crazy!*

It wasn't until he had reached his mountain bike that it occurred to him that he was still carrying the Filofax and the bag. What was he going to do with them?

Once more he looked around, but apart from the young man—who was already some distance away, climbing the embankment toward the road—there was still no one in sight.

Jonathan went over to one of the benches near the fitness area and sat down. He ran his hands over the leather cover of the diary. Hesitated a moment.

Then, finally, snapped open the tab and looked inside the little book.

*Your Perfect Year*

Those words, handwritten with a fountain pen, graced the first page in lavishly looped letters. Nothing else. No name or address, as were usually found in these personal organizers.

Jonathan leafed through a few pages and reached January 1 of this virginal year he was on the threshold of. The layout of the organizer was generous, with one day to a page, although these pages were filled with writing. The title was written in the same beautiful calligraphy:

*January 1*

*You can't give your life more days,*

*but you can give your days more life.*

*Anonymous proverb.*

Jonathan winced. What a trite calendar motto! Only *"Carpe diem!"* was worse. Or those often-quoted and flogged-to-death words misattributed to Charlie Chaplin, to the effect that a day without laughter was a day wasted. As corny as a cheap greeting card! And yet he found the whole thing fascinating, so he read the rest of the entry for that day:

*Sleep in until noon. Have your breakfast in bed with H., followed by a walk by the Alster including mulled wine at the Alsterperle.*

*In the afternoon: marathon DVD session. Possible movies:*

*P.S. I Love You*

*The Bucket List*

*The Notebook*

*The Silence of the Lambs*

*Alternative: all episodes of North & South*

*Evening: tagliatelle with cherry tomatoes and grated Parmesan, accompanied by a good bottle of rioja*

*Night: Cuddles, stargazing, whispering sweet nothings*

Jonathan had to laugh. What a choice of movies! What kind of "whispering sweet nothings" would follow *The Silence of the Lambs*? And whether there would be any time left over for eating or cuddling or anything else after all the episodes of *North & South* was extremely doubtful, since the series dragged on for hours.

Years ago, Tina had forced him to sit with her week after week watching the schmaltzy love story between Orry and Madeline—and as he recalled, he'd found the experience about as vile as watching ten chainsaw-massacre movies back-to-back.

His curiosity piqued, he turned the page. He was well aware that it wasn't right, since it was like peeking into someone's private thoughts, but he might as well be hung for a sheep as a lamb. As he skimmed page after page, an undeniable sense of admiration crept up on him. Here was someone who had made the effort to enter something for every single day of the year. All the pages through to December 31 had been filled out. Despite the numerous popular platitudes with which every entry began (*"It is only with the heart that one can see rightly; what is essential is invisible to the eye." —Antoine de Saint-Exupéry*), he couldn't help feeling a degree of respect.

Sometimes the plans were in greater detail, such as on August 25:

*Rent a camper and drive to the seaside at St. Peter-Ording, collect shells on the beach, have a barbecue, and sleep under the stars. Don't forget to take music!*

And there were smaller undertakings, like the one on March 16:

*H.'s birthday!*

*Take H. to the Lütt Café on Haynstrasse in the afternoon and eat cake until it makes us ill.*

On June 21 it simply said:

*First day of summer! Get up at 4:40 to watch the sunrise on the banks of the Elbe!*

As he leafed through, Jonathan felt a strange sadness rising up in him. Partly because this diary clearly wasn't meant for him—for one thing, he didn't know a single "H" apart from his neighbor on the left, Hertha Fahrenkrog. But even if that good woman's birthday were on March 16, she had to be over ninety and lived for no one but her poodle, Daphne. Jonathan could safely rule out the notion of her sitting down every day for weeks and filling out a diary for Jonathan in a spidery copperplate hand (which this wasn't, but which he associated with Hertha Fahrenkrog). And the thought of breakfast in bed . . . no!

In fact, the handwriting was the second reason for that strange feeling of melancholy—Jonathan felt oddly touched by it.

It took a while for him to realize why: the rounded script reminded him of his mother, Sofia, who had divorced his father when Jonathan was ten. Her writing had looked just like this, with all its long, looping tails. Jonathan hadn't thought about her for ages, but as he skimmed the entries, he recalled with painful clarity all the letters and notes she used to leave him throughout the house.

*Good morning, darling, have a lovely day!*—on the breakfast table next to his plate of scrambled eggs and bacon. And later, as he unpacked his sandwiches during the school lunch break, she would always have written *Enjoy!* on the parchment they were wrapped in, adding a heart in red ink. *Don't worry, your next attempt will be better!*—stuck in a schoolbook next to a flunked math test. *Sweet dreams!*—she had tucked the very same wish under his pillow every single evening.

But they were just notes. They didn't change the fact that Jonathan's mother had left not merely his father but him, her only child. Her sweet words had not stopped her from returning to her home near Florence, which she had reluctantly left after meeting Jonathan's father, who'd gone to Italy as a student in the late 1960s.

She had fled over thirty years ago, back to her beautiful, warm homeland, leaving Jonathan behind in the cool north with his equally cool father.

It was Jonathan's well-kept secret that the *N* in his name stood for *Nicolò*. He could almost hear his mother whispering, "Nicolino, my treasure." Right into his ear. *"Ti amo molto. Molto, molto, molto!"*

Well, *molto* or not, she had left. And after three years of her occasional letters, phone calls, and mutual visits, at the height of puberty, Jonathan had told his mother by postcard that as far as he was concerned, from that moment on she could stay where the lemons grew.

He had been astonished to find that she had taken him at his word—he hadn't heard from her since.

And yet here he was, staring at that handwriting, which so strangely reminded him of her.

A raindrop fell on the page, blurring the ink slightly, and Jonathan rubbed his right thumb over it without thinking. He was even more astonished to realize that it wasn't actually raining. How ridiculous!

He quickly snapped the diary shut, shoved it back in the bag, and drew the zipper closed. The best thing would be to leave the book here on the bench, where its owner would be sure to find it if he came looking. He had probably simply dropped the bag on the path nearby, and an observant passerby had hung it on his bicycle, assuming that it belonged there or would be more easily spotted.

Jonathan's hands trembled as he tried to enter the combination of his bike lock. No wonder—he was completely exhausted and hadn't yet had anything to eat. It was high time to go home and enjoy a sumptuous breakfast! He jumped onto his bike and pedaled off, his fitness band showing a pulse of 175 after a few yards.

Three minutes later he stopped pedaling and braked hard, almost propelling himself out of the saddle. *No.* He couldn't. It was wrong to leave the bag lying on a bench, an invitation for any stranger to pick it up.

So he turned. He would take the bag with the Filofax home with him and make the effort to trace its rightful owner. *Yes.* That was it. It seemed the only right thing to do.

# 4

## *Hannah*

***Two months before:***
***Sunday, October 29, 12:47 p.m.***

"If you don't answer the phone *now*, I'm calling the police! Or I'll have a heart attack! Maybe both!" Hannah yelled so loudly into the receiver that Simon, in his apartment over in Hohenfelde, could probably have heard it without a phone line.

"Tell him we'll have the Russian Mafia after him!" Lisa shrieked in the background. "And the Albanians as well!"

"Did you hear that?" Hannah bellowed. "That was Lisa, and she's not amused!" She waited a moment, but no sound came down the line apart from the white noise of the answering machine. Simon wasn't answering his landline, and her attempts to reach him on his cell phone had also failed dismally. Nothing, *nada, niente*—Hannah's boyfriend was nowhere to be found.

In a little over an hour the first visitors would be arriving for the opening party of Little Rascals. Everything was ready, perfectly prepared: the puppet-show people had arrived in good time and were shuffling from foot to foot outside; the two girls hired to do face painting were setting up on a table in the corner; the small bouncy castle had been inflated in the parking lot next to the entrance; the loudspeakers were playing a selection of children's favorites; the side table was groaning beneath the weight of not only the doughnuts and cookies but also a variety of cakes and other treats that Hannah's and Lisa's friends and parents had brought for them—but the five hundred balloons lay flaccid in a bag, and apart from tap water from the little kitchenette and Lisa's lukewarm half bottle of diet cola, there was a serious drought on the drinks front. Without the promised paper plates and cups, it didn't really matter anyway.

"Don't worry, I'll be there no later than eleven, blowing up balloons like there's no tomorrow!" Simon had promised the evening before, when Hannah had complained that he chose to spend the night before her big day not at her place but, as he did so often recently, in his own apartment. "I think I'm coming down with a cold, so I'd be better off having an early night with a hot-water bottle to make sure I'm ready for action in the morning."

*Ready for action! As if.* It was as though the earth had opened up and swallowed him. That in itself was not good. But since he had the helium tank for the balloons, and the plates and cups and drinks for the opening party, it was an absolute catastrophe!

She simply didn't understand it. Simon was normally so reliable. She had been over the moon when he offered to buy the things at the wholesale store, where his press pass still allowed him to shop. "Things are a lot cheaper there," he'd said, "and besides, you won't need to lug heavy bags around. I'll do it. And I'll pay, too—consider it my opening gift to you both."

"What are we going to do now?" Lisa asked. She ran her hands through her short black hair, transforming her tousled style into a just-out-of-bed look.

Hannah shrugged. "No idea."

"Do you think Simon will be offended by that business with the Russian Mafia and the Albanians? It just slipped out."

Hannah rolled her eyes. "You're not seriously worried about whether he'll take offense at your sass, are you?"

"No, of course not," Lisa replied quickly. But Hannah knew she was. She was like that.

"Well," Hannah said, "instead of concerning ourselves with Simon's sensitivities, we'd be better off finding a solution to the drinks problem."

"I could pop back to Wernicke's and see what kinds of water and juice they have. You never know, they might even sell paper plates and cups."

"Do you know how much that would cost? We pay two euros there for a stupid Capri Sun!"

"Do you have a better idea?"

Hannah thought for a moment, then hurried over to the kitchenette and grabbed her coat from the hook. "I'll drive over to Simon's place and see where he's hiding." She hurried past Lisa toward the exit.

"And what am I supposed to do while you're gone?" her friend called after her. "You can't leave me here on my own!"

"You can start blowing up balloons. If you're quick, you can get at least fifty done!"


Fifteen minutes later, Hannah screeched to a halt in her old Twingo outside Simon's apartment on Papenhuder Strasse. She threw the driver's door open and was halfway out when she almost strangled herself on her long scarf, which had wound itself around the steering wheel.

"Haste makes waste, Hannah," she told herself as she tried to release the stubborn fabric from the turn-signal lever. Ten seconds later she had freed herself and got out of the car—this time making every effort to act calmly. She slammed the car door shut and walked up to the redbrick building where Simon lived.

She rang the bell marked "Klamm." And rang again. A third try; this time, long and forcefully. Nothing happened. There was no response to a fourth, fifth, and sixth ring of the bell. Wasn't Simon at home? Where was he? Hadn't he told her that he wasn't feeling well and was going to be tucked up in bed with a hot-water bottle?

Or—the thought crept through her with unexpected fright—maybe Simon wasn't tied up with a "cold," but with something else. Could he be lying under the covers being warmed up by something—or someone—that wasn't a rubber bottle filled with hot water?

No. No question. Simon just wasn't the type. If it came to a sponta-neous fling, he simply wasn't . . . spontaneous enough. It had taken him weeks to ask her out on a date; he definitely wasn't a man to rush things.

But what if it wasn't a spur-of-the-moment fling, but someone he'd known for longer? Hannah tried to ignore the small, malicious voice in her head. It was a crazy notion. Everything had been fine between her and Simon until he lost his job, and in any case, there was no way he would get up to something like that just as she was embarking on her new career. Simon had a sense of decency; that wouldn't be his style at all.

"You've got such an imagination," her mother, Sybille, would say in such situations. Hannah had inherited her mainly positive outlook on life, while her father, Bernhard, was more like Simon, tending to see a bandit behind every bush. That was another of those turns of phrase that Sybille used, laughing, whenever her husband immersed himself in conspiracy theories about their peaceful neighborhood of Rahlstedt.

Bernhard Marx was convinced the Müllers had something against him because of a chance meeting in the supermarket when his neigh-bor's greeting hadn't been as friendly as usual—only to find out a few days later that Herr Müller had lost his glasses and simply hadn't rec-ognized him.

Another time, Hannah's father was convinced that the mailman was holding back a package he was waiting for urgently, out of pure maliciousness. A short while later, Hannah's mother had phoned the sender and discovered that they had not yet put the package in the mail. Sybille would complain to her daughter with exaggerated outrage about this "impossible man" who was slowly driving her "utterly mad."

Hannah cut short her musing about her mismatched parents and pressed the bell a seventh time. And then decided that she had waited for longer than was reasonable and now had every right to use her key and see for herself what had happened to her boyfriend.

Her anger was tempered by an uneasy feeling of concern as she hurried up the stairs to his apartment. Because if Simon was not answering his landline, his cell phone, or the doorbell, either he really wasn't there, had turned deaf overnight—or was dead.

# 5

*Jonathan*

*Monday, January 1, 9:20 a.m.*

After devouring a vanilla protein shake and lean turkey slices on two gluten-free, low-carb rolls, Jonathan sat in his comfy leather armchair by the large bay window in his study, enjoying the wintery view of Innocentia Park.

But the scene was littered not only with the debris of the New Year's Eve celebrations but also with the overflowing waste from his own and the whole neighborhood's recycling bins—they were only emptied every other Monday. The recycling had last been collected on the Monday before Christmas, but it now looked like the whole collection crew had been lying together under the Christmas tree singing "O Come, All Ye Faithful." Sure, everyone was entitled to take some time off for the holidays—but this just would not do.

Shaking his head, Jonathan N. Grief rose from his armchair, walked over to sit at his desk, and opened his laptop. A few minutes later he had called up the website of the Department of Public Works, clicked on the "Contact" button, and begun to write.

Dear Sir or Madam,

As the new year begins, I would like to take this opportunity to inform you that the state of the recycling containers in our beautiful city is currently unacceptable. The containers are overflowing— hardly an attractive advertisement for Hamburg!

I am aware that doubling up on collections to cope with public holidays can cause a certain backlog in emptying the bins, but I would really appreciate it if you would find an emergency solution in this case, one that would benefit both the citizens and taxpayers of the city and your employees.

Yours sincerely,
Jonathan N. Grief
(Resident of Innocentiastrasse, with full bins on my doorstep)

He scanned the text once again, then sent it off with a nod. *Yes, very good. He who hesitates is lost.* He liked to deal with things methodically and quickly; productivity of this kind gave him a warm sense of virtue.

After settling down once again in his armchair, he picked up the Filofax. Instead of losing himself in the quality of the handwriting and the various entries, this time Jonathan concentrated on searching for information that would give him a clue to the identity of the diary's owner.

It was in vain, apart from the note of the birthday on March 16. There was an occasional specific reference, such as the one on January 2 (*7 p.m., Dorotheenstrasse 20, second bell from the bottom*) but nothing that he could really use. Unless, of course, he was prepared to lurk around Dorotheenstrasse at seven the following evening in the hope of seeing someone wandering around asking all and sundry about a Filofax. Why on earth hadn't they put a name, instead of "second bell from the bottom"? That couldn't be Googled! Why so mysterious? It was all very strange—and not at all designed to make Jonathan's research any easier. He briefly considered setting off there and then and going to the address, but he soon dismissed the idea. It wasn't right to turn up unannounced on someone's doorstep on a holiday.

Then Jonathan had the idea of looking at the back, where most appointment diaries have an address book. Maybe he'd find a few names and phone numbers with which to try his luck the following day. He might get hold of someone who at least knew the diary's owner and had heard it had gone missing. Or something like that.

Once again, negative. Beyond the page for December 31 there was merely a "Notes" section containing rather a lot of empty pages, followed by the leather cover. Jonathan noticed a slight rustle. At the back of the diary was a pocket with the corner of a white piece of paper peeping out. Jonathan pulled on it and a second later was holding an envelope marked *Save for later!* The plot thickened.

He opened the envelope—it wasn't sealed, he reassured his conscience—and breathed in sharply. It was a good thing he hadn't left the bag lying on the bench! He quickly counted: five hundred euros, in fifties, twenties, and tens, had been tucked into the envelope.

Jonathan mentally summarized his findings. There was this diary, in which someone had made entries from the first to the last day of the year, which had then been lost near the Alster, then thrown away or deliberately left on the handlebar of Jonathan's bike. Then there was this envelope containing five hundred euros. Nothing else. No phone number or address, no clues whatsoever about the identity of the owner.

So what should he, Jonathan N. Grief, do about it? Obviously, he couldn't simply keep the diary; someone must be searching desperately for it.

A lost-and-found office. He'd take the bag and the Filofax to the local police station's lost-and-found desk—that was the easiest solution! Wasn't it what those places were for? Someone lost something, someone else found it and handed it in, then the owner went to collect it. Simple!

He was on the verge of returning to his laptop to look for the address and hours of the nearest police station with a lost-and-found facility, when he paused.

Was it really such a good idea? After all, the diary seemed to have great personal value. And then there was all that money! Five hundred euros was a tidy sum. How trustworthy were the officers who manned lost-and-found desks? Would they really catalogue the Filofax in the proper way and keep it safe until its rightful owner contacted them?

Or would they more likely take the money and then lose the diary on some shelf, where it would gather dust along with myriad other items until it faded into obscurity? How much did the people in lost-and-found offices earn? Not a fortune, certainly, so an unexpected financial bonus would be an irresistible temptation.

No, the lost-and-found wasn't such a good idea after all. The bag had been hung on *his* handlebars, so he was effectively responsible for making sure the diary found its way back into the hands of the person to whom it belonged.

Jonathan had a brilliant idea. He sat down at his keyboard.

Editor, *Hamburg News*
By email

I'm writing to you this time with a personal request. While out on my daily run by the Alster this morning, I found a bag containing an appointment diary near the fitness station at Höhe Schwanenwik. I'm reluctant to say any more about it, to reduce the risk of attracting the attention of possible opportunists.

If the rightful owner gets in touch with you and gives you a more detailed description of the diary and bag, please forward it to me. If it matches, I'll gladly return the diary to them through your editorial office.

Yours sincerely,
Jonathan N. Grief

P.S. Once again, I wish you a happy New Year!

# 6

## *Hannah*

*Two months before:*
*Sunday, October 29, 1:24 p.m.*

Simon wasn't dead, but he didn't look too lively either. Hannah was by his bed a few moments after arriving. He lay buried beneath several blankets, only his pale, snuffling face visible, surrounded by an unappealing heap of used tissues, the bedside table laden with a collection of pills, cough medicine, throat lozenges, and a thermometer.

"Simon! What's the matter?" Hannah asked.

Her boyfriend blinked in astonishment. "Hannah?" he said weakly as if an image of the Holy Virgin had appeared before him. Wheezing laboriously, he sat up and supported himself with his elbows on the pillow. "What brings you here?"

Until that moment, Hannah had been shocked by Simon's condition, but her concern turned to annoyance. Simultaneously relieved and angry that Simon clearly had not departed this life, she snatched the covers from him. The suffering patient was lying there in a sweatshirt and long johns.

"Hey!" he grumbled, wrapping his arms around his chest.

"I don't believe it!" Hannah's voice was now shaking with anger. "Are you seriously asking me what brings me here? Have you forgotten about the opening of Little Rascals?"

Simon turned even paler. "Little Rascals? Oh, no!" He flopped back onto the pillow.

"Oh, yes!"

"I'm so sorry!" Groaning, he sat up again and ran a hand through his bedraggled, greasy hair. "I meant to just take a little rest, but I must have fallen fast asleep. I . . . I . . ." He looked at her remorsefully and tried a crooked smile, failing miserably to impress. "Honestly, I . . . I'm so sorry."

"So am I!" Hannah couldn't stay too angry—Simon did look pitiful. He was drenched in sweat, his top and pants clinging clammily to his body.

Her concern regaining the upper hand, Hannah covered him up again, tucked him in, and sat on the edge of the bed.

"It's starting in half an hour, and I've been waiting for you since eleven." She'd meant it as a reproach, but even to her own ears it sounded merely sad and disappointed. He looked so sick—what could she do?

"In half an hour? Is that the time?" Simon made an attempt to get up, but Hannah grasped his shoulders and pressed him gently but firmly back down.

"Stay there. I can see how lousy you're feeling."

"I'm afraid I am." With a sigh and a groan, he sank down into the pillows, his eyelids fluttering. "And I've got a raging temperature."

"How high is it?" Hannah peered at the thermometer on his bedside table.

"It was just under 100.8 this morning."

"Well, well." She couldn't suppress a smile. "I think you'll survive. No need to call the emergency helicopter just yet."

"But I'm sweating like crazy." His justification sounded rather feeble.

"I would be, too, if I were lying under three layers of covers."

"My throat's all swollen, look!" He placed both hands beneath his chin.

Hannah leaned forward and felt Simon's neck. It was a little swollen. "It is," she said, frowning. "Is it sore?"

He shook his head. "Not particularly. But I've taken around ten throat lozenges."

"Was it as bad as that?"

He shook his head again. "Preventive, I guess."

"Ah." She wondered if it was just Simon, or merely a typically male trait, to gulp down half a bottle of pills despite an absence of real symptoms. She decided a few herbal lozenges from the box by the bed wouldn't do him any serious harm. Then again, they probably wouldn't help either.

"I feel totally whacked," Simon said, continuing his lament. "I hurt all over and I feel sick. My legs gave way under me earlier . . . I only just made it to the toilet."

"Then you'd better keep sleeping it off." She got to her feet. She didn't have time for any more sympathy. Simon's alarm clock showed in glowing red figures that it was shortly after one thirty. "I'll just grab your car keys and transfer the stuff over to my car."

"No, wait!" He heaved himself up again, but more slowly than before. "Give me ten minutes. I'll come with you!"

"Simon." Hannah looked at him with a mixture of concern and severity. "For one thing, I don't have ten minutes, and besides, you really wouldn't be any use in that state. You said yourself that you can hardly stand up. So you're better off staying here."

"Are you sure?" His body sank back in slow motion as he spoke.

"Totally sure. And now I really have to go."

"Just take my car, so you don't have to move everything over."

"Your car?" She couldn't believe her ears. Simon's old Ford Mustang was like a sacred cow to him. Well, a sacred car.

"Of course," he replied as though it were the most normal thing in the world for him to be suggesting Hannah get behind the wheel of his prized possession. He had done it only once before. That had been a good six months ago, on his thirty-fifth birthday, when he'd spent several hours trying to drink the bar of the Hans-Albers-Eck on the Reeperbahn dry with his best friends, Sören and Niels. They hadn't quite managed it, but when Simon had called Hannah late that night, to beg her to pick up him and his drinking buddies because there was no way he could leave the Mustang in the red-light district, he had sounded as though they were only a small beer away from succeeding in their mission.

It had been four thirty in the morning and Hannah had been really annoyed, after having gone home alone on the subway two hours earlier. Nevertheless, she had dutifully called a taxi, dashed over to the Reeperbahn, loaded the three wasted men into Simon's Mustang, and ferried them back to his apartment to sleep off their excesses.

When she'd reappeared at Simon's apartment around noon the following day with a large bag of buns and three two-pint bottles of orange juice, she had rolled her eyes at their loud complaints of headaches, and she'd let Simon know in no uncertain terms that when it came to her thirtieth birthday the following year, she would expect repayment in full.

But she hadn't really been annoyed with him; after all, in her eyes Simon hadn't been boisterous or irresponsible often enough in recent years. It had all begun with the death of his mother and made worse by the miserable atmosphere in the editorial department. Now he tended toward caution and, unlike before, checked five times in every direction before moving, to which Hannah often reacted with an exaggerated eye roll. To think he would lose his job not three months later . . . No one could have foreseen that.

"You must be feeling lousy," she said.

"Lousier than lousy," he replied, again attempting a crooked grin. This time he succeeded. "So you'd better split before I come to my senses enough to realize what I'm offering."

"Okay. I'll give you a call when we've finished," Hannah replied hurriedly.

"No, I'll call you. Maybe I'll sleep right through till tomorrow morning. I want to get back on my feet as soon as possible."

Again, Hannah felt a brief flash of mistrust. Why didn't he want her to call him? Did he actually have something to hide?

That was a stupid thought. One look at his pale face was enough to tell her that her boyfriend had nothing up his sleeve but a long sleep to help him recover.

Hannah quickly leaned down to him and kissed him goodbye. A second later she was out the door, sprinting down the stairs. Only twenty minutes left. She hoped Simon's pride and joy would show her what it had under the hood.

# 7

*Jonathan*

*Tuesday, January 2, 11:27 a.m.*

Mr. Jonathan N. Grief
By email

Thank you for your New Year greetings. We hope you have had a good start to the new year.

We always welcome feedback from observant readers—among whom we have counted you for many years—pointing out the occasional error that sometimes escapes our notice in the daily, often hectic routines of the editorial office.

Regarding your query about the bag and diary, we are sorry to tell you that we don't have a section for such matters in our newspaper. That said, you would of course be welcome to take out an ad at the usual rates. I am attaching the contact

information for the advertising department, along
with a price list. Personally, I would recommend you
take the bag and diary to your local police station.
I'm sure the relevant details will be easy to find.

Yours sincerely,
Gunda Probst
Reader Services, *Hamburg News*

Well, well. So the *Hamburg News* didn't have a section "for such matters"? As he cast his eyes briefly over the clumsy wording, wondering
about the best way to improve it, Jonathan's fingers were itching to
fire off a reply to that stupid woman, Gunda Probst, and ask her what
exactly the slogan "By Hamburg people for Hamburg people" was supposed to mean if they weren't prepared to concern themselves with the
kind of situation he had described?

But he let it be and closed his email program, silently fuming. Take
it to the police! What kind of dunce did this Gunda Blunder take him
for? As if he hadn't thought of that himself!

He snapped his laptop shut and gazed at the Filofax lying next to
it on his desk. He opened the diary again.

That handwriting! *Nicolino.*

A thought occurred to him. An incredible thought. Outrageous,
even.

He shut the diary again. Crazy! Why would his mother have hung
the bag with the Filofax on his bicycle? After all those years of complete
radio silence? It would mean that not only was she in Hamburg but
that she must have been watching her son and lying in wait for him.

No, no. Completely crazy.

Jonathan N. Grief jerked his office chair back and stood. He had
more important things to do. His CEO, Markus Bode, was expecting
him at noon for a meeting.

Bode's secretary had phoned that morning and made this "urgent appointment" with him. Jonathan wondered what could be so pressing—he had been in the office for the Christmas party less than four weeks ago. What on earth could have happened since then, with the holidays in between?

Punctual as ever, Jonathan entered the late nineteenth-century white villa by the Elbe, which had been in his family for generations and still housed Grief & Son Books, with its seventy or so employees.

This was where his great-great-grandfather Ernest Grief had founded the publishing house a century and a half ago. As always, when Jonathan climbed the sweeping blue-carpeted staircase to the second floor, he felt a combination of awe, pride, and unease wash over him.

This feeling usually reached its peak on the top landing, where the oil portraits of his ancestors hung on the wall: Ernest Grief; his great-grandfather Heinrich; his grandmother Emilie (they had been hoping for an "Emil" in the delivery room but proved flexible when the surprise arrived); and his father, Wolfgang. When he passed through the glass door on the left-hand side to the publisher's (therefore, his) offices, he always felt a weight lifting from his shoulders.

"Happy New Year, Mr. Grief!" His secretary, Renate Krug, turned from the rubber tree she was busy dusting to greet him. Putting down her duster, she came to him and held out her right hand, raising her left to adjust her glasses on her nose before deftly smoothing her dark-brown suit and primping her snow-white hair. This was piled up in a neat bun, as usual, and even Renate Krug's age—she had long since passed sixty—didn't change the fact that she was an exceptionally beautiful woman.

"And the same to you, Frau Krug!" Jonathan replied with his friendliest smile, shaking her hand and giving a nod before disappearing into his office with a muttered "Send Herr Bode in."

"I'll let him know," she called. Jonathan heard her pick up the receiver of the telephone on her desk.

Renate Krug had worked for his father for as long as he could remember—and that was quite some time. After his father retired, Jonathan had kept her on as his personal assistant, occasionally feeling a touch of remorse that she hardly had anything to do under him. Although she was now free to go on Friday afternoons and had a whole day off on Mondays, her twenty-eight-hour week was filled with about fifteen hours of actual work, if that.

On the other hand, Renate Krug was not far from retirement age, and she probably considered herself lucky to be spending her last years of employment . . . dusting rubber trees. And, of course, enjoying the wonderful view out over the Elbe.

Which was what Jonathan now did as he waited for his CEO to arrive. He looked out through the large lattice window to the river, where a huge container ship was gliding by. A few squawking seagulls accompanied the barge downstream toward the estuary, and Jonathan wondered briefly where the ship was headed. And—if only for a moment—believed he caught a glimpse of a pair of swans by the bank.

Looking more closely, however, he discovered that the birds were two flapping plastic bags. With a shrug, Jonathan turned away and went across the room to sit in one of the chairs to the side of his desk that he used for meetings.

"Knock, knock!" Markus Bode stood in the doorway, a briefcase tucked under his arm, and rapped his knuckles on the frame.

Jonathan got back to his feet and went to greet him.

"A happy New Year to you!" Bode said as they exchanged a hearty handshake.

"You too," Jonathan said, noting that his CEO looked somewhat worn out. He was usually meticulously attired, his well-tailored suit and neatly side-parted blond hair giving an impression of exaggerated attention to detail, but Jonathan was struck by today's five-o'clock shadow, dark rings under his eyes, and creased shirt, which aged him beyond his nearly forty years. He did not look good. Not at all.

"Well, now." No sooner were they seated than Bode came straight to the point. "We have a problem."

"Go on."

Bode opened a briefcase, took out a stack of papers, and placed them on the table. "During the holidays, I went through the provisional figures for the quarter and spent some time considering our plans for the next few months."

"Why would you do something like that?"

Bode looked at him, uncomprehending. "What do you mean?"

"Bothering yourself with work during the holidays. You should have been resting and spending time with your family." Jonathan knew his CEO had a gorgeous wife and two small children.

"Ah," Markus Bode replied, his expression, if anything, even more bewildered. "I'm the CEO of Grief & Son Books—my working hours are different from most people's. Comes with the job."

"Sure," Jonathan conceded. "But you have to think of your health. Even a CEO has to relax sometimes."

"Not when he's aware that we had a thirty percent shortfall on our forecast income over the last quarter." He coughed, lowered his eyes, and added in a slightly quieter voice, "And when his wife and children have just left him, he doesn't need much free time."

"Oh." Now it was Jonathan's turn to look bewildered.

"Yes, well."

"That's not good." Even to Jonathan's own ears the remark sounded hopelessly inadequate. But he had no idea what else to say. Markus Bode and he got along well, but theirs was a purely business relationship, and this personal revelation was too much for him.

"So. That's how it is." Bode slumped into himself a little more.

"Should we . . ." Jonathan paused and wondered where to go from there. What could he say in such a situation? What had his friends said to him when he told them his marriage to Tina was at an end?

Nothing, he recalled. He hadn't told anyone and had come to terms with the situation by himself. He hadn't felt close enough to anyone to share his private catastrophe with them. Apart from Thomas. But for obvious reasons, his shoulder was ruled out as one to cry on.

It wasn't until later, once the divorce had gone through, that a few acquaintances had asked how things were going, and by then it was mainly a matter of the financial arrangements between him and Tina—which had been totally unproblematic.

Markus Bode was looking at him, obviously waiting for his boss to finish his "Should we" question.

"Should we . . ." Jonathan repeated, feverishly searching for the right words, "should we go for a beer, perhaps?"

"A beer?"

"Yes, a beer!" Although Jonathan rarely drank alcohol, apart from the occasional glass of good red wine, it seemed like an appropriate suggestion. Men whose wives had just left them went for a beer, didn't they?

"It's only midday!"

"That's true." Maybe it wasn't such a good idea.

"I think we'd be better off discussing the figures." Bode seemed as though he was mentally squaring his shoulders. Suddenly he didn't look so disheveled.

"Fine." Even figures were a more attractive prospect than a heart-to-heart.

"As I said, we failed to reach our targets by thirty percent." Bode tapped the documents on the table with the index finger of his right hand. "You could call it a disaster."

"Have you analyzed the reasons?"

"To an extent," the CEO replied. "As you know, the whole sector is having to cope with falling turnover. Add to that the fact that the sales of our most important author, Hubertus Krull, are slowly falling off, and his serious illness means he won't be delivering a new title to us in the foreseeable future." He paused. "We can't profit from his backlist unless we have a new novel to draw readers in." Jonathan nodded pensively. It was his grandmother Emilie who had acquired Krull, recognizing him as the standard bearer of postwar German literature. She had gone on to establish him as an international bestseller.

"We've also seriously miscalculated on certain titles."

"Which ones?"

"For example"—Bode picked up the pile of papers, leafed through it, and finally took out a single sheet—"this one." He handed the page to his boss.

Jonathan glanced at it. "*The Loneliness of the Milky Way?*" he exclaimed in surprise. "But that was nominated for last year's German Book Prize!"

"That may be," Bode continued, undeterred. "However, not only did we pay too much for it in the first place, but we printed thirty thousand extra copies after the nomination, of which twenty-seven thousand are still in storage. And we're already getting returns from some booksellers."

"Hmm. Why's that?"

"I'd say it's because people don't want to read it."

"But it's a great novel!" Jonathan had read the manuscript because Bode had asked his opinion before they'd acquired the rights. He had been absolutely convinced that *The Loneliness of the Milky Way* was an important work of literature, one that satisfied all the right artistic criteria.

"You think so, I think so—but readers prefer one of those erotic potboilers or a Grisham." He sighed. "'Thinking of Germany in the night, puts all thoughts of sleep to flight.'"

"Precisely." Jonathan held back from remarking that Bode—like so many—was quoting Heinrich Heine's "Night Thoughts" completely out of context. The poet had composed the verse while exiled in Paris, as an expression of his homesickness and, above all, his longing for his mother, not as a criticism of Germany. "So what do you suggest?"

"That's what I'm asking you," Bode replied.

"Me?"

"Well, yes. You're the publisher."

"And you're the expert," Jonathan fired back reflexively.

Bode cleared his throat in a mixture of embarrassment and pride. "True. But I can't set the future course of Grief & Son Books on my own."

"Easy, now," Jonathan said. "Just as one swallow doesn't a summer make, one flop doesn't mean ruination. I don't think we need to be considering a new course just yet."

"But I'm sorry to say we're not talking about *one* flop." He slid a few more sheets across the table. "It's more a case of our whole list. And it's been going on for some time. I've simply been trying to tell myself that it's in line with the fluctuations in the rest of the industry. And we've always been able to milk Hubertus Krull for all we could. But we urgently need a new strategy."

"Hmm." Jonathan leaned back in his chair. "If you say so. But I'll have to think about it for a while."

"Of course, I'm not saying we should completely revise our whole portfolio starting tomorrow," Bode conceded. "But I had to let you know the current position. To make sure we keep an eye on things and react quickly."

"Yes, yes." Jonathan nodded. "Fine. So now I know."

The two of them sat pondering silently for a while. Jonathan couldn't help but think of the young man by the Alster who had reminded him of Harry Potter. What did he like to read? Maybe he should have asked the guy.

"Well, now." Markus Bode eventually broke the silence. "So, I . . . I'll leave the documents here for you to look through." He stood.

"Okay," Jonathan replied, also getting to his feet. "Thank you for keeping me informed." They shook hands. For a little longer than usual. Jonathan wondered again if it would be appropriate to say something. Anything. "I hope things sort themselves out for you soon," he said finally, clapping Markus Bode stiffly on the shoulder.

"Thank you very much," Bode said. "I only hope my wife doesn't come back."

"I'm sorry?"

"Joke."

With a shake of his head, Jonathan watched his CEO trot out of the office. What a weird sense of humor!

# 8

*Hannah*

"First, the good news: your car's outside, in perfect condition—not a single scratch."

"Oh, no!" Simon cried, pulling Hannah into his arms. "I'm soooo sorry!" he sobbed into her ear, holding her so tight that she could hardly breathe. "Honestly, I can't tell you how sorry I am!"

She disentangled herself from his embrace. "Why? Should I have driven it into the ground?" She struggled to suppress a snort of laughter.

"I don't mean the car!" Simon said. "But if that's the good news, then I'm guessing the bad news is that the opening was a complete washout. I'm such an idiot!" He smacked his forehead with his palm.

"We-e-ell." She was grinning broadly. "It was a total success!"

"But you just said you'd start with the good news."

"That's right. To be followed by the excellent news!" Hannah laughed cheerfully.

"Ah." Simon shook his head. "Let's go sit in the kitchen. I put the kettle on for tea." In his robe and slippers, he shuffled down the corridor ahead of her. Despite his "Pity me, I'm so ill" getup, he looked remarkably better than he had the day before. At least he was on his feet and able to walk unassisted. Good thing, too, as Hannah had a favor to ask him.

"So, how did it go?" Simon asked as Hannah took a seat in one of his Eames chairs and he poured the tea.

"Over a hundred children and their parents came!" she began excitedly. "We're more or less fully booked until Christmas, and it means we'll probably have to ditch our plan of only offering events in the afternoons and switch to mornings as well. The demand's incredible—people were practically snatching the registration forms out of our hands!"

"That's amazing!" Simon regarded her thoughtfully. "I have to admit I wasn't expecting that."

"And I expected you wouldn't."

"Why not?"

"Take a guess!"

"Silly woman!" he replied with a grin.

"And 'have to admit' sounds so negative, somehow," she added.

"Huh?"

"I mean the fact that you have to *admit* you weren't expecting it."

"I'm really not following you now."

"Forget it." She flapped a hand dismissively and laughed again. "The children were thrilled with the balloon thing."

Simon sighed with relief. "So you managed to inflate them all in time?"

"Of course not," Hannah retorted. "I was much too late getting back to the shop. We'd just thrown the plates and stuff on the table and set up the drinks when people started showing up."

"But—"

"It was a stroke of genius! We got the kids to join in blowing up the balloons. It was their absolute favorite part—they were lining up for a turn with the helium bottle! And the moment they discovered that the gas made their voices sound like Mickey Mouse, there was no stopping them." She put on a silly voice and plucked at a nonexistent Adam's apple. "Hello, I'm little Hannah!"

"So it wasn't such a screwup, that I forgot all about it?" Simon asked, regarding her as though fearing the worst.

"On the contrary. Things couldn't have been better."

Now her boyfriend was grinning with her. "Which only goes to reinforce your favorite saying, that some good comes from everything."

"Exactly, my darling." She leaned forward and gave him a smacking kiss on his red nose. "And to cap it all, you weren't standing around getting in our way and muddling things up. You could say it was a win-win situation."

He feigned offense. "What's that supposed to mean?"

"Nothing." She kissed him again, this time directly on his pouting lips. "I'm just over the moon because everything went so perfectly. Lisa and I will have to start looking for a couple of assistants immediately. We can't cope with the demand on our own."

"Hold your horses," Simon said. "How many confirmed reservations do you actually have?"

"Argh!" Hannah rolled her eyes and thumped Simon's shoulders. "There you go again. Spare me the negative vibes; you're polluting the very air I breathe!"

"I just think you shouldn't let your euphoria run away with you."

"Don't worry. I've always got you to put the brakes on."

"Ha ha. Thanks!"

"Seriously, though." She took his hands and squeezed them. "Don't worry so much. You know that worrying is like sitting in a rocking chair—you expend a lot of energy but you never get anywhere."

"You must have stolen that from somewhere."

"True, but I can't remember where, so it's mine now."

"I'm not worrying," Simon said, stroking her fingers with his thumb. "But I just don't want to see you disappointed. And that can happen if you always expect the best."

"Again, that's so typical of you. I'm telling you how wonderfully it all went, and there you are talking about disappointment."

"Ah, well." He raised his hands in apology. "I'm probably only jealous."

"I agree," Hannah said. "And I think we really need to turn things around." She stood. "So let's go!"

"Go? Where?"

"You can start with the shower. And then we're going to Little Rascals."

"Now?" He looked at her aghast.

"Yes," she replied simply. "You've had plenty of time for convalescence, and I've told you how desperately we need help."

"I've still got a cold, Hannah!"

"Doesn't matter." She grinned. "Ninety-nine percent of small children catch up to ten colds a year—no one will even notice. And we've got an endless supply of tissues."

"I hope you're joking."

"Not at all. You need something to drag you out of your pit of self-pity." She laughed. "Everyone has to have fun now and then. Stop looking at me like that and get yourself down to Little Rascals. You'll see—it'll do you good!"

"Um, what am I supposed to do when I get there?"

"You can begin by helping Lisa and me tidy up. And at two o'clock we need a clown."

# 9

*Jonathan*

Jonathan hadn't intended to make the first visit of the year to his father until Thursday, but after his meeting with Markus Bode, he decided on the spur of the moment to stop by the Sonnenhof Nursing Home that very day.

He knew only too well that he wouldn't be able to discuss the latest developments at the publishing house with his father—for one thing, his father's mental state made such conversations out of the question, and even if it were possible, it would excite Wolfgang far too much. But after half an hour spent lingering in silent communion before his father's portrait in the hope of inspiration, Jonathan had felt a sudden desire to see the old man.

Jonathan drove his dark-gray Saab up the broad white gravel drive that led to Sonnenhof. The modern building was bathed in the most magnificent sunshine that could be hoped for on a January day in Hamburg. The glass palace stood proudly on a slope high above the Elbe, the light reflecting from its numerous picture windows and fracturing here and there into glittering sparks. When the weather was like this, there were long-distance views far beyond the river, with the Airbus site to the left and the flat Altes Land, with its extensive fruit orchards, to the right.

Jonathan had wondered more than once whether his father had an inkling of the beauty of his surroundings. Mostly he sat in a wing chair in his room, headphones on, listening with eyes closed to compositions by Beethoven, Wagner, and Bach.

He was surrounded by relics from the past. A moving company had brought every item of his furniture and effects from the publishing house and villa to the nursing home. Craftsmen had been brought in to piece his Biedermeier furniture back together and to position the antique desk, at which Wolfgang Grief no longer sat, in the light from the window. They had installed the tall shelves and arranged according to a prescribed cataloguing system the extensive library—hundreds of books he would not or could not read anymore. They had even lined up the framed photos he no longer looked at on the mantelpiece of the false fireplace.

Only the bed and the chair were still used by Wolfgang Grief, today as all other days. After knocking and entering, Jonathan had to attract his father's attention. Every time he saw Wolfgang sitting there, immersed in his music, Jonathan paused and wondered whether he should disturb him. He looked so peaceful, so relaxed, enraptured. There was no trace of the man whom the employees at the publishing house used to describe in whispers as the "despot" and "crazy patriarch."

No, this man slouching in his armchair with closed eyes was merely a harmless grandpa, unwrapping the crackling gold paper from a toffee for his (nonexistent) grandson. His thick white hair stood out against the dark-red cushion; he wore a turtleneck and a checked cardigan with beige cords, and dark-gray felt slippers on his feet.

Wolfgang Grief had once measured a full six foot two, and even though he had shrunk considerably, he still towered over most men his age—although slumped in his seat as he was, no one would have guessed it—and he was still as slim as he had been in his younger days. But at seventy-three he was beginning to look distinctly doddering.

Jonathan felt sadness welling inside him. How would his own life be when he was in his seventies? Would he also succumb to dementia and end up in an old-people's home? Would he live like his father, who had no one to visit him but his son and Renate Krug, who had remained loyal to her former employer?

No, the truth was much more depressing, as to date there wasn't even the prospect of Jonathan receiving visits from a son. Or a daughter. Or even Renate Krug. He suddenly had more sympathy for Hertha Fahrenkrog with her little dog, Daphne.

"Hello, Papa," he said in a low voice, cautiously tapping Wolfgang Grief on the shoulder to prevent himself from sinking ever deeper into murky brooding that would do him no good.

His father opened his eyes. They were a clear, steely blue like Jonathan's, only rarely betraying the confusion that lay behind them.

For a fraction of a second, Jonathan felt himself back in his childhood. As a boy, he had been terrified of the severity of his father's gaze, imagining those merciless eyes penetrating the deepest corners of his soul.

"Who are you?" Wolfgang Grief asked in confusion as he removed the headphones, the sounds of Bach's "Air" whispering tinnily from them in his liver-spotted hands. The image he had just conjured of the strict father with the unforgiving expression collapsed abruptly, bursting like a bubble.

"It's me, Jonathan," he replied, drawing up a chair and sitting. "Your son."

"I know that!" his father snapped grumpily as though he'd never asked.

"Good."

"What are you doing here?"

"I've come to see you."

"Am I getting any lunch today?" He frowned. "I hope it won't be the same mush as yesterday! You can force that down yourself. I tell you, I won't touch it!"

"No, Papa." Jonathan shook his head. "I'm not here to bring your food. It's long past lunchtime. I'm your son and I've simply come to visit you."

"Are you the new doctor?" Wolfgang Grief was now looking at him suspiciously.

Jonathan shook his head again. "No, I'm your son. Jonathan."

"My son?"

"Yes."

"I don't have a son."

"Yes, you do, Papa."

His father turned his head away and looked through the window to the Elbe. He sat in silence for a long moment, lost in thought and chewing his lower lip. He turned back to Jonathan.

"Are you the new doctor?"

"No," Jonathan said again. "I'm your son."

"My son?" Wolfgang Grief sounded confused now. A few seconds later he smiled a little stupidly. "Yes, of course, my son!" He laid a hand on Jonathan's and patted it.

"That's right," Jonathan agreed, relieved, and patted his father's hand in return, though it felt strange. "And I've come to see you. It's the second of January. The start of a new year. I just wanted to make sure everything was all right."

His father looked surprised. His expression turned a few seconds later to disappointment. "What?" he yelled, so angry that it made Jonathan jump. "A new year?" He moved to rise from his chair.

"Sit down," Jonathan said, pressing him back by the shoulders.

"But I have to go!" he cried, pushing against his son with astonishing strength.

"Where do you want to go?" Jonathan struggled to keep his old man in the chair.

"To the office, of course! They're all waiting for me." He made another attempt to stand.

"No, Papa," Jonathan said without slackening his grip on his shoulders. "Everything's fine; don't you worry about a thing."

"Nonsense!" Wolfgang Grief shouted. "I'm not where I should be, so how can everything be fine?"

"I was just in the office," Jonathan said as calmly as he could. "Renate Krug and Markus Bode have everything under control."

"Ah, yes, Renate." Wolfgang Grief's agitation subsided as quickly as it had arisen, giving way to a satisfied smile. "Now *there's* a good woman!"

Jonathan nodded. "She is indeed."

"You must remind me to buy her flowers," his father said, winking at his son. "I've sent Renate Krug a bouquet of flowers every New Year for years. White carnations. She's particularly fond of those."

"I know." Jonathan realized with horror that he had completely forgotten the tradition he had inherited from his father. He made a mental note to take care of that as soon as he possibly could. "I'm on it."

"Good, good."

"So you see, it's all going great, and there's no reason at all for you to worry." As he spoke, he recalled the problem Markus Bode had raised with him only a couple of hours ago and felt like a complete hypocrite. But what else should he have done? It simply wasn't possible to discuss the matter with his father. Even when he wasn't mistaking Jonathan for his new doctor or one of the nursing assistants bringing his lunch, Wolfgang Grief would never be able to help run Grief & Son Books again.

A small, evil thought entered Jonathan's head, almost making him laugh out loud—why couldn't he tell his father all about the problems facing Grief & Son Books, outlining them in the goriest detail? After all, his father would forget it all three seconds later. Dementia wasn't all bad; sometimes it could even be a blessing.

But no, of course Jonathan wouldn't do such a thing.

They sat for a while facing one another, for all the world like the perfect image of a father and son on almost–New Year's Day, except that Jonathan was racking his brain to think of what he could say next.

He hadn't been there much longer than ten minutes; to take his leave so soon seemed not only impolite but callous, even though he had no idea whether his father appreciated his presence or didn't care one bit if he had company. Or whether he might actually prefer to be back in his own little world, immersed in his music.

He was like a coma patient whose friends and relations didn't really know whether he was aware they were at his bedside. The comparison was a bit shaky, since Wolfgang Grief was fully conscious. But he was no longer really there and hadn't been for a while. Jonathan had realized only recently that he'd begun to talk about his father in the past tense.

Jonathan had once been advised by the doctor who looked after his father—to Wolfgang Grief's eternal dismay, he was under the care of a female doctor!—that he should simply talk to his father. "Tell him something exciting or cheerful, little things from your everyday life. Involve your father in the regular things you do—it's especially important for him in his condition."

Huh. Easier said than done. Jonathan had absolutely no idea what to talk to his father about—there was too little going on in his life; it meandered along predictably, without any particular highs or lows. Not that Jonathan was complaining; on the contrary, that was how he liked it. But his daily routines were hardly the stuff of amusing anecdotes.

Once again he tried to conjure up a suitable topic for a harmless filial chat. Which excluded both what Markus Bode had told him earlier and the fact that Tina had sent him a New Year's greeting. Wolfgang Grief had never been his daughter-in-law's biggest fan, a feeling that was entirely mutual. Apart from those two nuggets, Jonathan's mind was blank.

"Oh, there's something I have to tell you!" he exclaimed suddenly, slapping his thighs in relief at having at last thought of something to tell his father. "Something really strange happened yesterday morning."

"Oh yes?" His father looked at him expectantly, apparently roused from his lethargy for a moment. Like a light being switched on in a darkened room, his eyes showed genuine awareness.

Jonathan nodded, still delighted that he had come up with a truly interesting story that would allow him a few minutes' stress-free conversation with his old man.

"So," he said, "I went on my usual run along the Alster, and when I finished and came back to my bicycle, I found a stranger's bag hanging on my handlebars." He paused for effect, blissfully ignorant of the fact that his father was completely unmoved by such dramatic flourishes.

"What was in it?" Wolfgang Grief asked, fidgeting impatiently in his seat like a child in the front row of a Punch-and-Judy show waiting for the puppets to appear.

"A diary," Jonathan said, dropping his bombshell with relish.

"A diary?" His father looked disappointed; he had clearly anticipated something more exciting. A briefcase full of money, perhaps, or the Golden Fleece. Or a suspiciously ticking package. But Jonathan was nowhere near the conclusion of his story.

"Yes," he continued undeterred, "a Filofax, already full of entries! Something there for every day of the coming year!"

"Hmm." Wolfgang Grief hardly seemed on the edge of his seat. "An old Filofax?"

"No," Jonathan corrected him. "Not an old one from last year, but a new one for this year!"

"So?"

"But, Papa, don't you find it strange? Someone's made plans for the whole year, written them down in a diary—and hung it on my handlebars?"

"Someone or other probably lost the bag and a passerby picked it up and thought it belonged on your bike."

"It's possible," Jonathan conceded. "But the burning question is: Who lost the bag containing the Filofax?"

His father shrugged, his face showing exaggerated boredom. "It's nothing to do with you. Hand it in at the lost-and-found and let that be an end to it. I'm sure you have better things to do than worry about such trivia." His eyes were now fully clear. Fully clear—and disapproving.

"There was an envelope containing five hundred euros tucked inside the back cover," Jonathan protested.

"You don't really need the money."

"That's not what I'm saying!" He fought against the growing disappointment, the helpless feeling of being casually dismissed like a silly little boy. He tried telling himself he was only here to exchange a few coherent words with his father, regardless of the subject matter.

But the disappointment was still there. So he continued his efforts to convince Wolfgang Grief of the extraordinariness of the incident. "You see, it's not as if the bag was simply lying around on the path—it had been hung on my bike. As though someone had put it there on purpose."

"As I said, it was probably a passerby."

"But it might not have been." Jonathan was not going to be brushed aside so easily. "And in any case . . ." He hesitated for a brief moment, uncertain whether it was right to tell his father exactly why the diary had cast such a spell over him. But ultimately, it was the only detail that truly mattered. "In any case, the handwriting looked almost as though *Mamma* had written it." He would have preferred to leave out the "almost," but as he spoke he thought it was probably for the best.

Wolfgang Grief said nothing more. He merely looked at his son, eyebrows raised, face frozen in a grimace of surprise as though he had just suffered a shock. A moment later, he turned his head and resumed staring mutely through the window, gnawing his lower lip as before.

"Papa?"

No reaction.

"Are you listening to me?" He put a hand on his father's shoulder. Nothing.

They didn't talk about Jonathan's mother. Never had, not for decades. After she left him, Wolfgang Grief had made it abundantly clear by dogged silence that as far as he was concerned, the subject was closed. And after Jonathan's postcard and the total silence that followed, her name had not passed either man's lips.

"It's more than strange," Jonathan continued helplessly. "I mean, I'm well aware, of course, that it's only a coincidence, simply someone who happens to have identical handwriting to *Mamma*'s—but for that to end up on my bike, of all places . . ."

"Sofia."

Jonathan shuddered as his father softly murmured the forbidden name, still staring expressionlessly out of the window. "Really," he replied uncertainly. "I was puzzled at first, as you can imagine."

"Sofia," Wolfgang Grief repeated. He closed his eyes, sighed deeply, and nibbled more urgently at his lower lip.

"Well, yes. I've been wondering whether I should try to find out who the diary belongs to," Jonathan went on, somewhat confused.

Silence.

"You mentioned the lost-and-found . . . I don't know; somehow it doesn't seem right. It's likely to simply get buried, or the owner won't think of asking there."

No reaction.

"I know I'd be delighted if I lost something like that and the finder made the effort to trace me and give it back."

Silence.

"That's why I think I should try to find the owner." Jonathan noted that he was speaking ever more rapidly—a useless monologue that no one was listening to. "I even wrote to the *Hamburg News* yesterday, to ask whether they could publish a notice, but the ignoramuses there refused point-blank and suggested I could pay for a small ad—can you believe it?" He gave a forced laugh. "'By Hamburg people for Hamburg people' indeed! You go to them with a real need and they simply brush you aside. Maybe I'll contact them again, but this time send my email directly to the editor in ch—"

"She's been here," his father interrupted.

"Papa, will you listen to me?" He wasn't prepared to go along with the abrupt change of subject, so typical of his father's behavior since his decline. Not this time. "Of course, I could give in and take out an ad."

"She—was—here!" The old man spoke the words so forcefully that Jonathan felt a shock run through his body.

"Who was?"

"Sofia." Wolfgang Grief turned back to his son and smiled, his blue eyes shining. "Sofia's been here."

"What?" Jonathan swallowed, an icy-cold shudder coursing through him. He must have misheard. "*Mamma's* been here?"

His father nodded.

"Here, you mean? At Sonnenhof? Recently?"

"Yes." He nodded again. "She comes to visit me regularly."

"Oh." Jonathan wanted to say something but was prevented by a lump in his throat.

"We talk a lot when she comes," Wolfgang Grief continued. "About the old times."

"I'm sorry, Papa," Jonathan said a little more calmly. "But that's impossible."

"She's forgiven me everything, you know," he went on as though his son hadn't said a word.

"What has she forgiven you for?"

"It was all so long ago, and we're both old now, so none of it matters anymore."

"What are you talking about? What has *Mamma* forgiven you for?" Thoughts were chasing themselves around his head. Not only was his father clearly imagining things, but Jonathan hadn't the slightest idea what he was talking about. One day his mother had simply up and left her family, so if anyone was going to forgive anyone else, it should be the other way around. But instead of a reply, Jonathan simply got another rapt smile. "Papa," he insisted, "please, will you tell me what you're talking about? *Mamma*'s been gone for years. We haven't heard a thing from her for ages. You're talking nonsense."

Wolfgang Grief's smile was replaced by a questioning frown. "Are you the new doctor?" His eyes roamed back to the window and stayed there.

# 10

*Hannah*

*Simon says . . .*

The music, which had been booming from the speakers at earsplitting volume, snapped off. Simon stretched his arms in the air and froze as nine giggling, screaming children copied him.

Hannah watched the scene in delight. Her boyfriend made a passable clown, even if the colorful costume was rather loose on him and the makeup on his sweat-drenched face was clearly beginning to run.

No wonder—for the last twenty minutes he'd been whirling like a dervish around the playroom, apparently finding their combination of Simon Says and Musical Statues as much fun as the kids did. Hannah's theory—that Simon would soon feel better once he'd roused himself—was proving correct.

The game itself was simple. As long as the music played, the children simply had to copy Simon's dance movements. The moment it stopped, they had to freeze in whatever pose they were in. Anyone who moved or fell over was out. Being out wasn't so bad, since it meant going to join Lisa in the kitchenette making popcorn, then forming it into chains with needles and thread.

Hannah had learned one essential aspect of childcare during her training: to avoid tears and tantrums, don't allow children to actually lose a game. And so the failed statues dashed enthusiastically to the kitchen, with one or two of the little scamps falling over on purpose so they could get ahead of the others at the popcorn station.

Yards of popcorn chains were already hanging from the ceiling of the playroom, and there would have been even more if half the popcorn hadn't ended up in the children's bulging tummies.

Feeling buoyant, Hannah pressed "Play." The familiar sounds once again filled the room, and Simon performed a series of wildly eccentric moves like some sort of 1980s aerobics celebrity.

"I hope you don't mind me sticking my nose in," Lisa murmured to her friend as she tacked the next popcorn chain to the wall behind her, "but don't you think it's time he took a break?"

"He's just hitting his stride," Hannah replied. "And the kids think it's a riot."

"You'll certainly have a riot on your hands if you're not careful," Lisa said, watching Simon with concern. "He looks like he could keel over at any moment. Look at his face—soaked with sweat. I bet he's glowing as red as a beet under all that makeup."

"At least he'll be sweating the last of his cold out."

"Is this revenge for yesterday?" Lisa asked.

"What's revenge got to do with it?" Hannah flashed her an innocent smile. "Simon left the two of us in the lurch, and he's simply making up for it. It's only right, and we're all benefiting. Anyway, it was his own idea to lead the dancing."

"Probably the result of a guilty conscience. I'd have one, anyway."

"Something else he can dance away," Hannah said with a laugh. "Let it all out—get rid of all those pent-up negative emotions."

Lisa threw her a look she couldn't interpret, and with a shrug turned to go back to the kitchen. She muttered something Hannah didn't quite catch, but which sounded suspiciously like "The girlfriend from hell."

Hannah pressed the "Stop" button on the CD player with a flourish. Panting, Simon and the children stopped in their tracks. A boy named Finn flopped, gasping, onto the floor, then scrabbled his way hastily toward the kitchen. Lisa did have a point, Hannah admitted to herself when she looked at her boyfriend more closely. He seemed totally wiped out; she'd bring it to an end after the next round.

She started the music one last time. The song would be over in a few moments and Simon could call it a day. It would be nearly five o'clock by then, in any case, and they could spend half an hour making and hanging popcorn chains before starting the tidying and cleaning as parents drifted in to pick up their children.

Hannah was putting this afternoon down as a complete success. Her little clients had partied like there was no tomorrow, joining in every game with gusto. There had been no arguments, crying, or demands of "I want Mom!" and—most importantly!—there had been no accidents.

Thanks to Simon, they had been able to accept twenty-four rather than sixteen children, which meant there'd been no need to turn anyone away. Hannah thought it important, especially at the start, not to have to send away any disappointed children.

And then there was the income: four hours per child at six euros an hour made . . . twenty-four times twenty-four . . . so . . . and then divide by two . . . well, by three . . . before tax, of course . . . that made . . .

"Argh!"

Hannah looked up from her fingers, which she had been using as a calculation aid. She saw a crowd of shocked children's faces all staring in the same direction. She stared too. And saw Simon, his right hand pressed against his chest, fall to the floor.

For a dreadful moment she simply gazed at the clown slumped facedown in the middle of the room. Then she heard a bloodcurdling scream. It was coming from her own throat. "Siiiiiiiimon!"

# 11

## *Jonathan*

*Tuesday, January 2, 4:04 p.m.*

Half an hour later, after several vain attempts to get his father to talk to him again, Jonathan was sitting at the wheel of his car, agitated and frustrated in equal measure. Transfixed and on edge, he couldn't even stir himself to start the engine. He had no idea what to think.

Although he was perfectly aware that dementia had long since carried Wolfgang Grief away into a parallel universe, Jonathan still found it hard to come to terms with his father's claim that Sofia regularly came to visit him. She'd been absent for decades, for God's sake!

Before leaving Sonnenhof, Jonathan had even talked to Dr. Knesebeck and two of the nursing assistants, half hoping, half fearing that they would confirm his father's story—but as he expected, they'd assured him that they had never set eyes on Sofia Grief. Nor Sofia Monticello, for that matter.

And no, there was no way they would have failed to notice a regular visitor; after all, Sonnenhof wasn't a railway station with people wandering in and out for fun, but "a first-rate facility." Dr. Knesebeck had repeated the latter assertion more than once, which sounded to

Jonathan like an attempt to justify the not-inconsiderable sum they charged him each month.

Nevertheless. A hint of doubt, a scrap of uncertainty, remained.

Whatever the nursing home's ratings, it wasn't Fort Knox either. Jonathan had strolled down deserted corridors on more than one occasion, and at midday, Sonnenhof was like an office building whose occupants had all gone to lunch. His father had talked about Sofia so clearly, with such conviction, that it was difficult for a healthy observer to believe that she had merely sprung from his deluded imagination.

And then, of course, there was the diary. As he thought of the Filofax on his desk at home, Jonathan realized that its existence had become even more of a mystery since the conversation with his father.

Could it be true? Was it *really* possible?

No, Jonathan silenced such thoughts. Even if his mother had decided to break her silence after almost thirty years and turn up in his life, surely there were far less complicated ways of making contact. She could have phoned, for example. Written a letter. Or come by his apartment.

*Well,* said the inner voice that had grown all too familiar, *maybe if your father's telling the truth, she did at least go to see him.*

However absurd it might seem, Jonathan simply *had* to investigate further, or the whole thing would never leave him in peace.

He pressed the little green telephone icon on his car's onboard computer with more force than needed, and with a voice command asked the system to put him through to Renate Krug. If anyone knew for sure whether or not Wolfgang had been visited by his ex-wife, it would be his longtime assistant.

"Hello, Herr Grief," Renate Krug said in her usual efficient but friendly tone.

"Yes, hello, Frau Krug."

"What can I do for you?"

"Do you know . . ." He gave a little cough. "I've just been to see my father . . ."

"Is he all right?" She sounded worried.

"What? Oh, no, not that, I mean, everything's fine. But I, ah, need to ask you, well, something strange."

"Something strange?" she echoed. "What is it?"

"Well, you may find this peculiar, but do you happen to know if my father's recently had a visit from my mother?"

Renate Krug said nothing.

"Are you still there?"

"Yes," she replied. "But I'm afraid I can't have heard you right. Did you say your mother?"

"I did," Jonathan confirmed. "I mean Sofia Grief. Or Monticello, maybe."

"What gives you that idea?"

"Papa said she'd been there."

Another brief pause, followed by "Oh, Jonathan." She never used his first name, or at least she hadn't since he'd reached the age of eighteen. Renate Krug was completely old school. But now she spoke to him as if she were talking to a young child she was looking after. "You know how it is with your father."

"Of course I do," he hastened to reassure her, immediately feeling stupid for broaching the subject. "I just wanted to make sure. Papa . . . well, he seemed so lucid at the time. Not confused at all."

"Yes, that's what's so tragic about his illness." He heard her swallow loudly. "The sufferer believes that everything they experience is the absolute truth. They think it's real."

"So you haven't heard anything about my mother being in Hamburg, now or recently?"

"No, Jonathan. I'm quite sure she isn't—or hasn't been."

"Have you . . ." Since he'd already made a fool of himself, he might as well go whole hog. "Have you heard or seen anything of her at all recently?"

"No, I haven't," Renate Krug replied. "No more than you or your father have."

"Do you know where she's living now?"

"In Italy. Somewhere near Florence, as far as I know."

"Even I know that. I just wondered if you had a current address for her."

"Unless it's the one she always had, I'm afraid I don't. Have you tried to contact her?"

"No," he admitted. "I didn't have any reason to before."

"And now you do?"

"Not really. It's just that . . . Well, after my father said she'd been to see him several times at the Sonnenhof, I just . . ."

"Well, if that's what's bothering you, I can assure you one hundred percent that it's impossible." She paused, as though wondering whether she really could rule it out. "In any case, how would Sofia know where your father is? She's never contacted me to ask. Has she been in touch with you?"

"No," Jonathan said. "Of course not." *Not for many years,* he added silently.

"There you go," Renate Krug said. "It's not only unlikely, but impossible that your mother went to the home."

"Hmm, yes, okay. Thanks!"

"Of course." She hesitated. "Is there anything else I can do for you?"

"No." He was about to hang up when something else occurred to him. "I mean, yes, there is."

"Yes?"

"My father mentioned that my mother had forgiven him something. Do you have any idea what he could have meant?"

"Not in the slightest," she replied.

"You don't know anything about an argument they might have had? Something that could have come between her and my father?"

"No, Jonathan, there was nothing of the sort. She wasn't happy here in the north and wanted to go home. That was all." She paused. "And it seems she'd imagined a rather different life for herself than to be with a man who worked as many hours as your father. As an Italian, she had a different set of values. I think that's what your father must have meant if he spoke of forgiveness—simply that he'd neglected her."

"Did my mother talk to you about it?"

Renate Krug laughed out loud. "Hardly," she said. "We weren't exactly friends. She was simply my boss's wife. But your father told me, and I saw no reason to doubt what he said."

*No reason to doubt what he said.* Well, *there* was something that had changed.

"Hmm," Jonathan said. "It's probably all just a figment of his imagination."

"I'm afraid so."

"Nevertheless, it's rather bewildering. He's never talked about her in all these years. And today he suddenly claims that he sees her often? It's weird!"

"Don't take it so seriously," Renate Krug replied. "People with dementia live more in the past than the present. It's completely normal. Things that happened many years ago suddenly seem closer to them than things from a moment ago."

"I know." He wondered briefly whether he should also tell his father's assistant about the mysterious diary, but he decided against it. They weren't particularly close, even though he had known her since he was a boy. "Thank you for the information, anyway."

"You're welcome."

"So, till next time. And, um, Frau Krug?"

"Yes?"

"Your New Year's bouquet is on its way. I'm sorry I forgot about it today."

Renate Krug laughed softly. "I don't mean any offense, Herr Grief, but I've always hated those carnations. I'll be delighted if they're not cluttering up the office this year."

"Really? Why didn't you tell my father?"

She laughed again. "You have a lot to learn about women."

"What do you mean by that?"

"Maybe you'll understand one day."

They said goodbye and hung up, leaving Jonathan alone in his Saab, his fingers drumming nervously on the steering wheel and a strange feeling in the pit of his stomach. How many things had his father been mistaken about? And just what, exactly, did he have to learn about women?

# 12

*Hannah*

"Yes, yes, and once again, yes! You were right. I'm the girlfriend from hell. Let's say the worst ever. Satisfied?" Hannah was sitting hunched over in the waiting room of the Eppendorf University Clinic emergency room, head in her hands, elbows on her knees, like a sinner before the doors of a church.

"Please don't feel bad!" Lisa sat by her side as they waited for the doctor to appear. "I'm sorry I said it; I really didn't mean it. Of course you're not the girlfriend from hell. And it's not a matter of whether I'm satisfied. It's Simon we should be worried about."

"Yes, of course." Hannah sighed. "I hope it's not too serious."

"I doubt it." Lisa put her arm around her friend and gave her a comforting hug. "It was probably all just a bit too much for him."

"It's so horrible!" Hannah said. "How was I supposed to know he was going to collapse?"

"You couldn't *know*," Lisa said with a crooked smile. "But you could sort of tell by looking at him. I was surprised when you dragged him into Little Rascals at lunchtime. I thought he looked like a man who belonged in bed, not in the middle of a noisy horde of little kids."

"You should have said something!"

"I did! Which part of 'Oh my God, he looks awful!' didn't you understand?"

Hannah shrugged. "I didn't hear you."

"So that's why you answered that no one would notice once you'd put his makeup on?"

"Stop!" Hannah snapped. "Anyway, you know Simon's tendency to exaggerate."

"Okay," Lisa agreed. "I do. I also know your tendency to see everything with rose-colored glasses. Or at least how it fits in best with your worldview." She elbowed her friend in the ribs. "Sorry, but you've got to admit it."

"It's better than always fearing the worst."

"Depends."

"On what?"

"Well, if we all end up in the ER, I don't really think it's for the best."

"For God's sake!" Hannah sat up abruptly and crossed her arms. "I've already confessed! I *am* the girlfriend from hell."

"Don't start that again. Sorry. Let's wait and see before we get all worked up."

"Okay."

They sat together in silence for a while. Hannah surreptitiously watched the other people in the waiting area. Most of them seemed to be there with someone else, like she and Lisa were, but here and there she spotted a bandage or a crutch. In the far-left-hand corner, a mother had a little girl in her arms, the child burying her head in her mother's neck and letting out the most heartrending sobs.

Hannah couldn't help thinking that although the situation was far from pleasant, at least they weren't there because of a child. She couldn't bear to imagine their first day ending with a trip to the hospital with one of their little charges. Not good advertising for Little Rascals.

They'd almost managed to see the funny side of having to call an ambulance for Simon and watching it screech up Eppendorfer Weg, siren wailing, just as the first parents were arriving.

The children had hopped up and down with excitement and watched with wide-eyed interest as the jolly clown was examined by a paramedic and then loaded onto a stretcher and carried out to the waiting ambulance. Pure drama!

Hannah had gone with her boyfriend, while Lisa followed half an hour later after reassuring all their clients and saying goodbye to them. By then, the ambulance team had carried Simon, groaning loudly, off to who-knows-where, and they had been sitting there waiting for news ever since.

Hannah heard Lisa let out a snort of laughter.

"What?"

She looked at her friend, who waved her away.

"Nothing."

"Tell me!"

"I couldn't help thinking of when the ambulance arrived."

"Me too." Hannah laughed with her.

"Not a bad show to put on for our first day."

"You could say that."

"Good publicity. Our fame will have spread all over the neighborhood by now. It's not every day that a semiconscious clown gets whisked off through the streets, let alone one surrounded by an excited gaggle of onlookers."

"Do you think it'll damage our image?"

"Only if the clown dies."

"Lisa!"

"Sorry," she said quickly. "That was a stupid joke." She placed a reassuring hand on Hannah's arm. "Everything's okay. I told the parents your boyfriend has been trying out a new diet and that's why he fainted."

"A diet? Simon's a string bean!"

"It was the first thing that came into my head. Or should I have told them that his girlfriend forced him into playing the entertainer despite a raging fever?"

"Ha ha."

"Don't worry. We've got a full house again tomorrow, starting at two."

"I hope Simon's better by then."

"You're not intending to sign him up again?" Lisa looked at her incredulously.

"Of course I am," she replied as seriously as she could. "If he can stand, he's got to play his part."

"Then I can only hope he takes a while to recover—you're going to kill him!" Their loud laughter drew bemused stares from the other occupants of the waiting area. But Hannah didn't care. It felt good to have a moment's light relief.

"Hannah Marx?" She hadn't noticed the white-coated young man in his early thirties approaching. He now stood looking down at them through rimless glasses.

Hannah's attempt to suppress her laughter ended in a shrill squeak.

"Um, yes?" she managed to say.

"My name is Dr. Robert Fuchs. And you are . . ." He opened the thin file he had been gripping under his arm and glanced at the contents. "You're Simon Klamm's wife?"

Hannah nodded, earning herself a sidelong look of astonishment from Lisa. When checking in, she'd thought it easier to say she was Simon's wife, since she was worried the situation might be too serious for her to be allowed in to see her boyfriend. She knew from *ER* and *Grey's Anatomy* that the poor girlfriends were always left hovering out in the corridor as loved ones underwent life-threatening brain surgery. Damned to nerve-racking ignorance, they had no legal right to know what was happening. The fear that such a thing could also happen to

Hannah in the Eppendorf University Clinic might be a bit of overdramatization, but better safe than sorry.

"You can see him now. Please follow me."

Hannah jumped up.

Lisa rose, too, and before the doctor could say anything, Hannah reassured him that "she's the sister."

"I like it," Lisa whispered as they hurried after Dr. Fuchs.

"What, that you're Simon's sister?"

"No. That you've decided to keep your maiden name. I'm sorry, but Hannah Klamm sounds awful!"

Hannah suppressed a laugh and thumped Lisa in the side. The last thing she wanted Dr. Fuchs to see was the worried wife in a fit of hysterical giggles.

They followed the doctor through seemingly endless white corridors, past patients and waiting relatives. The hospital was packed to overflowing; even the hallways were lined with beds where people slept or lay looking miserable.

Hannah felt anxiety overtaking her. She hadn't pictured the afternoon ending like this. Apart from the fact that no one in their right mind enjoyed spending time in a clinic, she suddenly remembered the period, about four years ago, when she had come with Simon to the hospital almost every day.

His mother, Hilde, had lain dying after fighting cancer for several months. An operation, chemo, radiation therapy—nothing had helped. She had a malignant tumor in her lung and had finally suffered a horrendous death—Hannah couldn't think of it any other way—that lasted for weeks. More than once Hilde had whimpered that she couldn't take any more and wished she could be released.

Simon and Hannah had only known each other for six months; it wasn't long after their picnic by the Elbe that the doctors told his mother there was nothing more they could do. Although they hadn't been together long, Hannah went with Simon on most of his visits, to support him during that difficult time. His mother was his last remaining family; his father had passed away over ten years before her, from the same evil disease.

Everyone knew that the death of a mother hit boys harder than girls. When Hilde died, Simon had been a young man of thirty-one, but he had cried like a little child at her funeral, and even months after her death he sometimes broke down in tears for no reason. Hannah felt helpless, with no idea how to comfort him.

Despite her reluctance to descend into the usual platitudes of "Time heals all wounds" or "We all have to go sometime," she was nevertheless unable to think of any more appropriate words of wisdom. So she had tended to limit herself to taking Simon's arm, stroking his head, and waiting for his tears to dry. Sometimes she thought it might have been easier if there'd been a brother or sister to share Simon's grief, but he was an only child like she was.

As she scurried after Dr. Fuchs with Lisa and thought back to those times, she resolved not to be so hard on her boyfriend in the future. After all, Simon had coped with some serious crises in his life, and it was unfair of her to brush them aside with her customary "It'll all be okay!"

She really had no right to talk. Her parents were both still alive and in the best of health. Even her grandparents on her mother's side— Marianne and Rolf, eighty-five and eighty-seven—gave the impression that they intended to roam this beautiful planet for a good few decades more. And at ninety, Hannah's paternal grandmother, Elisabeth, was the picture of sprightly vitality.

"Here we are," the doctor said, tearing Hannah from her thoughts. They came to a stop outside a white door. He pressed the handle and entered, Hannah and Lisa on his heels.

# 13

*Jonathan*

**Tuesday, January 2, 6:56 p.m.**

There was nothing to it, nothing at all. Jonathan would simply ring the bell at that address, introduce himself politely, and tell them why he was there. And a few minutes later it would all be dealt with. Whoever had an appointment at seven p.m. at Dorotheenstrasse 20, he or she would be delighted to get their diary back, and Jonathan would be convinced once and for all that the Filofax had nothing to do with his mother. As simple as that. Nothing to make a fuss about.

And yet, as he walked up and down in front of the late nineteenth-century white house, ready to press the second button from the bottom at seven p.m. precisely, he realized that his hands were damp with sweat. Unpleasant, and completely uncalled for. *There's no reason at all to be nervous.*

Jonathan muttered this over and over to himself like a mantra, swinging the bag with its diary in time at the height of his right knee. But he found it hard to convince his sweat glands and heartbeat. It was just as he'd felt before the oral exam at the end of his philosophy-and-literature degree. Even then it hadn't been so bad, as he'd prepared thoroughly and sailed effortlessly through his exams.

When the big hand of his watch showed one minute to seven, Jonathan N. Grief ascended the three steps to number 20 and looked for the right bell. There—second from the bottom. "Schulz."

Before he could have second thoughts, he pressed it. The intercom buzzed three seconds later. No "Hello?" or "Who is it?" Someone was obviously expected at seven o'clock. Either that or the occupant was a trusting soul; Jonathan could have been anyone. This was the time of year, for example, when the garbage collectors often went from door to door hoping for tips. Not that there was anything wrong with that—if they'd done their job well during the past year, why not?

Jonathan couldn't help recalling his email to the Department of Public Works. He hadn't received a reply yet, and he wondered if anyone was going to take notice. The bins outside his house still hadn't been emptied. But he told himself not to be impatient—and not to distract himself now, of all times, by thinking about garbage collection!

Slowly, with measured steps, Jonathan climbed the stairs to the third floor, where he imagined Herr or Frau Schulz to be waiting for him. He took his time. He didn't want to arrive out of breath or sweating, any more than he already was.

The stairwell was spacious, bright, and welcoming, the walls still decorated with their original colorful art nouveau tiles, finished at the top with an ornamental band. A well-kept house, it had to be said. His mother would have liked a place like this; as far as he could recall, she was typically Italian in her infallible good taste.

Moreover, the old building was at the heart of the central Hamburg district of Winterhude, with numerous cafés and shops at its doorstep. Sofia had always felt a little cut off at their family home on the Elbe, and she tended to suffer from boredom. She had often talked gushingly about the bustling streets of Florence—or, more precisely, the market-place of the little town of Fiesole, where she came from.

Jonathan could still vaguely remember his father responding to her complaints with a reference to the disastrous parking situation in the city center. Jonathan himself had just had to trail around the block in his Saab for a full quarter of an hour before bagging a legal parking space big enough for his car. Even then, he had to draw on all his parallel-parking skills, since the driver of the Golf in front had clearly deemed it perfectly acceptable to leave a two-foot gap between it and the tree at the end of the row.

When, after much meticulous back-and-forth, Jonathan had finally managed to squeeze into the space behind the Golf, he had taken out the notepad he always carried, scribbled a note to the parking lout, and tucked it behind the windshield wiper.

> Dear Driver,
> You have parked very inconsiderately. Your car is taking up the space of two! It has taken me great effort to fit into the space behind you. If you had only moved forward a few inches, you would have made the life of a fellow citizen much more pleasant.
> Yours sincerely,
> Jonathan N. Grief

As if that wasn't annoying enough, Jonathan had been faced with having to pay an exorbitant price to park. Four euros per hour! It felt like he wasn't paying to use the parking space, but to buy it! Another topic for the *Hamburg News*. Maybe he'd have to send another email to the editor drawing attention to the modern gangsters in charge of the city's parking. He was already composing it in his mind.

> Dear Editorial Team,
> As a citizen who drives a car in our beautiful city, I am writing to ask you to cover the subject of the highway robbery of parking prices . . .

He told himself now was not the time or place to get worked up. He needed to concentrate fully on the matter of the diary; after all, that was why he was here.

When he reached the third-floor landing, he saw a lady standing outside the door of her apartment, waiting for him with a smile. Jonathan was reminded of the singer Cher; this woman was equally beautiful, although without as much cosmetic surgery. He guessed she was in her midfifties, but she could have been a good ten years younger. Or older—it was hard to say.

Her long black hair fell in a shiny wave over her shoulders, and her striking features had something Indian about them. She was wearing a close-fitting anthracite-colored pantsuit that coordinated perfectly with her dark-gray eyes. All in all, she was a vision of loveliness. "Timeless elegance" would be the literary expression for it.

Jonathan cleared his throat as he approached and reached out to shake her hand. "Hello, Frau Schulz. My name is—"

"Shhh!" The woman cut him off with an index finger over her lips. She was still smiling, but somehow it now looked conspiratorial. "No names!" she purred in a dark, smoky voice. If Jonathan had needed to find someone to overdub the character of Frau Schulz, he would have chosen that very voice. Though maybe he would change the name Schulz; he wasn't too fond of that. "Come in." She swung the door open and stepped aside to let him past.

"Um, yes," Jonathan stammered as he removed his shoes, left them on the mat, and obeyed her invitation. "So, Frau Schulz—"

"Sarasvati," she interrupted again.

"Saras-what?"

"My name is Sarasvati."

"Really? Sarasvati Schulz?"

She laughed out loud, bright and bubbly. "You could say that. Sarasvati is my spiritual name. My soul name."

"Spiritual. I see." Jonathan fought an impulse to take his leave and vanish there and then. This lovely woman was seeming weirder by the minute.

He was reminded of Harry Potter by the Alster babbling about his "spiritual" swans. Was there something in Hamburg's water? What was going on? Of course, Jonathan didn't leave; his curiosity had already gotten the better of him. That and the feeling that he was embarking on an adventure.

"Sarasvati is the Indian goddess of wisdom and learning," Frau Schulz explained as she led Jonathan into the living room. The interior was stylish, with a blend of light, modern furniture and selected dark wood antique pieces, the most striking of which was a grandfather clock with filigree carving. The white woolen drapes hanging at the three large windows, the thick African patterned carpet, and the Moroccan ceiling light combined to give the room an exotic warmth and coziness.

Frau Schulz, a.k.a. Sarasvati, gestured for him to sit in one of the chairs around the teak dining table, which was dominated by a six-branched candelabra. Next to that was a crystal carafe of water with two glasses, and a pack of playing cards. "Do sit down, please."

"I'm afraid there's been a misunderstanding," Jonathan said without taking the offered seat. "I hadn't intended to come to you."

"Really?" Sarasvati raised a perfectly plucked eyebrow.

"Well, not exactly. But I've got something to hand over."

"You do?" She reached out a hand. "So give it to me."

Jonathan involuntarily grasped the bag harder with both hands and pressed it against his upper body. "No, I can't. It's not for you!"

"Not for me?" The second eyebrow followed the first. "In that case, I don't understand why you're here. You seem to be in a bit of a muddle, young man."

"Let me explain." He was quietly irritated by that "young man"—it was so patronizing. But he swallowed his scruples and told Sarasvati about his morning run by the Alster and the find that had brought him to her now.

"I see," she said, regarding him with amusement as his tale came to an end. "But you can leave the diary here with a clear conscience. I'll give it to my client as soon as he arrives."

"Your *client?*" Jonathan N. Grief looked once again around the room, trying not to reveal the thoughts that sprang into his mind.

In vain. Sarasvati laughed again. "It's not what you think!" She pointed to the table. "I read the cards."

"Cards?"

She nodded.

"So you're a fortune teller?"

"I prefer to call myself a 'life adviser.'"

"Ah." The thoughts now in Jonathan's head were more complimentary than the previous ones, but they did contain words such as *charlatan* and *hocus-pocus*.

"You don't think much of it, do you?" It seemed the lady was clairvoyant after all.

"Well," Jonathan said evasively, "I've never really tried it."

"You should. It's fascinating!"

"Yes, well . . ." He decided to ignore her proposal. "I just want to be sure the Filofax finds its way into the right hands."

"And you don't think my hands are the right ones?"

"What makes you say that?"

The fortune teller shrugged. "You don't want to leave the diary with me, even though I've assured you that I'll pass it on."

"Please don't take this the wrong way," Jonathan replied, "but I don't know you at all." He thought of the five hundred euros in the back pocket of the book and couldn't help thinking that a fortune teller hardly had the best credentials for such a duty of care. Call it prejudice.

"Please don't take this the wrong way yourself, but I don't know you either," Sarasvati replied. "Yet you're sitting here in my living room."

"You asked me in!"

"Because I thought you were a client."

"There you are," he said triumphantly, unable to suppress a smile. "That's exactly why you should always be cautious!"

She shook her head. "I hope you're not going to cause me trouble."

"What?"

She waved him away. "Forget it." She pointed again to a chair. "But how about this for a plan? You sit there and wait until the mysterious owner of the Filofax appears."

"Am I disturbing you?"

"No, not at all. I've kept the next three hours completely clear for this appointment, so we're free to spend the time together until my client arrives."

"Three hours?" Jonathan wondered as he sat down at the table and placed the bag on the floor next to the chair. "That's how long a reading takes?"

"For a first consultation," Sarasvati replied, moving to sit opposite him. "It can take up to five hours sometimes."

"Five?" Jonathan exclaimed in amazement. "What do you find to talk about for five hours?"

"Life. Believe me—some clients come back again and again, because the human experience is so complex. A single consultation is nowhere near enough."

"What do you earn?" he said without thinking, his curiosity getting the better of him.

"What do you earn from your job?" she countered. "What is it you do?"

"I'm sorry." He felt his cheeks reddening. "I shouldn't have asked." Once again, he couldn't help himself. "Anyway, if you're a psychic, you must know what I do."

"Life adviser," she corrected.

"Whatever. I didn't want to step on your toes. I was only interested to know what someone in your"—he tried his best to avoid the word *profession*—"in your line of business earns."

"It depends."

"On what?"

"On the people who come to me for advice."

"You decide on the basis of how much you like them?"

"That's part of it," she confirmed. "And on what the client can afford."

"So you offer discounts for the needy?"

"You could call it that," she said. "It also depends on the seriousness of the problem." She winked at him cheerfully. "It certainly wouldn't be cheap in your case."

"But you don't know anything about me!"

"I know enough." She smiled. "I only have to look at you."

"Really?" Jonathan crossed his arms, surprised to find he wasn't really offended but rather . . . fascinated. Even though it was, of course, utter nonsense, he had to admit that this Sarasvati had something about her. "Would you be prepared to tell me what it is you see? And how it all works?"

"There's nothing to tell," she replied. "I just know. It's a gift. You either have it or you don't."

"So why do you need the cards?" He pointed at the pack in the middle of the table.

"They're my tools, like a carpenter uses a hammer, or a painter uses a brush. I can use them to see the way things are going."

Jonathan leaned across the table toward her. "I'm sorry, but I find it difficult to believe."

"Believe what you want."

"I mean, they're completely normal cards, aren't they?" He couldn't let it go; the whole thing was simply far too interesting.

"They're tarot cards."

"And you shuffle them, lay them out, and presto! You know what's going to happen in the future?"

Her rippling laughter rang out again. "If you like, yes. Except I'm not the one who shuffles the cards; my clients do. And I don't see the future, but the possibilities."

"Ah!" He should have known. *Possibilities.* There were always plenty of those. For instance, he could step out of his house tomorrow and get run over by a truck. Anything was possible.

"If I can explain a little more," Sarasvati continued. She picked up the pack of cards and began to spread them out in front of Jonathan. "With the tarot there's what we call the law of correspondence." She placed one card after the other with a plop on the table. "All our feelings, our thoughts—all our hopes, beliefs, and fears—can be expressed in a picture."

"So far, so good," Jonathan said. "But what I don't understand is how the cards can possibly know what I hope or feel or believe."

"It's not the cards that know it. You're the one! Your subconscious reacts to the symbols in the pictures. It's like dream interpretation."

Jonathan shook his head skeptically. "But let's assume I shuffle the cards and pick a couple out—the outcome is pure chance and has nothing to do with what I know, consciously or subconsciously."

"Nothing in life happens by chance," Sarasvati said. "Everything's connected to everything else. The inner always corresponds to the outer."

He leaned back in his chair. "I'm afraid you've lost me."

"Shall I show you?"

"How do you mean?"

"Well, by reading the cards for you."

"What?" He raised his hands dismissively. "Oh, no, I'm not interested! I'm only here to hand over the diary, that's all."

"As you wish."

95

"Yes." He glanced at the grandfather clock. A quarter past seven. "There can't be much longer to wait."

"Would you like a glass of water?" She reached for the carafe. "It's been activated with healing stones."

Jonathan noticed for the first time that some purple stones lay on the bottom of the crystal pitcher. "No, thanks." Who could say what was floating around in that water? A cloud of bacteria, at best.

"Very well." She poured herself a glass of water and drank two big gulps before setting it down with a sigh of satisfaction. "Oh, that feels good!"

"Hmm." Jonathan wasn't sure what to say. The easy situation had all at once become suffocating, and he hoped the client wouldn't take too much longer to arrive. It really wasn't acceptable to arrive so late. When there was a fixed appointment—a professional one in Frau Schulz's case, after all—Jonathan was firmly of the opinion that being fashionably late simply wasn't an option.

The psychic didn't seem concerned in the slightest; she sat completely relaxed, drinking her healing water and looking at Jonathan with an open, friendly expression.

Neither of them said a word; only the ticking of the clock filled the room.

Shortly before half past seven, Jonathan decided to try the water. He passed Sarasvati his glass, saying casually, "I might as well have a drink." Smiling, she poured him a glass. He raised it to his lips and was surprised by how nice and fresh the water tasted. Whether or not it was "activated," he couldn't say—but it was no worse than the Evian he liked to drink.

A quarter to eight. Jonathan toyed with his empty glass. "It looks like your client isn't coming," he observed.

"It doesn't matter," Sarasvati replied.

"But you've put aside three hours!" How could she be so calm and casual about it? He would be fuming if someone wasted his time like that.

"They've paid up front."

"You take advance payments?"

"PayPal."

"How does that work?"

"It's very practical. The client simply uses their email address to send it to mine."

"Money by email? Don't you think it's a bit insecure?"

"No." She laughed. "Your account's managed using your email address, that's all."

"So that means you must know your client's name," Jonathan said.

"Not in this case," she replied, to his disappointment. "The email address used for the payment doesn't give a hint of a name. The meeting was booked as a gift via my website. There's a calendar where you can check for free time slots and reserve one."

"You have a website?"

"Of course. I have to move with the times."

"Yes, of course." He smiled. "You seem to be a very modern clair-voyant," he said appreciatively.

"Life adviser."

"Indeed."

They both fell silent again as the hands of the clock crept forward agonizingly slowly.

"Well," Sarasvati said as a deep bell rang out eight times. "You seem to be right that no one's coming. So it looks like I can't help you. And since you don't want to leave the diary with me—"

"Isn't there any way you can find out who made the appointment?" He could hear the despair in his own voice and felt embarrassed at his lack of composure. He couldn't explain the strength of his feelings.

Sarasvati frowned and looked at him searchingly. "Why is it so important to you?" she asked. "The owner has nothing to do with you."

"True, but . . ." But what? *The diary could be my mother's? The whole thing just feels important? Not a lot happens in my life, and this is the first time in ages that . . .* "Oh, I don't know. I suppose I'd better hand the Filofax in to the police and forget about it."

"You think that's for the best?" She stared at him so intently with her almond eyes that Jonathan felt warmth coursing through him.

"Well, if the owner hasn't turned up here and you don't know who he or she is . . ." He had a flash of inspiration. "You could send an email to the address they paid with! That way you could tell them I've found a diary and they can come see me to pick it up. I can give you my phone number."

"I could," Sarasvati agreed. "But why should I?"

"Um." He was momentarily speechless. "Out of the kindness of your heart?"

"I do have a kind heart, yes." She smiled broadly. "And because I do, I'm offering again to read the cards for you. The consultation's been paid for, after all."

"No, no," he said. "It really isn't my thing."

She wouldn't let it drop. "If you just allow yourself to think for one second that nothing in life happens by chance, and then wonder why you're sitting here with me—aren't you dying to know what the outcome could be?"

"Uh . . ." He hesitated. "No?" His determined statement came out as a question.

"I don't believe you."

"And I don't understand why you're so determined to look into my future!"

"Your possibilities," Sarasvati corrected.

"Whatever. I'm not interested." As if to give more weight to his words, he slapped the flat of his hand down on the table and moved to rise from his chair.

Sarasvati leaned back and looked at him for a moment, shaking her head. "Tell me," she said, "what are you so scared of?"

"Scared?" He laughed and sat back down. "I'm not scared!"

# 14

*Hannah*

**Two months before:**
**Monday, October 30, 7:53 p.m.**

"Hello!" Simon was sitting up in a hospital bed by the window. When they entered the room, he raised a hand in greeting and gave them a weak smile. He still looked very pale and had tubes running from his left arm to two transparent plastic pouches that hung from an IV pole by his bed. Hannah took one look at her poor boyfriend and her knees went weak, her heart clenched painfully, and her stomach turned queasy.

"Darling!" She drew up a visitor's chair and grasped Simon's hand. "What have you been up to?"

His smile turned roguish. "I could ask you the same thing—what have *you* been up to? With me?"

"I'm so, so sorry," Hannah said, glancing at Lisa as she said it again. "If I'd had any idea—"

"Don't worry," he interrupted. "I survived." He looked over at the doctor. "Dr. Fuchs says I suffered some kind of collapse, but nothing serious."

"That's right," the doctor confirmed. "But you don't want to be too casual about it," he added sternly. "You overexerted yourself, and when you have a lingering infection, that can be quite risky." He paused to allow his words to have the desired effect. They certainly affected Hannah, who sank visibly into her chair. Lisa, who was still standing by the door, also looked guilty, even though she had played no part in the situation.

Of them all, Simon, lying in his bed, seemed the most cheerful. Was Hannah mistaken or could she see a clear "I told you so!" in his expression?

"People often underestimate the impact a common cold can have on them—even young, healthy people," Dr. Fuchs continued. "In the very worst cases, cold viruses can attack other organs, which can lead, for example, to myocarditis. And in certain circumstances, that can be fatal." All three gasped.

"Oh, please don't tempt fate!" Hannah said reproachfully, as soon as she'd composed herself.

"Nothing could be further from my mind," the doctor replied a little complacently. "I'm not tempting fate; I'm just telling you what we doctors see here, day in, day out."

Simon wheezed. "Day in, day out?"

"Well, maybe not so often," Dr. Fuchs conceded and cleared his throat. "But often enough to prescribe complete rest for you for the next few days." He picked up Simon's chart and looked at the contents with the frown of a man studying the figures of a stock-market crash. "Well, Simon, your condition is stable now. As soon as the infusions are complete, one of the nurses will remove the drip and you can sleep in peace. If everything looks okay, we'll discharge you tomorrow morning." He leafed through the chart again. "Your blood pressure's very low, but I'm not surprised. Your blood test did show a couple of abnormalities. I'd have it checked again by your family doctor."

"Abnormalities?" Simon said.

The doctor snapped the file shut and looked him in the eye. "First, your inflammation levels are high, which is why we're giving you an antibiotic along with the saline solution." He tapped one of the plastic pouches on the IV pole. "Please continue to take the medication orally for the next six days. You'll be given a prescription when you're released."

Simon nodded obediently.

"There are also signs of slight anemia, which I believe is caused by the infection."

"Infection-related anemia?" Lisa asked.

"A consequence of the cold, which makes me think it might actually be influenza. Fortunately, there are no signs of pneumonia."

"Ah," Hannah said, feeling even worse than she had before. So it was flu now—and she'd forced Simon into a clown costume!

Oh well, at least it wasn't pneumonia. That was positive, surely.

"It should get better on its own. Flu's rarely a problem at your age," Dr. Fuchs said. "But I do recommend that you present yourself at your family doctor's office in a few weeks, once you're feeling better. You should be given another blood test and have all the indicators checked."

As the doctor went on about what Simon should and shouldn't do, Hannah was irritated by his pompous, self-important way of speaking. *Present yourself at your family doctor's office.* Honestly! "Hello, may I introduce myself? My name is Simon Klamm." Really, the good doctor looked so young but acted so stuffy!

". . . but the most important thing is complete rest over the next few days," the white-clad demigod said, ending his monologue.

"In that case, I'd rather stay here in the hospital," Simon said.

"I beg your pardon?"

"Well, if I need rest, I'd rather not go home." He grasped Hannah's hand surreptitiously. "I've no chance of recovering there, with my own personal slave driver forcing me into strenuous activity. I feel safer here in the hospital. A kind of refuge, you know?"

"Refuge?" Dr. Fuchs had an expression of complete incomprehension, while Lisa was doubled up with laughter and Simon was barely suppressing a smug grin.

"Just stop it!" Hannah complained. "I got the message, okay? You don't have to keep rubbing it in."

"Oh, come on, honey," Simon said, squeezing her hand again, this time in a soothing gesture. "I need to have some fun. Isn't that what you always say?"

"But it's all at my expense."

"Take your turn with everyone else," Lisa said.

"Well, I don't know about all that," the doctor intervened. "I'll leave you to it. My colleague Dr. Hausmann will be on duty tomorrow morning. If everything's going well, which I think it will be, you can go home." He hesitated a moment, as though wondering whether to add "If you want to." He held back, merely taking his leave with a brief nod and vanishing from the room.

"Huh!" Lisa said as soon as the door had closed behind him. "What a performance!"

"You can say that again," Hannah agreed. "I felt like I was confessing every one of my sins at the Last Judgment."

"It didn't last long enough for that," Simon said, bursting out laughing. Hannah gave him an evil look, and he raised his free hand defensively. "Actually, I thought the doctor was great. Someone who took me seriously, at last!"

"As if I don't take you seriously!"

"Oh, come here and let me kiss you, you impossible woman!" He pulled her to him and began to cover her face with kisses. She let him, laughing.

"It looks like it's time I went back to Little Rascals," Lisa said. "Someone has to clean up."

"Wait!" Hannah mumbled from beneath Simon's lips. "I'll come with you!"

"Don't worry." Lisa waved her away. "Stay here with our patient."

"Are you sure?"

"Of course!" She grinned from the doorway.

"I'll see you tomorrow?" Hannah asked.

"If Simon can live without you, of course!"

"Read my lips," Simon said. "I need *rest*!"

"Huh!" Hannah replied.

Lisa said goodbye and left them on their own together.

"Oh, my love," Hannah said and laid her head on Simon's chest. "That was quite some excitement."

"Absolutely wild." He laid an arm across her shoulders. "Actually, I like the way you're so concerned about me." He began stroking her hair.

"You know," she said, closing her eyes and enjoying Simon's touch, "I got the shock of my life when you keeled over."

"Really?"

"Yes." She raised her head and looked at him. "I was really scared for you."

"Nonsense," he said awkwardly. "It'd take more than that to finish me off."

"Glad to hear it." Her voice shook a little. "I hope you know how much I love you. When I thought I might lose you . . ."

"Shush!" He laid his index finger over her lips. Then he smiled, leaned toward her, and kissed her gently and cautiously. "I love you too." He kissed her again. "And you needn't worry. You won't get rid of me that easily."

"I hope not!"

"Definitely not."

"No?"

"No, not at all." He cleared his throat. "I just realized what it was I've been wanting to ask you all this time."

"Yes?" Hannah's heart paused for a moment, only to start beating wildly the next. Would this be the ultimate question, the one she'd secretly been waiting for? Here? In the hospital? But she didn't really care where Simon popped the question. The main thing was that he spat it out at last! Maybe that afternoon's scare had made him realize that the time had come? That life was short, and when it came to the things that were important to you, you shouldn't wait until it was too late?

"So, the thing is . . ." He trailed off. "Oh, I don't know how to put it."

"Just say it," she encouraged.

He took a deep breath, then began again. "All this time I've been wanting to ask you—"

"Herr Klamm!" The door flew open and crashed loudly against the wall. A strapping nurse strode in, her ponytail swaying back and forth with every step. "I'll remove your drip; it's finished now." She deftly removed the IV from Simon's arm and covered the puncture wound with a bandage. Then she gave them both a friendly nod and left, pulling the IV pole behind her. Hannah watched the door shut. The nurse was like an evil spirit, making a brief but effective appearance. She could have killed Nurse Ponytail! Why that very moment? *Why now?*

"Go on," Hannah told Simon as soon as they were alone again.

"No, I'd better not," he said, to her bitter disappointment. He yawned deeply. "I'm wrung out. I desperately need sleep."

"Are you sure?" She tried her best not to let that disappointment show, but she could already feel the tears springing to her eyes. "I could wait here while you take a nap."

"That's really sweet." He smiled at her as he settled down into his pillow. "But once I've nodded off I probably won't wake up again till morning."

"I don't mind," Hannah insisted. "I'll just stay here."

"Don't be silly. You need some sleep yourself."

"I'll sleep here."

"Where?" He blinked. "On that uncomfortable visitor chair?"

"I can lie on the floor if I have to." Even she could hear how silly it sounded. After all, she was hardly keeping watch over his deathbed.

"Go on now," Simon said with another wide yawn. "I'd really like to be on my own for a while."

"But don't you want . . ." She hesitated, but couldn't get it out of her mind. What had he wanted to ask her? What? She had to know! He'd been so close just then, so *close*! "Don't you want to get your question out of your system?"

"Another time, all right?" His eyelids began to flutter, and Hannah had to concede defeat.

"Okay, darling." She gave him another gentle kiss on the lips. "I'll be back tomorrow morning to take you home."

She got a light snore by way of reply.

# 15

*Jonathan*

"Well, it's looking very good already. You have a long and happy life ahead of you."

Jonathan N. Grief peered skeptically at the thirteen cards he'd selected and which Sarasvati had laid out in a pattern on the table. She called it the Celtic cross, but as far as Jonathan was concerned it could just as easily have been the Bohemian village.

He tapped his index finger on the topmost card. It showed a skeleton in knight's regalia, astride a white horse. "I don't like to contradict you, but the first thing I see here is death. It even says so on the card!" He shuddered.

"That's true," she replied—and the shudder intensified. "But death shouldn't be taken literally. It means letting go, a far-reaching change. A transformation."

"How reassuring." Jonathan gulped. "I mean, dying is quite a change—but one I'd rather not experience quite yet."

"As I said, your cards indicate a long, fulfilling life."

"How nice."

"But—"

"Ah, here comes the catch!"

Sarasvati Schulz silenced him with a stern look. "But," she repeated, bending over the cards, "you must also be prepared to allow these changes in."

"So, what are they?"

"Shhh!" She flapped a hand as though batting away a fly, then slowly traced her finger from one colorful image to the next. "I can see you're worried about something."

"Who wouldn't be worried, given the way the world's going?"

She looked up and clicked her tongue. "If you're going to interrupt every word I say, we certainly won't finish in the time we have."

"I'll hold my tongue."

She turned again to the tarot deck. "Yes, I can see it clearly. You're full of a great fear that's holding you back."

Jonathan swallowed the remark that he really wasn't afraid of anything. At least, not right then; things could, of course, change during the next hour and a half.

"You have to release yourself from your paralysis and approach things head-on." She tapped an image labeled "The Fool," which showed a youth balancing on the edge of a precipice. "The cards are advising you to lighten up," she said. "Let go of your cares, don't hang on to your pain, get rid of all your baggage."

"I don't *have* any cares!" Jonathan said again, more loudly than he'd intended. "In any case, if I may be so bold, that young man looks as though he could fall at any moment."

Sarasvati sighed and leaned back in her chair. "I'm sorry, but we're not getting anywhere. We'd better stop. There's no point with you." She made a move to gather up the cards.

"Oh, don't!" Jonathan cried, surprised. He shot his hands out and laid them on hers. Noticing her piqued expression, he cleared his throat in embarrassment and let go. "Sorry," he mumbled. "I won't say another word, promise!"

"Good." She tipped her head from side to side as if weighing whether or not to grant Jonathan his request. Then she began to trace her finger along the cards again. "This is the knight of wands," she said, indicating an image of a man who, like death, was dressed like a knight and rode a horse. In his hand he held a staff—or, rather, a branch, since on closer inspection Jonathan saw it had green shoots coming from it. "He indicates that you should act, tells you that something has to happen. The wands symbolize the element of fire; they represent vitality and movement." She nodded. "Yes, the time has come for you to embark on a whole new course."

Jonathan would have loved to ask what on earth she meant by a new course, but he didn't dare open his mouth again.

"You won't have to walk this path alone; you'll be given support." She tapped the image of a woman in a crown and yellow robe sitting on a throne, also holding a long branch. "Someone will give you the first impetus and point you in the right direction."

"A woman?" Jonathan couldn't help asking, as he was reminded of his mother.

"It's possible. In any case, you'll have a strong companion." She pointed to another card. "This is the queen of cups. This cup holds a secret that's connected with your emotions and your soul."

"A secret? What kind of secret?"

"That's for you to find out. In any case, it's a very emotional card that tells you to listen more to your heart and less to your mind."

"Huh." He was growing irritated at the vagueness of Sarasvati's pronouncements. They could mean anything—or nothing.

"Listen to your intuition," she advised. "If you look closely enough, you'll see the signs and be able to interpret them."

"Mm-hmm."

She seemed to notice Jonathan's dissatisfaction. "It's quite simple. Most people go through life with blinders on and never notice the clues fate keeps giving them. Open your eyes and your heart, be prepared to travel unfamiliar new paths, and you'll be given answers to all the questions that burn in your soul."

"Mm-hmm." It sounded ambiguous, to say the least. "Could you be a little more specific? I wouldn't know where to begin with what you've told me so far."

He feared another scolding from Sarasvati, but she nodded with a smile. "Allow me," she said, and let her finger move over three cards lying side by side. "This year you'll enter into a very close, fruitful relationship."

*Now* things were getting interesting! "A very close relationship?" he asked. "What kind of relationship? A professional one?" For quite a while now, he had been considering elevating Markus Bode from CEO to partner, with a share in the profits of the company. Bode was a capable man, and their most recent conversation alone showed the extent to which he felt bound to Grief & Son Books. Would now be the right time to reward his dedication?

"Well." She smiled broadly. "I can't say for sure, but when I look at this combination of cards, I might even say you could be getting married soon."

Jonathan couldn't help barking out a laugh. "Getting married? I might have known!"

"Our subconscious knows things our conscious minds have no idea about."

He laughed again. It sounded a bit hysterical to his own ears. "Okay, you know what? You were right. So far I've had nothing to be afraid of, but if you're telling me now that within a year . . . Well, in that case I *am* afraid. Very afraid."

"There's no reason to worry."

"I'm not. Because your claim is absolute lunacy. I don't even have a girlfriend." He threw her a look of triumph. She wouldn't have guessed that he was most definitely single, light-years away from a relationship.

Sarasvati seemed calm and unimpressed. "The year is yet young," she said.

"Believe me"—he was still grinning—"even if I walked out that door right now and bumped into the most beautiful woman in the world, I wouldn't rush headlong into marriage."

"Really? Why not?"

"Because it would be completely reckless."

"Sometimes recklessness is the right thing."

"That may sound good, but it's hardly applicable to real life."

"You seem to know all about that!"

"What?"

"Real life," she mimicked. "I'm guessing you're in your early forties, and if you still haven't found a partner, it looks like it's not going to happen."

"Now, listen here! I've been married once!"

"In the past tense. There must be a reason you couldn't keep the lady."

"Is that intended as an insult?"

"Yes."

"Thank you very much!"

They stared at one another for a moment. As their eyes locked, Jonathan felt a tingling sensation creep through him, an almost electric crackle between him and the attractive Sarasvati Schulz. He couldn't remember the last time he'd felt anything similar. If ever. His time with Tina seemed like a thousand years ago.

It wasn't unpleasant; on the contrary. Goaded by the unfamiliar feeling, Jonathan let out an uncharacteristically impertinent remark: "And you don't seem to have found anyone, either, so we're both in the same boat."

"Oh? And how would you know? Are you a psychic now?"

"Life adviser," Jonathan corrected.

"Touché!" They both laughed.

"So, is there someone in your life?" Jonathan asked as the laughter subsided. He couldn't say what had come over him, behaving like a sassy teenager, but he had to admit it was great fun.

"Yes," she said simply, "but this isn't about me. In my opinion there are plenty of areas in your life you should be examining."

Jonathan leaned back and crossed his arms. "So if I may be allowed to summarize: There are a few radical changes ahead of me. I'm going to enter into a close relationship, possibly even marry. And I should be aware of any signs and act on them."

"Yes, you could put it like that."

"The question remains: How will I recognize these signs?"

"That's relatively easy."

"Oh?"

"You just need to learn to say yes."

"Yes? As easy as that? I don't get it."

She rolled her eyes. "I really have to spell things out for you, don't I?"

"You do?"

Sarasvati gave an exaggerated sigh. "You're so good at it."

"At what?"

"At acting dumb."

"I'm sorry, I'm not acting."

"Fine, I'll explain. In the next few days, just try saying yes instead of no to everything that happens. It could be an invitation, for example, that you wouldn't normally accept."

"What good would that do?"

"In order to gain new experiences, to expand your horizons, to give fate—or serendipity or whatever you want to call it—a chance. And that only happens if we say yes to things."

"You mean like just now, for example, when I turned up here unexpectedly with the diary and it led to you reading my cards?"

"Eureka! He's got it!"

"It wasn't *that* difficult," Jonathan replied, a little sniffily.

"Please pick another card," Sarasvati said, ignoring his tone. "As you do, concentrate on something you want to know."

"Okay." He allowed his left hand to wander over the cards fanned out in front of him. As he did, he wondered where the Filofax had come from and what he should do with it now.

He was surprised to feel a sudden tingling in his fingers. He placed his index finger on the card beneath his hovering hand. "This one."

"Good. Now turn it over."

He did, and he and Sarasvati found themselves looking at the wheel of fortune.

"Perfect!" the tarot reader cried out, clapping her hands in delight. "It couldn't be clearer!"

"It couldn't?"

"The wheel of fortune represents the meaning of life. It turns unceasingly." She looked excited, positively euphoric. "Please, can you tell me your date of birth?"

He told her.

"I should have known!" Sarasvati exclaimed after writing down the date and adding the figures together using a system unknown to Jonathan. "Your date adds up to ten."

"And?"

She tapped the *X* on the card he had just drawn. "The wheel of fortune also has the number ten in the major arcana of the tarot. So this year will be influenced by not only a major change, but also good fortune. Everything you do this year will succeed."

"You can see that?" Jonathan asked in astonishment. "That's amazing!"

"Yes, it really is. I'd say you've got a perfect year ahead of you! All you need is the courage to get on with it."

"A perfect year?" He looked at her dubiously. *Your Perfect Year.* He hadn't mentioned the heading on the first page of the diary. It couldn't be pure coincidence; it felt prearranged. "Are you sure you don't know who the Filofax belongs to?"

She blinked in confusion. "No, honestly I don't. What made you ask that?"

"It just occurred to me." Jonathan searched her face for a hint of anything that might give her away, but he found none. Could his suspicion be wrong? Since yesterday morning the craziest things had happened; maybe this was just one of them. "Well," he said, "in any case, it looks like I'm extremely well prepared for the coming year."

"Do you have any more questions? We've got a little time left."

"There are so many things I'd like to ask. But I'm sure we couldn't begin to touch on them this evening."

"You're welcome to make a second appointment with me."

He raised his hands dismissively. "Oh, no, thanks all the same. It was a very entertaining introduction to the world of the supernatural, but I think it's enough for now."

Sarasvati sighed. "You still don't get it. None of this has anything in the slightest to do with the supernatural. You should think of it more as a dialogue, a glimpse into your subconscious, a mirror of what really drives you."

"Whatever." He glanced at his watch. "It's time I was making tracks. My parking expired over two hours ago, and I've got a few things to do." The last part was a lie, but he had no desire to let Sarasvati know that he was usually in bed by ten with a good book. He could imagine what she'd say to that.

"So what will you do with the diary now?"

He shrugged. "I suppose I'll just hand it in at the lost-and-found. That would be the most logical thing to do."

"The least reckless, perhaps."

"What do you mean?"

"Think about it."

When Jonathan returned to his car, he saw that:

a) the Golf had gone, and

b) he had been given a ticket for overstaying in the parking space, and

c) a second note had been tucked beneath his windshield wiper.

He grabbed the scrap of paper and read:

> Dear Jonathan N. Grief,
> I wish you a wonderful day and a life full of happiness and love, in which trivia like slightly tight parking spaces are so insignificant that you no longer even notice them. And I'm really sorry about your parking ticket!
> Yours,
> The Inconsiderate Driver

With a sigh, Jonathan picked up the parking ticket from beneath his wiper and crumpled it in his hand. He was surprised to find himself laughing out loud.

# 16

*Hannah*

"Brrr, it's cold outside! I'm like an icicle on legs. We could use a hot chocolate—right now!" Lisa's cheeks were glowing as she tumbled through the door of Little Rascals dragging seven shivering children behind her. She had spent a good hour with them in Eppendorfer Park after the little darlings demanded a snowball fight. Now, despite woolly hats and scarves and waterproof coats and snowsuits, they were frozen through, although they all had cheerful grins on their faces.

Hannah had to smile at the sight. Romping in the snow was the absolute best for little kids—nothing had changed in that respect since her own childhood. Armed with a fat, hard-packed snowball, whooping for joy when a well-aimed missile hit a friend smack in the middle of their back, they never noticed the subzero temperatures and numb feet. As a little girl, she had always felt the excitement from the moment the first flake of snow fell. Her parents would get the old wooden sled from the cellar and tow her behind them to the nearest park, where she would enter into hard-fought snowball battles with her father.

"Hello? Earth to Hannah. We need hot chocolate!" Lisa was standing right in front of her, staring in amusement.

"Sorry, I was miles away."

"So I saw. You were all glazed over." Lisa winked. "Let me guess—it involved Simon."

"Wrong. I was lost in memories."

"Dreaming of a white Christmas."

"You got it." She gestured toward the kitchenette. "The hot chocolate's ready and waiting on the stove."

"Great!" Lisa rubbed her hands. "We might just get away without freezing to death." She took off her winter jacket, hung it in the coatroom, and busied herself releasing one child after another from snowsuits and winter boots.

Hannah went back to the playroom, where she had been keeping eight other kids busy making stars of Bethlehem and angels out of gold paper in a cozy indoor temperature of over seventy degrees. A third group, watched over by Hannah's mother, Sybille, had left at noon for a tour around the local police station and were expected back at any minute.

Their optimistic forecast had proved true and more. The huge interest since the opening of Little Rascals had not only been maintained but had even increased. Word-of-mouth publicity was proving an outstanding success, and the four articles on the Little Rascals that Simon had produced for them—sadly, as press releases, so unpaid—had brought Lisa and Hannah a rather sour telephone call from their last boss ("You could have said something!" "We did, but you weren't listening.") and children from more far-flung districts such as Blankenese and Sasel. Hannah and Lisa were forced to put off new parents temporarily and add them to a waiting list.

In addition to Lisa's and Hannah's mothers—Barbara and Sybille—a number of teaching students and trainee childcare workers came to Little Rascals as assistants. The two friends needed the extra help because the huge demand meant they had to extend their hours to include mornings, and they were also offering sleepovers every other weekend. In short, the Little Rascals business was an out-and-out success. It looked like they would have more Christmas money to spend than in recent years. They'd even been able to give each of their employees a small Christmas bonus of fifty euros.

Sometimes Hannah caught herself thinking what a pity it was that she hadn't plucked up the courage sooner to turn her idea into reality. But it didn't really worry her; she had no time for might-have-beens, and it was better late than never. She was already considering expansion, but kept that to herself for the time being. She didn't want Simon or Lisa to think she had delusions of grandeur, and she thought it better to wait and see whether their business model continued on its stellar trajectory.

In any case, however sweet the taste of their success, the fact that there was still nothing doing with Simon put a bit of a damper on her enthusiasm. Sadly, since his collapse a few weeks ago, her boyfriend had still not asked her the mysterious question, nor had he found another job and with it a better mood.

And he hadn't really made much progress on the health front either. He spent most of his time at home, slouched on the sofa watching some TV series, sending out the occasional lackluster application and spending the rest of the time bemoaning the fact that he still wasn't properly back on his feet. It was enough to make her weep!

Of course, like most men, Simon was a master of complaining about his regrettable situation—but actually doing something about it and getting the medical advice Dr. Fuchs had clearly recommended seemed not to enter his head.

Hannah suspected she knew what his problem really was—she was convinced that he was suffering some kind of depression that he couldn't shake off. His physical complaints were merely a symptom of his mental state—as well as the perfect excuse for letting himself go.

Yesterday morning, after yet another night she had spent alone because Simon had wanted to creep into his own bed alone, she had felt it was time to take action. She had ferried him to his family doctor, determined to make sure he had a thorough examination before Christmas. The laboratory results were due that afternoon, and Hannah had been waiting hours for his call, fully expecting him to say meekly that the doctor had prescribed him a few vitamin supplements and recommended he get out his jogging clothes and prepare to engage with life again.

But he hadn't yet been in touch, and Hannah was slowly but surely starting to feel nervous. She was reluctant to call him; she had already put enough pressure on him and certainly didn't want to keep fussing over him until he was incapable of standing on his own two feet.

"Do you have any time?" Lisa asked at a quarter past six, after saying goodbye to the last of the children along with Hannah's mother, and clearing the chaos in the playroom with a few deft movements. "I thought we could discuss the plans for next week. Only if you have a minute, of course." They had decided not to shut Little Rascals over the holidays, after it had become apparent that at this time of year in particular, their clients—stressed out by all the Christmas and New Year's goings-on—were practically weeping for joy at the prospect of being able to drag their precious little ones from the TV screens at home for at least a few hours. Of course, it meant that Hannah and Lisa would have to manage without help that week, as their assistants had all arranged time off. And Simon—well, Simon.

"Of course," Hannah replied. "I've got nothing else to do." She was unable to stop a loud, deep sigh from escaping.

"That doesn't sound good. What's the matter?"

"Oh, nothing," Hannah said defensively, but immediately corrected herself. "Well, you know, I'm worried about Simon."

"Is he getting worse again?"

"Not really. But he's not getting any better."

"Has he been to see the doctor?"

"Yesterday morning," Hannah replied. "I practically had to drag him there. We're expecting the results of the blood tests today, but he hasn't been in touch yet."

"That means it can't be anything serious. No news is good news, right?"

"That's true. But I'd just like him to call and tell me the 'no news.' I've been waiting for hours."

"Men!" Lisa rolled her eyes. "It's a well-known fact that they live in another time zone. He's probably lost in some fantasy world on his computer and it simply hasn't occurred to him that his girlfriend's biting her nails to the quick."

"Huh." Hannah shrugged. "You're probably right." She must have looked unhappy, because Lisa immediately turned sympathetic.

"I'm sorry, that was a bit insensitive. You really are worried, aren't you?"

"Whatever!" Hannah waved her right hand as if to drive all her unpleasant thoughts away.

"It *is* unusual for him to be so run down for so long."

"But, Lisa, you just said it's probably nothing serious."

"True, but—"

"If you ask me, it's his unemployment getting him down. That's all."

"I have to say, the connection between 'no job' and 'one infection after another' doesn't seem immediately obvious," Lisa said.

"Everything's connected to everything else."

"True." Her friend grinned. "Amen!"

Hannah's cell phone rang. She dashed over to her jacket and grabbed it out of the pocket.

"Ha!" she said as she saw the display. "Speak of the devil." She answered the call with a breathless "Hello, devil!"

"Hello." Simon sounded slightly muffled. And that single word was very, very quiet. Hannah's knees suddenly threatened to give way under her as they had in the hospital. She had to reach out a hand to support herself against the wall. "It's me," he said, not making the slightest reference to her peculiar greeting. Hannah found that strange.

"Is everything okay?"

"Yes."

That one syllable shot a wave of relief through Hannah. Her body turned hot, then cold, then hot again in rapid succession. "Thank God!" she whispered, briefly closing her eyes. Only now did she realize how right Lisa had been—that she had been seriously worried, but had not wanted to admit it. "So, what did the doctor say?" she asked as she opened her eyes. Lisa smiled and nodded, giving her a cheerful thumbs-up.

"It doesn't matter," Simon replied. "What does matter is that you get home as quick as you can, change into your best dress, and wait for me to pick you up in exactly one hour from now."

"What? I don't get it."

"You go home," Simon repeated patiently; even through the phone she could hear his grin. "Change into a pretty dress and make sure you're ready by half past seven."

"Ready for what?"

"I'm not telling. A surprise."

"Let me guess." Her voice tripped over itself in excitement. "You've found a new job!"

"I'm afraid I'll have to disappoint you there," he replied. "I'm still unemployed."

"Enough of this mystery! Please can you just tell me what's happening?"

"You'll see in good time."

"Simon!" she pleaded. "I want to know right now what you're plotting."

"No." He said nothing more, but simply hung up. Hannah looked at her cell phone with a frown.

"What's up?" Lisa asked.

"No idea. I'm supposed to change into a dress and wait for him to collect me."

"Does that mean he's got a new job?"

Hannah shook her head. "Not that."

"Hmm." Her friend looked at a loss for a moment, then her expression brightened and she clapped her hands in delight. "He-e-e-y!" she cried out. "This sounds much more promising!"

"Promising? I've no idea what you're talking about."

Lisa looked at her sternly. "Isn't it obvious? You're not usually so slow on the uptake."

"What's so obvious?"

"Tonight's the night—he's going to propose to you!"

"You really think so?"

"Of course! What else could it be, if it's not a new job? I seriously doubt Simon would ask you to get all dressed up for a night out with him so he can tell you about his blood cholesterol levels."

"You're right."

"How wonderful! Something's happening at last!" Lisa broke into a crooked smile. "Even if it's not in my life."

"Excuse me," Hannah said reassuringly, "I'm sure that the right guy will turn up soon. But in the meantime"—she made an expansive gesture encompassing the premises with both arms—"just take a look around! I'd say rather a lot has happened in the last few weeks."

"True," Lisa conceded. "But I was talking about something really important. Something significant. Something . . ." She paused, searching for the right words. "Something life changing!"

# 17

*Jonathan*

**Wednesday, January 3, 9:11 a.m.**

After his morning run, followed by his customary shower, change, and breakfast, Jonathan sat at his desk and looked at the pile of documents Markus Bode had left with him the day before. He knew that as publisher it was his responsibility to deal with them, but he didn't have the slightest inclination to do it.

As far as he was concerned, Markus Bode could have complete freedom to do whatever he thought fit—Jonathan had the greatest trust in him. It was just that saying such a thing directly would have been equivalent to professional suicide, so his only choice was to at least make an attempt to look through the heap.

His eyes wandered over the endless columns of numbers. Here and there Bode had marked something with a highlighter, but Jonathan felt stupid as he admitted to himself that he had no idea what his CEO meant by it. It was embarrassing to admit such a failing, even to himself, but he felt like he was wandering through a dark vale of cluelessness.

On hearing Jonathan's decision to study philosophy and comparative literature, his father had given him a kindly smile and merely remarked that he would learn the business side of publishing later, "by getting thrown in the deep end." This had not ultimately proved necessary, since Wolfgang Grief had at some stage decided that his son would be better suited to the role of representative for the publishing house. Jonathan did not know to that day what had led to his father's decision, but deep down he wasn't bothered by it, since he'd always liked the role.

Jonathan moved in the PR side of publishing, making sure the authors felt well cared for. And who wouldn't appreciate a job that involved dining out and enjoying conversations with knowledgeable people about quality literature? The really important decisions were made by his father, even for a long time after his official retirement, when he hovered in the background as a kind of elder statesman.

Given the way their affairs had been arranged until Wolfgang Grief had become so ill, Jonathan had lost the capacity to use his own initiative in the company. Which was not the end of the world, since Markus Bode was an outstanding CEO, and business was going well. Jonathan would happily have allowed things to go on as they were. Until now. Now he recognized the quandary in which he found himself: Should he confess to his CEO that he understood absolutely nothing about running a business, especially not the accounting side?

Jonathan stared at the documents for a few more minutes before shoving them aside with a sigh and reaching instead for the latest edition of the *Hamburg News*. He'd go back to the publishing-house affairs later. Right now, he preferred to start the day with a pleasant perusal of the morning headlines.

He was annoyed to see that the front page of the newspaper was torn. He would have to have a serious word with the delivery person, tell them they should take greater care when placing the paper in the box. That was why Jonathan had installed it. Was it really too much to ask that his newspaper was properly rolled up and pushed without mishap into the generously proportioned tube by his front door? Hardly.

He skimmed the latest news articles with interest, highlighting a typo or grammatical error here and there with a sharpened pencil. He skipped the sports section—for Jonathan, the only point of sports was in taking an active part, not reading about the achievements of others—and finally he immersed himself in the arts-and-culture section.

As he folded up the newspaper a short hour later and set it down on his desk, a missing-person notice at the bottom of page 1 caught his eye.

Huh. Thanks to the careless delivery person, the article ended before it began. The corner had been torn off—the very corner where Jonathan imagined further information and a photo of the missing person would be. What a nuisance!

The name Simon Klamm rang a faint bell. But why? Did he know the man? No, he'd remember if he did; he was blessed with an excellent memory. He had probably read articles by him, as he seemed to belong to the *Hamburg News* staff, and Jonathan had been a subscriber for years.

Before he could brood on it any more, the doorbell made him jump. He glanced at his watch. It was already ten o'clock, and as he so often did, he had forgotten that his housecleaner, Henriette Jansen, came at this time every Wednesday to ensure that his bachelor pad was clean and tidy.

He leapt up, ran downstairs to the dining room, and with a clatter gathered his breakfast dishes, hurrying to the kitchen and shoving them hastily into the dishwasher. The bell rang a second time and he skidded to the front door, tearing it open with a cheerful "Happy New Year!"

"To you, too, Herr Grief." The compact woman, as broad as she was tall, marched in purposefully, laid a fresh bouquet of amaryllis on the telephone table in the hall, and began to untie her head scarf, revealing her blue-rinsed perm. "Well? Have you dashed around clearing up again? I can see the kitchen door swinging." She gave him a cheerful wink, a million crow's-feet forming around her eyes.

"Of course not. That's what you're here for!"

"Precisely." She shook her head in amusement, removed her boots, and reached into the hall closet for a pair of sturdy sandals that lay next to the felt slippers he kept for guests. "Anything in particular today?"

"No, everything as usual."

"I'll get started."

"I'll be out of your way in a minute."

As Henriette Jansen disappeared into the kitchen, Jonathan went upstairs to grab a good book from his study.

He intended to go to a café and read for the five hours it would take his cleaner to whirl through his house. This had been their arrangement for years; Frau Jansen hated people looking over her shoulder as she worked.

She had told Jonathan more than once that he could give her a key to the house so he didn't have to wait and let her in, but he had never been keen on the idea. It wasn't that he suspected his cleaner of doing anything wrong, truly not—Henriette Jansen had worked for him since the days when he and Tina had still been together in the villa, and she was above all suspicion. It was just . . . just that he didn't feel quite comfortable with it.

Jonathan stood in front of the large bookshelf in his study, browsing the generous array of books. What did he feel like reading? Poetry? Not really. Nonfiction? Definitely not. A novel? Not quite right for today; he found himself somehow unable to concentrate. His eyes jumped from spine to spine, with nothing drawing him in.

He could print out one of the constant supply of manuscripts the editors sent him to review, but since that fell into the unappealing category of "publishing house and its finances," he really wasn't in the mood. So today he'd go for a little walk instead of concerning himself with literature.

He broke into a sweat as he recalled that the documents Bode had given him were lying open on his desk, and much as Henriette Jansen might have his complete trust, the economic position of Grief & Son Books was no concern of hers.

He went to his study, picked up the pile of papers that included the figures, and shoved it between the pages of the *Hamburg News*. He hesitated a moment before slipping the newspaper right at the bottom of the recycling bin by his desk. Better safe than sorry.

With some relief, he went back down to the ground floor, put on a winter jacket, and poked his head around the kitchen door to say goodbye to Henriette Jansen.

"I'm off," he said.

"Okay," she replied without looking up from the counter she was busy wiping.

"Oh, one thing: you don't have to empty the recycling today. The bins outside are overflowing. There's no room for anything more."

"So I saw. No problem."

"Good. Till next Wednesday, then!"

His hand was on the doorknob when his eyes fell on the bag hanging from a hook in the entrance hall, previously hidden by his jacket.

The bag with the diary.

Ah, now he knew how he'd spend his time until Henriette Jansen finished her work. He'd go to the lost-and-found in Altona and hand in the Filofax.

Hadn't he done everything he could to track down the owner? From now on, fate would decide what happened to it. Yes, fate.

Sarasvati Schulz had said as much herself.

# 18

*Hannah*

*When the moon hits your eye like a big pizza pie, that's amore . . .*

Dean Martin was belting out his hymn to love at full volume as they entered the Italian restaurant Da Riccardo on Mansteinstrasse. Hannah was more excited than she'd ever been in her life—drunk with anticipation that fluttered around her stomach like a wild cloud of butterflies.

As arranged, Simon had come to collect her at precisely half past seven. Like a true gentleman, he had offered her his arm, led her to the car, opened the passenger door, and closed it once she was comfortably seated.

Now, in the cozy light of the little restaurant, he helped her out of her coat, looked at her appreciatively, and said, "You look wonderful!"

"Thank you very much." Naturally, she had taken great care getting ready for her unexpected date. She'd spent half an hour with the straighteners working on her red hair, which usually reminded her of an exploded cushion, but which now fell over her shoulders in soft waves. (With a bit of luck, it would stay that way for at least ten minutes.)

She wore the small gold shrimp earrings Simon had once given her for Christmas, and for the first time since her teens had delved deep into her makeup bag and searched out the "smoky eye" eye shadow. She had read somewhere that the look was particularly mysterious and sensual with green eyes like hers.

But looking in the mirror, it had struck her that *bank robber* might be a more apt description. She had removed it all and used a more subtle palette of natural colors, rounded off with a touch of lip gloss. She felt much better, more genuine, that way, and she had no desire to give Simon the slightest excuse to associate marriage with a prison sentence.

As her boyfriend had requested, she had put on her best dress for the occasion. The choice had not been too difficult, since she only possessed one. In her everyday life there were few situations that weren't best faced in a pair of pants, so it had taken her a while to find the little black number in the farthest corner of her closet, before unearthing a pair of tights without runs at the very bottom of her sock drawer. She had last worn her black pumps for Simon's mother's funeral, but she hoped that if he noticed at all, he wouldn't automatically think *funeral shoes*. In any case, she sincerely hoped that her boyfriend would have other things on his mind that evening than what she wore on her feet.

"You look amazing too!" Hannah said as Simon returned from hanging up their coats. It was true: she rarely saw him looking so elegant. He'd become rather neglectful of his personal appearance since losing his job.

Tonight he was wearing a dark-gray pinstriped suit that highlighted his tall, slim figure to perfection. The collar of his white shirt was crisply ironed, he had on a burgundy tie, and silver cuff links shone from under the sleeves of his jacket. He had obviously paid a quick visit to the barber, as his dark-brown hair was tamed back into something that could be called a style. His narrow face was clean-shaven, so that

Hannah could once again enjoy a full view of the attractive dimples on his cheeks. Simon had even left his glasses at home and was wearing contact lenses, which Hannah knew he usually reserved for especially important occasions, such as an interview with an A-list celeb. *Maybe also for a marriage proposal?*

"*Buonasera!*" A waiter approached with a friendly smile. "I'm Riccardo."

*Wow, the owner himself!*

"Good evening," they replied in unison.

"Do you have a reservation?"

"Yes." Simon nodded. "Klamm."

"Please follow me," Riccardo said without hesitating for a second, or suppressing a smile or betraying any other reaction to Simon's name—a rare occurrence, since most people seemed unable to resist making some comment when Simon introduced himself. Hannah took this to be an indication of a wonderful evening to come, because "funny" quips such as "Clam? I'm sure you'll appreciate our seafood menu, ha ha" gave rise to little more than a yawn from either of them. Maybe it was simply that the man was a foreigner, to judge from his accent, and the meaning of the name simply didn't occur to him. But whatever the reason, it was a good sign!

The waiter led them past six occupied tables to the back, whisking aside a curtain to reveal a private booth.

"Oh!" Hannah exclaimed. A small table was laid for two, with highly polished wine and champagne glasses sparkling in the light of three candles in a silver candelabra. The cutlery was also silver, the tablecloth of starched white damask, and the cloth napkins deep red, a shade that perfectly matched the single long-stemmed rose lying on one of the two china side plates.

"Are you sure you haven't brought me here to celebrate you getting a new job?" Hannah looked at Simon in delight mixed with an equal dose of bewilderment. "Come on, you can tell me—you're the chief editor of the *Spiegel* as of today!"

"Sadly not," Simon replied, smiling. "It's something else."

"I'm on tenterhooks. Can't wait!" If Hannah had still been harboring the slightest doubt about Lisa's guess, it dissolved the moment she saw the romantic table laid out before her. It could only be a proposal; anything else was unthinkable. And if it was something else, she would have something to say about Simon's sense of humor!

"Signora?" Riccardo drew back the chair on the side with the rose and gestured for her to sit.

"Signorina," she corrected, taking her seat with an arch smile. It might have been silly, but she couldn't resist the little tease, giving Simon a conspiratorial wink. He didn't seem as if he had understood her innuendo or was at all amused.

On the contrary, as he took his seat, also drawn back for him by the waiter, he looked horribly serious, his features tense, almost grim. Hannah decided to avoid cracking silly jokes for the rest of the evening, since Simon seemed excessively nervous. Which was, of course, understandable, since it wasn't every day a man was called upon to propose marriage.

"Champagne?" Riccardo asked. With a clink, he drew a bottle from the ice-filled cooler next to the table.

"Thank you, that would be lovely!" Hannah held out her glass but immediately withdrew it, flustered, when she saw the astonishment on the restaurateur's face. Clearly that wasn't the thing to do; such behavior was for bars, not elegant restaurants.

With a slick gesture and a quiet pop, Riccardo opened the bubbly, poured some into first Hannah's and then Simon's glass, put the bottle back in the cooler, and nodded discreetly before vanishing through the curtain without another word.

Simon raised his glass. "So?" He smiled at last.

"To us!" Hannah said, touched her glass to his, raised the champagne flute to her lips, and savored the prickling sensation in her mouth.

*Bells will ring, ting-a-ling-a-ling,* Dean Martin sang again. *Ting-a-ling-a-ling* echoed the butterflies in Hannah's stomach.

They sat looking at one another in silence for a moment. Hannah imagined that she was glowing like a thousand-watt light bulb; they probably had no need at all of the candles. A pair of sunglasses each would have been more appropriate.

*Hearts will play, tippy-tippy-tay . . .*

"So, what's the reason for this beautiful occasion?" she burst out when it became clear Simon was making no move to break the silence. As soon as the words left her, she was annoyed with herself. She hadn't intended to initiate the proceedings or push things; she had firmly decided to leave it to Simon to guide them through the evening. *His* invitation, *his* pace!

But her mouth had acted independently, bypassing the synapses of her brain (no doubt causing a short circuit!) and simply blabbered on autopilot. She lowered her eyes in embarrassment. She would never ever manage to become a demure, patient, polite girl. Well, the time for the *girl* was long gone, but Hannah had little better expectations for the woman.

"There's no hurry, darling!" Simon reached across the table, took her hand, and squeezed it. Surprised by how cold his fingers were, Hannah startled and looked back up at him. "First, I want to enjoy the evening and an excellent meal with you. We've got plenty of time."

"Yes, of course." She felt like shouting out loud and stamping her foot. It was pure torture! How, exactly, was she supposed to enjoy the evening and the food, when the anticipation was not only giving her minor electric shocks, but bringing a lump to her throat?

She couldn't even face a single one of the olives that had been placed in a little bowl on the table. She would have found it difficult to get a pea down; swallowing was nearly impossible! She picked up her champagne glass and emptied it in a single gulp. Ah, she could swallow, after all.

"To this evening!" she said, hoping she didn't sound too anguished. She also hoped that Riccardo would reappear soon to refill her champagne glass. Grabbing the bottle herself would probably be her next big faux pas.

"Oh, darling!" Simon laughed. "I know I'm asking a lot of you."

"I won't argue with that."

"I can assure you that it's for the best if we just enjoy this evening." He leaned across the table to her, lowered his voice, and narrowed his eyes. "Before things get serious."

"Yes, okay." She had to swallow again, this time without champagne. Good grief, Simon was making such a drama of the whole thing; until that moment she'd been unaware of his acting talents.

"Then first of all, let's eat." As if on cue, the curtain swished open and Riccardo appeared, heaving a blackboard with *"Proposte del giorno"* onto a stool he'd brought with him for the purpose. After studying the menu carefully, Simon picked mixed antipasti and grilled sea bream, while Hannah ordered *vitello tonnato* and a seafood pizza. They ordered a bottle of Gavi to go with it.

"Wonderful," Riccardo said after writing it all down. He picked up the blackboard and was about to disappear.

*"Scusi?"* Hannah called him back and indicated her empty champagne glass. Whether this was the right way to do things or not, without it she would scarcely be able to contain her nerves. And besides, the bottle of bubbly must have been paid for and therefore needed finishing before the Gavi arrived, didn't it?

*"Certo!"* Riccardo took the bottle and poured Hannah a generous measure. He started to do the same for Simon, who declined with a glance at his almost-full glass. Fine, Simon needed to keep a clear head. He had the major part to play, whereas all Hannah had to do

was whisper "I will" at the right moment, and she could manage that regardless of her alcohol intake.

*When the world seems to shine like you've had too much wine, that's amore . . .*

"So, what did your doctor have to say to you?" Hannah changed the subject once they were alone.

"Nothing in particular," Simon replied.

"Nothing?"

"It doesn't matter." He waved the question away. "I don't think it's the best subject for our romantic dinner."

"Then tell me what subjects you feel comfortable with."

"Hey, no need to take offense!"

"I'm not taking offense!" Hannah said, offended. "I just think you're being a bit unfair to me."

"Being unfair?"

"Yes." She nodded. "You know perfectly well that patience isn't one of my strengths."

"'Not one of your strengths' is a gross understatement."

"You see? You know it's my greatest weakness, yet you're torturing me with the suspense when there's really no need." She had never said it out loud, but she believed this was a symptom of the biggest problem in their relationship: Simon's pace, or lack of it, often drove her to distraction. Now more than ever.

Her boyfriend laughed. "Please, Hannah, don't spoil our evening."

"Oh? So now I'm spoiling the evening?" She knew she was on the cusp of doing just that—and that it would be for the best if she changed tack as soon as possible. But her nerves were stretched to the breaking point; she could hardly bear it. A lump was already forming in her throat. It wouldn't take much more for her to burst into tears.

Simon seemed to sense it. He looked at her with the greatest tenderness, took her hand, and gently stroked her skin.

"Darling," he said quietly, "I don't want to upset or torment you. And I certainly don't want to make you cry." He sighed. "I'd simply hoped for a carefree evening, but if that's so difficult for you, then I'll tell you here and now what it's all about."

"Oh, no!" She didn't know what she was supposed to say. Of course she was burning to hear the magic words at last—but at the same time she felt bad that she couldn't even manage to wait a short while longer, until the moment seemed perfect to Simon.

"It's okay," he said. "Maybe this is the best way, otherwise I might lose my nerve at the last minute."

"In that case I'm all ears right now!"

"So, Hannah." He was still holding her hand, but a little harder, as if he were afraid she might jump up and run away. Which was of course crazy. Why would she do such a thing? She wanted the exact opposite, to be together with Simon for the rest of her life.

"Yes?" *GET ON WITH IT!* her small inner voice argued.

He cleared his throat. "First of all, I want to tell you again how wonderful you look this evening."

"Thank you." *NOW—BRING IT ON!*

"The first time I saw you, when I came to collect Jonas, it was love at first sight."

Hannah giggled and murmured bashfully, "Get out of here!"

"It's true. I saw you and at that moment I knew that you were the right woman for me. And that hasn't changed one bit, to this day."

"Hmm." A flush rose to Hannah's cheeks. She had to admit that for once Simon's pace suited her incredibly well. He was welcome to crawl toward his proposal at a snail's pace, provided he did so with such spellbinding words.

"You're so full of energy, so full of life! Your spark attracted me from the start, even if I did wonder at times if it wouldn't be better for you to shift down a gear or two."

"Well, I . . ."

"Shhh! I'm talking now."

"Okay."

"Sometimes I thought to myself that I hoped our children would take after you more than me." He laughed. "That would mean they wouldn't only inherit your wonderful stubbornness and positive attitude, but also your red hair."

Coughing slightly, she ran a hand through her hair, wondering whether her style was still in place or her hair had reclaimed its independence.

"Honestly, Hannah! You're the embodiment of everything I've ever wished for in my life. You're my dream woman, best friend, adviser, emotional support—all rolled into one. Any man would want to find a woman like you!" His voice had risen and now sounded so euphoric and loud that Hannah was beginning to feel embarrassed. She hoped that no one out in the main dining room could hear this completely over-the-top tribute and Simon's inordinately flattering words.

"Thank you, Simon," she said. "But maybe you should cool it a bit?"

"No," he replied. "I'm not going to cool it. You're the love of my life."

"And you're mine."

He swallowed deeply. "That's why what I have to say to you doesn't come easy."

Now it was her turn to press his hand in encouragement. "Just say it."

"Hannah . . ." He closed his eyes for a moment. When he opened them again and looked at her fixedly, she felt faint. His gaze contained so much emotion, so much love, that she wanted to believe every one of the words he'd just spoken, however over the top. "And that's why . . ." He paused briefly. "That's why, Hannah, I'm setting you free."

"Yes!" she exclaimed joyfully. "I will!"

She jumped up from her chair, ready to run around the table and throw herself on Simon. Midmovement, it struck her, what he had actually said. She dropped back down in the chair in bewilderment.

"I'm sorry, but . . . what did you say?"

"That I'm setting you free," he repeated. "I'm letting you go, so that you can make someone else happy. You don't know how hard this is for me, but I'm not the right man for you."

"I beg your pardon?" She shook her head to drive away the hallucination that was clearly plaguing her. It was hardly possible that two glasses of champagne could cause such a lapse of consciousness! She jerked her hand away from his. "Did I understand you right? You're breaking up with me?" What a bizarre sense of humor!

"No," he replied calmly. "I'd never split up with you, never!"

"You just did."

"Please." He moved to take her hand again, but she laced her fingers together. "I understand that I'm confusing you."

"Oh, really?" She could feel her eyebrows leaping upward. "I wonder what makes you think that? Of course, it's totally normal for your boyfriend to give you a long speech declaring that you're his absolute dream woman before breaking up with you."

"Please let me explain," he said. "I'm not doing this because I want to."

"You're being forced to?"

He shrugged. "In a way."

"Uh-huh." She really didn't understand a thing. "So who's forcing you? Are you leading a secret life as a spy that I know nothing about? Do you need to go underground? A witness-protection program?"

"No, Hannah." He looked at her, full of sadness. "But I want you to be happy. And you won't be with me."

"What the hell are you saying?" Now she really was about to cry. None of it could be true; she must be dreaming. She was having a nightmare!

*When you walk in a dream but you know you're not dreaming . . .*

"The thing is, Hannah . . ." He cleared his throat again, picked up his napkin, and began to knead it nervously. "It looks as though I've got less than a year to live."

She stared at him. Stunned. Waves of hot and cold ran through her and she felt dizzy. She felt bad. Very, very bad.

"What?" Her voice shook. "I don't understand what you just said."

"I'm sorry. I'll probably be dead before the year's out."

*"Allora!"* The curtain was whisked aside and Riccardo approached the table. With a flourish, he held a bottle under Simon's nose. "The Gavi!"

# 19

*Jonathan*

**Wednesday, January 3, 10:47 a.m.**

No, it wasn't right. What had Madame Sarasvati advised? From now on, he should say yes to everything and pluck up the courage to face the year head-on. What he was intending to do now was the exact opposite of that. It was a clear no. He nevertheless parked outside the lost-and-found office and considered handing the diary over to some official and having nothing more to do with it.

That was definitely the sensible thing to do, sure. But was it the *right* thing?

What if the diary contained a secret that Jonathan ought to get to the bottom of? The fortune teller had talked about something like that, about a secret that was connected with his emotions and his soul . . .

With an expansive gesture, Jonathan tore his car door open and put his feet firmly down on the sidewalk. He wasn't about to take the groundless musings of a psychic seriously!

He was standing by his car, diary in hand, ready to march into the lost-and-found office and plonk the thing down on the counter—or wherever you handed over found articles—with a decisive clunk. The little book didn't belong to him, so there wasn't the slightest reason for him to have anything more to do with it.

But he found himself hesitating again. *Right or wrong? Wrong or right?* He sighed, sat back down behind the steering wheel, and closed the door. If he simply handed in the Filofax now, he would never know what it was all about. Who did it belong to? Who had filled out the pages? Who was it intended for? And how on earth had it landed on the handlebar of his bike? Would the uncertainty continue to plague him? To drive him mad, never leave him in peace? Ever?

He had no need to answer those last two questions, since the diary was already doing just that: driving him mad, giving him no peace.

However improbable it was, he couldn't completely shake off the possibility that his mother, Sofia, might have something to do with it. And the possibility that, even if that were not the case, Jonathan might be missing out on something interesting.

Or maybe not. He picked up the diary and opened it once again. He leafed through to the entry for today, January 3:

*There are only two days in the year when nothing can be done.*

*One is called Yesterday and the other is called Tomorrow. Today is the right day to Love, Believe, Do, and, mostly, Live.*

*Dalai Lama*

Oh yes, whenever people were unable to think of anything else, they quoted—or misquoted—the Dalai Lama; they'd always find something there. Jonathan had to admit that he could see the logic in this one. Of course you couldn't do anything yesterday or tomorrow; you didn't have to be a genius—or even the Dalai Lama—to send such wisdom out into the world. Such sayings were little more than pop philosophy. But it sold well.

He thought of the books by Paulo Coelho, Sergio Bambaren, François Lelord, and the like, whose sentimental scribblings drove hordes of people into raptures and sat on the bestseller lists for months. His father, Wolfgang, had always called that kind of thing "the opium of the people," after Karl Marx, and stressed that Grief & Son Books had no need for that sort of "cheap success," since good money could also be made from serious literature. At such times his father always nodded toward the leather-bound volumes of Hubertus Krull's works that stood proudly in a prominent position on his bookshelves.

Well. If Jonathan interpreted the words of his CEO, Markus Bode, correctly, it seemed the press urgently needed a few successes. Especially cheap ones. Or quick ones, at least.

Before he could digress again, he turned his attention back to the diary, since there was more on the page for January 3. The writing was so small here that he had to reach into the glove compartment for his reading glasses. He put them on and studied the rest of the text.

*A task for every day from now on:*

*Every morning, in the "Notes" section at the back, write down 3 things for which you're grateful. Something from the heart—the sun is shining, your friends, love, the fact that you can walk, anything that occurs to you.*

*In the evening, write down 3 things that were good today: a nice meal, a friendly conversation, hearing your favorite song on the radio.*

*Go for it!*

Well! Now it was becoming truly adolescent. What was this non-sense supposed to mean? Who had time for that? And above all, what was the point?

Jonathan knew what he was grateful for in his life; he didn't have to spend time writing it all down. Unlike his father, he didn't have dementia, so he didn't run the risk of forgetting.

For example, he was grateful for . . . for . . . grateful for . . .

For what, exactly?

# 20

*Hannah*

**Fifteen days before:**
**Tuesday, December 19, 9:23 p.m.**

They didn't drink the Gavi. Nor did they eat the sea bream, *vitello tonnato*, or seafood pizza. They ate nothing. Instead, they talked. No, Simon talked.

He told her how he'd spent half the day in the hospital after being sent there by the doctor. How they'd turned him inside out with physical examinations, further blood tests, and an ultrasound. How at some stage he'd found himself sitting in front of a triumvirate of doctors with identical expressions of concern, who had informed him they believed he had lymphoma and advised him to come for a biopsy as soon as possible for further clarification of the type and progress of the disease.

How he had left the clinic with his head spinning. Panic stricken, in despair, scared. How he had at last ended up at home and done some internet research. And how he had made the shattering discovery that he would certainly be dead within the next twelve months.

At this point, Hannah interrupted him, bravely suppressing her tears. "But what makes you think that? You don't know for certain yet that—"

"Hannah! You weren't there. But I saw the expressions on those doctors' faces. The way they looked at me, the way they felt me from head to toe, shaking their heads all the while. The way they studied my lab results and scans with their eyebrows raised, exchanging gloomy looks with one another. Believe me, the cancer has spread all over my body. This 'further clarification' they spoke of is just for reassurance. To make sure I don't jump straight off the nearest bridge." He laughed bitterly. "I'm afraid I know what's what with cancer. The doctors were always trying to give my parents hope, but in the end it only led to years of suffering for each of them."

"You don't know about your own situation!" The words tumbled out of Hannah's mouth.

"I do," he said. "For one thing, I've got a genetic predisposition and have always carried an increased risk of cancer." He counted off on his fingers. "Also, I appear to be suffering already from B symptoms."

"B symptoms?"

"It seems that what I thought was a stubborn but harmless cold is actually a side effect of the lymphoma."

"It seems."

"It's more than my own opinion. The internet is full of stories about people who experienced exactly the same things. Most of them were dead within six months. The cancer grows really quickly, especially in younger people like me. Just Google 'lymphoma' and you'll see what I mean."

"For God's sake, Simon!" She slapped the flat of her hand down on the table and stared at him, stunned. "I hope you're not intending to rely on Dr. Google for such an important thing."

"Of course not. But don't forget, I'm a journalist. I know which sources are to be trusted and which aren't. And I'm not a daydreamer who always sees the best in everything and tells himself it's not going to be so bad."

"Are you talking about me?" She swallowed the next sob.

"No," he replied quickly. Then he checked himself, searching for the right words. "Hannah, I simply don't have your positive outlook; it's not one of my gifts. I don't think you're a daydreamer—just look at the success you've made of Little Rascals—but deep down, we're very different. And I prefer to look reality in the eye and acknowledge that I'm likely to be dead within a year. I can't fool myself."

"I refuse to listen to this garbage!" Hannah felt an impotent rage rising up inside her over Simon's stubborn refusal to rule out any possibility that things might not be as bad as he feared. "We're going home right now, and we'll sit down and think calmly about where we go from here. If I have to, I'll take you from one expert to the next—a whole string of them. There's no question of you just giving in!"

"No," he said. "There is no 'we' anymore."

"No! I won't let you go! We'll see this through together!"

Simon didn't reply but simply looked at her sadly.

"Come on." She stood. "We'll pay at the door."

He made no move to rise, and she sank back down into her chair. She suddenly saw that he, too, was fighting tears. And she felt what she hadn't allowed herself to feel until that moment: fear. Fear that grabbed her around the throat and pressed hard with an icy grip.

"Simon," she whispered. "Please."

He took her hand again. "I know how difficult this is for you. But I'm sticking to my decision. My mother watched my father die for ten long years. Constantly veering between worry and hope, day in, day out. All the operations and chemo, the sleepless nights of pain and sickness, the weeks-long hospital stays, over and over and over again. The small steps of progress that only led to the next horrid setback. Mama totally neglected her own life; she put it on hold for Papa's sake. And then? When he finally died and she could have enjoyed her remaining years, she got sick herself and died a hideous death. I don't want to think of that happening to you—it's out of the question!"

Hannah swallowed hard. The way Simon described it, it sounded dreadful.

"I hear everything you're saying, but I'm not going to leave you."

"You don't have to." He dug into the side pocket of his sports jacket, took out his wallet, and removed two fifty-euro bills, which he laid on the table. "I'm leaving you. I'm sorry." With these words he shoved his chair back and stood.

"You can't do that!" Hannah also rose, so forcefully that she almost tipped the table over. In a single leap she was by him and threw her arms around his neck, clasping him tightly to her. "I love you!" There was no stopping her tears now; they fell, uncontrolled, over her cheeks.

"I love you too." Simon wrapped his arms around her and pressed her to him. He gently stroked her hair, bent his head down to hers, and kissed her ear softly. He was crying as much as Hannah, shaken by sobs and hugging her more tightly to him, so that she was convinced the spell would never be broken and he would never let her go.

But he did.

After a few minutes he drew away from her gently but firmly. He looked at her sadly, wiping his face with a hand before brushing Hannah's tears away too.

"I want to go home," he said.

"Can I come with you? Please!"

"No, Hannah. I need to be alone."

"You don't have to, you—"

"Please," he repeated. "Today's been bad enough."

"And I'm making it worse?" She couldn't keep the hurt from her voice.

"Yes," he said, but he immediately withdrew it. "No, of course not. But . . ." He sighed. "Don't make it so hard for me."

"But I want to make it hard for you!" She tried to smile. "You can't expect me simply to accept it and let you go."

"Give me a few days, okay? Everything's all over the place in my head. I need some space, some peace and quiet."

"And then you'll take back what you said about separating?"

"Oh, Hannah!" Once again he drew her to him and kissed her on her brow. "Hannah," he murmured. "My crazy, sweet, wonderful Hannah."

She pushed him away a little, raised her head, stood on tiptoe, and gave him a long, tender kiss. "We'll get through it," she said softly after drawing apart from him.

Simon said nothing.

"I'm convinced you shouldn't give up. Once you've recovered from the initial shock, we'll find out how to help you." Hannah heard herself starting to babble nervously, but she couldn't help it. "And of course you'll survive the coming year! You have at least fifty good years ahead of you, I'm totally sure of it! Oh, what am I saying? 'Good' years? I mean wonderful, perfect years!"

Simon still said nothing.

"For instance, I could—"

"Let's go," he said. "I'll take you home and then go lie down."

"I told you—I want to come with you!"

Now he smiled, for the first time. "I know. But I'm taking you back to your apartment, you stubborn little mule! We'll talk about it all another time."

# 21

*Jonathan*

**Wednesday, January 3, 4:44 p.m.**

Darkness had almost fallen by the time Jonathan steered his car into the driveway in front of his house. He switched off the engine and sat for a moment, feeling ashamed of himself.

After walking aimlessly through the city and making a few minor purchases (he'd run out of low-carb bread and turkey slices), he had sat on a bench in the Planten un Blomen park, opened the Filofax, and whipped out his pen.

He'd felt the urge to write down his personal list of things to be grateful for. Just for fun. Because after all, he was supposed to say yes, not no. That was the only reason he'd wanted to try out this little exercise. And it wasn't as if he had anything else to do; he was simply passing the time until Frau Jansen finished her work. Why not draw up a little gratitude list? He could easily tear out the ring-bound page without leaving a trace; even if the diary eventually found its way to its rightful owner, no one would notice.

And then . . . nothing.

An absolute vacuum in his head. He couldn't think of a single thing he was grateful for.

Yes, of course, there were platitudes such as "For not being in a wheelchair," "For having a healthy bank balance," "For having enough to eat," or "For being a well-regarded and respected man"—he could dredge up a few of those.

But sadly, he could think of nothing for which he was really, *truly* grateful. From the bottom of his heart. Something that was actually worthy of gratitude, that filled him with joy, happiness, and contentment, something he could think of the moment he got up in the morning and at night before he closed his eyes.

And why would he? His wife had left him for his best friend, and he was alone. His father was wasting away, and his mother had left him when he was a little boy. He had recently found out that all was not well in his business, so that he might end up on the streets. The developments in the wider world, and the actions of his fellow humans in particular, filled him with despair more often than gave him cause for gratitude. He only had to think of the dog mess along the banks of the Alster.

No, he wasn't ungrateful or unhappy, it wasn't that. His life was . . . okay. But nothing more. His life simply happened, from one day to the next, without any particular highs or lows. It . . . *functioned*. He functioned. Even though, if he were honest, there was nothing important to function for. He had arranged his life to be as free as possible. Free of responsibility, perhaps, but also free of euphoria.

Depressing. Yes, he had to admit the thought was rather depressing.

He had finally snapped the diary shut in annoyance and decided to go back to the lost-and-found after all. Why should he bother with something that shook him from his comfortable middle ground?

The hours of the lost-and-found desk in the police station made him think again. He'd stood in front of the locked doors and registered with disbelief that it was closed all day on Wednesdays and Fridays, open just until one p.m. on Tuesdays, and only on Thursdays did the employees stay until six.

Jonathan's annoyance had increased to anger. What kind of a dump was this? No wonder the country was going downhill, when the officials worked only half days or not at all!

In order to calm himself down, he had gone to the fitness studio he visited occasionally and worked out manically for three hours—in jeans and socks, since his gym bag was, of course, back at home, where Henriette Jansen didn't want to be disturbed. So Jonathan had braved the looks of astonishment from his fellow gym-goers, doggedly pumping iron and telling himself over and over again that the gratitude list and other such nonsense was for little girls, not a fine figure of a man like himself.

In any case, what was the big deal about gratitude? Grateful to whom, for goodness' sake? To fate? To almighty God? What did it mean, what was it supposed to achieve? If you weren't grateful right now, would the world come to an end? And conversely, were you allowed to be *ungrateful* for everything that didn't go your way? Of course, the same question applied: To whom were you supposed to be ungrateful?

Jonathan N. Grief sat in his car in the drive in front of his house turning crazy thoughts around in his head. The damned diary was still on the passenger seat, clinging to him like a ghost he would never be rid of. But he hadn't summoned it! He hadn't.

Or had he?

"Oh, to hell with it!" he swore out loud. Grabbing the Filofax, he got out of the car and marched up to the front door.

As he entered the hall, he was met by the fresh smell of lemons. He loved the way Henriette Jansen always finished her cleaning by polishing all the floors with that particular product, so the scent hung in the air for days.

And, crazy as it might be, at that moment he understood what it was about. The smell reminded him of his childhood, as his mother had always used the same cleaning fluid—always under protest from his father, who was of the opinion that none of the Grief women should turn her hand to menial housework. But Sofia had brooked no argument. As a true Italian *mamma*, she would never agree to handing over that part of her domain to a woman from outside the family.

His mood improved, Jonathan removed his jacket and hung it on the coat stand. He ran up the stairs to his study and threw the diary down on his desk.

He wasn't about to be intimidated by this little book and allow it to spoil his mood. *No way!* He'd simply let it lie there on his desk until he once again felt inclined to seek out the lost-and-found office during the thirty seconds it was open. Until that moment, he wouldn't give it another thought; he had better things to do. For example . . .

Jonathan's eyes fell on the recycling bin.

On the *empty* recycling bin.

Empty.

How come?

Hadn't he specifically told Henriette Jansen not to touch it?

Yes, he had.

As he felt a sudden light-headedness coursing through him, he couldn't at first say what bothered him more—the fact that his cleaner hadn't obeyed his instructions, or that the latest figures for Grief & Son Books were now lying somewhere in a heap of wastepaper. The latest alarming figures, freely visible to anyone who happened across them.

Jonathan shook himself from his paralysis, turned on his heel, and ran down to the ground floor. He tore the front door open, jumped over the threshold, and stumbled to the still-overflowing recycling container. As soon as he lifted the lid, he could see that Markus Bode's documents weren't there. On the top lay the little gift bag in which Tina had given him the chocolate chimney sweep (Jonathan had polished off the sweep himself; no point throwing something like that away).

But where were the budget figures? Where had Henriette Jansen put the contents of the box?

Jonathan stormed back into the house, snatched the telephone from its cradle in the hall, and dialed his cleaner's number.

"Jansen."

"Yes, hello, Jonathan Grief here."

"Hello, Herr Grief! Did I leave something behind?"

"No, I just wanted to ask where you put the wastepaper. You know, the pile from the bin next to my desk."

"The wastepaper?" She sounded surprised. "I recycled it."

"I told you not to do that!" He could barely stop himself adding, "Why did you disobey my instructions?" But that hardly seemed reasonable.

Henriette Jansen laughed. "Oh yes, so you did. Nevertheless, I took the liberty of throwing it away."

"Where, if I may be so bold as to ask?" He felt beads of sweat forming on his brow.

"In the paper-recycling container, where else?"

"But there's no sign of it in the one outside the house!" he yelled.

"Why are you so mad about it?"

"I'm not mad!" He made an effort to sound a little calmer. "I'm afraid I threw away a couple of documents that I now need urgently."

"Oh, silly me!" Henriette Jansen sounded taken aback. "I honestly thought you'd be pleased if I—"

"Where is it now?"

"Across the road in the recycling dumpster in the park. There was still some room in that one. I thought that would probably be emptied soon, so I—"

"Great, thanks!" He hung up and sprinted out of the house once again, this time to the paper-and-glass-recycling containers in Innocentia Park. He prayed he'd find the documents there.

He couldn't bear to think what would happen if those figures got into the wrong hands! In his mind's eye he could already see the headlines in the local section of the *Hamburg News*: "Longstanding Hamburg Publisher About to Go Under!"

He made himself stay calm. Running through disaster scenarios wouldn't help one bit, and there were no grounds for his fears. For such a thing to happen, the documents would have to catch someone's eye from among all the wastepaper. Then he or she would need to realize what the figures meant and also somehow come to the conclusion that the information might be of interest to the media. And that person must also be of the opinion that Jonathan's business was exciting enough to be the subject of a newspaper article. All in all, more than improbable. Grief & Son Books might be encountering a few difficulties at the moment, but they were far from going to the dogs. At least, Jonathan hoped so, despite his poor head for finance.

Nevertheless, his pulse was racing as he reached the paper-recycling dumpster. He was lucky and unlucky. The container had narrow slits for pushing paper into, but it also had a large blue flap on one side for bigger boxes.

This was easy to open, and Jonathan peered inside the container. He was met by pitch blackness and could make nothing out. He leaned as far as he could into the container, feeling around in the hope of his fingers meeting something. But his hand kept sweeping through empty space; unlike his household bin, it looked like this container had actually been emptied recently.

Breathing heavily, he raised himself on tiptoe, grasped the edge of the opening with his free hand, and pulled himself so far into the container that he almost fell in headfirst. Now, at last, his fingers touched a piece of paper. He grasped it and pulled. It slipped away from him, so he tried to shift himself a little closer to his goal.

By the time he realized his body's center of gravity had slipped a little too far forward, it was too late. Jonathan lost his grip, tipped head over heels into the container, and landed inelegantly with his face resting on a piece of cardboard that smelled suspiciously like pizza.

He groaned out loud.

"Ouch!"

Jonathan started. He hadn't said anything. The voice belonged to someone else.

# 22

*Hannah*

"I'm sorry, but you have to calm down—I can't make out a word you're saying. You sound like a three-year-old with a pacifier in her mouth."

"I . . . I . . ." Try as she might, Hannah couldn't get any other words out. All she could do was sob out those simple sounds between wails. No wonder Lisa had no idea what was going on.

Hannah's call had torn her friend from her bed three minutes ago. Lisa had actually apologized for not picking up on the first ring, and if Hannah had not been preoccupied with more pressing issues, she would have reassured her that there was no need to apologize for failing to sleep with her phone beneath her pillow.

"Calm down, Hannah," Lisa said again. "Take a deep breath. Slowly, calmly, in and out. And another . . . and out!" She guided her like a yoga teacher, breathing loudly into the receiver to demonstrate.

"O . . . okay." Hannah made an attempt to follow her friend's advice. She would never have thought that the mere act of breathing could be so difficult. But it was. Her ribcage felt like it was about to explode.

She had still been feeling fine—considering the circumstances—until half an hour ago. Simon had dropped her off at home and left her with a hug and a kiss. He had promised to contact her the next day and reassured her that he wasn't about to jump off a bridge. And that if he did somehow find himself on the wrong side of a set of railings, he would call her from there. So far, so good.

Hannah had remained astonishingly calm. She had undressed, removed her makeup, moisturized her face, and brushed her teeth. Then she had slipped into her nightgown and gone straight to bed, exhausted by the evening's events.

But no sooner had she switched out the light and closed her eyes than she was wide awake. There they were, all of a sudden: the dreadful thoughts and images.

The horrific fear that Simon's guess was true and he would die during the next few months. That the cancer had already spread through his whole body, that no one and nothing could help her beloved. That she would soon be alone.

Hannah had tried to drive the dread from her mind by displacing it with lovely, happy memories. She had even begun to sing softly to herself in the hope of stopping the manically racing thoughts. She had failed utterly.

*Dead.* Vanished. No longer there, gone, away, forever. *Ashes to ashes, dust to dust.*

The prospect was monstrous. It was . . . unimaginable.

Hannah had never had any experience of death before, aside from Simon's mother, and she had only been involved there at the end of her long illness, had only lived through the last few months of Hilde's suffering. Of course, Hannah had been sad at the time, but mainly for Simon, the fact that he had lost someone so important at such a relatively early age. Hannah had firmly believed that for Hilde Klamm death had been a release; the way she died had proved the cliché.

But this was completely different. For the first time ever, she was directly affected herself; for the first time, it was a person she loved. And for the first time—she was ashamed to admit it, but it was true—she had been made aware of her own mortality. Painfully aware.

Along with the fear of losing Simon, a thought had appeared as if from nowhere, a concept that until then had seemed alien to her: *One day you, too, will be dead; one day you, too, will have to depart this world.*

Of course, she'd known that day would come. Everyone knew it.

But it was a vague, abstract certainty. Something that—absurd though it may sound—had nothing to do with Hannah. Not yet, at least. She wasn't even thirty, and Simon was only six years older! Dying—something that happened in the unspecified future, somewhere on the dim and distant horizon. Dying—something that only affected others.

*Everyone dies in the end.* As Hannah lay in her bed, that sentence, which her grandmother Marianne liked to repeat whenever the subject turned to life's end, played over and over in her head. Until then she had laughed at it, amused by her grandmother's sense of humor, and agreed with her. In the end, yes. An end that's a long, long way off.

Simon's revelation had brought death tangibly close, sneaking into her own reality, catapulting her into a fog of fear. Panic had shot through her veins like an evil poison, latching on to her like a destructive parasite.

Then came the shame, the disgust with herself that, on discovering that Simon was gravely ill—maybe even terminally ill!—she could do no better than worry about the transience of her own life. It wasn't about her; she was unimportant in this. It was Simon who was threatened by cancer. She had no right to feel so bad. On the contrary, it was her duty to be strong for him.

Ultimately, Hannah had seen nothing to do but call Lisa, whatever the time. She wanted to talk to her, she had to talk to her, to stop herself from turning in circles and doing something stupid. Like running out into the street shouting for help, or driving to Simon's place and begging him through tears to let her take him straight to the hospital to have all the necessary further tests done on the spot.

She knew that would be wrong and would have the opposite effect, causing Simon to close off from her completely. He had told her clearly enough that he needed time and space to allow what the doctors had said to seep in and to process it. Hannah wanted to allow him these things, even if being condemned to inactivity drove her crazy.

So she had dialed Lisa's number. But now, with her friend on the other end of the line, as she tried to follow her instructions and do nothing but breathe slowly, the panic refused to ebb. In fact, it seemed to be getting worse. Hannah was now struggling with light-headedness and dazed confusion.

"Any better?" Lisa asked.

"Yyyyyyy . . . Nnnnnn . . ."

"Listen. I'm getting straight in the car and coming over, okay? It'll take a few minutes, I'm afraid, but I'll be there as soon as I can!"

"Nnnnnn . . ."

"I'm on my way!" Lisa hung up.

Hannah crawled on all fours back to her bedroom, climbed into bed, and drew the duvet up over her head. Then she waited, her heart thumping, for this damned terror to go. And for Lisa to arrive.

# 23

*Jonathan*

"Is someone there?" Jonathan asked in consternation as he flailed his arms around, trying to lever himself upright.

"Yes, you idiot!" a male voice hissed out of the darkness. "I'm here. And you just landed on my head!"

"Sorry!" Jonathan replied. "So who are you?" He squinted but couldn't make out a thing in the darkness.

"A rather more interesting question would be, What are you doing in my container?"

"Um, *your* container?"

"Oh, forget it!"

Jonathan heard paper rustling, then a movement right next to him. He sprang back so hard that he hit his head with a metallic *boing* against the outer wall of the dumpster.

"Shit!" the man swore.

"I'm sorry," Jonathan repeated, although he was the one who'd just hit his head. "I didn't know there was anyone in here." He coughed nervously. "It's kind of peculiar, isn't it? Besides, I only fell in here by accident. I—"

"Shut it!"

Out of the corner of his eye, Jonathan could now make out a shadowy figure rising up close by him.

"So, if you'll pardon my intrusion . . ."

"No, I won't pardon anything!" A head shot past him, outlined against the open hatch. Jonathan heard a groan of effort, closely followed by a flapping and the muffled sound of shoes landing on asphalt. Whoever had been here with him among the paper recycling was outside now.

Despite the unevenness underfoot, Jonathan also managed to stand. He gripped the edge of the opening with both hands and heaved his upper body out. Now he could see the man standing in front of the container. He was wearing a dark-blue army coat and glaring at Jonathan with eyes full of hostility.

"Hello!" Jonathan said in as friendly a tone as possible. He reached out a hand, keeping a tight grip on the edge of the opening with the other. His container companion ignored the gesture, looking at him even more mistrustfully.

"Well." Jonathan tried to defuse the embarrassing situation as he moved to climb out of his prison. It wasn't so easy, as somehow the opening seemed to have become smaller since he had fallen in. The stranger watched Jonathan's floundering efforts for a while, and then, with a sigh, he moved a few steps toward him and reached out a hand.

"Thank you." Jonathan gripped it and the man pulled him out, supporting him as he landed.

"Very kind of you," Jonathan said once he was back on firm ground, vainly dusting off his clothes. He had the impression that he now smelled of pizza. Honestly, didn't people know that dirty paper and cardboard belonged with the household garbage?

"You're welcome," the man replied with a slight smile that made him look much friendlier. His chin was covered with white stubble, and his long white hair was tied back in a ponytail. His coat, which reached almost to the ground, was threadbare enough to be a rummage-sale reject. He looked pale and worn out. The deep furrows lining the man's face suggested that he must be in his late fifties at least. "You gave me a real shock there," he said.

"And you me!" Once again he held out his right hand. "Jonathan Grief."

The man hesitated briefly before grasping and shaking it. He wore fingerless gloves, but his handshake was firm. "Leopold," he said.

"Leopold? What an extraordinary name! Especially here in the north—it's more of a south German name."

"My pals call me Leo." He grinned. "So, Leopold to you."

"No problem," Jonathan replied before realizing exactly what the man had just said.

"So, John-Boy. What were you doing in my container?"

"I was looking for something."

"What?"

"Some documents. Nothing important." He waved his hand dismissively, unwilling to go into the details with this peculiar man.

"Important enough for you to jump on a man's head in the deepest, darkest night."

"First, it's not nighttime but still afternoon," Jonathan corrected him. "And second, I had no idea you were in the container." He stared at Leopold with undisguised curiosity. "What were you doing there?"

"What do you think? Keeping warm."

"In the recycling?"

The man nodded. "Yes. It's a good insulator."

"Why don't you just go home?"

Leopold laughed out loud. Loud enough to make Jonathan jump. "You're a character!" he snorted, slapping his thigh. "Did they let you out for good behavior?"

"I'm sorry?"

"Ha!" The man wiped a couple of tears from the corners of his eyes. "You know what?" he said between gasps. "My town house is being renovated at the moment, I'm afraid, so I can't go back there right now."

"Really?" Something told Jonathan the man was pulling his leg.

"Jesus, boy! Which tree did you just drop out of? Take a look at me! I'm homeless!"

"Oh." Jonathan N. Grief had no idea how to respond to that. He suddenly felt extremely stupid.

"Oh, yes!" Leopold nodded. "And on particularly cold days like today, I sometimes grab a little shut-eye in the dumpster."

"Isn't it dangerous? The thing could be emptied while you're asleep."

"True." Leopold tapped his temple. "But I have all the collection times in here."

"Glad to hear it."

"I just hadn't anticipated someone jumping on my head."

"As I said, I'm sorry."

"Don't worry about it. No damage done."

"Fortunately not."

"So, did you find what you were looking for?"

Jonathan shrugged. "Not a trace. I'd hoped the papers would be on top of the pile."

"Hmm. I'm afraid I stirred it all up when I was making myself at home in there."

Jonathan almost laughed out loud at "making myself at home." He'd never associated the words with a dumpster.

"Do you have a flashlight?" Leopold asked.

"Yes, over in the house." Jonathan pointed toward his villa across the street.

Leopold let out an indefinable sound. "Wow! You live there? Not bad!"

"Um, yes." The thought immediately leapt into his head that it might have been a mistake to show the man his house like that. One never knew . . .

"Let me make a suggestion," Leopold said. "You go get your flashlight. I'll climb back into the container and you can light it up for me."

Jonathan hesitated.

"Your papers can't be that important."

The headline of the *Hamburg News* once again appeared before Jonathan's inner eye.

"They are," he said. "But it's a hassle—I don't want to take up any more of your time."

"No hassle. And time's the one thing I have plenty of."

Jonathan pondered for a moment longer, then accepted Leopold's offer gratefully. He went home to fetch a flashlight from the cellar.

Leopold was waving out through the slot in the container as he returned. "Good. So what are we looking for?"

"A stack of papers covered in numbers."

"Could you be a bit more specific?"

"Someone made a few notes here and there in red pen and highlighter."

"Okay. Preparing to dive!" He vanished into the depths of the container. Jonathan leaned in as far as he could with the flashlight and lit up the area around Leopold.

"That's good," he said in a muffled voice, quickly followed by "Ugh!" A banana skin flew past Jonathan's head, brushing his left ear. "People are such pigs, the things they throw in here!" Leopold muttered. Jonathan had to agree. Pizza boxes might be forgiven, but organic waste really did not belong here. He immediately felt a closer bond with his new acquaintance, who seemed to share Jonathan's view of right and wrong.

"Is this it?" Leopold called out, waving a crumpled piece of paper through the slot. Jonathan took it and glanced at it.

"Yes," he said with a relieved smile. "But only some of it."

"Hang on, I can see some more."

"Take care, now."

"Take care?" Leopold said in a pained voice. "You've got me rummaging around in the trash for you and now you tell me to take care?"

"I don't want you to get hurt in there." Jonathan held back from pointing out that the whole thing had been Leopold's idea.

"How many more pages to go?"

"I don't know," Jonathan replied. "Let me check; they're numbered." He pulled out the flashlight and held it over the pages.

"Hey!" Leopold complained. "Let there be light!"

"Coming right up. I can't see what I'm doing without it." Jonathan gripped the flashlight between his teeth and searched the crumpled sheets for page numbers. He saw *3 of 12* in the bottom-right corner of a page. He began to sort them. *1, 2, 3, 4 . . . 8, 9, 10, 12.* "There are four pages still missing," he called in to Leopold.

"So shine that light in here!"

Jonathan shone the flashlight back into the container, and Leopold crawled from left to right, rummaging through the paper and cardboard. "I hope this is really important."

"It is," Jonathan assured him.

"So what in God's name is it doing in the recycling?" A plastic bottle whizzed past Jonathan's head.

"A mistake," he said as he ducked. "Can you . . . please could you look where you're throwing things, or at least give me some kind of warning?"

"Sorry." He could practically hear Leopold's grin. "I'll *take care*, promise." A moment later, a cushion flew past, followed shortly by an "Oops!"

"You should keep that," Jonathan joked and threw the cushion back. "It'll make your night cozier."

"I won't be needing it," Leopold replied. He poked his head through the slot and triumphantly held up four more crumpled pages. "I'd say I've earned myself a night somewhere warm."

"Oh yes?" Jonathan asked, taking the pages gratefully. "Where's that?"

Leopold grinned. "Guess!" He gestured with his chin toward Jonathan's villa across the street.

"No!" Jonathan N. Grief wanted to cry out. "No way!"

But then he thought of Sarasvati's advice. "Yes, of course, be my guest!"

# 24

*Hannah*

When her friend rang the doorbell thirty minutes later, Hannah summoned all her energy and stumbled to the door to let her in. As soon as she saw Lisa, Hannah fell into her arms, sobbing.

"Hannah!" Lisa cried out in shock as she caught her. "What happened?"

Hannah cried harder, released by the security, wanting to be held like a little child who runs to Mama for comfort.

Lisa said, "I'm sorry it took me so long, but—"

"Shhh," Hannah said, silencing her. She didn't care how long it had taken, the main thing was that Lisa was with her.

"Will you tell me what's happened?" her friend eventually asked, stroking Hannah's hair. Lisa gently took hold of her arms and steered her into the little living room, where they sat together on Hannah's wicker sofa, snuggled beneath a blanket.

Lisa listened without interruption as Hannah told her about the evening at Da Riccardo. The words tumbled out of her, streaming faster and faster from her mouth as though she'd opened a floodgate. She told Lisa about the cancer diagnosis the doctors had given Simon. About his conviction that he'd be dead in a year, and about his refusal to undergo further tests because he thought it pointless.

About the fact that he wanted to leave her because he believed it wasn't fair to expect her to stay under these circumstances—that he didn't want to subject her to the same fate his mother had suffered.

And Hannah even admitted to her friend the fears she had been fighting with herself, the way she'd been overcome by panic as she was forced to face her own mortality. How ashamed she was of that. Ashamed, ashamed—ashamed to the bottom of her heart.

"But that's completely normal," Lisa soothed. "It doesn't make you a bad person."

"You don't think so?"

"Of course I don't. Every one of us has thoughts like that. When we see a serious accident on the freeway or read something horrific in the newspaper—a natural disaster or a terrorist attack—we immediately get to thinking, 'What if that had been me?' Or, even worse: 'Thank God it wasn't me!'"

Hannah sighed in relief. "I'm glad you don't think I'm a monster. I'm already feeling a little bit better."

"And so you should." Lisa hugged her. "It's bad enough without you beating yourself up—that's the last thing you need."

"Says the woman who apologizes for every stupid little thing and constantly has a guilty conscience."

"True." Lisa laughed. "But as you've said yourself: it's usually only about stupid little things."

Hannah sighed. "And there I was thinking Simon was inviting me to a lovely romantic dinner in order to propose to me. To ask me if I'd stay with him until the end of my life." She gave a bitter little laugh. "I had no idea it was about the end of his life. And certainly not that the end would be so soon."

"Stop! It's not a question of who's going to reach the end of their life when."

"Try telling Simon that! He's probably out there looking for his final resting place and designing his gravestone."

"Give me the phone. I'll call him."

"No way!"

"But you said I should tell him."

"Yes . . . I mean no." Hannah was still having difficulty concentrating. "Simon's completely lost it. If we put any pressure on him, it could make things worse. I don't think it'd be a good idea to lay into him right now. Besides, I'm not sure he'd be happy that I've told you all this."

"Not sure he'd be happy?" Lisa said incredulously.

"It's kind of private," Hannah said. "He might be ashamed—"

"Ashamed about what?" her friend interrupted. "Your boyfriend's told you he's got cancer, not that he robbed an old lady!"

"Oh, Lisa, you know what I mean."

"Yes, I do." She nodded decisively. "You were right to call me. What did Simon expect? That he'd hit you with news like that and you'd just shrug and go back to your everyday life as though nothing had happened? That you can cope with it all on your own, that you'll set up a profile on an internet dating site tomorrow while he goes off looking for a place to die like a frail, elderly elephant?"

"I never said that was what he expects."

"But you're wondering in all seriousness if he'd mind you telling me about it. Honestly, it's the sort of thing I'd wonder about—but not you!"

Hannah smiled. "That's true, at least."

"Like I said!"

"I still don't have the slightest idea what to do. What I *can* do."

"It's a difficult question," Lisa said. "You're probably right that too much pressure would be counterproductive."

Hannah, who'd felt helpless and sad until now, exclaimed angrily, "I just don't get how someone can be such a blockhead, refusing more tests like that! Simon's just come up with his own diagnosis and then takes it as a given. If I were in his shoes, I'd already have contacted the ten best oncologists in the world—and he does nothing, just gives in, rolls over, and accepts his fate?"

"Well, I can understand he may need some time to let it all sink in."

"What is there to sink in? If it's really as bad as he thinks, then he hasn't got a day to lose!"

"I have to contradict you there," Lisa said. "If he's truly afraid it's as bad as that, I can see why he wouldn't want to go running to the next expert."

"Really?" Hannah raised her eyebrows in astonishment. "Help me understand."

"For one thing, Simon's already had bad experiences with cancer through his parents, and I can imagine that there are some things you'd really rather not know in gory detail."

"Even if they're as important as in Simon's case?"

"Maybe he'd prefer to leave room for a small amount of uncertainty."

"Uncertainty?"

"It's possible!" Lisa said. "If he refuses a biopsy, he's not only rejecting the possibility of the doctors telling him it's not so bad after all and they can help him—he's also avoiding the risk of someone telling him, 'I'm sorry, I'm afraid there's really nothing more we can do for you. You'd best go home, you've had all the treatment you can.' Just think, he's avoiding the risk of seeing his death sentence written out irrevocably in black and white."

Hannah burst into tears again.

"I'm so sorry!" Lisa slapped her palm to her forehead. "I'm such an idiot! How could I say such a thing?"

"Noooo," Hannah replied between sobs. "You're right." She wiped both hands over her face and attempted a smile. "It's just so difficult for me to get my head around it all. Me, I'd always prefer to know exactly where I stand rather than stumble around in the dark. That's the only way I can come to terms with it."

"Hmm. Are you sure that's what you'd do? You've never been in that situation."

"I'm still certain!" Hannah replied without hesitation. "I'd want to know."

Lisa thought for a moment before voicing her next thought slowly and carefully. "Let's say someone could see your future with one hundred percent accuracy—"

"Impossible."

"Never mind; just assume they could. And that someone could also tell you the very day you'll die—would you really want to know? Or wouldn't you prefer death to hit you one day out of the blue, without warning?"

"What a horrible question!"

"But that's the question Simon's facing right now."

"Not exactly," she countered. "Simon knows he's ill, so there's no question of 'out of the blue.'"

"Well, the diagnosis has fallen on him out of the blue."

"Out of a cloudy sky, more like," Hannah said. "He hasn't been feeling well—physically or mentally—for several months."

"Just think about what I asked you."

"Okay," Hannah said reluctantly. She didn't need to think for long. "I'd want to know, whatever the situation," she said emphatically. "Then I could experience the time left to me fully aware. I could savor every day. I could get my affairs in order, as people so nicely put it, say good-bye to the people I love, or travel the world—and at the end, maybe even throw a wild party."

"Fine," Lisa said. "Just as I thought. That's what you're like."

"Like what?"

"Pragmatic."

"Pragmatic?"

169

"Always looking ahead," Lisa said. "Not allowing things to get you down and making the best of everything—and that's fine, in a way. Except that everyone's different, and Simon seems to be choosing a different way."

"He's not choosing any way, he's standing still!"

"Doing nothing is also a decision."

Hannah regarded her in astonishment. "Since when have you spouted wisdom like a guru?"

Lisa blushed. "I, um, I read that somewhere recently."

"Where? In *Spiritualist Weekly?*"

"Don't laugh at me! I'm only trying to help."

"Sorry, I didn't mean it like that." She nudged her friend in the ribs.

"Apologizing's what *I* do, remember?" Lisa said and nudged her back. "Anyway, you're the one who's always talking about seeing crises as opportunities and all that—I thought I'd try it out."

"Ha ha."

They smiled in silence at one another for a moment. Hannah was so glad her friend was with her. It didn't make the situation any better, but it was somehow more bearable.

"What about you?" Hannah asked eventually. "Would you want to know when you were going to die?"

"No idea. I never think about things like that."

"Huh!" Hannah rolled her eyes in mock irritation, then wagged her index finger. "Not so easy! You can't wriggle out of it like that. You have to answer the question!"

"Have to?"

"Yep."

"Well, then, let me think." Lisa leaned back on the sofa and closed her eyes. Thought about it. For a long time. A very long time.

"Have you gone to sleep?" Hannah asked impatiently.

"No." She opened her eyes but remained silent and unmoving, staring at the ceiling as if there were something interesting there.

"It can't be that difficult," Hannah said after another two minutes had gone by. "You're just stalling!"

Lisa finally turned to her. "No," she said, slowly shaking her head. "I wouldn't want to know the day I was going to die. No way. And if anyone wanted to tell me, I wouldn't let them. I wouldn't want to know when anyone else was going to die either. It would be horrible to know when *you're* going to die . . . or my parents."

Hannah raised her hands defensively. "No need to make a speech about it! Don't worry, I can't tell you."

"Sorry."

"Now what for?"

"That you think I'm speechifying."

"Doesn't matter," Hannah said. "I'm just amazed that you're suddenly taking it so seriously."

"It's a serious subject."

"We're just playing with ideas. Since no one can reliably predict when we're going to die."

"No," Lisa agreed. She smiled. "I just had a thought."

"What?"

"Can't tell you."

"Why not?"

"Because it makes me feel uncomfortable. Embarrassed."

"Now you've really got me curious."

"Sor— I didn't mean to." A flash of guilt flitted across her face.

"Don't be sorry, just tell me!"

"Okay," Lisa said, beaten. "I just remembered how a tarot reader once wanted to tell me the day I'd die. And how dreadful I found it."

"What?" Hannah looked at her in surprise. "You once went to a tarot reader?"

"Not just once." Lisa looked uncomfortable. "To be honest, I go regularly."

# 25

## *Jonathan*

**Wednesday, January 3, 5:46 p.m.**

"What a fantastic house!" Leopold stood in the hall and looked around appreciatively. "I've seen some digs in my time, but this is a place you could photograph for a lifestyle magazine without having to run around with the vacuum cleaner first."

"Um, thanks," Jonathan replied, feeling a mix of pride, embarrassment, and concern.

The pride had the upper hand.

He felt embarrassed because the presence of this man in his worn-out army coat was making Jonathan feel like a repulsive snob. Like a glutton who happily tucks into a ten-course meal in front of a group of starving people, and then throws anything he can't eat into the trash without a care.

The large vase by the door, in which Henriette Jansen had tastefully arranged the fresh bouquet of amaryllis, as she did every week (a tradition introduced by Tina and retained automatically by Jonathan), had alone cost probably as much as Leopold would need for a month's comfortable stay in a quality hotel.

The terra-cotta floor tiles were, of course, from a small Italian ceramics factory, and the hand-woven runner adorning the staircase to the second floor had been in Jonathan's family for generations; he couldn't begin to guess what it was worth.

He had never been so aware of his wealth as in that moment, standing next to a man he had just accidentally fished out of a dumpster. So *unpleasantly* aware.

But at the same time, this very circumstance caused Jonathan N. Grief to worry. Had he committed a serious error with his spontaneous invitation, or rather his enforced agreement to the suggestion? Was it not extremely dangerous to allow a stranger, a homeless man to boot, into his own four walls? Sure, Leopold seemed likable. But what good would that be to Jonathan when he ended up in his bed with his throat cut? And what on earth did "I've seen some digs in my time" mean? Could Leopold be a crafty character who made a habit of inveigling his way into gullible people's homes? Someone, God forbid, you could never get rid of?

He feverishly wondered if he could come up with a not-too-flimsy pretext for neatly getting his unwanted visitor back outside.

His gaze wandered to the glazed window in the door. In the glow from the outside light he could see snowflakes dancing. No. He couldn't in all conscience do such a thing.

And the pages Jonathan was still holding in his right hand reminded him that Leopold had undeniably done him a great service.

He could barricade himself away in his bedroom that night—then the worst that could happen would be that Leopold made off with a few valuables. Better than being murdered, at least.

Or he could lock Leopold in, maybe secretly, after he had gone to sleep. The guest room—formerly Tina's territory—had its own bathroom, so his visitor would be able to see to his bodily needs. It seemed incredibly unwelcoming, though. Well, it not only seemed unwelcoming, it would *be* unwelcoming.

Even then, *unwelcoming* was merely a euphemistic way of describing what could more accurately be termed *unlawful imprisonment*.

"Let me guess!" he heard Leopold saying.

"What?" He looked in confusion at his guest; he realized he must have been standing in the hallway silently brooding for several long minutes.

"You're racking your brains trying to think of how to get rid of me."

"Nonsense!" Jonathan N. Grief countered vehemently as his cheeks turned red.

"You are," Leopold retorted, not looking the slightest bit annoyed or offended—more amused. "It's obvious from your face, written in block capitals on your forehead. And I can understand it, too." He laid a hand on the front doorknob. "So I'd best be—"

"No!" Jonathan cried, his voice all the louder for the embarrassment at how bluntly his expression betrayed his thoughts. "Believe me, you couldn't be more wrong!" He indicated the coatrack almost obsequiously. "Please, take your coat off and make yourself comfortable!"

Leopold's look of amusement faded. He hesitated and glanced shyly at the jacket and coats hanging by the door. "Are you sure? I'm afraid mine's rather dirty and . . ." He looked to the floor without finishing.

"Not a problem," Jonathan said, a little too calmly to be entirely convincing. "Just hang it on one of the free pegs. Then I'll show you your room."

"I'm getting my own room? I'd be quite happy with a sofa. Even the floor would be heaven!"

"Feel free to sleep on the guest-room floor if you prefer."

"No, of course not—I'd love to sleep in the bed!" Leopold replied quickly as he removed his coat and his heavy boots. The socks that he revealed caused Jonathan to swallow hard, as both of Leopold's big toes were sticking out. But what did he expect from a vagrant? Luxury men's socks from Hugo Boss, like the ones he wore? Jonathan opened the left door of the hall closet and got out a pair of felt slippers. "Here."

He pressed them into his guest's hand. Leopold took them gratefully and immediately slipped into them, visibly eager to hide the holes in his socks. "Let's go."

It was a strange feeling to enter his ex-wife's room with Leopold. He hadn't set foot in here for years; only Henriette Jansen entered, to vacuum and dust every few weeks.

Even though Jonathan had called it "the guest room" since the divorce and kept it ready, with made-up bed and clean towels in the en suite bathroom, for the eventuality of overnight guests, no one had ever actually come to stay.

It simply hadn't happened. Since Jonathan had not only been born and bred in Hamburg, but had also never left the city for more than three weeks at a stretch, he had no friends or acquaintances in other cities or countries who could have or would have wanted to come stay with him.

And even if they did, his potential visitors would probably be in a situation similar to his own and would prefer to stay in a hotel rather than invade another person's private space.

Any contact with the Italian side of Jonathan's family had been cut off once and for all with the departure of his mother, or at least with his final postcard to her, so he could hardly expect visits from those quarters. Jonathan knew his mother had a sister in Italy; he had seen her a few times when he was a boy. But he couldn't even recall her name with certainty—something like Gina or Nina.

In any case, Jonathan had no reason at all to enter Tina's old room, as the rest of the house gave him more than enough space. So now, as he stood with Leopold surrounded by the colorful patchwork world of his ex-wife, he felt queasy. The whole room exuded her presence, as though her ghost still lingered within the four walls.

In contrast to the rest of the villa, Tina had not decorated her own personal space with cool practicality, but in a cheerful interpretation of the country-house style.

The double bed was covered with a colorful quilt and had a canopy of heavenly swags of lace; the rest of the furniture—the wardrobe, book-shelves, dressing table, and stool—had been refinished by Tina herself (in her phase of giving meaning to her life through DIY), so that the grain of the wood showed through the varnish. She had chosen a light-apricot pastel shade for the walls, with a flowered border all around and curtains to match.

All in all, the room was a young woman's dream, as only found these days in romantic hotels, and the little dressing room to the left was the icing on the cake. With a pang of embarrassment, Jonathan remembered how, when Tina had presented her finished work, he had said something to the effect of "Are you reliving your teenage years?" Tina had burst into tears, and not even an invitation to dinner in her favorite four-star restaurant, or the expensive gold chain he bought her, had succeeded in cheering her up.

All his subsequent reassurances that the room was now "very beau-tiful" had been countered with "You don't really mean that" and "You hurt my feelings." It was true that, in the cold light of day, they hadn't been well suited for each other. Strangely, when he showed Leopold Tina's former refuge, Jonathan had to admit that the guest room was genuinely lovely and inviting. Not at all to his own taste—but cozy nevertheless.

"Oh," Leopold said, "Laura Ashley is alive and well!"

"Who?"

"Laura Ashley," Leopold repeated. "Don't you know her?"

"Never heard of her. Who's that?"

"I think she invented this style—inspired by the British landed gentry and the like."

"You're a font of knowledge, aren't you?"

"Not what you expected of me, hey?" He grinned. "It may surprise you to hear it, but I wasn't born in a dumpster."

"Um, yes, of course." Jonathan felt on the verge of turning red again, so accurately had Leopold hit the nail on the head for the second time in quick succession. "You can make yourself at home here," he said in a clumsy attempt to change the subject.

"Thank you. I'm sure I will."

"Yes, well . . ." Jonathan looked around hesitantly, then squared his shoulders. "Let me just show you the kitchen."

They went back downstairs and crossed the hall to the spacious designer kitchen. Jonathan told his houseguest where to find the dishes, cutlery, and glasses, and a case of mineral water; he told him there were juices and milk in the fridge, along with butter, cheese, and deli meats. "Help yourself to what you like," he said as he opened up the bread box on the counter.

"That really is very, very kind and generous of you!"

"Think nothing of it, my man," Jonathan replied with a half smile. They caught each other's eye and laughed.

The ice was broken.

A second later it froze over again.

"So." Jonathan clapped his hands. "I'd say you have everything you need, so I'll be off upstairs. I'll see you tomorrow morning."

Leopold looked at him, taken aback. "You're going to leave me here alone?"

"Yes, why not?" Jonathan paused. "Do you need anything else?"

"It's not that. I just thought . . . Well, I assumed we'd spend the evening together."

"We'd spend the evening together?" Jonathan echoed.

Leopold gave a little cough. "Now that you put it like that, it sounds strange. I mean, I thought we might cook something together and hang out. A guys' night. I could really enjoy that. I'm so often . . ." The same look of embarrassment as he'd had by the coatrack crossed his face. He shook his head and dropped his eyes. "No, forget it," he muttered. "It was pushy enough of me to invite myself here." He turned toward the kitchen door. "I'll go upstairs and take a shower, okay?"

Jonathan laid a hand on his shoulder from behind and held him back.

"A guys' night sounds kind of good."

Leopold turned back to him. "Really?"

"But you'll have to cook. I can only do fried eggs and bacon."

"Why do you have this contraption with six gas burners, then?" his guest asked, nodding toward the huge freestanding island in the middle of the room. "And why eight stainless-steel pots and four frying pans?" He indicated the array of professional equipment hanging from a rack above their head.

Jonathan shrugged. "No idea," he confessed. "But it looks good, doesn't it? And you don't cook a fried egg in your hand!"

"It's such a shame!"

"That you can't cook a fried egg in your hand?"

"No." Leopold laughed. "That a lovely kitchen like this is wasted on a man who doesn't know its true value."

Jonathan N. Grief spread his arms in an expansive gesture. "As I've said, make yourself at home! *Mi casa es su casa.*"

"You speak Italian?"

"It's Spanish, actually." Jonathan thought as he said it that no, he couldn't speak Italian.

Also a shame.

# 26

*Hannah*

"The guy was a real creep."

Hannah listened with interest as Lisa told her about her experiences in the world of clairvoyants. She could hardly believe that her friend had been having her cards read every few weeks for years—and had never mentioned a thing about it.

Hannah felt a tiny spark of disappointment and hurt, since she had thought the two of them were close enough for Lisa to have shared it. She tried to push aside her feelings about this "betrayal," which in fact wasn't one, and simply listen to her friend's account. Didn't everyone—even Lisa—have a right to their secrets?

"I should have known," her friend said, continuing her account of her visit to the self-styled "psychic" who had tried to tell her the unwanted date of her death. "I mean, what else could I have expected from someone who calls himself Mr. Magic?"

"Mr. Magic?" Hannah almost choked. "You can't be serious!"

"*I'm* not," Lisa said. "But he was."

"How did you end up going to see him?"

She shrugged. "Found him on the internet. Despite the crazy name, his website looked good. I just wanted to try it."

"Well, anyway, what did you say when he threatened to tell you the date you'd die?"

"What do you think? I got up and walked out!"

"That's what I'd have done too."

"You just claimed the exact opposite—that you'd want to know."

Hannah rolled her eyes. "And I would. But not from a tarot reader. Anyway, I don't believe it *is* possible to predict the day you're going to die."

"I don't really believe it either," Lisa said. "But trust me, the moment someone says they can see when you're going to die, you get a real scare."

"If that someone goes by the name of Mr. Magic, I'd be more likely to have a laughing fit."

"You weren't there." Lisa pouted.

"That's true. I'd never have gone to someone with a name like that in the first place."

"That's easy to say after the fact. Anyway, there are others out there besides Mr. Magic."

"I should hope so."

"Seriously, now." Her friend was getting irritated. "Some of my consultations have been a great help."

"With what?" Hannah couldn't keep the skepticism from her face.

"With making decisions, for example."

"Name me one!"

Lisa thought for a moment. "For example, when we were considering whether to go it alone and set up the Little Rascals business—"

"You're saying that when we were deciding whether or not to take this crucial step, you sought advice from some psychic guy?"

"From a life adviser." Her friend's lips were pursed in offense. "Anyway, it was a woman."

"Oh, that makes it *completely* different."

Lisa sighed. "Forget it! I don't see the point in saying more."

"No, please go on. It's really exciting."

"Nah," Lisa said. "I'm not interested anymore."

"Please," she pleaded.

"No."

"Please, please, please! It'll be a nice distraction from these horrible worries about Simon."

"Now you're resorting to emotional blackmail. That's unfair. How can I refuse?" She crossed her arms and regarded her friend reproachfully.

"Oh, go on!" Hannah continued to beg. "I won't interrupt again."

"You won't be able to resist."

Hannah turned an imaginary key over her mouth and threw it in a vast arc. "Hmph."

"Very well," Lisa said generously. "Of course, I didn't base my decision entirely on what the cards said. The consultation merely strengthened my conviction that we were doing the right thing, because all the indications pointed to success."

"Gla' t'ear i'," murmured Hannah through semiclosed lips, earning herself another stern look from Lisa.

"In fact," she said, "you only give yourself the answers you already know deep down. You just don't see it, and the cards help reveal it. Get it?"

Hannah nodded.

"Let's take another example." She seemed to have regained her flow. "I know you and Simon have been wondering when I'll finally get around to looking for another boyfriend. But to be honest, I haven't wanted a man in my life for ages, because deep down, I knew the time wasn't right. After I split up with my last one, there were more important things going on."

Hannah pricked up her ears. "Aha," she said. "You said 'were,' in the past—has something changed?"

"You're still not allowed to talk, but yes."

"Yes? You've met someone?"

"Not yet, but I will soon."

"Soon?"

"It just so happens that the single life has suited me fine over the last few years," Lisa said. "I don't feel like I'm missing out—I've really enjoyed doing and not doing whatever I want. And the cards always confirmed it—that things are perfectly good as they are." She paused. "It wasn't till a few weeks ago, when we started Little Rascals . . . How can I put it? I feel so good and happy since we've been running the business that I find myself thinking how lovely it would be to have a partner to share in my happiness."

"Really?" Hannah took Lisa's hand and squeezed it. "I can't tell you how relieved I am to hear it. Sometimes I worry a bit about having talked you into quitting your job. It could all go wrong."

"It was totally the right thing to do! If I'd known how wonderful this would be, I'd have wanted to do it much sooner."

"I'm glad." Hannah grinned. "And now I know that we've also got the backing of a tarot reader, I won't worry. If we end up going bust, I can simply blame it all on her—she should have seen it in her crystal ball."

"Cards," Lisa corrected. "Sarasvati reads the tarot for me; she has nothing to do with crystal balls."

"Sarasvati?"

"Hmm," Lisa said. "It just slipped out."

"Out is out," Hannah said cheerfully. "Sarasvati sounds even crazier than Mr. Magic!"

"She's brilliant," Lisa said defensively. "And so far, everything she's said has come true."

"Can you ask her for the lottery numbers?"

"Don't be stupid!" Lisa looked really wounded.

"Sorry, I didn't mean to upset you." Hannah backed off. "Go on! So this Sarasvati thinks you'll have a man in your life soon?"

"She didn't say anything about a 'man in my life.' But when I went to see her two weeks ago, she said that during the next year I'll have a special encounter."

"'Special encounter' sounds like something that can mean whatever you want it to."

"According to Sarasvati, it's related to a partnership."

"Maybe she meant me? We're partners."

"For one thing, I already know you, so that rules you out. And for another, the cards indicated a man."

"Okay." Hannah winked. "I'm not a man."

"That's true. Though you often act like one."

"Thank you very much!"

"It was meant as a compliment."

"I said thanks, didn't I?"

They laughed, and then Hannah turned serious again. "I'm glad you had good predictions about Little Rascals and your dream man—but what am I going to do about Simon?"

"I don't know," Lisa admitted. "Wait, I guess."

"I'm finding it difficult. I feel like dragging him by the hair into the hospital for more tests."

"You can't force him. He has to choose it himself."

"I know. But if only we could convince him somehow that even in this situation he shouldn't lose the will to live. That he must have more than a year ahead of him. That he's gearing himself up for a worst-case scenario totally unnecessarily."

"How can you convince him of that? You don't actually know it yourself."

"I do!" Hannah said. "I'm certain of it."

"How can you be?"

"No idea. I just know it. Simon can't be going to die soon, simple as that. I won't allow it!" Tears sprang to her eyes again. She knew that her arguments were childish, no more than magical thinking, a desperate attempt to close her ears to what she didn't want to hear.

Lisa looked at her sadly. "Sometimes things that seem so horrific that we can't face them are nevertheless true."

"Yes," she said quietly and sobbed. "They are. Unfortunately."

They sat side by side, two friends who no longer knew what to say. Lisa began to stroke Hannah's hair again, as though she were comforting her for a cut on her knee. But this was a serious, deep wound. So deep that it might never heal.

Lisa eventually broke the silence. "I have an idea."

"What?"

"We could send Simon to see Sarasvati, get her to read the cards for him."

Hannah straightened and looked at her doubtfully. "I don't think so. He'd never go along with such 'humbug,' as he'd call it, and in any case, we don't know what would come of it. She might tell him he doesn't have a chance—and then what?"

Lisa shook her head. "She wouldn't do that. She's not Mr. Magic. Sarasvati shows her clients the possible ways. She helps them discover their own opportunities."

"Whatever. Simon won't go along with it. I'm sure of it." She almost laughed. "I can just imagine saying to him: 'Listen, I know you think you're going to die soon, but here's the address of a brilliant psychic. You ought to go see her.' Honestly, he'd tell me where to stick it."

"It was just a suggestion." Lisa sighed. "I've got no idea how to help him either."

"Oh, don't worry. You're helping me just by being here. I don't want to have to be alone tonight."

"That goes without saying." Lisa smiled, leaned over, and kissed her cheek. "And I'm sure we'll find a solution together." She yawned widely and scrunched down a little into the sofa. "But maybe not right now. Everything will look a little better in the morning."

"I hope so."

Hannah laid her head on Lisa's shoulder and closed her eyes. Although she was also bone tired, her thoughts continued to run amok. If only she could think of something to drag Simon from the hole he'd sunk into! How could she breathe a little of the will to live back into him? How could she convince him that he most certainly wouldn't die in the coming year?

Maybe a session with Lisa's tarot reader would be the right thing? No, it was nonsense, it wouldn't achieve anything.

From the depth of Lisa's breathing, Hannah could tell that her friend had fallen asleep. She wished she, too, could drift off and escape from her brooding, at least for a few hours. But there was no way; despite her exhaustion she simply couldn't rest. After trying for a few moments longer, she threw the blanket aside and stood up, taking care not to wake Lisa.

Deep in thought, she watched Lisa sleeping. Hannah was really glad she had her. Not only because together they had brought a successful business into being, but above all because without her friend, she would have had no idea how to survive this night.

Hannah went to the bedroom, sat on the edge of the bed, and took her cell phone from the bedside table. She usually switched it off at night, as she did her house phone, but tonight she had kept it ready and waiting in case Simon called. A glance at the display told her he hadn't been in touch. She hadn't expected him to.

Nevertheless, she had hoped. Wished. Wished that he'd sent her a message before going to sleep, a little *I love you and I'm thinking of you*. Or even a *Don't worry, I'm fine*. Anything.

Hannah opened the web browser. However great the temptation to do a sneaky search for information on lymphoma, Hannah resisted. She didn't want to risk being driven crazy like Simon had by Dr. Google.

No, she'd leave it and not allow herself to go into a downward spiral toward death by the opinions of people whose specialized medical knowledge came from browsing the pharmacy shelves.

Instead she searched for inspiration on the themes of life, optimism, and joy. For stories proving that there was a way out of any situation, however hopeless it appeared.

As she read and read, a single question ran through her head: *How can I get Simon to tackle the coming year with optimism, despite his illness?* How could she convince him that he held the key to the way the next twelve months would turn out? That he shouldn't lose faith. And that it was a matter of taking each day as it came, each hour and each minute; that he should savor and enjoy them fully.

Ultimately, it made no difference how long someone lived—what mattered for everyone was the here and now, living in the moment.


Her phone display was showing *6:23* when the idea came to Hannah's rescue. She let out a cry of joy, so loud that she heard a clatter from the living room indicating that Lisa had rolled off the sofa.

A second later her friend was standing in the bedroom door.

"What happened, for God's sake?"

"Nothing," Hannah replied with a laugh. "I've just had a stroke of genius, is all."

"And what's that?" Lisa plonked down next to her on the bed and looked at her expectantly.

"It's simple."

"So tell me!"

"You and I, we're more or less event managers, aren't we?"

"Well, maybe that definition's a little ambitious."

"Then we'll aim high. What I mean is, every day we make sure the kids in our care have a wonderful time."

"I'm sorry, I'm not quite following you."

"It's simple: what Simon needs is a wonderful time!"

"A wonderful time?"

Hannah nodded. "Exactly!"

"Uh-huh." A thousand question marks were written on Lisa's face.

"I'm firmly convinced," Hannah continued, "that Simon's actually suffering a kind of depression. His mother's death and the loss of his job—he's slid into a crisis situation and can't find his way out."

"You're forgetting that he's just been told he has a terminal illness."

"No, I'm not forgetting it. I'll come to that later. Can I go on?"

"Sorry. Yes, of course!"

"So, I've been wondering how I can get Simon to rediscover more joy in his life. And the answer's obvious: he has to *live* more. That's all! Simon needs to *move*."

"How? If I understood correctly, right now he's planning his own funeral. It's probably not the best moment to tell him that he's damn well got to start enjoying life."

"Wrong!"

"Wrong?"

"It's the best possible moment. What time could be more appropriate than when your own mortality is staring you in the face? When you're given a blindingly clear reminder that none of us lives forever?"

"You think so?"

Hannah nodded energetically. "Absolutely."

"So what exactly is your plan?"

"I'm going to write out a diary for him."

"A diary?"

"Yes!" Hannah nodded again. "I'm going to start today. I'll plan Simon's year for him, think up a whole range of lovely dates, appointments, and things for him to do."

"You mean you're going to dictate what he should do for the whole year?"

"What do you mean, 'dictate'? They'll be suggestions. Three hundred sixty-five ideas, one for every day!" Her words almost tripped over themselves in her excitement. "I'm going to show him tracks into the future."

"Tracks into the future?"

"Yes," Hannah said.

"I don't understand."

"It's a really simple principle. When you lay down tracks into the future, you behave as though whatever you wish for has already come true today."

"I still don't get it."

"A practical example: You buy a pair of pants in size six, although your size is eight—because you want to lose weight until the smaller size fits you. By already buying something that *will* fit you, you're laying down tracks to the future."

"Uh-huh."

"It really is that simple! Our energy is guided by the focus of our attention," she said, telling Lisa what she believed from the innermost depths of her heart. "So when we turn our thoughts to what we want, the probability of attaining it is so much greater than if we're constantly wrestling with what we don't actually want. In that case, we're focusing our attention on precisely what we *don't* want to happen."

"Excuse me, but if I'm understanding you correctly, your logic would make it foolish to fasten your seat belt when you get in the car."

"My turn—you've lost me."

"It's obvious: if I fasten my seat belt, I'm laying the track into the future that says an accident could happen."

"That's not how it works," Hannah said with irritation. "Laying a track into the future doesn't mean I've completely lost my mind and intend to cheerfully jump from the roof because I believe I can fly."

"That's a shame."

"Stupid woman!"

"Stupid woman yourself!"

Hannah couldn't suppress a giggle. "For someone who embraced self-employment on the basis of what a psychic said, you're being a touch critical!"

"Life adviser," Lisa corrected. "Anyway, I'm only trying to see things from Simon's perspective, giving you advance notice of his possible objections. Personally, I'd find such a diary an excellent idea—but we're not talking about me."

"Whatever he might say, I'm going to do it anyway! Simon believes he may not even have a year left to live—so I'm presenting him with the next year, laying down his tracks into the future, so that he has down in black and white all that he has to look forward to. It kind of means it's not possible to die his way out of it, since the diary leaves him no space to do that!" Her enthusiasm was returning.

"I don't want to take the wind out of your sails," Lisa said, once again playing devil's advocate, "but do you seriously believe he'll be open to something like that right now?"

"As I said, this moment is particularly appropriate."

"Your plan is all well and good, and it even sounds logical—but there's a massive difference between theory and practice. And everyone's different. One person discovers they're about to depart . . ." She paused with a small "Sorry."

"Doesn't matter, go on!"

"Well, one person discovers they'll soon be kicking the bucket and that makes them really go for it, like you would. But there are others who shut themselves off entirely."

Hannah didn't reply but simply stared at Lisa.

"Did I say something wrong?"

"No," Hannah replied thoughtfully, her brow creased. Then she beamed at Lisa. "On the contrary!" she exclaimed. "You've said something wonderful!"

"Have I?"

"Yes. A bucket list—that's what the diary should be!"

"What do you mean, a bucket list?"

"Like in the film—you know?"

"I've never seen it."

"You have to—it's brilliant! It's about two men with incurable cancer—"

"Great! Especially given the current situation."

"That's really not the point. These two become friends and start to draw up their bucket lists together. A list of all the things they still want to do before they—"

"Kick the bucket."

"Exactly."

"And what happens in the film?"

Hannah couldn't meet her eye. "Well, they both die in the end. But before they do, they've actually done all the items on their bucket lists."

Now it was Lisa's turn to stare at Hannah. "Oh, terrific! So they go to their graves completely fulfilled."

"Oh, you have to have seen it. Then you'd understand what I mean."

"I understand perfectly," Lisa replied. "You want to make Simon draw up his bucket list. To say to him, 'Hey, why don't you just write down all you want to do before you kick the bucket. You may believe you only have a few months or even weeks, but we can cram in a quick trip to the Heide Park Resort. And if we're lucky, the theme-park rides will get you so excited that you forget all that death business.' Seriously, if you're worried about it, he could always hit you over the head with your diary—that way, your bucket list would be sure to get a reaction!"

Hannah looked unhappy. "Of course I wouldn't call it a bucket list. My plan is that he shouldn't have to write it for himself, but that I do it for him. That's what the diary's for—I'm effectively outlining his bucket list."

"So what's going to be in there? Apart from the trip to the theme park, I mean?"

"I don't know yet," Hannah admitted. "I've only just had the idea; I need some peace and quiet to think about it." She wrung her hands. "A few nice things we can do together, for one thing. Going to the seaside. Walking barefoot through a flower meadow, dancing through the night until five in the morning—"

"I'd seriously advise against that in Simon's condition," Lisa interrupted. "Sorry," she added immediately, on seeing Hannah's face. "Just saying."

"The diary bucket list can have anything at all. They don't have to be massive events," Hannah continued. "Little things, anything that makes him feel good. And a few comforting thoughts, though I've no idea what yet." She pondered for a moment. "For example, I'd set a date and time when he should finally sit down and start writing his novel."

"Could turn out to be a morbid one. And unfinished to boot."

"Lisa!"

"Sorry," she said again, lowering her eyes. "I just don't want you to be disappointed."

Hannah sighed. "Things can't get any worse than they are now. I've got to try it. And if Simon really thinks he's going to die in the next twelve months, what does he have to lose?"

"Nothing."

"Exactly. If I ask him to get into the spirit of it for my sake and at least try, maybe he will? Simply because he still has a small place in his heart for me and I'm important to him?"

"Could work," Lisa agreed.

"I hope so."

"But what about his illness? He can't just ignore it; he really needs to go to a doctor or back to the hospital."

"I don't know about that. Of course, I'm hoping I'll stir up enough energy in him that he'll take up the fight and get some help." She smiled sadly. "And if it really turns out that Simon's right with his gloomy prognosis and he doesn't have much time left, then it should at least turn out to be the best time of his damned life!" Hannah swallowed hard and, before she knew it, had begun crying again. "Shit!" She banged her hand down on the duvet. "If it really is his last year, I'll make sure it's a damned perfect year for him!"

Lisa laid an arm around her shoulder.

"You'll do that," she said softly. "And I'm going to help you."

# 27

*Jonathan*

Twenty minutes later, Jonathan and Leopold were sitting at the long teak table in the dining room over plates of scrambled eggs and ham. Not only did Jonathan not know how to make anything else, but he had nothing else in the house to cook.

He had offered to run out to the supermarket and pick up a few things, if Leopold helped him make a list, but his guest had dismissed the idea, saying he merely wanted "something warm."

Leopold had excused himself and taken a quick shower, returning to the kitchen a quarter of an hour later wrapped in the flowery bathrobe that hung in Tina's bathroom. Whistling cheerfully, he had taken a box of eggs from the fridge and set to work.

The result was not too different from Jonathan's usual staple of fried eggs, but the taste was worlds away. Leopold had helped himself to the spice jars and put together a blend that, without overdoing it, resulted in the best scrambled eggs Jonathan had ever tasted.

"Amazing!" he told his new acquaintance.

"Thank you."

"Where did you learn to cook like that?"

Leopold grinned. "Scrambled eggs are hardly the pinnacle of culinary genius."

"These taste like it." He nodded in confirmation. "Yes. Exquisite, if I may say so."

"When you live on limited means, you learn to make the best of what you have."

"Understood."

"Besides, I'm a trained chef."

"That explains a thing or two."

"Here." Leopold held out a basket containing a few slices of mixed-grain bread. "Have a piece; it'll taste even better."

"No, thanks," Jonathan said. "I don't eat carbs after six o'clock in the evening."

Leopold almost choked on his eggs. "Are you serious?" he wheezed, holding a napkin in front of his mouth as he spoke.

"Totally serious. Foods containing starch eaten in the evening are a veritable poison for an organism."

"Says who?"

Jonathan shrugged. "It's common knowledge."

"Oh, really?"

"Well, I read it somewhere and it seemed to make sense."

"Fair enough." Leopold picked up a slice of bread and took a hearty bite. "Here's to common knowledge," he said as he chewed.

"However, I can offer you something else, something that's very digestible at this time of day." Jonathan rose and went into the kitchen, returning with a bottle of red wine and two long-stemmed glasses. "A Bordeaux—an excellent wine for special occasions," he announced as he sat back down, setting a glass in front of each of them and beginning to uncork the bottle.

"I feel very honored," Leopold said, looking a little sheepish, "but I'm afraid I have to be a spoilsport. I don't drink alcohol."

Jonathan paused with the corkscrew. "But this is only wine!"

"I'm sorry. I'm a complete teetotaler, and that includes wine."

"Hmm." Jonathan looked at him helplessly, unsure whether or not to open the bottle anyway. At the same time, he realized how surprised he was that a homeless man, of all people, didn't drink. It might be a cliché, but he'd always been firmly convinced that everyone who lived on the streets brightened up their lives with liquor. And a chef, to boot! He thought they were all on the bottle. Half a bottle of wine in the sauce, half inside the man making it. "Have you always abstained?" he asked.

Leopold laughed. "No, not always. On the contrary, I used to love drinking. Too much. That's why I don't touch a drop now."

"Ah." Jonathan was still paused, the corkscrew twisted halfway into the cork, with no idea what to do with his hands. Or the bottle.

"Not a big deal," Leopold said. "You go ahead and enjoy your wine. It doesn't bother me."

"You sure?"

"Totally sure." He smiled. "If I couldn't bear to see people drinking in my presence, I'd have to move to a desert island. And even there I'd probably run into some shipwrecked soul with a hip flask. So go for it!"

The cork slid from the neck of the bottle with a loud pop. Jonathan poured himself a small measure, swirled it around the glass, and finally brought it to his lips.

He held back on any words of appreciation, since he already felt like a criminal drinking a drop in front of a recovering alcoholic. If he'd had the slightest idea, he would have stuck to the water he'd already poured for them.

"It's not long behind me," Leopold said, leaning back in his chair.

"What isn't?"

"The drinking."

"Oh?"

He nodded. "I ended up back in the clinic six weeks ago. The police hauled me in from the Reeperbahn, where I'd settled down for the night in the doorway of an amusement arcade. My blood alcohol was over 0.3 percent when I woke up in the rehab clinic."

"Over 0.3 percent?" He almost added a breathless "Respect!"—but managed to suppress it.

"Yes." Leopold's expression betrayed an uneasy blend of remorse and belligerence. "After a week, my head was so clear that I swore it would be the last time I ever ended up in an institution like that, and I'd immediately take back control of my life."

"But you're still living on the streets?"

"What do you mean, 'still'? Things don't move that quickly," Leopold said. "I've only just begun."

"Doesn't everyone get welfare assistance?" Jonathan wasn't too familiar with the welfare system—why would he be?—but as far as he knew, no one in Germany who didn't want to was forced to live on the streets.

"Now there's a subject that could drive me back to drink," Leopold said, raising his hands to make it clear he was only joking. "It's complicated. Homelessness is a vicious circle that isn't so easy to break out of. It takes time. Time and staying power."

"Can I . . ." Jonathan hesitated just in time to stop himself from finishing the sentence with ". . . help in any way?" He instead blurted a somewhat awkward ". . . hear more of your story?" It was nice sitting here with Leopold, but he wasn't about to let a spur-of-the-moment emotional impulse compel him to offer to take the man in.

"Oh, no," Leopold replied with a dismissive gesture. "It's not particularly interesting. I'd rather hear something about you. I don't know anything about you. Apart from the fact that you have an amazing house with a wonderful kitchen you don't use. And that you throw away important documents."

"To be honest, there isn't really much more to say about me."

"I don't believe you."

"It's true, though."

"Prove it!"

"Very well." Jonathan took another drink of wine. "I'm the last in the line of a Hamburg publishing dynasty. So I haven't earned most of my income—I inherited it. My father's a tyrannical figure, but he now suffers from dementia and is mainly harmless. I haven't seen my mother for thirty years. I'm divorced and childless, and I spend the majority of my time reading, walking, and exercising. That's it."

"Any hobbies?"

"I go running every day and read a lot."

"And?"

"And what?"

"What else do you do in your free time, which you clearly have a lot of?"

"What am I supposed to do?"

"No idea," Leopold replied. "Whatever you do when the world's your oyster. Traveling, for example. Or managing some charity project or other. Sailing, playing polo, golfing—whatever people like you do."

"The publishing house has a foundation that supports young authors, but the staff see to that. I'm afraid of horses, sailing bores me, so does golf, and since my wife left me, I haven't had much desire to travel. I actually like spending time at home."

Leopold stared at him expressionlessly. Then, for the second time that day, with an unmistakably ironic undertone, he added, "Wow!"

"I told you there wasn't much to say," Jonathan replied defensively.

"Sure," Leopold agreed. "But *so* little?"

"Most people don't live their lives like Indiana Jones."

"There's quite a gap between that and meaningless existence."

"And just how meaningful is an existence in a dumpster?" Jonathan fired back.

Leopold's eyes narrowed to slits. The relaxed atmosphere was suddenly charged with hostility, and Jonathan had the feeling his new friend was soon to become an ex-friend. He imagined him getting up and leaving the house. If Jonathan was unlucky, Leopold might even land one on him on his way out.

But nothing of the kind happened.

Instead, Leopold raised his water glass, smiled, and toasted him with a "Touché!"

"Cheers." Jonathan picked up his wineglass and clinked it against Leopold's.

"So, back to getting to know each other," Leopold said after they had both drunk. "Of course, I'm itching to know what you were looking for so urgently in the recycling. It obviously wasn't a love letter." He winked.

"Oh, that . . ." Jonathan hesitated. And then decided to tell him. After all, Leopold had confided in him about the alcoholism, so it was only fair to return the trust. Besides, it was highly unlikely that the two of them had any mutual acquaintances, so he was unlikely to be able to do anything with the information. And even if he could, Jonathan's intuition told him that this man was a decent guy. Battered by life, perhaps, but respectable. "Those were my publishing company's latest financial statements, and they probably don't look too rosy. So I was afraid that someone might find them and use the information."

"Probably?" Leopold echoed. "The statements *probably* don't look too rosy?"

"I hadn't had a chance to look at them closely."

"But it's your company, isn't it?"

"Yes, it is." A feeling of unease spread through Jonathan. He should have kept this to himself. Too late now. "My CEO looks after the operational side of things; I don't . . ." He stopped.

"You don't have a clue about it?" Leopold suggested.

"Not as such," he conceded.

"Aren't you interested?"

"Yes, well, I . . ." He searched for the right words. "I don't know. I'm passionate about books. It's just that . . ." Jonathan fell silent and looked at Leopold helplessly.

"Don't you think you're capable of running your own show?"

"Of course I do!" Jonathan cried. And drank another mouthful of wine.

Leopold shrugged. "Well, if it's not that, it must be that you're not really interested."

"It's not as simple as that."

"It is. It's very simple, in fact. I'll tell you one truth: if life's taught me anything, it's that you should only do what excites you. Everything else is a waste of time. No one should act against their heart and their own convictions." He slapped the flat of his hand down on the table for emphasis.

"Excuse me," Jonathan said. "I really don't want to offend you, but when I see where this philosophy has led you, then—"

"Wrong!" Leopold interrupted. "It's because I've only recently adopted this philosophy that I'm in this predicament. I never used to act according to my convictions; I did things that made me so unhappy that I turned to drink. I threw my marriage and family to the wind, lost my job, and ended up on the street. Unfortunately, I recognized it way too late. It only really became clear to me the last time I was in the hospital. It was like scales fell from my eyes and I saw that I'd been on the wrong track for decades."

"Oh?" Jonathan replied cynically. "And since you saw the light six weeks ago, you're now evangelizing?"

Leopold shook his head. "No, not at all. But I look at you and think I'd give anything to be fifteen years younger and able to do it all differently."

"With respect"—Jonathan coughed for emphasis—"I'm neither on the bottle nor on the streets."

"But your marriage is down the drain, and you told me yourself that your finances probably don't look too rosy. And a pad like this doesn't run itself on fresh air."

"Yes, but—"

"At your age, I, too, only enjoyed a glass or two here and there," Leopold continued without taking any notice of him, "and I was way up the career ladder."

"As a chef," Jonathan replied drily.

"No, you dunce!" His voice was raised now. "I wished I'd stayed a chef! I enjoyed it; it was my passion. But I always hankered after more—nothing was ever enough. So I went to night school and got a degree in business administration, and over the years I worked my way up from managing director of a chain of restaurants to the board of a major group of food companies."

"Doesn't sound too bad."

"No, of course not. It was all wonderful! A massive salary, fancy company car with chauffeur, fancy house, fancy yacht, very fancy friends in the very best society. Massive ego. And massive depression, because endless work I didn't actually enjoy meant that I no longer knew who I really was. When things began to go downhill, my wife and kids did a disappearing act along with all my fancy friends, leaving me alone with my schnapps and a huge mountain of debt. Or that's how it seemed. Anyway, I advise you to stop and take a good look inside yourself. If the publishing house isn't your thing, then sell it."

"Sell it?" Jonathan laughed indignantly. "That's impossible—it's a family firm with a long tradition behind it."

"If family tradition is the only reason, you really should sell it."

Jonathan opened his mouth to object. And closed it. He was speechless. Who was this man? How had he come to be sitting at Jonathan's table?

A thought occurred to him: it was no mere coincidence! So many strange things had happened over the last two days—something fishy was going on!

No, that was crazy: of course it was coincidence. No one could have imagined that Henriette Jansen would throw the papers into the recycling and so lead Jonathan to Leopold.

But it was uncanny. The kind of thing that happened in fairy tales. There was always a wizened little old man turning up in storybooks who set the hero back on the right track.

Or the wrong one, depending on the story.

"I'm sorry." Leopold jolted him from his thoughts. "It really wasn't my place."

"No problem," Jonathan said. "It was . . . interesting, anyway."

"No, really, it was excessive. I don't know you at all, and I haven't the slightest clue about your life. Things seem to be going just fine for you; I really shouldn't have assumed otherwise."

"No. No one ever should." All the while, he was thinking, *Leopold's right. Things are going fine. It's just that there's nothing more to it than that.* "You know," he said, "something strange happened to me the day before yesterday."

He went on to tell Leopold about the diary. His new friend listened attentively.

*A quarter past three. A quarter past three in the morning!* Jonathan couldn't remember the last time he had sat over a glass of good wine until the small hours, chatting with someone. If ever in his life. He was no night owl; sleep was just as important to a man as having enough to eat and drink.

But after he'd told Leopold about the Filofax and then shown it to him, they had begun to speculate: where it could have come from, and for whom it was intended (Leopold considered the theory about Jonathan's mother to be absurd). What he should make of his visit to Sarasvati and what the relevance of the money could be. And, of course, they discussed what was now the best thing to do. Leopold was strongly against Jonathan taking the diary to the lost-and-found, because he thought it highly unlikely it would find its owner that way. He also regarded the whole situation as far too exciting to end it just like that.

"If fate deals you a hand like this, you can't just ignore it," he had said.

"Why's everyone suddenly so concerned with fate?"

"It's a question that merits consideration," Leopold had said, grinning enigmatically. At least that was how it had seemed to Jonathan, though it could have been a result of the wine—since, contrary to his usual habit of enjoying no more than an occasional glass or two, he had single-handedly downed almost the entire bottle over the course of the evening.

He was now lying in bed at a quarter past three in the morning. His head was spinning, which definitely had less to do with the wine than with the many thoughts casually playing ping-pong in his mind. They weren't bad thoughts, just unusual ones. He closed his eyes and sighed. The last few days had certainly been eventful.

He was on the brink of falling asleep when something occurred to him.

He sat up with a start, switched on his bedside light, and reached toward his night table for the Filofax. He opened it and picked up the pencil he kept tucked between the pages. He began to write.

*I'm grateful for meeting Leopold and the good conversations we've had with one another.*

He looked at the entry with satisfaction. There! He did have something to be grateful for, genuinely and from the bottom of his heart. And that had nothing to do with the wine, either, even if a loud hiccup escaped as he smiled.

He was about to close the diary again, but he paused and added something:

*Tomorrow I'm going to invite him to stay in Tina's room for the time being. If he accepts, I'll also be grateful for that, because it's good to imagine him living in my house.*

Jonathan N. Grief set the diary down on the bedside table, hiccupped again, switched the light off, and slid back down under the duvet.

*This is going to be great,* he thought before his eyes finally closed. *A housemate. Why not?*

# 28

*Hannah*

***Three days before:***
***Sunday, December 31, 11:59 p.m. and 59 seconds***

As the first rocket shot up into the Hamburg sky, Hannah didn't know what to say.

"Happy New Year"?

No, that wouldn't do.

She was standing with Simon on the small balcony of his apartment, and together they looked out over the Alster at the fireworks being sent up to celebrate the beginning of the new year. He had wrapped both arms around her from behind, his chin resting on the top of her head, and Hannah wished she could stay with him like that forever.

But she knew it wasn't to be. They had a few more minutes of enjoyment, of losing themselves in the pretense that this was simply a New Year's Eve like any other—but at some point they would go back inside. And then the hour of reckoning would be upon them both. Except that Simon suspected nothing, and Hannah was terrified. How would he react to her gift?

They hadn't spoken a word more about his illness since the evening at Da Riccardo. Hannah had tried to broach the subject only once, the following day, but Simon had asked her to leave it be until he felt ready to face the matter again.

Hannah had accepted that; of course she had. She was pleased that it also meant no further mention of their separation, of him cutting her out of his life completely. That should have been enough for the time being. Part of her had even been a little relieved—the part that preferred to hide from reality, like a little child who closes her eyes in the belief that she can't be seen.

But she had only partly managed to suppress her worries, and she had used the following days, during which she and Simon had acted as though nothing had happened, to put together the diary she was composing for him. She'd begun the morning after the night Lisa had spent with her. She'd bought a particularly nice Filofax in an expensive stationery shop, a fine volume bound in dark-blue leather with white stitched seams, that nestled cozily in her hand.

Hannah liked the idea that the leather would become softer and softer over the years, so soft that Simon would secretly hold it against his cheek from time to time just to enjoy the feel of it. Over the years— many, many years.

Hannah had not hesitated one moment when it came to the first of the ring-bound pages. She had written *Your Perfect Year* with a fountain pen she had also bought in the stationery shop. Then she had got down to work with feverish enthusiasm, thinking, with Lisa's help, about what Simon enjoyed, what would jolt him from his lethargy and inject some enthusiasm into him. What would help him forget how things were, and might even inspire him to face up to his illness and start fighting it.

Hannah had written out everything she believed and lived by. All of it. She had spent hours on the internet searching for words of wisdom that were inspiring but not clichés, and in the frequently recurring moments when despair threatened to overcome her, she had taken hold of herself, carried on and carried on and carried on, in the hope that what she was doing would convince Simon not to give himself up to his perceived fate.

Hannah had been conspicuous in her absence from Little Rascals since Simon's revelation, and she was grateful to Lisa and both their parents for supporting her project without objection. She would otherwise never have managed to complete the diary by New Year's Eve, but they had all agreed there was no question that she should hand over the Filofax to Simon on that symbolic night.

A wake-up call, a "Get set, go!"—this was the purpose of the diary, and Hannah had put all her energy, all her love, into every single entry. As Lisa had noted appreciatively on reading the finished work, she had surpassed herself. The two friends had fallen into each other's arms in tears. Lisa was particularly moved that Hannah had actually made an appointment with Sarasvati, for January 2. "Because ultimately," Hannah had explained, "it's all clutching at straws. Things can't get any worse."

Hannah had then copied the pages of the diary for herself, so that she could support Simon in living his perfect year and always knew to the last detail what was coming up. She hoped so much that he would not only understand the Filofax but really get into it.

"Come on, let's go in. You're shivering." With these words, Simon gave the signal for the most difficult moment in Hannah's life to date. She had no idea whether the diary she was about to give him would serve its purpose. Whether he would be as moved as Lisa had been, or whether . . .

No, she wasn't going to allow any "or." *Watch your thoughts; thoughts become reality!* If these words she had heard her mother say since she was tiny contained the slightest hint of truth, then now was the very moment she should be taking the advice to heart.

"Why are you looking at me like that?" Simon asked as soon as they settled on the blanket he'd spread on the floor in front of the sofa.

Hannah had asked him if they could celebrate this New Year's Eve like their very first evening together on the banks of the Elbe, with a picnic on the ground, in the hope of creating an atmosphere that would support the success of her impending mission. He had agreed to her request with amusement, calling her "my little romantic," and then begun to move the food he'd prepared earlier from the table to the blanket. "Is something wrong?"

Hannah swallowed hard, trying not to break out in hysterical laughter. He was seriously asking her if something was wrong? But instead of yelling at him that nothing was right—nothing at all—since he'd told her he was expecting to pass away soon, she picked up her large shoulder bag and took out the lovingly gift-wrapped parcel.

"Here, this is for you."

"What is it?"

"Open it."

"Since when have you given presents on New Year's?"

"Since today."

"I can't wait." With excruciating slowness, he carefully peeled off every strip of tape—Simon always unwrapped packages that way, a trait that drove Hannah crazy.

Once again she had to control herself, this time to keep from grabbing the parcel from his hands and ripping the paper off herself. Her patience was seriously put to the test—no amount of chanting *om* would have been enough to soothe her frazzled nerves. And then, finally, at last, on what felt like the following New Year's Eve, the Filofax was in his hand.

"A diary?" He looked at her in amazement.

"Yes." She nodded. "For the coming year."

"But . . ." He said no more. Simply "But." The single word held a hundred thousand phrases, Simon's expression more than a million objections. Everything Hannah had feared resonated in that "But." *But*

*I don't have another year left. But I'm going to die soon. But I don't believe I'll be able to use your gift. But I know there's no hope left for me. But I . . .*

"I've filled it out," Hannah said to shut off the silent drone of Simon's words in her head. "I thought of something for every day. All I want is that you accept my gift and at least try it. Please! For me. For us."

Instead of replying, Simon undid the snap and opened the diary. He began to leaf through the pages, silently reading entry after entry, frowning occasionally. He read and read and read without saying a word.

Then, after reaching the last page, he looked up.

He was totally pale.

"I . . ." Hannah began, but fell silent as Simon set the diary aside, took her hands, and drew her to him. He held her as tightly as he had that evening at Da Riccardo; she could feel his heartbeat and how hard he was trembling.

"Thank you," he whispered in her ear. "No one's ever given me such a wonderful present. Thank you."

"So you accept it?" She moved back so she could see his face.

Simon smiled. "Why wouldn't I?"

Laughing with relief, Hannah fell on his neck. "It'll all be okay, my love!" she said. "You'll see. We can do it! Cancer won't bring us to our knees. You'll be well again, I just know it!"

"Yes," he replied slowly, "I believe so too."

"I can't tell you how happy I am to hear you say that! As soon as the holidays are over, we'll look for a good oncologist. Oh, what am I saying, 'good'? The best! Even if we have to go to the ends of the earth! If necessary, we'll hitchhike. We'll walk! We'll find a specialist, the top in his field! He'll take care of your body, and the diary will nourish your soul."

"It sounds great. We'll do it."

Hannah giggled; she couldn't help it.

"What's so funny?" He studied her.

"Nothing at all. I just love you crazily, madly, that's all."

"I love you too. Crazily, madly."

It was still dark when Hannah woke in Simon's bed.

It was there again! Exactly the same feeling she'd had on the morning they opened Little Rascals—that incredible fluttering of sheer excitement and love. Except that it was now many times stronger than it had been a few weeks ago.

Hannah turned to snuggle up to Simon and wake him gently. She wanted a little more of what they had shared during the night, more of the passion with which they had made love to the point of exhaustion.

He wasn't there. The bed was empty; Hannah was alone.

The clock on the bedside table showed 7:59. Simon never got up at that time, even when he had been working as a news editor—they had never started work at the paper until ten in the morning, instead working until late into the evening on the next day's edition.

She sat up and stretched, listening for sounds from the living room, expecting to hear the shower, the gurgling of the coffee machine, or the TV. But it was deadly silent; only some twigs tapped softly against the bedroom window.

"Simon?" she called. "Where are you? Come back to bed!"

No reply.

"Simon?"

Nothing. Hannah wrapped herself in the sheet and scooted down the mattress to the foot of the bed, where she peered out into the darkness of the hallway. "Siiimon!" she called a little louder. "Where are you?"

When he still didn't answer, she stood and left the room as fast as the sheet would allow. She glanced impatiently into the living room. Everything was just as they had left it the previous evening, except there was no trace of Simon. It was just the same in the bathroom and the kitchen. It was as though the earth had opened up and swallowed him.

She calmed herself with the thought that he had probably gone to the bakery, and decided to wash away the brief night under the shower.

On the way to the bathroom, the front door caught her eye. And the folded piece of paper lying on top of an envelope in front of it. Together with Simon's keys. She could see from where she stood that the note said more than simply *I've gone to get some rolls*.

She went up to it, bent down, and picked up the note. As she read it, her knees turned so weak that she leaned against the door before sliding down to the cold floor tiles.

> My dearest Hannah,
> I'm so very sorry to do this to you and cause you so much pain—but by the time you find this letter, I won't be alive anymore.
> I'm sure this will have shocked you. Maybe you're angry; I even hope you are. But I can't do anything else; I don't have the courage to face up to this disease. My parents' suffering lasted for far too many years, and I'm scared of sharing their fate. I'm even more scared of making you go through the very same things my mother had to. You don't deserve that. No one deserves that!
> Last night made it clear that you won't leave me. And however lovely it is for me to be certain of your undying love, it's also terrible. Because I can't bear to leave you.
> The gift you gave me is so wonderful, so incredibly magnificent, that I don't have the words. But I can't find it in me to keep my promise to accept it. I don't have a year left.
> Hannah, please believe me when I tell you I know it. I can sense the cancer, and I know that I can't defeat

it; it's much too late for that. I don't need a doctor to tell me.

To be honest—and if not now, when should I be honest?—I've realized for a long while that things haven't quite been as they should. You were right when you told me I'd changed, that somehow I'd lost my vitality.

I'm afraid it was true. I don't know if it began when Mama died or when I lost my job. Maybe a combination of the two, or maybe before that. The truth is, I didn't send off any applications—not a single one. I lied when I claimed to be looking for a new job. I lied that I'd received nothing but rejections—it was all lies, all of it!

I believe it isn't really the cancer that's killing me. Something's been dead inside me for a long time; it's just that before now I didn't dare to draw the logical conclusion. I once read a very comforting thought in a book: when you die, you return to the same state as you were in for millions of years before your birth—you're physically absent. It's not a bad thing at all that every one of us must leave this world sometime; we simply return to the universe where our souls have been and will be for the vast majority of time. This moment has now come for me. I can feel it so clearly.

Please, Hannah, forgive me and be happy without me. I know you can do it. I'm convinced you'll have a wonderful life, one that's much better without me than with me.

What is it you always say? Some good comes from everything? Believe me, there's good in this. It's the decision I've made for myself. It's what I want for myself.

Please be kind enough to give my apartment keys to my landlord. You can simply have it cleared out, but there's no rush. The balance in my account is enough to cover a few months' rent, so don't give up the apartment until you're ready.

Please keep the car keys—the Mustang is yours now. You can drive it yourself or sell it. The documents are with the keys on the chest of drawers in the living room. The large envelope contains a full power of attorney, hopefully giving you all the rights you need to sort everything out. I'm afraid it isn't an official form, but I'm sure it will be valid, as my signature's on it.

If there's any money left in my account by the end, it's also yours. I'd like you to invest it in Little Rascals—use it to help your wonderful idea grow.

Hannah, I love you! And I'm so proud of you!

But however sorry I am, this love isn't enough for me to carry on.

Simon

Hannah stared at Simon's words, reading them over and over again. And as she became aware that the letters were blurring and dancing in front of her eyes, that she was on the verge of fainting, she bit her lower lip so hard that she gasped in pain and tasted blood.

*This love isn't enough . . .*

She stood, allowed the letter to fall to the floor, went into Simon's living room, and picked up the phone. She was calm—her fingers weren't trembling in the slightest—as she dialed 110. It only rang once before a policewoman answered.

"Please come quickly," she said slowly and clearly into the receiver. "My boyfriend's about to commit suicide."

# 29

*Jonathan*

When Jonathan N. Grief didn't wake until shortly after ten the follow-ing day, he felt no pangs of conscience. It had been a long evening, so it was hardly surprising that he didn't jump out of bed as he usually did at six thirty. But he felt a slight malaise, a certain wistfulness, an indefinable . . . well, an indefinable feeling.

No sooner was he out of bed than this small, intangible worry vanished. A glance at the Filofax reminded him of the decision he had made only a few hours ago: he would invite Leopold to stay with him for a while.

In a cheerful mood, Jonathan marched into the bathroom, took a long shower, and got dressed. Not in his sports gear—that would be ridiculous after a shower—but in pants and a turtleneck sweater. He could catch up on his daily jog later. Or—a reckless notion—even miss it altogether for one day. He simply didn't feel like it, and Leopold's advice to live life more on a what-makes-you-happy basis seemed to make at least as much sense as avoiding carbs after six in the evening. At least as much.

He went downstairs, approached Tina's room, and knocked.

As he opened the door, Jonathan took a step back so as not to embarrass his guest, who might not yet be dressed.

"Leopold!" he called through the door. "Good morning! It's me, Jonathan!" While waiting for a reply, he smiled at himself for announcing his name. Who else would it be? Silence reigned in the room, so Jonathan knocked again. "Leopold? Are you awake? Come on, rise and shine!" No reply. Jonathan knocked again, then entered.

Tina's room was empty. The door to the bathroom was open; Jonathan saw no one there either. The bedclothes were rumpled with the flowery bathrobe and a used towel on top. But these clues aside, there was nothing to indicate the presence of another person.

Puzzled, Jonathan went out into the hallway. Where had Leopold gone? He looked over to the coat stand—the army coat had vanished, as had his new friend's boots.

Jonathan felt a sudden apprehension. Was he really such an idiot? Had he thrown all his reservations to the wind, only to discover that he'd been taken in by a trickster, a swindler? A man who had used his hospitality and had taken off with as much as he could carry? Jonathan hadn't even locked the important rooms like the study or the dining room (the fine family silver!)—he had simply stumbled into bed in a wine-fueled haze.

Was he really such a—how had Leopold put it?—such a dunce?

Apparently so.

Jonathan could hear his father laughing at him, loudly and with schadenfreude, on seeing that his "feckless son" had once again proved his inability to cope with life. Intuition? Ha, what intuition?

*No.* Jonathan N. Grief squared his shoulders. It could have happened to anyone. Anyone who, like he did, still believed in morality and respectability, who . . .

Oh, why stand here talking to himself? He would be better advised to figure out as quickly as he could which valuables Leopold had made off with, and then inform the police. Let the officers have a good laugh at his expense; the main thing was that they did their work and caught the thief. Leopold wouldn't get far in his worn-out old boots.

Half an hour later, Jonathan had turned the house upside down. Nothing.

Nothing at all was missing. Not the silver, not the money he kept in a cash box on his desk, not a single cuff link, not even the empty bottles in the plastic bin on the terrace, which could have been returned for cash. It was all still there. Everything except Leopold.

Somewhat bewildered, Jonathan went into the kitchen to make himself a cup of tea. That was when he noticed his wine rack. There *was* something missing: the gap was enough to hold three, maybe four bottles. Jonathan spun around and ran into the dining room to check his liquor cabinet. He immediately saw that bottles were missing there too. Jonathan moved closer and saw that the whiskey and gin were missing. The expensive grappa he had once bought for visitors and hadn't yet opened was still there. Except that the bottle was almost empty.

Jonathan sighed deeply. Then he noticed the note beneath the grappa bottle. He picked it up, sat down at the dining table, and began to decipher the practically illegible scrawl.

> My dear friend,
> It looks as though I ran into the guy with the hip flask on my desert island. I'm sorry, the temptation was too much in the night. I thank you most sincerely for a lovely evening and for your hospitality—and I'm ashamed to have disappointed you like this.
> Yours,
> Leo

P.S. If I were you, though I'm sincerely glad I'm not (I'm sure you'll take this little sideswipe in the right spirit, my friend) I'd open up that diary and get to work on the contents. You don't get a gift like that every day. I wish I'd received something like that myself.

Jonathan read the note twice more. Then he took a pencil from the case on the sideboard next to the table and added the comma that was missing after the parentheses. Without giving it a further thought, he went into the kitchen and threw the pencil and the note into the trash.

# 30

## *Hannah*

Three days. Three days like three years. Like ten years, like fifty, one hundred. Like Sleeping Beauty's thousand-year slumber. In a dark, gloomy sleep behind a yards-tall hedge of nothing but thorns, without a single rose. But no one came to wake Hannah from this nightmare. No one came to kiss her.

First, they came to pacify. Uniformed police officers, talking to Hannah in soothing tones, assuring her that they would find her boyfriend soon. Telling her insistently that suicides announced beforehand only rarely came to pass. And yes, of course, they would do all they could to find Simon. They would put out a search for him; every patrol would be on the lookout, although they drew the line at the dog team and the divers in the Alster and Elbe that Hannah had asked for, saying they would be neither useful nor feasible given the size of the city. On the second day came appeals to local radio listeners. On the third, a notification in the papers, along with requests from the police that Hannah should go home; there was nothing she could do.

But she wouldn't, simply couldn't, go home. She was incapable of anything except sitting in Simon's apartment waiting for him to come through the door and tell her his letter had been a mistake. A joke, a sick joke. A new twist—not an April Fool's trick but a New Year's prank, ha ha!

Yes, he'd admit it had been tasteless, thoroughly tasteless. He'd be sorry, but he'd been put under so much pressure by her, driven into a corner and overwhelmed by her expectations, to the extent that he had simply . . . Yes, he'd understand if she was mad at him. Truly, truly angry, furious as hell. He'd accept if she never wanted to say another word to him despite a commitment to go for further tests and even live according to her childish diary.

Over three days. Seventy-four hours and fifty-four minutes. That was how long she had sat in his apartment with nothing but these thoughts for company, waiting for him. Wearing the black dress she had worn again on New Year's Eve, so soon after the evening at Da Riccardo, she could do nothing but wander aimlessly between the bedroom, living room, kitchen, and bathroom, suppressing a scream every time the doorbell or her cell phone rang.

But it was never him, never. It was always Lisa, or her mother, Sybille, who were taking turns keeping an eye on her throughout the day and bringing her something to eat. Who told her that they were managing just fine at Little Rascals without her (as though Hannah had the slightest interest in the business; with all due respect, she didn't); who brought regular reports that Simon had not turned up at Hannah's apartment, where Sybille had moved in for the time being. And who, just like the police officers, begged her over and over again to relinquish her vigil, or who brought copies of the *Hamburg News*, as they had yesterday, so that Hannah could see for herself that the missing-person notice for Simon really was on the front page, as his former colleagues had promised.

As Hannah stared into space in Simon's apartment—simply vegetating, checking her cell phone every ten seconds, remotely checking her voice mail at home and scanning her email inbox, in the faint hope of receiving some message from her boyfriend—she knew the whole time. She had known from the moment she'd read his farewell letter. That she could scream and rage and cry as much as she liked, but Simon no longer existed.

He had not, as one of the police officers suggested, simply run off; he had not burned all his bridges, nor was he sunning himself somewhere under a palm tree with a cocktail in his hand. No. These were nothing more than empty words to help Hannah hold out, to stop her from rampaging through the city lashing out at everything and everyone in her way.

It was crazy; she was crazy. For although she knew deep down that Simon was not a man to make empty promises, never had been, she clung in utter desperation to every possibility, however improbable, even if it was only a goddamn cocktail under a goddamn palm tree.

But there was his Mustang—he would never have left that behind. However absurd and painful this notion was, it was so true. If he had paused even for a second to consider the idea of a drink under the palm trees rather than suicide, he would have slid behind the wheel and driven off. Hannah couldn't rule out that if he did, he might leave her behind. But his car? No, never. The car keys on the coffee table in the living room, together with the farewell letter and the power of attorney (or copies of them—the police had the originals), were compelling evidence of all that Hannah didn't want to contemplate.

The only thing she hadn't been able to find was the diary. It wasn't in the apartment nor outside in the trash, where she had looked in the certainty of finding it there.

That damned Filofax, tossed in among the sticky eggshells and coffee grounds by Simon as his last deed. That miserable effort Hannah had put together in her stupid delusion that it would all turn out right.

In the naive belief that it would take no more than a bit of attention, a cheerful song or two, and some "every cell in my body is happy" drivel to free her boyfriend from his mortal dread.

The very thought made Hannah want to do the same as Simon. To grab a sharp knife from the kitchen and slash open her wrists or leap from the fourth-floor balcony—the only logical punishment for what she had done.

It was probably her constant urges to action, her insensitive some-good-comes-from-everything, crisis-as-opportunity, and finding-light-in-the-darkness platitudes that had driven him to despair in the first place.

Some good comes from everything? What, exactly, was this situation good for? Apart from driving Hannah humbly to her knees and showing her that real life had nothing to do with her colorful Pollyanna world? Nothing in the slightest.

The *ping* of her cell phone made Hannah jump. A new email had arrived in her inbox. Another message from her parents or Lisa, or the newsletter of some online shop, or a message to say that some deceased Nigerian multimillionaire had declared her his sole legal heir.

None of those. It was from Sarasvati.

Hannah took a moment to process the name. The day on which she had written to Lisa's psychic and explained the situation, asking her to throw out her professional ethics and hold a "very special" session for Hannah's terminally ill boyfriend, which might renew his will to live a little (and, for the love of God, not to let him know she'd received prior instructions from Hannah)—it seemed to have happened in another life.

Sarasvati—Hannah remembered. She opened the email.

Dear Hannah,

Normally I don't ask any questions if someone misses an appointment, because I don't want to put pressure on anyone. But I'm making an exception in this case, because I can't get it out of my head.

Your boyfriend, who you wrote to me about, didn't turn up. Instead, there was a man who had found his diary by the Alster. I can't tell you any more than that, and I didn't tell him the circumstances of our appointment, because I wasn't sure you would have wanted me to say anything.

Now I'm wondering whether it was maybe a mistake. I've got a very strange feeling about it. I therefore just wanted to check whether everything was okay with you. How is your boyfriend?

Light and love,
Sarasvati

Hannah had never dialed a number more quickly in her life. Her fingers flew over the keypad of her phone as she entered the numbers at the bottom of Sarasvati's email.

A few seconds later she had the life adviser on the line.

"Th . . . this is Ha . . . Hannah Marx," she gabbled, tripping over her words in her haste.

"Hello, Hannah," a friendly, warm voice said. "I didn't expect you to call me so quickly."

Hannah got straight to the point. "My boyfriend's disappeared. He wrote me a goodbye letter. He said he was going to kill himself."

"Oh my God!" There was complete silence for a long moment, until Sarasvati asked Hannah what had happened.

"I gave Simon the diary—the one I told you about—on New Year's Eve. And he promised he'd try to follow it. That he wouldn't give up the fight." She swallowed hard as she remembered their last evening together. "The next morning, he'd disappeared and left me a suicide note. The police have been looking for him ever since. I have, too, of course."

"God, I'm so sorry!" Sarasvati blew her nose audibly. "How foolish of me not to have realized something was wrong when that man turned up at my door with the diary. But I simply thought your boyfriend hadn't liked the idea. As you said in your email, you weren't sure he'd go along with it. How stupid of me!"

"Who was this man? What was his name?"

"I don't know, I'm afraid." She sounded truly remorseful. "I didn't ask him. I don't, usually. If I do, many people think I've got some secret device in my ear to access the internet and find out all about them."

"Do you know how he came by the diary?"

"He said he found it in a bag hanging on the handlebar of his bicycle."

Hannah's heart sank. She had fervently wished and prayed that Simon had handed the Filofax to someone in person, given it away as a gift or asked someone to keep it safe for him. That he had exchanged a few words with whoever it was—had maybe even told them what was wrong and what exactly he intended to do.

Hannah sometimes felt it was easier to open up to a complete stranger than to someone she was close to. She had no other way of explaining why Simon hadn't told her the extent of his despair.

She corrected herself silently. Yes, he *had* told her. Not in so many words, but he had told her. It was just that she hadn't listened closely enough. She hadn't listened at all, but drowned him in a sea of her over-whelming optimism. "So the bag was just hanging on the handlebar of his bike?" she asked, cutting short her self-recrimination.

"That's what he said, anyway. Apparently on January first, like every other day, he went jogging by the Alster, and when he got back to his bike, the bag was just there."

"Did he say anything else?" Hannah was gripping the telephone so hard that her fingers hurt and her knuckles were white. "Did he notice anything unusual? Did he see Simon, maybe?"

"Not that he told me. He said he'd like to know himself who the diary belonged to, and that the only reason he came to the session with me was because the date and time were in it. He believed the owner would turn up at my place."

"So he only wanted to give the diary back?"

"That's what he told me," Sarasvati said. "He seemed incredibly eager to find out who the Filofax belonged to, so he wanted to wait until the owner arrived. To pass the time, and since the session was already paid for, I gave him a consultation. He was an odd guy."

"Did you tell him what I'd asked you on Simon's behalf?"

"Of course not!" Her voice was gentle but firm. "And I'd only have told your boyfriend what I actually saw for him in the cards, even though I'd have been fully aware of the circumstances myself." She paused, then added, "Of course, I'll refund what you paid for the session."

"There's no need," Hannah assured her. "The only thing I'm interested in is finding Simon. So on New Year's morning, he must have been somewhere near the Alster . . . It could be a small clue, a tiny one. But better than nothing!"

"What do the police have to say?"

"They don't know yet that he was near the Alster, but I'm going to call them as soon as we've finished."

"I meant, what have they done so far?"

Hannah sighed. "If you ask me, not much. The police are looking for him and have put out a missing-person notice, but he could be anywhere." She stopped herself from even thinking *If he's still alive, that is,* let alone voicing it. "His cell phone's at his apartment, so they couldn't locate him that way. But now at least there's a starting point for a search. Maybe some dog walkers or locals saw him by the river."

"I really wish I knew the name of the guy who turned up here."

"What did he look like?"

"Around forty, quite good looking. You don't see blue eyes like that very often, especially not with dark hair. Expensively dressed and very polite. That's about it. Oh, and he seemed tense and nervous, but that only occurred to me in hindsight."

"That doesn't give us much to go on."

"No," Sarasvati agreed. "In any case, he didn't see hide nor hair of your Simon; he only had the diary."

"But if someone talks to him, he might remember something. A minor detail that he thinks is unimportant and only means something in context. Of course, I don't care about the Filofax itself, but without it we don't have the slightest clue where to start, and if there's a chance that someone saw Simon alive, I have to pursue it."

"Yes, I can understand that. I wish I could help you. But he left after the session and took the diary with him. If only I'd—"

"Did he say what he was going to do with it?"

"Yes. He was going to take it to the lost-and-found at the nearest police station."

"I'll call them immediately! Maybe they keep a record of finders' details," Hannah said optimistically. "If they do, the officers dealing with Simon's case will need to know right away."

"It's worth trying."

"It certainly is," Hannah said. "Thank you for getting in touch."

"Oh, sweetheart!" Hannah was surprised to find she liked the sudden familiarity. "I wish there was more I could do." Sarasvati paused for a moment. "Would you like a consultation yourself? I could read the cards for you."

"Is it possible we could trace Simon that way?"

"No." Hannah hadn't expected any other reply. "But we might discover something else."

"It's really kind of you. But I don't want to discover anything except Simon."

"I understand. Feel free to get in touch anytime. And please let me know how the search for your boyfriend goes."

"I will," Hannah promised. They said goodbye and hung up.

She immediately phoned the police officer who'd left her card and told her to call anytime if she had any new information.

"Simon was by the Alster!" she yelled into the phone as soon as the woman picked up. "You need to send some people down there, right now!" Then, even though it indicated a rather pessimistic expectation of the outcome and was therefore contrary to her belief in "laying tracks into the future," she demanded: "And please, will you finally get a diver on the case?"

"We'll send officers to the banks of the Alster first," the police officer said calmly. "We'll take it from there."

Hannah ended the call and took a deep breath. *Good.* The police would now intensify their search for Simon, this time with specific information about where he was last seen.

Next, she Googled the number of the lost-and-found office at the local police station, and asked the man who took her call about the Filofax. Nothing. No one had handed in anything that remotely resembled a diary since New Year's Eve. Hannah asked the man to call her the minute anyone appeared with a dark-blue leather appointment diary. She couldn't help sympathizing with his rather surly reply that he was not a personal secretary, so she explained the situation briefly. The official apologized and promised to call her immediately if he or one of his coworkers were handed a diary.

Hannah thanked him courteously and hung up. What now? What could she do?

She picked up her cell phone a third time and called the editorial office of the *Hamburg News*. She gave them the information and asked them to publish another missing-person notice the following day, telling them to ask the finder of the diary or any other possible witnesses who might have seen Simon by the Alster to get in touch immediately. They promised to make room for it on the front page again.

She thought feverishly about what steps she could take next.

She had to find the man who had the diary! Why hadn't he handed it in at the lost-and-found as he said he would? What had he done with it instead?

Well, he probably didn't realize that he could provide valuable information, that on New Year's morning down by the river he had become entangled in what was literally a matter of life and death. He couldn't know how desperately she was looking for him. The thought that time was passing without any new information coming in made Hannah feel helpless, impotent, and furious. How could she get hold of the guy who had found Simon's diary? How on earth?

She had no idea. The finder had visited Sarasvati. Maybe he'd make further attempts and turn up for another appointment before going to the lost-and-found? Sarasvati had said that he really wanted to know who the diary belonged to; Hannah didn't care whether he was driven by sheer curiosity or a strong sense of civic duty. It was a small chance, but she dug the copy she'd made of Simon's diary from her bag and leafed through the pages with shaking hands. Where was the next entry containing a date, time, and place, where the mysterious diary finder might appear?

She was disappointed to see that there wasn't one for another ten days, on January 14. Ten days! If Simon hadn't turned up or been found by then . . .

Forbidding herself from completing the sentence, she turned back to the entry. For January 14 at seven p.m., she had noted a talk by Sebastian Fitzek at the Kampnagel theater. Fitzek was Simon's absolute favorite author; he idolized him and had devoured all his thrillers with gusto.

Hannah couldn't understand how anyone could of their own free will fill their head with murder and death (*Watch your thoughts!*), but

Simon had always explained it by saying that, for him, it was a kind of mental hygiene. "After a good read by Fitzek, I'm immune to all the horrific stories I have to read or write as a journalist, day in, day out. Unlike thrillers, those are *real* and *true*."

She had been delighted to discover in September that the author would be coming to Hamburg to give a talk. She had seen it as a fateful sign (rather a pompous description of an author talk, but that was how it had felt), hoping that going to see his favorite author would gently ease Simon in the direction of finally starting his own book. She'd immediately bought two tickets online. She had originally intended to give them to him for Christmas, but soon repurposed them for his perfect year.

The tickets would be available on January 14 at the box office, with reference 137, as she had noted in the diary. She had wanted to leave it to Simon whether he would ask her to go with him or, if he'd prefer, Sören, who shared his liking for grisly stories. She wouldn't have minded, either—as she entered the event in the diary, it had suddenly occurred to her that with Fitzek's stories she might be trading one living nightmare for another.

Now she would put up with any number of nightmares, and Simon could spend the evening with whomever he wished. She hoped at least that the man who had found the diary hanging from his bicycle would turn up at the theater box office to see who came to fetch reservation number 137.

But there were ten days to go—a painfully long time! She couldn't wait that long; she'd go mad by then. Why hadn't she made more specific arrangements? Why had she wanted to take things slowly at first, and after the "kickoff" with Sarasvati had chosen mainly tasks that Simon could do at home, alone?

Assuming that they'd have to plan for a lot of doctor and clinic appointments in the early days of the new year, she'd kept the days free from activities. Besides, she'd still had to consider her own work, which she was now seriously neglecting, albeit with the blessings of the others—but she'd had no inkling of that when making entries in the diary.

Now she cursed herself for failing to arrange something for this very day, something with a specific time and coordinates precise to a fraction of an inch, something there was no way anyone could miss. But here, too, it was a case of *if only*.

If only, if only, if only. If only she had half a clue how to find this stupid jogger!

*This stupid jogger?*

Sarasvati's words echoed in Hannah's ears. *Apparently, on January first, like every other day, he went jogging by the Alster.* THAT was it!

Twenty minutes later she went tearing down the stairs to the front door, clutching a box of thumbtacks and fifty posters she had printed out on Simon's computer.

She ran along Papenhuder Strasse and turned onto Hartwicus Strasse so quickly that she almost fell, keeping herself on her feet with great effort. She could see the lake at the end of the street and headed straight for it with her posters. She intended to plaster every bench, every tree, every bush, and every single blade of grass with her notice, which showed a picture of the diary that she had downloaded from the manufacturer's website, and a photo of Simon. Underneath, she had written in bright red, *Has anyone seen this man or this diary???*

If the guy who turned up at Sarasvati's really did come running here every day, Hannah didn't want there to be the slightest chance that he would miss her notices. And even if the man himself didn't stumble over them, someone—anyone!—must have seen Simon. Because her boyfriend had been there on New Year's morning!

Gasping for breath, Hannah stopped by the Alsterperle restaurant. She'd begin at the popular day-trip destination. As she pinned the first poster to a tree, she began to feel better. At last there was something she could do!

# 31

*Jonathan*

Dressed in his running gear, Jonathan N. Grief was sitting on the small telephone-table seat in the hall, putting on his jogging shoes for his rather belated riverside run, when he paused, laces in hand.

Was this the right thing to do? Carrying on as he always had, after the previous evening? Acting like a wet dog that shakes the water drops from its coat and then trots on its way without a care, as if it hadn't seconds before been chasing after a tempting bone only to find it was a stupid stick?

That was just how Jonathan felt. Disappointed, cheated. With a hint of guilt and shame, as he feared he was not completely innocent in the matter of Leopold's relapse. He'd made sure his valuables were safe, and that he didn't come to any physical harm, when he would have been better off ensuring that Leo didn't have access to his well-stocked liquor cabinet. He wondered if he had even provoked the man to run off into the night and the fog with an assortment of wines and spirits. Would it actually have been better if he'd refused to take Leopold in, and simply left him there in the recycling container? But of course he'd never have dreamed of doing that. Jonathan silenced his self-reproach with a sigh.

He had believed it would all be so great—so refreshing, so invigorating. He and Leopold, an oddball pair of housemates. The hobo and the publisher—his father would have had something to say about that! At least, he would if he was having one of his more lucid moments when Jonathan told him about his new friend, and could actually grasp that there was something worthy of comment.

Ha! Hamburg's answer to *The Odd Couple*—the stuff novels were born of! Popular fiction, of course, so not something that Grief & Son Books would ever entertain, but novels nevertheless.

Jonathan stretched out his legs and stared into space. Played through the previous evening and night once again in his head. The things Leopold had said to him—that open, confiding conversation between buddies. And the two entries he had drunkenly scribbled in the diary after going to bed. Yes, damn it, he felt guilty and bad. But what was he to do about it? Should he get out there and search for Leopold, in the hope of tracking him down and marching him back to the house? By force if necessary?

But he was neither a social worker nor a therapist; maybe such a move would be overreaching. Not to mention that Hamburg was a big city, and the probability of finding the guy was pretty close to zero. So should he simply forget his new "friend," put on his Nikes, and slip back into his daily routine?

No, that didn't feel right either.

Jonathan N. Grief kicked his sneakers aside decisively and went upstairs in his stocking feet to his study. The Alster would still be there tomorrow. Today, at least, he would take Leopold's advice and delve into the diary.

He settled into his favorite reading chair and opened the Filofax at January 4. Read the entry and laughed out loud. Leopold may have vanished, but his views had clearly remained.

*Life is too short to concern yourself with things you don't enjoy.*

*Write out two lists today: One of everything that makes you happy. And one of everything that you do but don't enjoy at all.*

*Then delete everything on the second list and live according to the first! Only that! Also, write out what would make you happy—and do it! TODAY! However crazy. Do at least one thing from the first list RIGHT NOW!*

Well, *there* was an order! Rather an unrealistic one, when Jonathan thought about it. For who could run their life purely for pleasure, following their moods and doing only what they enjoyed? No one—apart from some very privileged members of society. Or maybe those who were so close to dying that it didn't matter at all how they frittered away their remaining time. Everyone else had to bow to social conventions and perform at least some activities that secured them a living. And if that meant standing on an assembly line screwing together ballpoint pens, then you just had to stand on that assembly line and screw together ballpoint pens. Whether you enjoyed it or not.

On the other hand, why was Jonathan lapsing back into brooding about other people? After all, he was in the privileged position of being able to do or arrange for what he wanted, as Leo had so rightly pointed out. Who if not Jonathan could allow himself the luxury of this little game of make-believe?

He whipped out a pen. So, what did he want to do? What did he enjoy?

He hadn't completed the *J* of *Jogging* when he stopped.

He went running every day, but as he was writing it down, he wondered if he actually *enjoyed* it.

231

It had never occurred to him to wonder about it. Why should it? Everyone knew exercise was healthy. The daily run was as much a part of his life as brushing his teeth, there was no doubt about it. Or was there?

He chewed pensively on the end of his pen, trying to imagine he was out on a run. Did he enjoy it?

Not really. It was more a case of fulfilling a duty. The moment *after* a run came closer to enjoyment. Once the grind was over, when he was doing his stretching and reveling in the achievement of conquering the bugbear of getting up early and pushing himself to run, and appreciating the result.

He picked up the pen again and wrote:

*I enjoy having been jogging and having done sports activities.*

He looked at his entry and felt at a loss. What did it mean? *Was* jogging one of those things that belonged on the enjoyment list and should be continued? Or not? The very thought of ceasing his daily run just like that was out of the question.

If he knew anything, it was that all psychologists, sports doctors, and even the *Bild* tabloid recommended physical fitness as a wonder cure for almost everything. Whether it was physical health or mental troubles, nothing helped so much as making sure the "human machine" was running properly.

So exercise was and remained a duty. Except—did it *have* to be a jog down by the Alster? If Jonathan were honest, he could think of more enjoyable pastimes than jogging through the empty city in the gray morning mist, in all weathers, alone and distracted from the boring monotony of his steps only by the occasional irritation of dog excrement or kamikaze cyclists.

Personally, he had never experienced that oft-mentioned "runner's high," the addictive state described by many that drove you to do nothing but pound the miles—it had always been down to his own perseverance.

Could it be . . . that running wasn't the right sport for him?

*Tennis.* The thought came from out of the blue. He had enjoyed playing tennis as a boy. Not too well, and not as a member of a club, but every so often he and his mother had hit a few balls over a washing line strung at an appropriate height in the garden of their villa by the Elbe. Yes, he had enjoyed it—very much, even, despite the fact that he hadn't continued with the game. Golf was the Grief family's game. His father had taught him from a tender age that the golf course was where the best business deals were made.

Which was idiocy; Jonathan had never bagged a major deal wearing checked pants and spiked shoes. Maybe because, ever since his father's illness had propelled Jonathan to the forefront of the publishing business, he'd been relieved to put away his clubs. He'd always found golf to be dreadfully boring. Besides, he wasn't the one responsible for major business deals—that was why he had Markus Bode.

*Bode.* It really was high time that he made contact with his CEO, who was probably waiting for his call.

But first he wanted to work on his enjoyment list a little more—and telephone conversations with Markus Bode on the future of the publishing house definitely weren't on the list. So, tennis.

He wrote it down: *Playing tennis.*

He immediately scribbled below it: *Singing.* He had completely forgotten about that! As a small boy, Jonathan had really enjoyed singing, warbling along to the Neapolitan folk songs his mother had often given full, passionate voice to.

*Huh.* His father had naturally thought his son should concentrate far more on chasing after a small ball than singing, so Jonathan's musical ambitions had come to an end with Sofia's departure. After his voice broke, he had even stopped singing in the shower.

Jonathan took a deep breath and composed himself.

*Guarda, guarda, stu giardino*
*Siente, siesti scuranante . . .*

He broke off abruptly. It sounded hideous! If he didn't stop immediately, Daphne, the poodle next door, would soon be howling with
wild abandon. And he was having difficulty remembering the lyrics.
Which pained him, as he could clearly remember knowing every word
of "Torna a Surriento" as a boy.

Lost and buried, like so much else.

Tennis and singing. *What else?* Deep in thought, he tapped on the
paper with the tip of his pen, mentally spurring himself to action. Surely
he could think of more than these two pitiful examples!

Nothing.

So—to the list of things he didn't enjoy doing. Jogging? Yes? No?
Yes?

His phone rang.

The display showed *Markus Bode.*

Coincidence? Or a reminder—as clear as a smack on the head with
a golf club—of the things he hated? He picked up.

"Jonathan Grief," he said.

"Hello, Mr. Grief. Markus Bode here."

"Mr. Bode! How lovely to hear from you! I was about to call you."

"Have you been thinking about what I said? Had any ideas?"

"Quite a few," Jonathan replied.

"Shall we meet at the office?"

"No."

"No?"

"No." Jonathan grinned. "I've been doing some serious thinking.
And I've been wondering whether you play tennis, my friend."

"Tennis?"

# 32

*Hannah*

*The same day:*
*Thursday, January 4, 4:14 p.m.*

Although an unpleasant sleet had set in, covering everything in a cold, wet, icy blanket, Hannah was sitting on a bench by the Krugkoppel Bridge, clutching the last of her printouts. She had kept one back from her poster campaign so that she could thrust it under the noses of passersby. Except that this weather meant hardly anyone was out walking, and the sheet of paper, which she could only half protect beneath her coat, was already in a very sorry state. She should have put the posters into plastic pockets, but she'd been in such a hurry to implement her plan.

She would come back and put up new, protected posters tomorrow; after all, she had nothing else to do. And she'd stay on her bench for the rest of that day. She'd sit there for as long as it took to find someone who could help her, who might have seen something. Or until she froze. She suspected the latter might happen first.

She had covered miles of the Alster's banks pinning up her posters, until she had only this one left. Along the way she had met two police officers who said they'd keep an eye out for Simon. At least *something* was happening!

Of course, the officers had both suggested she go home, and after looking at Hannah's posters, they'd said with a hint of offense that they would do their job, she had no need to worry about that. But Hannah Marx wouldn't be Hannah Marx if . . . if she wasn't Hannah Marx.

Her cell phone rang. With stiff fingers she fumbled it from her coat pocket and answered.

"Hey, you're not still out there in the cold?" Lisa had already phoned her three times. She had liked Hannah's idea of the missing-person posters but believed that her friend should now go home, because in this crap weather she'd be more likely to catch her death than find Simon.

"I want to wait till it gets dark."

"Just look up at the sky! It's happening as we speak."

"The paths are well lit. I'll be fine."

"Hannah!"

"Please stop it. I know what I'm doing—really I do."

"I'm sorry, but I'm not so sure of that. It's not going to help Simon if you catch pneumonia."

"And what if I leave now and two minutes later someone comes along who's seen him?"

"Who do you think would be out for a riverside stroll in these freezing temperatures in the sleet?"

"I'm only going to stay another half hour, I promise!"

"Where are you, exactly?"

"By the Krugkoppel Bridge."

"At least go indoors somewhere. There's the Red Dog around the corner, for instance. You can get a nice hot cup of tea there."

"I don't even know if they're open."

"Then go and look!" Lisa's voice combined affection and impatience. It was the same tone she used when trying with amazing forbearance to persuade a child to please, please put their hat and gloves on.

"But if I hide away in there, I won't be able to see—"

"Any crazy walkers. True." Lisa sighed. "Listen, sweetie, you've done everything you possibly can. You have to leave a little to the fate you're always talking about. It's not all down to you alone."

"I know that." Hannah sobbed loudly and involuntarily. She had no idea how many tears she had shed in the last few days, but it was certainly more than in the rest of her life put together.

"I'd come out to you, but I'm afraid I can't. I'm still surrounded by a noisy crowd of twenty or so kids; I can hardly leave them to our two mothers."

"No." Hannah was overcome by a guilty conscience. She did have something better to do than sit helplessly on this bench in the sleet. Or if nothing better, then at least something different. "Listen," she said, "I really am going to stay here for another half hour, and then I'll come over to Little Rascals and help you clean up, okay?"

"That would be great! We could go for something to eat together afterward."

"Um . . ."

"Or go to Simon's apartment and have a pizza delivered there? And a nice bottle of wine?"

Hannah smiled into the phone. "I love you!"

"You too."

At a quarter to five—after thirty minutes during which not a single person walked past her—Hannah got up from the bench as promised. Her joints were painful from the cold, and just putting one foot in front of the other made her legs ache as if she'd run a marathon without training.

She briefly considered calling a taxi to get her to Eppendorfer Weg, but when dashing out that morning she had not only failed to think of plastic sleeves for the posters, she had forgotten to bring any money. Which meant a visit to the Red Dog Café would have been pointless in any case. But if she had to walk back, at least she could show her poster to anyone she passed on the way.

"Some good comes from everything," she told herself loudly and forcefully, then tramped off toward Harvestehuder Weg. If she walked quickly, she could reach Little Rascals in twenty minutes. A few stops to question passersby would make it thirty, and it would warm her up enough to rule out pneumonia. She coughed.

After nine minutes, Hannah was more than halfway, since she had run more than walked, and apart from a couple of cyclists and a man who responded to her inquiry with nothing but a bewildered stare before walking on, she had not encountered another soul.

What was wrong with the people of Hamburg? Surely a little bit of sleet like this wasn't enough to keep them huddled on their sofas at home. A true northerner ought to be a hardy being, unafraid of storms, possessing at least three oilskin jackets and a sou'wester ready for action.

By Innocentia Park, Hannah hurried along the slushy sidewalk in the shadow of the nearby town houses. By now, she was frozen enough to consider pneumonia a real possibility. She should have taken a taxi after all, and borrowed the money for the fare from Lisa when she arrived, but her stubbornness had once again blinded her to common sense. And now it was hardly worth getting her cell phone out and calling a cab.

Thirty yards away, in the glow of a porch light, Hannah saw a small figure stepping out onto the sidewalk. A child? She picked up speed—child or not, she wanted to show at least one other soul her missing-person notice, hopefully ensuring that her arctic expedition would at least have yielded some results.

As she approached, she saw that it was not a child but a small old woman with a poodle on a leash. She was wearing a raincoat and a plastic head scarf; the dog was also tucked into a little coat.

"Hello!" Hannah called and pounced on the woman, who jumped. "Don't worry, I only want to ask you something."

Instead of replying, the little woman shot with amazing speed back into the entrance of her villa, dragging the poor little dog behind her.

"Hello!" Hannah called again. She waved her soggy poster in the air, bounded toward the dog walker, and laid a hand on her shoulder from behind. "Please wait!"

"Let go of me right now!" She was astonishingly fast and had an even more astonishing voice. Her reaction shook Hannah to the bone. Shocked, she withdrew her hand. The old lady spun around and looked at her angrily, but with a touch of fear. Hannah immediately felt apologetic. "What do you want from me?" the woman snapped. "Leave me alone!"

"I'm sorry, I only wanted . . ." Hannah took a step toward her, reaching out her hand in an attempt to appease her.

"Help!" the woman cried. She followed this with a command that seemed incredible given the appearance of the dog: *"Daphne, get her!"*

The poodle neither bared its teeth nor growled but began to yap frantically, causing Hannah to leap back in fear that the grumpy mutt might soon be hanging from her leg.

"You've completely misunderstood," she said, trying to sound as reassuring as she could while raising her hands defensively. "I . . . I . . ."

"What's going on here?"

Both women turned abruptly toward the man's voice. In the darkness of the porch of the house next door, two indistinct figures were peering out.

"Is everything all right, Frau Fahrenkrog?" the man asked.

"Everything's absolutely fine!" Hannah said before the lady could resume screaming bloody murder. "Just a misunderstanding!"

Then she marched away in the direction of Brahmsallee as quickly as she could while retaining her dignity. She could still hear Daphne yapping behind her, but at least the old lady wasn't screaming anymore, and the figures from the next-door villa didn't seem to be coming in pursuit.

She almost had to laugh. She had clearly come within a hair's breadth of being arrested for assault, but she had only wanted to ask the dog's owner about Simon. What had the woman been scared of? What on earth did she think Hannah wanted? To sell her a magazine subscription? That thought really did make Hannah laugh, even though the situation was anything but funny.

# 33

*Jonathan*

"My goodness, Bode! Respect!"

Jonathan was sprawled over a leather armchair in the living room of his house, where he had invited his CEO for "one for the road"—a refreshing glass of iced tea—after their tennis match. He grinned; he was exhausted but also euphoric. Yes, he had really, really enjoyed the game with Markus Bode, even though the balls had done little more than fly past his ears, and every muscle ached as if he'd been run over by a truck. "I wouldn't have had you down as such a genius with a racket!"

"Why not?" Markus Bode also grinned, with an unmistakable glow of pride.

"No idea." Jonathan shrugged. "I just wouldn't have thought it."

"Just like I'd never have thought you were so bad," Bode replied with an even broader grin. "After all, it was you who suggested the game. I assumed you could actually play."

Jonathan laughed. "Well, I'd no idea I was up against a second John McEnroe."

"Thanks for not comparing me with Boris Becker." Markus Bode smiled. "But seriously, you did improve with every minute."

"You don't need to flatter me because I'm your boss."

"I mean it. I could tell you've played in the past; you're just a bit rusty. How long since your last match?"

"I wouldn't say 'match,'" Jonathan replied. "When I was a little boy I used to hit balls around in the garden with my mother; it was never anything more than that."

Bode raised his eyebrows quizzically. "So what gave you the sudden idea for a game today?"

"Oh . . ." There was no way Jonathan was going to tell Bode that he was following the instructions of a mysterious diary. "No idea. I just thought I ought to try a few new things in the new year. I want a bit more oomph in my life and decided to start with tennis."

"I see." Bode nodded thoughtfully and looked down at his half-full glass of iced tea. "The new year's going to bring a few changes for us both, isn't it?"

"It looks like it." Feeling obliged to ask, he added, "How's it going with you at the moment?"

"I'm managing. My wife and I are talking it over, as people so neatly put it."

"Oh? Well, that sounds promising."

"It depends what's being talked over. To be honest, in our case it's the lawyers who are doing the talking for us, and it's basically all about the amount of alimony and child support I'll have to pay and how often I'll be able to see the kids."

"Oh." Jonathan looked at him apologetically. "That doesn't sound promising."

"Not really."

"Well, my dear fellow." He noticed himself floundering and slipping into forced joviality, but felt he had to say something suitably wise.

"As a man who has all that behind him, let me assure you that it'll all pass one day."

"Hmm." Bode nodded. "But you and your ex-wife didn't have any children."

"That's true," Jonathan admitted.

"And as far as I know, she was more than reasonable after you separated and didn't even want any alimony from you."

"How do you know that?" Jonathan asked in surprise and some embarrassment.

"I've been at Grief & Son Books for fifteen years—as CEO, too, since your father left. In case you hadn't noticed."

"Yes, of course. But what does that have to do with it?"

"Let's just say that my job includes keeping myself informed about everything that affects the business."

"I didn't realize my failed marriage was something that affects the business." Jonathan was unable to conceal his indignation.

"No, of course not," Markus Bode said hurriedly, turning red. "I'm sorry, I didn't mean—"

"Don't worry. It doesn't matter."

"No, no, I *am* sorry. But as owner of the publishing house, you're at the center of things. It's inevitable that people will talk."

"People?" Another wave of embarrassment washed through Jonathan. "What people?"

"Well, the employees, your staff. They're bound to be interested in their boss."

"Ah." The thought of his private life being a topic of discussion among his workforce was extremely uncomfortable. He would never have thought such a thing. He had always assumed that they viewed him, the head of their company, simply as a gleaming figurehead—or some kind of figurehead, at least—who appeared every now and then and was otherwise of little interest to them. And now here was Bode telling him it wasn't so. It was . . . it was . . .

"You really mustn't worry about it," Markus Bode said, interrupting his train of thought. "It's completely normal—gossip and chitchat are basic needs for most people. It's like a TV series or a popular novel."

"You're not seriously comparing my life to the plot of a soap, are you?"

"Oh, come on! What was that Oscar Wilde quote? 'There's only one thing in the world worse than being talked about, and that is *not* being talked about.'"

"He would have known," Jonathan said. "Didn't the beleaguered Mr. Wilde spend his last years in the most unjust, degrading conditions in jail and die shortly after his release, alone and penniless?"

"Nevertheless, he said some wise things."

"They didn't do him any good, did they?"

"But they've been a great boon to posterity."

"I'm sure that must be a real comfort to him from beyond the grave."

"Huh." Markus Bode spread his arms. "Isn't it what we strive for on a daily basis? To bequeath great literature to future generations?"

"I'd prefer it to be valued and acknowledged in the present day."

Markus Bode immediately sat to attention. "Shall we discuss business now, maybe?"

"Um." *Damn, damn, damn!* He'd managed to maneuver himself onto a sheet of thin ice, when he'd intended to avoid the subject for as long as possible. *Great!* But since he couldn't think of an avoidance tactic on the spot, he considered himself beaten and decided to go on the offensive. "Gladly," he said. "But since you've emphasized your many years' experience with the press, why don't we kick off with your suggestions?"

"I feel the exact opposite," Bode replied. "I'd like to hear what you, as head of the publishing house, think about the current developments that the accounts indicate so clearly."

"Please, after you!"

"No, no. You go first!"

Jonathan gave a little cough. What was going on—*Candid Camera*? Why was Markus Bode so reluctant to share his opinions? Could he . . . could he be scared?

Scared of him, Jonathan N. Grief? He could hardly believe it; after all, he wasn't his father. In any case, Jonathan was the one who felt scared.

Had that thought really just crossed his mind?

"Seriously, Markus," Jonathan said, making an effort to sound authoritative. "You're responsible for the operational side of the business, and you're far more familiar with the figures and the developments than I am. You have a better overview of the market, so it would be silly of me not to hear your expert opinion first."

"You really think so?"

"Yes, of course."

"So you want to hear my frank, honest opinion?"

"I'm asking you for it."

Markus Bode hesitated a moment. Then he put his glass down on the coffee table, shuffled forward to the edge of his seat, placed his feet square on the ground, and clasped his hands in his lap.

"If I'm honest, I think it's like this: the direction the press has taken since it was founded is no longer sustainable. We're no longer competitive."

"Could you give me a few more details?"

"Grief & Son Books is synonymous with high literature. But that's not a genre that many people are buying anymore. If you ask me, we urgently need to move in a more popular direction."

"More popular?" Jonathan spat the words as though he had a nasty taste in his mouth.

Markus Bode nodded.

"What do you mean?"

"I mean we urgently need a few popular-fiction titles. Romance novels. Crime novels and thrillers. Historical sagas."

"Never!"

"I thought that would be your reaction. But I don't see any other way around it."

"That's not what Grief & Son Books is about!"

"If things continue like this, Grief & Son Books won't be about anything for much longer."

"Nevertheless," Jonathan insisted, "if you have a screw factory, you can't suddenly change your mind and sell dowels just because there's more call for them."

Markus Bode looked at him in some confusion. Jonathan didn't blame him. He didn't know himself which corner of his brain had suddenly produced the screw-factory analogy. It must have been some kind of panic-stricken short circuit, and it sounded bizarre even to his own ears. "No," his CEO conceded. "You simply have to sell different kinds of screws. If you don't want to do that, you have to close down your factory because it's not working anymore."

"Oh, don't overdramatize!"

"Have you had a good look at the figures I gave you?"

"Of course I have!"

"Then it must have been obvious to you that I'm not overdramatizing."

"But . . ." Jonathan struggled to find the right words. "But I'm determined that we're not going to contribute to the world's dumbing down in order to make a profit!"

"Where do you get your pathological aversion to anything with even the slightest hint of popular entertainment?" Bode asked.

"It's not an aversion!" Jonathan replied snippily. He wondered whether he and his CEO were actually having a serious argument. It sounded like it.

"No?"

"I'd always thought we were singing from the same hymn sheet and you were fully behind our list."

"I am! Except it's not simply a matter of my own personal taste—or yours—but also what sells. Grief & Son Books is a business, after all, and has a responsibility toward its employees."

"It's primarily a business built on a long tradition as a family firm. I also have a duty toward that tradition."

"I understand that," Markus Bode said placatingly. "I'm not suggesting that we should publish nothing but Westerns from now on. Just the occasional more popular title that's likely to sell in decent numbers, in order to finance our core list."

"I'd call that hypocrisy!"

"I'd call it wise."

"Then we'll have to agree to disagree."

They stared at one another. Neither said a word or even blinked. *High Noon* by Innocentia Park.

Jonathan was about to clear his throat and de-escalate the situation, saying something to the effect that they may have spoken in unnecessary haste, when he heard a loud cry from outside.

"Let go of me right now!"

Jonathan leapt from his seat as if he'd been stung. Markus Bode did likewise, and the two men dashed down the hall to the front door.

"Help!" The voice was screaming now. *"Daphne, get her!"*

"That's my neighbor, Frau Fahrenkrog," Jonathan said as he tore the door open and peered out. "What's going on here?" he asked.

Markus Bode remained close by his side. Jonathan saw the old lady a few yards away, on the sidewalk outside their villa, standing in the twilight facing another woman with whom she was obviously arguing.

"Is everything all right, Frau Fahrenkrog?" Jonathan called to her, about to rush to her assistance.

"Everything's absolutely fine!" the unknown woman replied. "Just a misunderstanding!" There was something reassuring about her voice, and for a moment Jonathan really did believe everything was all right.

But then she hurried off so quickly that Jonathan would have had to run to catch up with her. His priority was to see to his neighbor, however.

"Are you okay?" he asked as he approached her.

"Yes." Little Frau Fahrenkrog was trembling like a leaf. "I'm fine, thank you." As if to confirm it, Daphne gave a belligerent *woof.*

"What did the woman want?"

"I don't know." She sounded pitiful. "She suddenly descended on me, just like that."

"Should I call the police?"

Hertha Fahrenkrog gave him a weak smile. "That won't be necessary, Herr Grief. Nothing actually happened, thanks to you."

"Are you sure you can manage?"

Hertha Fahrenkrog nodded. "I'm going back in to make myself a nice cup of tea."

"Good idea," Jonathan replied. "And if there's anything else, you know where I am."

Another smile, this time more relaxed. "That's good to know." She nodded to him, tugged Daphne's leash, and made her way on unsteady legs up her garden path.

Jonathan was about to turn and go back into the warmth, when something else occurred to him.

"Oh, Frau Fahrenkrog?" he called.

She turned. "Yes?"

"When's your birthday?"

"In May. Why?"

"Not March sixteenth?"

"No." She gave him a puzzled look. "May seventh. I'm not so doddering yet that I'd forget something like that."

Your Perfect Year

"Of course not," he replied. "Well, I wish you an uneventful, relaxing evening."

He went back to his front door, where Markus Bode was still standing.

"What was all that about?" Bode asked once they were both back in Jonathan's hallway.

"My neighbor was approached by a complete stranger."

"Around here?" His CEO shook his head in amazement. "Who'd have thought it?"

"Yes, I was rather shocked myself."

"Was she on day release from the psychiatric ward?"

"It's possible, though she sounded normal."

Markus Bode nodded. "They're the worst."

"Shall we go sit down again?"

"I'd love to, but I'm afraid I have to go now." He looked pointedly at his watch. "I've got an appointment with my lawyer, you know? So we'll have to continue our . . . our discussion another time."

"What a shame," Jonathan said. And thought: *Hurrah!*

# 34

## *Hannah*

**Friday, January 5, 6:53 a.m.**

Seven o'clock. Why on earth didn't the bakery on the corner open until seven? Weren't there enough people who had to get to work by then? Some of them might even have already put in half a day. What about them? Were they forced to start their mornings without rolls and coffee?

As Hannah shuffled from one foot to the other outside the locked door of the Hansa Bakery, she wondered whether to jump in the car and drive to the gas station at the Horner traffic circle. They were open 24/7 and were also sure to have today's edition of the *Hamburg News* on the shelves.

She had wanted to dash over there at three in the morning to grab a copy of the late edition, but after sharing a bottle of red wine with her, Lisa had talked her out of getting behind the wheel of her Twingo. She had been forceful, taking the keys from Hannah's hand and sternly instructing her to "go get at least six hours' sleep!"

Despite her friend's orders, Hannah had spent the night awake, tossing and turning in Simon's bed, her mind filled with dark thoughts, while her friend enjoyed the sleep of the just on the living-room sofa.

Hannah had got up and, unwashed and bedraggled as she was, hurried out to the Hansa Bakery.

Here she was, scruffy as a stray cat, resisting the temptation to rattle the metal shutters and yell at the top of her voice for them to let her in.

It was 6:56. The gas station? But even Hannah could see that it wasn't worth the effort and expense for four minutes, and that if she left her vigil by the door now, it might actually take longer to get her hands on the *Hamburg News*. She hoped the bakery had already received its deliveries. If not, she'd collapse in a fit of hysterical tears on the spot.

At 6:59 she heard the longed-for rattling of a key turning inside, and a few seconds later the shutter was rolled up. The elderly lady behind the door looked quite indignant at the way Hannah stormed into the shop the moment she opened, demanded a copy of the *Hamburg News* without so much as a "Good morning," marched over to the counter, and picked up a copy from the pile there.

"You've forgotten your change!" the lady called dutifully as she looked at the five-euro bill in her hand. But Hannah was already out on the street.

Breathing heavily, Hannah stopped and unfolded her newspaper. She was relieved to see the editors had kept their word. The missing-person notice about Simon was in a visible place at the bottom of the front page, with a large photo of her boyfriend and even a picture of the diary. If anyone had seen Simon by the Alster on New Year's morning, or if anyone had the Filofax, this article would be sure to help her find them. Guaranteed. Anything else was inconceivable.

# 35

*Jonathan*

**Friday, January 5, 6:15 a.m.**

The alarm ringing caused Jonathan to sit up in bed with a jolt, as he did every morning. It took him three seconds to realize there was no reason to be startled awake; on the contrary, the time had come for him to slow down his routine, as his daily predawn run was now history.

Tennis was the new jogging, so Jonathan silenced his radio alarm with a well-aimed thump and sank back onto his pillow, pulled the duvet up over his nose, and sighed with pleasure. *Wonderful!* He could stay here for as long as he wanted to.

And he *did* want to, very much. Apart from his company's unpleasant financial situation, and the fear that Markus Bode wouldn't let it go, he felt better than he had for a long time. He couldn't really say why, as nothing had actually happened. But there it was.

He woke for the second time at half past eight. Jonathan N. Grief grinned boldly as he peered at his alarm clock. Half past eight on a weekday—that was more like the right time for a man of the world, a bon vivant, as he was going to consider himself from that day forward.

He could even get rid of his alarm clock altogether; he had no reason at all to be harassed out of bed at some ungodly hour every day.

He sat up, slipped into the felt slippers he kept by the side of the bed, picked up his robe from the rocking chair. Now for a cup of good coffee, a freshly baked croissant, and the newspaper. That was the way to start the day!

As he went downstairs to the kitchen, he found it hard to believe that he had always spent this first part of the day in running gear, usually tired and sullen. What had got into him for all those years? And why, for goodness' sake, had he gone off jogging in the middle of the night, when he, a man of independent means, had absolutely no reason to indulge in such madness?

It must have been force of habit. He had gone on a morning run for years, since he was first a student, and over time this ritual had got so deeply under his skin that he'd never questioned it. He silently thanked the diary; without its prompt he would probably have tormented himself on the banks of the Alster morning after morning until he had to be pushed along the route by a paid caregiver.

After switching on the coffee machine and placing a croissant on a baking sheet in the oven, Jonathan went to fetch the *Hamburg News* from the tube by the front door and laid the paper on the dining table, ready to be unfolded and read at leisure. The coffee was not yet ready, so he hurried back up to his study to fetch the diary. He'd begin with that, before reading the paper.

He intended to make it a new daily ritual to read the day's entry every morning, taking care not to look ahead, however great the temptation. He had already skimmed some of the entries, but that didn't count—he'd been given no choice if he wanted to trace the owner.

But from now on he wanted to think of the Filofax—which no one missed, it seemed, or which had been gifted to him by fate, yes, *fate!*—as something like an Advent calendar: only one door at a time could be opened, otherwise you'd earn yourself a rap on the knuckles. This way, he'd start each day with a pleasant surprise. With his personal grab bag, his morning oracle, his . . . well, yes, his secret variety show.

Ten minutes later, he was sitting at the large table in the dining room, at peace with himself and the world. He took a hearty bite of the warm, delicious croissant, opened the diary at January 5, and began to read.

*Go on a media diet!*

A media diet? What on earth was that? He read on with interest.

*Our energy is fueled by mindfulness. So don't be distracted by bad news: no newspapers, no TV, no radio (not forever; just for a while). You know that the news in the media is mostly negative, so don't have anything more to do with it!*

*Your task instead is to think about how you would like your life to be. Make a list of everything, big and small, that you wish for. Success, money, love, a new hobby, ten children . . . Look for pictures in magazines, cut them out, and stick them on some posterboard. Then hang it up where you can easily see it. This is your "vision board." Lay your tracks into the future. The images will help your subconscious make all your dreams come true! Because: "If one does not know to which port one is sailing, no wind is favorable." (Seneca). And another: "Wishes are things that we can make come true." (Johann Wolfgang Goethe).*

Ah. Making something. That had been absent from his life for even longer than tennis. He vaguely remembered fiddling with colored paper and scissors in nursery school. Never mind; it sounded amusing enough. And he liked the Goethe quote, of course. Even if the writer of the diary had carelessly left out the *von*. Jonathan picked up a pencil and squeezed a *v.* in after *Wolfgang*. The author had been given his title in 1782 by Emperor Josef II, so people should be used to it by now!

He turned his attention to the vision board. He knew full well where this was supposed to lead. He wasn't stupid. This exercise was obviously designed to make him more aware of the things that were truly important to him, and to keep them in mind—in sharp focus, so to speak—by means of the images.

A familiar theme: once you began thinking about something, you suddenly bumped into it around every corner, just as pregnant women suddenly saw nothing but baby carriages and babies. That kind of thing. Jonathan had never been pregnant, but his imagination could stretch that far.

He found himself thinking of another Wolfgang: his father. How had Wolfgang Grief parried suggestions from employees who'd been so bold as to offer "new visions" for the publishing house? He'd parried them with that famous quote from the late chancellor Helmut Schmidt: "People with visions should go see a doctor." Wolfgang Grief had liked this and had trotted it out frequently, preferably in public and in front of a gathered workforce. Then he would roar with smug laughter.

Whenever Jonathan had been present, he had always found himself in a dilemma, caught between pride in and awe of his omnipotent father, and a sense of secret shame about the man's overpowering authoritarian airs.

Jonathan gave himself a mental shake. He had inherited none of his father's manner. On the contrary, as his nanny had put it, he had no gumption. Wolfgang Grief had taken it as a personal insult, but Jonathan had never been able to change it. He simply lacked the Grief family's alpha gene; it must have been the Italian blood running through his veins. At least, that was what he supposed—he had no idea what his Italian family was actually like.

What would his father have to say about Markus Bode's proposal to make the press a bit more "popular"? Jonathan could just imagine it. And for that reason alone it made no sense to expend even a single thought more in that direction. Let people say what they liked about his father's interpersonal skills, he certainly knew how to run a success-ful publishing house! Though on paper Jonathan was now in charge, since Wolfgang Grief was only partially *compos mentis*, he nevertheless considered it his duty to continue the business along the lines of proven tradition.

He had no doubt about Markus Bode's competence—in fact, he had a very high opinion of his CEO's abilities. But . . . but . . . but . . . A small rebellious thought popped into his head. Harry Potter was one instance where his father had been wrong; the young wiz-ard had certainly encouraged more young people to read than Grief & Son's educational but loss-making line of children's books, a sector that he had already shed on Bode's advice. Hubertus Krull, valued so highly by Wolfgang Grief, had not even been his discovery but that of Grandmother Emilie. And if Jonathan were being honest, he didn't find Bode's suggestion so utterly lacking in appeal.

He squared his shoulders. What he was thinking of here was . . . was mental patricide! How could he take sole responsibility for the business? Could he? Should he? Or would it not be much better to leave everything exactly as it was? Such a far-reaching decision as the complete overturn of the Grief & Son Books portfolio couldn't be made in passing.

Before risking becoming more deeply submerged in these rumina-tions, Jonathan decided to take a shower, get dressed, and devote him-self to today's task set by the diary. He'd make himself a vision board, though not with scissors and paper—he wasn't so behind the times! No, he would prepare a highly professional document on his laptop. A PDF with images of all the things he dreamed about and wished for.

For example . . . a really good tennis racket. *Ha!* He had the first image already. This was child's play! And if he searched the internet, he was bound to find a photo of the tennis club where he had played yesterday with Markus Bode. He ought to become a member, or at least book a few lessons. Laying tracks into the future—that was how it was done! And after that, Jonathan would at last terminate his membership at the golf club, which he had kept up for decades without once darkening the door. Although he could never tell his father.

Elated, Jonathan sprang from his chair, driven by the impulse to act. He was halfway out of the door on his way upstairs when he turned again and picked up the *Hamburg News*. He'd throw it straight into the recycling—after all, wasn't he on a media diet? In any case, he had more exciting things to do today than to get worked up by those unqualified pen pushers and send in corrections that probably went unheeded.

Four hours later, Jonathan N. Grief sat back and looked at his handiwork. He was delighted and amazed at himself. And a little embarrassed. He had no intention of hanging up this collage, which he'd made using photos from the internet and then printed out. At least, not in a place where anyone else could catch sight of it, not even Frau Jansen. His cleaner might be totally beyond reproach, but could she be trusted in such matters?

During the course of his work, Jonathan had been like a man possessed; there was no other way of explaining what was now set out in black and white—or, rather, four-color printing. For the rackets and the tennis-club logo had been joined by pictures even Jonathan found it hard to explain to himself. As though he had somehow chosen them under a spell.

Well, he could explain the singer with the microphone; hadn't he only recently acknowledged that singing was a deeply buried passion of his? Same for the photo of the old Ford Mustang. For years he had driven only Saabs, because along with Volvos, he believed there was nothing more reliable—but whenever Jonathan saw a Mustang, he couldn't help thinking how great it would be to be barreling along Route 66 with the top down and cool music playing. Staying the night in run-down motels and spending the evenings sitting out on the porch, a cold Budweiser in his hand, watching the other guests come and go.

Years ago, when he had suggested to Tina that they go on such a trip, she'd reminded him that he always called beer a "proles' brew," and that, given the cockroaches that were surely infesting the establishments along Route 66, he would never be done composing letters of complaint to the motel managers. This remark (maybe a small act of revenge for his "reliving your teenage years" comment about the patchwork room), had wounded him but had hit the nail firmly on the head. So it had remained a purely theoretical "Should we, maybe, one day?" idea.

Next, Jonathan looked at the house by the sea, tucked away in a secluded location behind dunes and wild marram grass. That did not belong to the "under a spell" images, either, since if he weren't tied to the business and his life in Hamburg, he could see himself living in just such a place: in seclusion, surrounded by untamed nature, not a single person in sight to disturb him. Off the beaten track on the North Sea coast somewhere, or even on a small island, in the best of all possible worlds, without internet or cell-phone signal. Not that Jonathan's phone was always ringing or he was constantly receiving email, but something deep inside him occasionally longed for monastic seclusion.

Which made the photo of the two little children, which Jonathan had downloaded on an impulse, all the more inexplicable. It simply didn't compute! As unlikely as the couple holding hands as they walked along a beach in the sunset.

Sure, like the house, they were by the sea, and the children were also playing in sand, but that was all the pictures had in common. Add to these the picture of the people sitting cheerfully around a large table in a garden enjoying a meal together, and there was only one possible conclusion: split personality. His collage indicated a certain degree of split personality.

But it had always been so. Jonathan enjoyed peace and quiet—solitude, even—because he was comfortable in his own company, but on the other hand he had really enjoyed the evening with Leopold and the tennis match with Markus Bode. And the fact that he didn't have children did not necessarily mean he didn't want any.

When he had still been married, he had thought a lot about children, if only because it went with the package. The idea had been negated by Tina's departure, but it seemed the subject still concerned him, deep down, although the "outer" Jonathan had already dismissed it.

He ran both hands over the vision board, as though he could feel which of the pictures meant the most to him. He would have to get rid of one or two of them, since you couldn't have everything you wanted in life.

*According to . . . ?*

Who had ever actually said that you couldn't have everything you wanted in life? Was it an immutable law? Sure, it was in line with a healthy way of thinking, but was it actually true?

Jonathan N. Grief stood to go downstairs and make himself another coffee. He would have to think about that one for a while longer.

# 36

*Hannah*

Nothing.

Nothing, nothing, nothing. Nothing at all for five days. The article had not had the slightest effect; it was as though it had not been read by a single soul.

Hannah's posters by the Alster, which she had renewed twice, had brought nothing more than one call to her cell phone, and that was only someone wanting to tell her that he'd recognized the photo and thought he'd gone to primary school with Simon.

Hannah had been tempted to yell at the man, asking him if he was out of his mind contacting her with such nonsense and risking giving her a heart attack. But she had simply thanked him meekly and hung up.

The police had found nothing new, either, although the officer who was Hannah's contact no longer sounded as optimistic as she had when the case was opened. She didn't say directly that she now assumed Simon would not be found, but her gentle, comforting tone of voice made it clear—that cautious manner with which they attempted to help friends and relatives come to terms with the fact that there was no longer any hope.

It couldn't be true; it *mustn't* be true! But where was Simon? Where . . . was . . . he? The question chased itself in endless circles around Hannah's head. It plagued her now, lying as she so often did on Simon's bed, tightly wrapped in his duvet, breathing in the faint traces of his scent that still lingered on his sheets.

She sobbed; sobbed like a little child. She felt so empty and weak, lonely and helpless, that she believed she would never again be able to get up from this bed. She would lie here until the end of her days. Or until Simon was finally back with her.

"Please," she whispered softly. "Please, dear God, let him be alive. Make him come back to me. Or at least let him be somewhere in the Caribbean sipping a cocktail. Anything would be better than this nightmare. Please, dear God, help me! Please, please, please!"

# 37

## *Jonathan*

**Sunday, January 14, 9:11 a.m.**

Jonathan N. Grief was content. Like every morning for almost ten days, he was sitting in his bathrobe at his dining table with fresh coffee and a warm croissant, about to turn eagerly to the diary. What did his grab bag have in store for him today? By accepting the Filofax as his guide, he'd already had a variety of interesting experiences. Such as finding out he was not missing a thing by not looking at the paper over breakfast, disposing of it unread in the recycling. The world continued to turn whether or not Jonathan knew precisely how.

He was already weighing whether to cancel his subscription, so little was he missing his daily reading. And he could hardly say that his letters to the editor—or to Gundel Thingamajig in Reader Services—had ever drawn much of an enthusiastic response. It followed that to stop reading the paper wouldn't be a great loss for either party.

Instead Jonathan had, as recommended, written down three things every morning and every evening for which he was grateful—and he was finding it ever easier to think of what to write.

There was his growing enthusiasm for playing tennis. He had met Markus Bode for a game on three evenings during the last week and a half. From one man's suffering came another man's joy—Jonathan considered it a minor stroke of luck that his CEO currently had nothing to do after work apart from sit alone in a hotel room. Or knock about a few balls with him.

Jonathan was delighted to have made rapid progress, especially with his forehand. He had secretly given himself the rather childish nickname "Jonathan Boom Boom," and the day before yesterday he had bought himself a professional-quality racket and a stylish tennis outfit. The Rothenbaum Center Court better watch out—Jonathan N. Grief was on his way!

He and Bode had said nothing more about the future course of the publishing business; Jonathan managed to skillfully avoid the subject. He put off Markus Bode somewhat vaguely by saying he wanted to wait and see how the current fiscal year developed, while hoping that it would all somehow turn out well of its own accord. Perhaps Hubertus Krull would make a miraculous recovery and sit there at his computer typing out one stirring chapbook after another. Or maybe all the enthusiastic critics who had been sent copies of *The Loneliness of the Milky Way* would have an effect on the sales figures after all.

Jonathan had tried to help things along a little by rearranging his vision board with a small photomontage: he had printed out the ranking of the hundred most successful publishers from the *Buchreport*, boldly glued the Grief & Son Books logo in the number-one slot, scanned the page, and placed it prominently in the middle of his collage.

He opened up his wardrobe several times a day now—he had hidden the board in there, behind his shirts—and contemplated his visions for the future. If it really was true that by so doing he was programming his subconscious to fulfill his dreams, then his subconscious should soon show what it had in store for him!

Like a diligent schoolboy, Jonathan faithfully carried out all the tasks the diary had assigned him so far: He'd spent a whole day smiling cheerfully at everyone he met, getting generally happy reactions in return. (Okay, one elderly gentleman had wanted to know whether he was feeling ill and needed help, and a couple of giggling teenage girls had ignored him, but everyone else had returned his smile.) He'd begun to meditate for a few minutes every day and, after some initial difficulties, had realized how much good it was doing him. Every so often he would sit in his armchair, composing himself, thinking of nothing at all and simply being in the here and now.

Twice already, when the diary had recommended *Today, do nothing but what you feel like doing*, he had gone to the sea "just because" and walked for three hours along the beach in the icy wind. He was now singing with gusto, even if only in the shower or the car.

Jonathan had even hugged a tree in Innocentia Park, fervently hoping that no one was watching, but had ended up putting this little exercise down as nonsense. Apart from a large stain on his lambskin jacket, it had done nothing for him.

Much more to his liking had been his visit to the flea market prescribed for the previous Saturday. He had driven to the Flohschanze market with the task of buying himself "something special." Jonathan had never done anything of the kind, because he had never seen the point of all those secondhand stalls. He had been all the more delighted when, between two bustling stalls offering all manner of junk, he had discovered a real gem: a volume of poetry by Joseph Freiherr von Eichendorff dated 1837 (!) in excellent condition, which he had snapped up for 120 euros, although he knew the book was worth ten times the amount. It wasn't Jonathan's fault that people had no idea about the things they were selling. The little book was now displayed proudly on the shelves in his reading room, and he felt a surge of pleasure whenever he looked at it.

Taking a bite of his croissant, Jonathan opened the diary for that Sunday, eager to see what it had in store for him next.

*Your favorite author is reading at the Kampnagel today— and you're going! Two tickets are waiting for you and a companion of your choice at the box office under order number 137. Doors open at 7 p.m. Enjoy!*

*P.S. If you don't know who to take, I can think of someone* ☺

Jonathan was electrified. A reading!

Not that he was a particular fan of them—most events of that kind involved a pasty-faced character in a turtleneck sweater mumbling into his glass of water, boring Jonathan horribly and confirming his belief that a writer should write and not give readings. However, several times now he'd sensed some mysterious personal connection with the diary, and this entry reinforced his suspicion once again. After all, it was a curious coincidence that he, a publisher, was being invited to a reading.

It would be an even more curious coincidence, however, if his favorite author really did show up at the Kampnagel that evening. For that was Thomas Mann, and he'd been dead for quite a while.

# 38

*Hannah*

"When did you last have anything to eat?"

Lisa looked thoroughly shocked as she arrived at Simon's apartment to pick up Hannah for the Sebastian Fitzek reading at the Kampnagel.

"What?" Hannah asked distractedly as she fumbled to fasten her coat. Her fingers were trembling so much that she was hardly able to push the buttons through the narrow slits. She felt weak and drained, as though she might keel over at any moment. But she wouldn't do that; she would go with Lisa to this reading, because it was the last glimmer of hope she had.

"Everything's fine," she muttered. "Let's go."

"Hannah!" Lisa laid her hands on her friend's shoulders, her face a picture of concern. "You look awful. Like a ghost of yourself."

"I'm fine," Hannah insisted. "Really."

"I don't believe you." Lisa sighed. "If I'd known you were on a hunger strike, I'd have dragged you back to my place ages ago and fed you."

"I *have* eaten."

"A week ago?"

"Forget it! Let's go, or we'll miss the reading."

"We've still got plenty of time," Lisa said firmly, taking hold of Hannah and gently steering her back into the apartment. "I'm going to make sure you eat at least a slice of bread and butter before we go."

"Fat chance," Hannah said. "The fridge is empty."

"Okay, then we'll pick up a snack on the way."

"That'll take too long. Please, Lisa! I have to be at the box office as soon as it opens. If someone comes to pick up the tickets, there's no way I'm going to miss them!"

Her friend took her hand and led her out of the door. "Don't worry, we'll be there on time. But you're going to eat something, even if it's only a pretzel stick from the gas station. I won't take no for an answer!"

"Okay," Hannah replied in a small voice and shuffled obediently after Lisa. She was feeling so lousy that it was actually nice to be bossed around in such a caring way.

She knew she couldn't manage by herself for long. She knew that the last week and a half (when, apart from the occasional trip to the riverbank to check her posters, she'd done nothing but lie on Simon's bed, crying and checking to see if her cell phone was still working) had pushed her to her limits. That she couldn't continue like this without falling apart, that nothing she did for the rest of her life would bring Simon back.

As she stumbled down the steps after Lisa, her thoughts were already at the Kampnagel. Would her prayers finally be answered? Even if not Simon himself, would the person who had his diary turn up? And would they be able to tell her what had become of her boyfriend?

She doubted very much that any of it would happen, but concentrated with all her might on imagining someone standing before her and telling her he knew where Simon was. And telling her that the talk of suicide had simply been a massive misunderstanding, that of course her boyfriend was in the best of health.

But however much she tried to imagine this misunderstanding, and however much she tried to conjure up a tangible image of her unknown redeemer, Hannah lacked the strength. It would take more than a pretzel stick to revive her unshakable belief that everything would somehow turn out right in the end.

# 39

*Jonathan*

Jonathan had never been to a rock concert in his life, but this was how he imagined it to be: an incredibly long line of waiting people snaked from the entrance of the Kampnagel theater all the way to the multi-story parking garage—a line consisting mainly of giggling, chattering girls.

He was confused. Had he come to the right place? At the right time? He took the diary from his briefcase and opened it to the appropriate page. Yes, here it was: Sunday, January 14, seven p.m. at the Kampnagel.

But why were so many people here? Surely they hadn't all come for a literary reading! In his experience, these events attracted a limited but, well, reverential audience. So reverential that the readings put on by Grief & Son Books authors generally reached the volume and exuberance levels of a dignified funeral. The similarity was reinforced by the soft rustling of handkerchiefs and the average age of those who had come to listen, which, regardless of the age of the author, was always somewhere over seventy.

But the crowd here? It seemed more appropriate for a Rolling Stones gig. Though the audience was too young for that; Jonathan was surrounded by teenagers. It wasn't possible! Not only *exuberant* people, but *young* ones—even less fitting for a cultural event!

"Excuse me." He turned to the two girls standing in front of him in line. "Who's doing the reading here this evening?"

The two of them stared at him wide-eyed as if he'd just asked whether the world was in fact flat. "Sebastian Fitzek," the one on the left squeaked excitedly.

"Fitzek?"

"Yes." The one on the right nodded. "It's his anniversary tour," she added, giving Jonathan a look that suggested he wasn't in his right mind.

"Thank you." The girls turned back to the front and put their heads together, giggling, as Jonathan looked around once again at the crowd.

Someone like Fitzek appealed to so many readers? He knew that the author was hugely successful, but he could never have imagined such audiences in his wildest dreams.

Now he noticed that a not-inconsiderable number of those waiting had several of the author's books clasped under their arms, and some of them were even holding large photos of him, which indicated to Jonathan that they were hoping to get his autograph. Every now and then, cell phones were whipped out by the girls so they could take selfies of themselves and their friends, in order to capture such a significant moment and share it on social media.

*Astonishing. Truly astonishing.* Jonathan would never have even considered coming to a Sebastian Fitzek event. But now he was interested to find out what this veritable fan cult—he couldn't think of it in any other way—was all about. At the same time, he was amazed that the Filofax had suggested this. It had only been a few days ago that it had ordered a media diet, designed to prevent him coming into contact with any negative news or information. As far as Jonathan knew, Fitzek's books were brutal thrillers, and he would dearly have liked to ask the author of the Filofax about this contradiction.

Jonathan had stood in line for a quarter of an hour before reaching the box office. He was glad he'd left himself plenty of time, as he always did, although he hadn't anticipated such a commotion surrounding the event.

He was about to state his order number to the man behind the counter, when he was shoved so violently that he lurched to the side. The culprit, a woman yelling loudly into her cell phone, didn't even notice, but elbowed her way through the waiting crowd toward the door, followed by a friend.

Goodness, that had almost been life threatening! It was doubtful that this crush was in accordance with the fire regulations; if anything happened to cause a panic, the masses in the foyer would be in all kinds of trouble.

Peeved, Jonathan watched the two women leave, but a rough shove from the girls behind him and a loud "Get on with it!" told him in no uncertain terms to stop holding things up.

"Good evening." Jonathan turned back to the man at the ticket counter. "I understand two tickets have been reserved for me under order number 137. I only need one of them."

"Just a moment," he replied and leafed through a box full of white envelopes. "Here." He took one out. "Number 137. Here you are!"

"As I said, I only need one of the tickets."

The man shrugged. "They're already paid for. Give one of them away. The reading's in room K6."

"Thank you." Jonathan took the envelope.

At that moment he felt a hand on his shoulder. Jonathan was about to spin around and bark at the disorderly girl when a voice said, "Hello. I'll take the second ticket."

Jonathan started. He hadn't expected that. He turned, expecting to see the owner of the diary at last.

# 40

*Hannah*

After a sandwich and a pint of orange juice, Hannah was feeling physically better, but mentally she was going through hell as she stood with Lisa next to the box office, staring eagle-eyed at everyone who had come to the reading. Her friend had been true to her word. They had reached the Kampnagel before the doors opened and were able to take up their positions as the first people were allowed in.

Lisa held Hannah's hand and kept squeezing it as they watched people, mainly teenage girls, pick up their tickets. There were only a few boys and older men and women. Hannah held her breath with every man who came up to the counter—she knew from Sarasvati that it was a man who had found the diary.

But she had been disappointed every time; none of them mentioned number 137. Hannah felt as though she were waiting for the lottery numbers to be announced, or playing bingo—wringing her hands in anticipation of a life-changing number being drawn. But it simply didn't happen.

"He's not coming!" she complained as yet another male attendee presented the wrong number. "He's just not coming!"

"Calm down," Lisa said, squeezing her hand yet again. "There are still so many people out there; he could still show up."

"I hope so," Hannah said, and nervously chewed her lower lip. "I really hope so!"

The next moment, she heard a quiet ringtone and felt a vibration in her back pocket. For an instant she wondered whether to ignore it and concentrate instead on not missing a single moment of what happened at the box office. But she relented, took out her phone, and glanced at the display.

Her eyes widened in shock and her hand flew to her mouth—she recognized this number, having dialed it more or less constantly in recent days. It was the policewoman who had told Hannah she could call her anytime.

Lisa noticed Hannah's reaction and raised her eyebrows. "Who is it?"

"The police," Hannah said, her voice faltering. She took the call and closed her eyes. "Marx."

"Hello, Hannah." She was right; it was the officer. "Where are you now?"

"At the Kampnagel," she replied.

"Are you on your own?"

"No. I've got a friend with me."

"Good." She paused briefly. "Could you both please come to the station? The precinct on Wiesendamm is just around the corner."

"What's up?" Hannah's voice shook.

"Please come; we'll tell you then."

"No!" She was shouting now. "Tell me right now!"

The policewoman said something that Hannah didn't catch, because some girls nearby broke out in raucous laughter.

"Just a moment!" she yelled into the cell phone. "I can't hear a thing; I'm just stepping outside." She shoved through the waiting people, taking a direct line to the exit and ignoring the angry murmurs of those she barged into on her way. Lisa followed at her heels.

"What did you say?" Hannah yelled as soon as they were outside.

"I'm asking you to come to see us at the station," the policewoman repeated.

"No," Hannah insisted. "Please tell me right now what's going on, or I'm not moving an inch. Have you found Simon?"

There was silence at the other end of the line.

"Hello?" Hannah shrieked. Her nerves were at the breaking point. "Have you found him?"

"Yes," the police officer replied softly. "We've found him."

Hannah closed her eyes again. She found it hard to breathe and felt as if her knees could give way at any moment. "Is he okay?" As soon as the words left her lips, she knew what the answer would be.

"No," the policewoman said. "I'm sorry. Simon Klamm is dead. Some walkers discovered his body an hour ago."

"Are you sure? Are you absolutely certain it's him?"

"I'm afraid so. We were able to identify him by the ID card he had on his person. But in order to make it official we need to wait for him to be examined by the forensic pathologist."

"So there could be a mistake?"

"Hannah, I really need you to come to the station."

"Tell me first if it's possible there's been a mistake!"

The police officer sighed. "Theoretically, and only theoretically, there is. We really do think it's him."

"Where?" Hannah yelled. "Where was he found?"

"He was lying on an embankment by the Mühlenteich lake. It looks like he drowned."

Hannah gasped, started to crumple, and was caught at the last moment by Lisa. "Fine," she croaked into the telephone. "We're on our way."

# 41

## Jonathan

**Sunday, January 14, 6:50 p.m.**

"Well, well. Who do we have here? So you're going to a Fitzek reading? Now you really *have* surprised me!"

It wasn't a stranger wanting his diary back, but Markus Bode. Clearly amused, he was grinning from ear to ear.

"Well"—Jonathan forced a laugh—"I thought I'd come check it out. Research, if you like. I need to get an overview of the market." He had an unpleasant feeling of being caught out, having argued with his CEO not long ago that books like Fitzek's spelled the end of cultural civilization as they knew it. It felt like Bode had spotted him in the act of entering a swingers' club or porn shop. Except in this case, Bode was also there, putting the pair of them in a stalemate that ought to be embarrassing for both or neither of them. Bode had already admitted that, for financial reasons, he had recently taken quite an interest in swingers . . . wait, no, in popular fiction.

"You really don't have to justify yourself to me," Bode said. He sounded patronizing. "On the contrary, what a lucky coincidence! The reading's completely sold out, and I'd hoped to grab a ticket at the door.

It looks like I'm in luck." He smiled. "At least, if you'd be so kind as to take me in with you."

"Yes, um," Jonathan replied. "True, what a coincidence! And of course you can have my second ticket." He opened the envelope, took out the two tickets, and gave one of them to Markus Bode.

"Thank you very much," he said, taking it with a nod. "What do I owe you?"

"Please!" Jonathan was appalled. "You're my guest, of course." *Well, not mine, exactly,* he added silently.

"Thanks again," Bode replied. "Let's go see what it's all about."

They allowed themselves to be swept along by the chattering crowd of people toward K6, stood waiting in line once again, and finally handed their tickets to the usher at the entrance. He tore them and let the two men into the auditorium.

"Wow!" Markus Bode exclaimed, standing rooted to the spot. It was a fitting description of the scene before them; everything about it was "Wow!" And it had nothing in common with any author talk that Jonathan had ever been to.

On the right-hand side of the hall was a huge stage that could have comfortably accommodated a ten-piece rock band. There were several microphone stands surrounding a drum kit in the middle, which was bathed in color by rotating spotlights. Directly above this, a large screen hung from the ceiling, with the cover of Fitzek's latest thriller projected onto it. Drum kit? Screen? What were they about to see?

Clearly quite a lot, judging from the crowd of euphoric faces in the audience. Hundreds (hundreds!) of audience members thronged the stands (stands! Not rows of chairs, but real stands!) and the atmosphere was charged like a World Cup final featuring Germany versus Brazil; only the vuvuzelas and flags were missing. There wasn't a single seventysomething with a handkerchief in sight, but there were pretty girls selling ice cream and soft drinks. And there was popcorn. It crunched under Jonathan's feet as he and Bode squeezed through the throng to take their places.

They were sitting close to the front with a good view of the stage—the anonymous donor had chosen excellent seats. Jonathan glanced at his watch; the spectacle would begin in a quarter of an hour.

And begin it did. At precisely half past seven, the lights went out, music blared at an earsplitting volume, and on the screen appeared a larger-than-life image of Sebastian Fitzek, closely followed by a fast-paced trailer for his new book. The audience yelled, and there was thunderous applause, increasing in waves and breaking out into wild stamping as the author himself finally took to the stage. "Good evening and welcome, Hamburg! My name is Sebastian Fitzek!" he cried into his headset.

Ecstatic screeching, people leaping up from their seats in a rapture of delight—Germany scores, one-nil! What an entrance. If Jonathan had not been there and seen it with his own eyes, he would never have believed it possible. Heavens!


"Huh." At first Markus Bode said nothing more, as they sat together in a corner of a wine bar after the reading, to discuss their opinions of the evening over a good glass of wine.

"Well," Jonathan agreed. They looked at each other in silence, both rather shaken. Sebastian Fitzek had spent the last two hours delivering an absolute fireworks display of light entertainment.

He had conducted the evening magnificently, reading some gripping passages from his thriller and explaining the background of the story with the help of a slick PowerPoint presentation. He had interviewed himself, invited members of the audience onto the stage, and cracked one joke after another. Then a band had played the "soundtrack to the book," Fitzek taking his place at the drum kit, driving the spectators wild at regular intervals. There were no panties flying through the air, but Jonathan wouldn't have been surprised if there had been.

Following the reading, the author had made his way to a table in the foyer, and hordes of people had flocked to it to have their books signed, get an autograph, or have photos taken with him. It was highly probable that Fitzek would still be sitting there the following morning dealing with the onslaught. The whole thing had the air of a crazy pilgrimage.

"Huh," Markus Bode said again, interrupting Jonathan's thoughts. "Now do you see what I mean when I say we need an author like that on our list? For each author of the caliber of Fitzek, we could support ten literary-prize winners."

"I'd say twenty," Jonathan replied, nodding. "Yes, I totally get what you mean." Not only that, but he had to admit to himself something he would never reveal to Markus Bode: he had really enjoyed it. The whole evening had rushed by like a speeded-up movie.

There was no comparison with the readings he usually attended. He'd always found them rather oppressive: every minute the author spent reading self-importantly from their work had stretched out like a well-chewed, stale piece of chewing gum. "Well," he asked diffidently, "have we been sent any manuscripts in any of the popular genres?"

"Not yet. We don't tend to get them, since as you said yourself, Grief & Son doesn't deal with that kind of book. We'll need to scout around." He looked hopefully at Jonathan. "Shall I do it? I could call a few agents and ask them to send us some suitable submissions."

"Let me think about it," Jonathan said in an attempt to rein in his enthusiasm. "I can't decide so quickly." He wanted to talk to his father. And for that he had to catch him in one of his more lucid moments. He hoped that Wolfgang Grief still had enough mental capacity for such a conversation, at least for a few minutes. Otherwise, Jonathan would have to make the decision himself, and that . . .

The next morning he'd go straight to the Sonnenhof home and pay his father a visit.

# 42

*Hannah*

**Monday, January 15, 8:05 a.m.**

*Sometimes things that seem so horrific that we can't face them are neverthe-less true.*

The sentence ran through Hannah's head again and again. That dreadful sentence Lisa had said to her only a few weeks ago. And she was right: It was horrific. And it was true. Simon had killed himself. He really had done it.

Hannah hadn't actually seen his body, which had been discovered by an elderly couple out walking by the Mühlenteich lake the previous evening, but the police were 99 percent certain that the dead man was Simon.

The officers didn't consider it necessary for Hannah to identify him (indeed, they had strongly advised her not to see him). The final confir-mation would come with the forensic pathologist's examination ordered by the public prosecutor, since the cause of death was still not clear.

They were assuming that he had drowned, had taken his life in the ice-cold water—as suggested not only by his final letter, but also the fact that initial investigations showed no sign of third-party interference—but Hannah's personal contact had told her they wanted to carry out a postmortem to be absolutely sure. There had been no eyewitnesses to attest to suicide, so all the indicators needed to be substantiated with hard facts.

Hannah no longer needed this certainty. She had known deep down in her heart all along, even if she hadn't wanted to believe it. On that New Year's morning when she had been sleeping, blissfully unaware in his bed, and woken still believing that she had reached him with her diary, had succeeded in giving him new hope—on that very morning, he had killed himself. He had made a solitary decision, had left Hannah behind, not even given her a final chance to talk to him about it and try to find a solution together, opting instead for the ultimate, final escape route.

She sat in Simon's kitchen, on one of his Eames chairs, feeling like a block of stone. She had sent Lisa home an hour ago, after her friend had spent the first half of the night with her at the police station and the second half in Simon's apartment. Lisa had been at a loss. Speechless. Apart from her usual "I'm sorry," all words had failed her. But what could anyone say? Except that they were truly sorry.

About Simon. About Hannah. About all that could have been and now would never again be possible. Over. Finished. Forever.

"Are you sure you'll be all right on your own? I'll call your parents if you like," Lisa had said after Hannah asked her to leave because she wanted space to dwell on her thoughts.

"I don't want to see anyone. But it would be really nice if you could ring Mama and Papa and tell them what's happened. I'm just not up to it right now," she had replied, surprising herself at how calm she sounded. Even at the police station she'd been unnaturally self-controlled, as if in a trance or under the strongest medication. The collapse she and everyone else had expected never came; she was in a state of shock. "Don't worry about me. I'll manage. And you need to take care of things at Little Rascals later."

"Don't you even think about that! It's not important right now."

"Yes, it is. It's the only thing I have left. As soon as I'm feeling a bit better, I'll be back. Just give me a few days."

"Take all the time in the world. I'm there and I can hold the fort, with the help of our mothers."

"What for?" she had asked. "What do I need all the time in the world for? To sit around here and think about how Simon's really dead? That he's really, truly never coming back? That I'll never again be able to hug him or kiss him, that none of that will ever, ever, ever happen again?" Then, finally, the release came in the form of tears that fell in torrents. Hannah had sobbed so violently and so loudly that her whole body shook.

"Shhh!" Lisa had taken her in her arms and gently rocked her. "It'll be okay, darling. It'll be fine."

But it wasn't fine. Nothing was fine, and nothing would ever be fine again. Hannah knew it with brutal clarity as she sat alone in Simon's kitchen. She suddenly felt out of place, here in a dead man's apartment.

What was she doing here? These weren't her belongings that surrounded her, and their owner didn't need them anymore. Not his beloved Eames chairs, not his high-tech Italian espresso machine, not the dishes and cutlery in the cupboards or the stupid stoneware mug with *Chef* on it, not the clothes that were still in the dryer, not the rows of books on the living-room shelves, not the racing bike that hung on the wall in the hallway, and not even his dreadful Birkenstock slippers which, when she first saw them on his feet, Hannah had said would be legitimate grounds for divorce.

He needed none of it, nothing, nothing, *nothing* anymore. They were only things! Dead, lifeless things, completely useless without the man they had belonged to.

Hannah sprang up from the kitchen chair and wandered restlessly through the apartment. After the tears came the anger. The raging, immeasurable anger with Simon for being such a coward.

Coward, coward, *coward!*

Suicide was such a thoughtless, *spineless* solution! To throw it all away without sparing a single thought for those you left behind. Simply to pull the plug and *après moi le déluge*—it was so egotistical, so mean, so . . . so absolutely inhuman! Yes, it was easy for the departed, it was all the same to him afterward, he didn't feel anything. Let the rest figure out their own way to get through it, to rebuild the ruins, to somehow find their way back to life and carry on.

Bang! With a violent swing of her arm, Hannah swept the espresso machine from the counter. It landed on the kitchen floor with a crash, breaking two tiles. It felt good. Very good.

She tore open the cabinet doors and swept everything from the shelves, watching as plates, cups, and glasses fell and smashed. With every item that shattered she felt the hairline cracks of her heart tear apart too. They were followed by packets and jars of pasta, jam, tea, sugar, salt, flour; she violently flung it all to the floor, until the kitchen looked like a battlefield.

Continuing her work in the living room, she overturned the TV, hurled a vase together with its flowers from the table, tore pictures from the walls and smashed them against a corner of the windowsill, dragged all the curtains from their rods and sent the CD collection flying.

"Asshole!" she yelled as she grabbed a framed photo of Simon and herself, which had been standing on the bureau by the sofa. She smashed it against a wall with all her might. "You great big damn asshole! How could you do this to me?"

She stamped her foot, screamed "Asshole!" again, this time so loudly that she feared the neighbors would come ring the bell. How could Simon have done this to her? However scared he had been, however worried that she would suffer the same fate as his mother, this was unfair.

It was unfair because it had robbed Hannah of the chance at least to say goodbye to him. At least to hold his hand one last time, to take him in her arms and tell him everything she had wanted to tell him. He had simply walked away and left Hannah speechless with a ridiculous letter and the remark that *his love was not enough for him to carry on*? Aaaargh!

Hannah's eyes fell on the car keys on the bureau next to the documents. Simon's Mustang. His sacred relic.

She grabbed the keys, stormed out of the apartment, and was downstairs by the car a moment later. At first she wanted to destroy it, to smash the headlights, snap off the windshield wipers, break the mirrors, drag the key along the dark-red paint with a screeching noise and leave deep, scratched scars. As deep and sharp edged as the cracks in her heart.

But then she came to her senses. Breathing deeply, she stood by the Mustang as calm gradually descended on her. She had ranted and raved enough, given herself sufficient release. Instead of reducing the car to scrap, she got in and started the engine.

She had other plans for Simon's treasured possession.

# 43

*Jonathan*

**Monday, January 15, 8:33 a.m.**

It was incredible. No sooner had Jonathan decided on his plan of talking with his father than his intention was validated by the mysterious diary.

*We cannot solve our problems with the same thinking we used when we created them.*

*Albert Einstein*

This quote headed the entry for today, and Jonathan found himself nodding in agreement as he read it. He also liked the rest of the text:

*Today, do the exact opposite of what you normally do. And look forward to seeing what happens as a result. Change means changing your ways—only by so doing can you have new experiences that may surprise you. Make a break with your habits, test yourself, expand your horizons! If you usually hold the phone in your right hand, use your left. Do your shopping in a different supermarket and buy different brands, take the bus instead of the car, be particularly friendly to people who usually irritate you. If you eat out, order food you don't usually eat. Experience the world around you as something completely new, as though you were a different person and not yourself. Enjoy!*

*P.S. And since our dear Mr. Einstein has said so many wise things on the subject that I really couldn't decide which to use, here's a second quote from the master of relativity: "The definition of insanity is doing the same thing over and over again and expecting different results."*

Jonathan laughed and shook his head. He had never seen it like that, but it was so true. It *was* insanity!

Most people did the same things over and over, following their habitual paths and always being surprised at the end that they yielded the same results. Jonathan himself was no exception. It was only since he'd found the diary that his life had become filled with unusual happenings.

Sarasvati, Leopold, playing tennis with Markus Bode, and, not least, the Sebastian Fitzek reading that he would never normally have attended: he had, in fact, been doing exactly what the Filofax was exhorting him to do today—it was just that he had been unaware of it.

So today, he would have that conversation with his father. He had felt a slight fluttering in his stomach when he considered revealing to his old man that Grief & Son Books was experiencing a few difficulties, forcing him to look for new solutions. But now he saw that it was the right thing at least to try.

What was the worst that could happen? The most probable outcome would be that Wolfgang Grief wouldn't be able to follow what his son told him, and Jonathan would ultimately be no wiser than before.

After having breakfast, showering, and getting dressed, Jonathan picked up his briefcase, along with the diary and his car keys, ready to head for the Sonnenhof on the Elbchaussee.

Out in the driveway, he clicked open the doors of his Saab and was about to get behind the wheel when he paused. The diary had suggested he go by public transport today. If he got into his car now, it would mean disobeying the instruction, so he dropped his car keys into his coat pocket and marched off on foot.

A few minutes later, he realized he had no idea where he was going, since he had not been on a bus or U-Bahn train since he was a boy. Why would he have? He had a car, so there was no reason to bother with Hamburg's public transportation.

He didn't know how to get from Innocentia Park to the Elbchaussee. He only knew it was quite a distance, one that took him half an hour with his own four wheels. How long would the door-to-door journey take if he caught a bus? At least an hour, for sure. That would be a waste of time, wouldn't it? And Jonathan had a pathological dislike of waste in every aspect of his life.

He went back to his car. In this, he would just have to ignore the recommendation of the Filofax, since he didn't have time to waste.

Once again, he clicked open the doors—but paused again. Hmm. It didn't feel right, as if he were doing something forbidden. As if he were about to drive away without a license (which, of course, he would never, ever do). *Click.* He locked the car, turned, and walked back down the street.

But where to?

He turned and went back to his driveway.

Shortly before he reached it, he turned again.

Maybe he could compromise and take a taxi. He whipped out his cell phone to call one, but lowered it again.

No, he shouldn't kid himself: a taxi would be a lazy compromise, a complete sham. After all, this was about new experiences, about expanding his horizons, and how did he expect to do that in a taxi? Unless Jonathan happened to get a driver who shared some new experiences with him. No, a taxi ride would be cheating.

"Good morning, Herr Grief!" The voice from behind caused him to spin around. Hertha Fahrenkrog walked up to him, as always with her poodle princess at her heels. "What are you doing, standing there like a lost soul?"

"I'm sorry?"

"Well," she said, smiling, "I've been watching you from the kitchen window and couldn't help noticing that you look rather confused. The way you're walking back and forth, it's as if you don't really know where you want to go."

"Yes, I do," Jonathan replied. "I'm going to visit my father. I just don't know how I'm going to get there."

"Has your car broken down?"

"No. But I thought I'd take public transportation."

"Why?" She stared at him. "If you want my opinion, if your car's not broken down, then you should go in that."

"Yes, um . . ." How could he explain? A bus ride as a trip to self-discovery—he doubted that Hertha Fahrenkrog had the mental faculties to understand it. "I need to visit the optician afterward," he lied, hoping he wasn't turning bright red. Normally the slightest white lie couldn't leave his lips without it being obvious to all the world. His father had found it hilarious, whereas his mother had seen it as a sign that his heart was in the right place. "I'm having my eyes examined," the man with his heart in the right place continued, "and they'll be giving me eye drops, after which I'm not allowed to drive."

"Ah." Hertha Fahrenkrog nodded. "Cataracts, is it? My Heinzi had that." She sighed. "God rest his soul. He could hardly see a thing at the end." She bent down to her poodle. "Isn't that right, Daphne—Papa could hardly recognize us at the end."

"Uh-huh," Jonathan stammered.

"But that's age for you," his neighbor continued with a smile. "We all have to put up with a few ailments."

"True." Jonathan recalled that over breakfast he'd been reading that he should be friendly toward people who would normally irritate him. And so he was friendly toward Hertha Fahrenkrog. Very friendly. Friendly enough to hold back from pointing out that he was only forty-two and, unlike her dear, departed husband, didn't go back to the days of the German Empire. For even though he had never had the opportunity to meet the beloved Heinzi, since his good neighbor Frau Fahrenkrog was not far from her centennial, it was safe to assume—

"Why don't you just call a taxi?" she said, rescuing Jonathan from getting lost in an increasingly complex sentence.

"A very good question!"

"So why not?"

"Because . . . because . . . because I just want to go by bus today." Why shouldn't he simply tell the truth? It didn't matter!

"By bus?" Daphne whined in sympathy. "You?"

"Why not me?"

"Well, you've got enough money for a taxi."

"Just because I have enough money doesn't mean I have to throw it to the wind!"

Hertha Fahrenkrog laughed.

"What's so funny?"

"Nothing," she replied. "I just can't imagine you on a bus."

"And why not?"

"Well," she began. "It's more something for ordinary people."

"And you don't think I'm ordinary?"

"Not at all."

"The way you said it didn't sound like a compliment."

"That's up to you."

"What is?"

"How you interpret what I say." She gave him a cheerful grin. Jonathan was rather shocked to find that this small, shriveled woman's mind was as sharp as a honed blade. Amazing! Was she on medication for it? Or did Daphne keep her in good mental shape? Maybe he should consider getting a dog, in case his father's dementia turned out to be hereditary.

"However you meant it," Jonathan said, "I've decided to take the bus and train to the Elbchaussee."

"Like Günter Wallraff," his neighbor said, on the attack again.

Jonathan was able to parry that one. "Exactly! *Jonathan N. Grief, Lowest of the Low*," he said, adapting the title of Wallraff's book from the 1980s that had made his name as an undercover journalist. As far as Jonathan knew, that had been another bestseller the likes of which Grief & Son Books urgently needed. One way or another, he was constantly brought back to this subject; the vision board seemed to be doing its work. "Well, then!" He raised a hand in farewell, turned, and walked off.

"Where do you think you're going?" Hertha Fahrenkrog called after him.

He turned back to her. "To catch the bus."

"If I were you, I'd head in the other direction," she said. "You won't find a bus over there."

"Of course not," he replied and set off in the opposite direction.

"In any case, if it's the Elbchaussee you're going to, I'd take the U-Bahn."

He stopped again. Gave in. It was madness to act as if he had the slightest idea where he needed to go. He'd be better off allowing a hundred-year-old to explain to him how to get where he was going on public transportation.

Twenty minutes later, Jonathan found that the Wallraff comparison wasn't so far off the mark. From his seat on the U3 line train heading from Hoheluftchaussee toward St. Pauli (where he was to take the number 36 bus heading for Blankenese, his neighbor had impressed upon him), it was clear that there were a good number of people who considered beer to be a suitable breakfast.

Feeling slightly scared, he sat hunched into the corner of a seat and watched two men swaying in the aisle not far from him, each with a can of Astra lager in hand, arguing so loudly that they were almost coming to blows.

Jonathan feared that they could at any moment descend into a brawl, and he could himself get drawn in. He kept his eyes averted so he wouldn't accidentally provoke the two beer drinkers, and looked around at the other passengers instead.

Most of them were reading, though they weren't absorbed in newspapers or books but were tapping on their cell phones and tablets. Interesting. And alarming.

He clearly remembered a discussion a few years ago at Grief & Son Books about electronic books, which his father had nipped in the bud by declaiming forcefully, "The e-book is just a passing trend and we're having nothing to do with it! At Grief & Son Books, we print on paper and that's that!" Nevertheless, Bode had shortly afterward insisted that the relevant reading devices were obtained for the editors, because, as he had explained, slightly shamefaced, it made checking manuscripts so much more efficient that the editorial staff refused to be without them a moment longer. Now, to judge from what Jonathan could see as he looked around the carriage, it wasn't only his editors who saw the virtues of digital books.

He left the train at St. Pauli Station, although when the two beer drinkers also got off there, he seriously considered staying on. The poster by the station exit announcing that weapons and glass bottles were strictly forbidden in this area did nothing to make him want to linger here any longer than strictly necessary.

He saw with relief that the bus stop for route 36 was only a few yards away, so there would be no need for him to cross the Reeperbahn and run the risk of bumping into any shady characters who paid no heed to the poster with its arms ban.

He went to stand by the stop and wait for the right bus. According to the timetable, one should be along in a few minutes.

A passing dark-red car caught Jonathan's eye. It was an old Ford Mustang—a particularly nice, well-maintained model. The car stopped at the Millerntor junction traffic lights, and he saw that the driver was a red-haired woman.

Jonathan had to smile, not only because an image from his vision board had more or less materialized in front of him, but also because he caught himself buying into a stereotype. In this district he would have expected a woman to be in the passenger seat, the car being driven by a pimp. But he had probably simply spent his childhood and youth hearing too many cautionary tales about the Reeperbahn from his parents, whose mission in life had been to keep him away from Hamburg's red-light district.

Successfully, too, he had to admit. He had never been here, not even as an adult. Why not? Hadn't every Hamburg citizen had at least one wild night out on the Reeperbahn? From Saturday night into early Sunday morning, with a prawn sandwich from the fish market as the crowning glory of a great night out.

As he stood there looking over at the Mustang, his thoughts miles away, he felt a desire to do it sometime. Apart from the prawn sandwich, of course—he couldn't stand those. But the rest of the plan sounded remarkably appealing. Maybe Markus Bode would be a suitable companion for a drunken night out in the red-light district? Anything that wasn't a lonely evening in his hotel must raise a certain enthusiasm, surely?

The light turned green; the woman in the Mustang stepped on the pedal and soon vanished from Jonathan's sight. He sighed and turned away, a little saddened. It was a really, really good car.

# 44

*Hannah*

Udo Lindenberg's homage to the Reeperbahn was playing on the radio as Hannah drove Simon's car toward the Millerntor high-rise blocks that marked the entrance to the red-light district. Despite her mood, she sang along with a kind of dark, gallows-humor cheer.

She had been driving around the city in the Mustang for an hour and a half, full of qualms about whether she should really do what she intended to, or whether she was overdoing it in her self-righteous anger. She had finally come to the conclusion that she was perfectly within her rights to overdo things and that she had to take some kind of action to vent the worry, the pain, and, yes, the rage that still boiled within her.

To make her mark. A loud, thunderous mark that would shove Simon from his cloud or wherever he was lounging around. So she headed for the red-light district, in an action that seemed like the only logical consequence of the way Simon had betrayed her.

At this hour of the morning, the entertainment district had none of the glitzy fascination of the night, when it drew in hordes of pilgrims eager to hit the town. No colored lights, no neon ads, no dolled-up women, and no loud music from the bars that lined the street. Everywhere there was dirt, dirt, dirt, and gray misery; the St. Pauli district had hung its pretty dress out on the line to shake off the dust, waiting for the next night. Groups of punks were hanging around on the sidewalk with their huge dogs; here and there outside closed amusement arcades and bars, sleeping bags were huddled where the homeless slept off their last high.

As she drew level with McDonald's, Hannah saw a vacant parking space that was big enough to maneuver the Mustang into without mishap. She indicated and turned the steering wheel. A sign announced that the parking spaces here were reserved for taxis from eight in the evening, but if things went according to Hannah's plan, the Mustang would be long gone by then.

She switched the engine off and left the ignition key in place. Then she left the documents lying on the passenger seat in full view of anyone passing by on the sidewalk.

She got out. Shut the driver's door. And walked away in the direction of the U-Bahn station, whistling.

# 45

*Jonathan*

*Monday, January 15, 12:03 p.m.*

Shortly after midday, following a brief odyssey—the woman and her Mustang had distracted him so much that he boarded the wrong bus, number 37, and didn't notice until he reached the end of the line—Jonathan entered his father's room in the Sonnenhof, where he found Wolfgang Grief standing by the window, staring out. A rare sight. And a hopeful one; Jonathan had clearly caught his father on one of his better days.

"Hello, Papa," he said.

Wolfgang Grief turned to him with a smile. "Hello, son." He nodded toward the outside. "Lovely weather today, isn't it?"

"Yes." The sky was cloudy and the light rather gloomy, but at least it wasn't raining. Given Hamburg's climate and the fact it was January, it wouldn't take too much imagination to describe it as "lovely."

"How's your dear mother?" his father asked as he sat down in his wing chair.

Jonathan's spirits sank. So it wasn't such a good day. He had long since dismissed the possibility that Sofia might actually be in Hamburg and had given her son the diary—not least since his mother had never spoken German so well, or written it with such correct punctuation. No, there was no way that the Filofax could have been her work; that had merely been wishful thinking on Jonathan's part.

"You mean Sofia?" he asked. Maybe his father had been talking about another lady, although he couldn't think off the top of his head who it might be.

Wolfgang Grief laughed cheerfully. "Do you have another mother?"

"No," he replied. "Of course not."

"There you are. So, how is she? Will she be calling to see me later?"

"Papa . . ." He hesitated. How should he answer that one? He decided to play along, even though it wasn't a game. "I think so."

"How lovely!" his father said. "We can take a little outing together. I would love to have coffee and cake at the Witthüs in Hirsch Park." He licked his lips in anticipation. "Yes, a nice piece of fresh cherry streusel cake is definitely on the menu for me today!"

"Good idea, Papa," Jonathan said, suppressing a sigh· "We'll do that."

"Let's hope your mother comes soon, then."

"Hmm." He sat down. Earlier, he'd been pleased to have reached the nursing home at all, but now he thought he could just as easily get up and leave. This time by taxi.

But he didn't want to be unfair. Seeing his father in such a good mood was something to be pleased about, although it seriously disturbed Jonathan that his father's moods were in direct proportion to his mental derangement. He clearly had two choices: a father capable of reasoning but grouchy, or one who radiated naive cheerfulness but whose thinking was at the level of a little child.

"So, what's new?" Wolfgang Grief asked.

Jonathan paused briefly. Should he make an attempt? Although the venture was probably hopeless, he should at least try. "I'd like to talk to you about the business," he began.

"Go ahead, boy! Is all well?"

"If I'm honest, not entirely."

His father looked at him in incomprehension, as though Jonathan had spoken a foreign language. "What do you mean?"

"There are a few problems with the sales figures."

Wolfgang Grief's eyes narrowed to slits. "Define 'a few problems.'"

"Well, the current list is going really badly."

"What are the numbers?"

Amazing. It was truly amazing. Regardless of his dementia, it was as though someone had switched a light on in Wolfgang Grief's mind. He suddenly seemed wide awake, the angry furrows on his brow standing out. His steely blue eyes fixed his son with the very look that had terrified Jonathan all his life.

"There's been a drop of thirty percent that—"

"Thirty percent?" his father snapped. "Show me the latest accounts!"

"I don't have them with me, but—"

"How can you come here bringing me news like that without the relevant documents?" His father thundered.

"Papa, it's—"

"Do you actually have any idea what you're doing? And you call yourself a businessman!"

"Well, I—"

"Oh, why am I getting so worked up?" He shook his head. "It's always been obvious you're not cut out to be an entrepreneur. I should never have retired from the operational side of the business!"

"No, really, it's—"

"What does Markus Bode have to say?"

"That's the whole point," Jonathan replied. "Bode thinks we should have a few mass-market titles on our list. Yesterday, for example, we went to a reading by Sebastian Fitzek—"

"Fitzek? Did you just say Fitzek?"

"Yes, I did." Jonathan squared his shoulders determinedly. He wasn't going to be treated like a little child by his demented father a moment longer—he was a mature man, damn it! "And if you'd been there yourself, you'd have a different opinion of him. In any case, I find the idea of having a few such titles on our list to be quite—"

"Jonathan, please! You're not seriously trying to suggest that Grief & Son Books should lower itself to the depths of popular fiction? That's absurd!"

"I don't think it's all that absurd," Jonathan replied. And it was true; he no longer did find it so absurd. Especially since his father, a businessman through and through, had begun by asking about the figures. Maybe he simply refused to see that the times had changed and there were ever fewer people who wanted to pay for high literature. Wasn't it Jonathan's task—no, his duty—to inform his father?

"No, my boy, there's no point in discussing it any further. Bring me the latest figures, then we'll see how best to proceed."

"But I think that—"

"And I think not!"

"Papa, I—"

There was a knock at the door, and a second later Renate Krug came in.

"Oh, hello," she said. "Am I interrupting you?"

A smile leapt to Wolfgang Grief's lips. "Sofia!" he cried, approaching his former assistant nimbly and hugging her. "I'm so glad to see you! Of course you're not interrupting us! I was just saying to Jonathan how much I'd like a little outing with the two of you."

"But of course, darling," Renate Krug said, and laughed as though it were the most normal thing in the world—first, that Wolfgang Grief took her for his long-lost wife, and second, that he wanted an outing with her and his son as a family.

"Um . . ." Jonathan looked at Renate Krug in some confusion. She responded with a conspiratorial nod as if to say, "Let your father believe it if he wants to."

Jonathan sighed inwardly yet again. Okay, so he'd go for a little outing with his father and his "mother."

# 46

*Hannah*

"What have you done? Are you crazy?" Lisa stared at Hannah, aghast. "Oh, I'm sorry," she added quickly, looking even more aghast. "I didn't mean that. You're not crazy, of course not, it just slipped out, but—"

"No problem," Hannah said casually. "Maybe it is crazy. But one thing's for certain—it felt really good."

"But you can't simply leave Simon's car, keys and all, standing around in the red-light district!"

"Don't worry." Hannah laughed and realized she sounded a little crazy even to her own ears. "I'm fairly certain the Mustang won't be standing around there anymore. Someone's sure to be off into the sunset with it by now." She grabbed a caramel from the open packet on the counter of the little kitchen, popped it into her mouth, chewed with relish, and gave Lisa a carefree smile.

"Come on!" her friend cried, putting on her jacket.

"Where are you going?"

"Where do you think? To the Reeperbahn. We're going to get that car back! It might still be there."

"No," Hannah said resolutely. "We're most certainly not. We're going to take our time preparing for an afternoon with the children, and we're going to carry on as usual."

"But it's completely crazy! You can't just . . . Simon's car must be . . . Well, I've no idea, but it must be worth a few thousand euros!"

"I'd guess about ten," Hannah replied unperturbed. "It's very well maintained and a real collector's piece." She nodded. "Yes, so I'd say at least ten thousand euros—that's what Simon always used to say."

"You really *are* insane." Lisa shook her head. "How could you just park it up in the red-light district? Didn't it occur to you what we could do with that kind of cash? Here—at Little Rascals? We could build the best monkey bars and buy whatever other equipment we need!"

Hannah shuddered; she felt a twinge of guilt for a fraction of a second. Then she shook her head slowly but determinedly.

"You could be right," she admitted. "But I really wouldn't want to use the money for Little Rascals. If we bought something with it, every time I looked at it I'd be reminded that the money came from Simon's Mustang. And that would somehow . . . Oh, I don't know, it'd feel a bit like grave robbing."

"Grave robbing?" Lisa replied, bewildered. "Simon said to you in his letter that you should invest his money in our business, since—"

"Lisa, please! I've made my decision and I'm sticking to it."

"You're still in a state of shock. You're bound to regret it in the morning."

"No, I won't. And I'm not in a state of shock—I'm thinking more clearly than I have for a long time." She had hardly finished the sentence when she burst into tears.

"Hannah." Lisa threw her arms around her, drew her close, and stroked her hair. "It's all right, let it all out."

"I . . . I . . . I . . ." Hannah stammered, clinging to Lisa as though she were the only thing left to hold on to as she teetered on the brink of an unfathomable abyss.

"I know, darling, I know . . ."

"How can I go on?" she sobbed. "What's going to happen?" She wiped the snot from her nose with the back of her hand. "It's a complete nightmare! It can't be true. I keep thinking I'm going to wake up soon. How can I go on? How's it supposed to work?"

"With small steps and by taking one day at a time. There's no other way." Lisa stepped back and looked at Hannah encouragingly. "We're never given a burden bigger than we can bear."

Hannah looked at her friend through her tears. "Do you really think so?"

Lisa thought for a moment, then shook her head slowly. "No. To be honest, that's utter nonsense. Just a stupid quote for people who have no idea. I'm afraid there are burdens that are way too much for anyone, so I take it all back and I'm now saying the opposite."

Hannah had to laugh despite herself. "Thanks for trying."

"You're welcome."

"Come on." Hannah wiped her face again. "Let's get going. I think work's going to be the best distraction for me."

"You're sure you don't want to go get the car? Totally sure?"

"I'm sure. I've already given it over to the universe." She sighed. "It's one less thing to think about. I'm dreading giving up Simon's apartment and having to deal with everything." She shuddered. "The funeral . . ."

"Don't worry about that now. I've already talked to your parents, and we've agreed to arrange the funeral and take care of everything. If you want, we can also clear out Simon's apartment together."

"It's very kind of you, but I can at least manage to deal with that on my own; it feels more right than if strangers . . ." She broke off. "Sorry, I didn't mean it like that."

"It's okay. But if you want me to, just know that I'll be glad to help you any way I can. We'll get through this. It won't be as bad as it feels right now."

"Thank you," Hannah said. "I don't know how I'd make it without you."

"You can depend on me, it goes without saying."

"No, it doesn't." Hannah began to cry again. "It definitely needs saying—I thank you from the bottom of my heart."

# 47

*Jonathan*

*Monday, January 15, 6:08 p.m.*

"Well, Frau Krug, there's something I'd really like to know."

Jonathan N. Grief sat next to his assistant in the back of a taxi, trying to put his thoughts into some kind of order. The afternoon had been enjoyable if completely absurd.

The three of them had taken a walk by the Elbe and then gone to the Witthüs for coffee and cake. Just like a normal family on a completely normal afternoon. Except they weren't a family at all, certainly not a normal one, with a papa suffering from dementia and a mama who wasn't related in any way.

Nevertheless, Wolfgang Grief had insisted on calling Renate Krug "Sofia," and she hadn't made the slightest attempt to disabuse him of the notion.

*Absurd, strange, like a screwball comedy!*

"How long has my father been thinking of you as my mother?"

"Well . . ." She examined her fingernails as though checking whether it was time for a manicure. "I'd say for about six months."

"And you never thought to tell me? Even when I asked you outright?"

"I admit that was wrong of me." A defiant look came to her face. "But it doesn't make any difference what your father thinks. If he's happy believing I'm his wife, who's it going to bother?"

"Um, me, for one?"

"Why?"

"Because you're simply not my mother!" He cleared his throat. "You can't just act as though you are."

"I don't see any reason why I shouldn't."

"Apart from the laws of common decency."

"Oh, decency!" She gestured dismissively. "Decency is overrated. Your father's very ill, and what matters right now is to make sure he feels good."

"I understand. So it's all right for us to treat him as though he's mentally deficient."

She said no more, but Jonathan knew what she was thinking. Because deep down, he was thinking it himself. His father *was* mentally deficient; his mind was in complete chaos. Such chaos that he now took his former assistant for his wife.

"I just don't understand where he got the idea," Jonathan finally continued. "My mother has had absolutely no place in his life for years. Why this sudden change of heart?"

"As you're well aware, people suffering from dementia live mainly in the past. Feelings and desires that have long been buried start to resurface."

"So you think that my mother's return is a long-buried desire of my father's?"

"It seems so. Clearly there's something there that he hasn't fully processed."

"I can imagine. How *can* you possibly process the fact that the woman you love simply vanishes overnight?"

"Hmm." Renate Krug sighed. "It's difficult."

"Anyway," Jonathan said, "it doesn't feel right to reinforce my father's delusions."

"I don't think we're doing any harm or making his situation any worse."

Jonathan thought about it. "No," he said. "Probably not. It's just so sad to watch that brilliant mind falling apart."

"That depends."

"On what?"

"Don't you think there's also some good coming from your father's illness?"

"What do you mean?"

"Well, he's much easier to be around than he was."

"I'm surprised to hear you say that. I thought you got along well with him."

Renate Krug laughed out loud. "Your father was a tyrant!"

"To you too?" He would never have believed that the apparently loyal Renate Krug would think so critically of his father.

"Especially to me, I have to say it. He took it all out on me—every mood swing, every little irritation."

"So why did you stay with him? I'm sure you could have found another job."

She lowered her eyes. "Because, apart from all that, he was also a great man. A striking personality, someone who knew exactly what he wanted. That's a rare find."

"Huh. Others would call it pigheaded."

"Weren't you just talking about the new plans you have for the publishing house?" Jonathan looked at her in surprise, while Renate Krug averted her eyes in embarrassment. "I was standing outside the door for a while. I couldn't help . . ."

"You were listening in," Jonathan said.

"I wouldn't say that. I simply didn't want to disturb you, and I happened to overhear a thing or two."

"Ah." Jonathan couldn't suppress a grin. "So, since you 'overheard a thing or two,' I'd value your opinion."

"My opinion?" She looked stunned.

"Of course!"

"Oh." She waved him away, blushing a little. "I've got no idea about such things. I'd rather stay out of it."

"Frau Krug," Jonathan insisted, "I'm not expecting you to give a detailed analysis. I'd simply like to know what you think about Grief & Son Books bringing out a few popular novels."

"I really couldn't say—"

"Come on! What do you like to read yourself?"

Her color deepened a touch more. "Um . . . it's a bit embarrassing."

"As bad as that?"

Renate Krug nodded. She reached for her purse, fumbled it open, and took something out. "This, for example." She handed Jonathan a small tattered book.

He looked at it, suppressed a gasp of surprise, and tried to compose himself. "Oh."

Renate Krug quickly tucked the book back into her bag.

They spoke no more about it and continued on their way in silence. Jonathan was fighting back peals of laughter, giving them free rein only once they had reached Renate Krug's apartment in Eimsbüttel and his assistant had left.

By the time the taxi stopped in front of Jonathan's villa fifteen minutes later, he was still laughing. Loudly and cheerfully. Renate Krug had surprised him more than once that afternoon. But the fact that she read novels with such titles as *In the Heat of Passion* was the icing on the cake.

What was he supposed to say to that? And above all, what would his father say?

# 48

*Hannah*

"And my soul spread its wings out wide, sailed o'er quiet lands as though in homeward flight."

Hannah silently mouthed the words as the pastor spoke them at Simon's grave to conclude the funeral. She had chosen a quote by Joseph Freiherr von Eichendorff that Simon had loved.

So here she was, at the graveside of the man with whom, until recently, she had thought she would spend the rest of her life. *Ashes to ashes, dust to dust.*

Standing next to her, Lisa squeezed her hand. True to her word, she had stayed by her friend's side during the recent days and lived through everything with her. Together with Hannah's parents, she had accompanied her to the meetings with the undertaker and the pastor, had helped her choose a plot for the grave at Ohlsdorf Cemetery, and had drawn up and sent the invitations.

More than two hundred people had come to pay their final respects to Simon. The editorial team of the *Hamburg News* had turned out in full, and of course all his friends had been there, as well as the pitifully few remaining relatives: an uncle and a cousin.

They all filed past in an endless line of condolences. Hannah shook hand after hand, let one expression of sympathy after another wash over her, and wondered how much longer it would be before she could at last be back at home on her own and give in to the next emotional crisis.

She felt like she would break down at any moment, collapse into herself like a burst balloon. She had managed to hold it together fairly well until the previous afternoon. But then the nice policewoman who'd given Hannah her number stopped by her house and gave her—Simon's "fiancée"—the confidential results of the postmortem.

Yes, Simon had drowned; there was no doubt about that. And the pathologist was certain about something else: he really hadn't had much longer to live—a few months at most. His cancer had been far too advanced for any chance of successful treatment.

Hannah's reaction had shocked the police officer. She had burst out in hysterical laughter, and the poor woman had been unable to calm her for several minutes. Hannah hadn't understood it herself. The others probably thought that this information would help reconcile her to Simon's suicide, since she now had proof that he'd been right, that he didn't have much longer to live—and in that respect it had made some sense to cut off a long, agonizing illness with a quick death. After all, everyone had the right in such a case to determine the way they died—at least, that was what Hannah had always believed.

And yet. And yet this news had pulled the rug from beneath Hannah's feet, since it made her gift for Simon, which in hindsight had to be viewed as her farewell gift, look merely cynical and repulsive.

Who was she, Hannah Marx, to have had the hubris to have known better? Oh, the arrogance with which she had brushed aside Simon's fears and worries, actually believing she could help him close his eyes to the facts with her stupid life-is-what-you-make-it diary.

She was ashamed. There was no other way of describing the feeling that had raged inside her since the policewoman's visit except deep, hideous shame.

And even now, as Hannah shook the hands of all those people expressing their sympathy, she couldn't rid herself of it. She felt like a total hypocrite. As though she didn't have the right to be here at all, in mourning as Simon's "widow." She had even falsely identified herself as his fiancée to ensure that the police gave her every bit of information, to make sure she had the right to be kept informed of the progress of the investigation.

Simon's fiancée. Hannah closed her eyes and forced down another sob. She had intended the engagement to happen on May 11, the anniversary of the day they'd met. She had thought it all out so beautifully! Had chosen a pair of engagement rings of beaten silver from a small jeweler on the Eppendorfer Landstrasse and set them aside, telling the manager that someone would come to fetch them.

She had hoped Simon would buy the rings, and had tucked an envelope containing five hundred euros into the pocket of the diary. The jeweler had been quite taken with her romantic plan, and had almost whooped for joy when Hannah had told her to give the purchaser— assuming he collected the rings—an envelope that contained all the further instructions: that Simon should come at eight that evening to Da Riccardo, where Hannah had reserved "their" table for the two of them. And where she had intended to propose to him when he arrived.

But "life is what happens to you while you're busy making other plans." John Lennon had nailed it. There would be no more proposals, at least not from her to Simon. The rings would eventually be bought by someone else; another couple would use them to declare their undying love and fidelity.

Hannah knew she ought to tell the jeweler that no one would be coming to pick up the rings, that they should be put back in the display window and that her engagement to Simon had fallen apart before it had begun. But Hannah simply couldn't bring herself to phone the shop and break off her engagement with such finality. It felt like yet another betrayal, like she'd be trampling on Simon's memory. She consoled herself with the thought that May 11 would come and go, and when no one appeared to collect the rings, the jeweler would simply put them back on sale. What did a few weeks matter? Nothing, compared with the eternity Simon had now entered without Hannah.

"I still can't believe it." Sören, one of Simon's best friends, was standing in front of Hannah offering his hand. He looked like she felt: his eyes red and swollen, dark shadows beneath them.

"Me neither," Hannah said softly. "Me neither."

"Are you managing?" Sören asked.

She shrugged. "What's managing? I have to go on somehow."

"If you need anything, you know where I am, okay?"

"Yes, of course, thanks."

"What are you doing with Simon's apartment? Do you need me to help clear it out?"

"No," she replied. "It'll get done. There's enough money in his account for the rent. There's no hurry."

"Wouldn't it be better for you to get it over with as soon as possible?"

"I . . ." Hannah swallowed with difficulty. She thought of the scene of devastation she had left behind in Simon's apartment. Of course she'd tidy it up, would clear out her boyfriend's things and hand the keys back to the landlord. She'd do it eventually, but the way she felt at the moment, it was enough simply to be able to breathe. "I just can't right now."

"I can understand that," Sören said. "Feel free to give me a call whenever you're ready."

"I will." They hugged, then Hannah turned to the next mourner.

Just under an hour later, Lisa dropped Hannah off outside her apartment in Lokstedt. There had been no reception after the funeral—the very idea of marking Simon's death with even coffee and cake turned

Hannah's stomach. After shaking the hands of the last mourners, she had simply wanted to go home, crawl into her bed, pull the covers over her head, and wait as long as it took for the pain to finally subside. Although she couldn't imagine that it ever would.

"You should go lie down," Lisa said. Hannah had already said she didn't feel like company.

"I will." The two friends looked at each other for a moment in silence, then Lisa leaned forward, took Hannah in her arms, and held her tight.

"I'm so, so sorry," she said softly. "I wish you'd been spared all this."

"So do I."

# 49

*Jonathan*

**Friday, March 16, 2:23 p.m.**

*"La professoressa è nell'aula. Nell'aula ci sono anche gli studenti."*

Frowning with concentration, Jonathan repeated the sentences. He had no idea if he would ever be in a situation where he needed to tell an Italian that not only the teacher but—surprise, surprise!—also the students were in the classroom, but nothing was ever certain.

In any case, the authors of the Italian course he had downloaded to his cell phone must have intended something by it, even if the teacher, students, and classroom were only a device to drum into Jonathan those damned Italian prepositions. *Nel, sul, dal, nella, sulla, dalla*—his head was spinning as he tried to repeat the phrases as correctly as he could. At the same time he wondered whether he would have been better off enrolling in a course at the local college. But the idea of sitting at a row of desks with a bunch of suburban housewives (a cliché, but probably true) hadn't appealed too much, and so when the Filofax suggested, a couple of weeks ago, that he should learn a completely new skill, he had opted for the electronic version.

He hadn't done too badly so far, and had surprised himself with his progress to date. He was already able to ask for a room with a shower (*una camera con doccia*); an ashtray (*un portacenere*), although he didn't smoke; and water with no ice (*un'acqua naturale senza ghiacco*). He could also introduce himself without mishap (*Mi chiamo Jonathan Grief* ) and say where he was from (*Sono di Amburgo in Germania*).

Maybe it was because of his knowledge of the venerable Latin tongue that Jonathan found it relatively easy to get a grasp of Italian—apart from the pesky prepositions, which defied all logic. Maybe his origins gave him an advantage too. Every now and then, he even recognized a phrase or two from his childhood, although his mother had almost always talked to him in German, since his father didn't believe in a bilingual upbringing but was firmly of the opinion that "the boy" should learn "decent German" above all. Whether Sofia's German, which she had learned as an adult, could be considered "decent" was open to question, but she had nevertheless obeyed her husband's instructions.

Only in the evenings, when Jonathan's mother tucked him into bed, had she sat with him for a few minutes and sung him something from her homeland. *Se sei felice tu lo sai, batti le mani.* As he recalled those evenings, he could clearly hear her warm voice in his head. *If you're happy and you know it, clap your hands!*

Jonathan was strangely happy. Not enough to whoop for joy or go around shouting it from the rooftops, but when he thought about how he'd felt during the years since his separation from Tina (or longer, to be precise; things hadn't been right while they were still married), he was feeling much better about life now. He was more satisfied. More balanced. At peace with himself.

Almost. He hadn't made much progress with the business. Jonathan simply didn't know what was the right course for Grief & Son Books. However often he weighed the arguments for a more popular list against those for maintaining the status quo, he remained undecided.

It was not only a matter of the publishing house's reputation and tradition, but a fundamental issue of its economic viability. And he wasn't convinced that all they needed to do to bring their accounts out of the red was to publish a few mainstream titles.

No, such a venture could fall completely flat if the trade and readers refused to accept their change of direction. They could become a laughingstock, have people telling them to stick to what they knew. It could be as though the magnificent Berlin Philharmonic suddenly released an album of show tunes—there would be uproar and indignation on the cultural scene, and rightly so! Jonathan strongly believed that if they went in that direction, it would make it impossible to match their earlier sales figures for more literary projects.

Markus Bode had suggested they simply establish a new imprint, a subsidiary press, for the popular titles. Sweeping aside Jonathan's objection that such a move would be thoroughly hypocritical with an airy "Oh, everyone's doing it!" he had added that it would make sense to test the market before discussing how to proceed from there.

Bode had set to work enthusiastically and asked a number of agents about suitable titles, even though Jonathan hadn't given him a definitive go-ahead. One of the agents had already called Jonathan and asked him in some confusion whether his CEO's email requesting a few "good reads from the 'landscape of love,' 'happy tears,' 'urban fantasy,' and 'cozy crime' subgenres" was correct.

"Oh, there must have been some mistake!" Jonathan had told the agent, thoroughly embarrassed by the mere mention of the subgenres. Cozy crime? What on earth was that, exactly?

"So, should I send you some manuscripts or not?" the agent had asked.

"Um, no, well, yes," Jonathan said, backpedaling in confusion.

"Would you like me to send you something, or not?" he repeated.

"Yes, please do."

"Are you okay?"

"Yes, never better!" He had cleared his throat. "We're just . . . trying out some new ideas. A kind of . . . literary experiment."

"Ah." The agent had paused, somewhat at a loss. "All right, I'll send you and Markus Bode some projects in the next few days."

The "projects" were still lying untouched on Jonathan's desk: five thick manuscripts with such suggestive titles as *In the Golden Glow of the Steppe* and *The Prima Donna Conspiracy*. Even if these works had come from the pen of Hubertus Krull himself, there'd be no taking such titles seriously!

And as if it weren't bad enough, Markus Bode had in a rush of blood bought copies of all the novels jostling for position in the top twenty of hardcover and paperback bestseller lists. Two copies of each, no less.

"So we can both gain a good overview," he had proudly told Jonathan when he called at the villa three weeks ago with two large boxes of books. Jonathan's ineffectual protests—that he still firmly believed they should wait until the end of the fiscal year so they could make a more informed decision about how things stood with the press—had fallen on deaf ears. "It won't do us any harm to read all these—then at least we'll be up to date with the publishing world."

He had taken out one of the books with a grin and passed it to Jonathan. "I can particularly recommend this one to you. It's a wonderfully warmhearted story about a paraplegic man who wants to commit suicide until a young, rather gawky caregiver gives him a new lease on life."

"Um, yes, that does sound wonderfully warmhearted," Jonathan had replied with more than a hint of irony, wondering what had got into Bode. They had always seen eye to eye on literary quality; maybe his separation from his wife had shaken him more than was immediately apparent. While he seemed outwardly the same as always, descriptions like "wonderfully warmhearted" gave more than a little cause for concern.

Jonathan dismissed his thoughts about his CEO's private life and concentrated on the Italian phrases coming from his earphones. It was his ambitious aim to complete the first module by the end of the month, despite a recommended study period of six months, so that he could move on to the advanced lessons. He wasn't too sure what he was going to do with his mother's language, as he had no intention of traveling to Italy—since his parents' divorce, the country had been . . . there was no other way to describe it . . . emotionally contaminated. But it had been his first impulse when the diary urged him to learn a new skill, and he had followed his instincts.

The voice in his ear, telling him to find the right preposition without prompting, was interrupted by a melodic ringing. Jonathan looked at his cell phone; it was two forty-five p.m., and he had set the alarm to remind himself that he had an appointment. At three he had to be at the Lütt Café on Haynstrasse, where he would eat cake until he felt ill. Or a slice of cake, at least.

He switched the alarm off, rose from his armchair, went downstairs, and grabbed his jacket. It was about a ten-minute walk to the café, which meant he'd be there promptly at three—even though it wasn't really a matter of promptness, since the diary only mentioned *in the afternoon*. But in Jonathan's opinion—and, so he believed, that of most people—the afternoon began at three o'clock these days, so he had decided to allow himself a short break from his Italian course to go for a coffee. Jonathan had long since given up hope of finding the diary's owner (if he was honest, he no longer even wanted to), but following the instructions in the Filofax to the letter had become a habit. And why not? There was no harm, and he enjoyed it.

He cheerfully swung the front door open. Although he rarely went for coffee and cake in the afternoon, if for no other reason than to preserve his ideal body-mass index, he was actually looking forward to a little walk in the spring sunshine with a slice of something sweet to round things off. They might even have gooseberry meringue tart at the

Lütt Café. That had been a favorite of Jonathan's since his childhood. His grandmother Emilie had not only a talent for spotting literary genius but also for making an excellent gooseberry tart with heavenly sweet meringue topping.

After his habitual checks that his door was properly locked, and setting the burglar alarm, Jonathan turned with a smile that immediately turned to astonishment.

"Hello, Jonathan."

"I didn't expect to see you here!"

# 50

## *Hannah*

**Friday, March 16, 2:17 p.m.**

"*Happy birthday to you! Happy birthday to yooou!* Wakey, wakey, rise and shine!"

"What's going on?" Dazed and confused, Hannah fought her way out from under her quilt, her eyes watering as she blinked in the daylight. "What's all this noise?"

"Out!" Lisa said. She was standing at the foot of Hannah's bed, grinning mischievously.

"Lisa, please! Go away," Hannah grumbled. She grabbed her duvet and pulled it back over her head.

"Sorry," came the muffled voice of her friend, "but there's no way I'm going to do that!"

"Go away!" Hannah muttered into the sheets, thrashing her legs in annoyance. "And you'd better leave your key here!"

"Noooo," Lisa sang out cheerfully. A second later, Hannah felt a hefty tug that left her exposed, without her protective cocoon.

"Leave it alone!" she yelled as she sat up. A mistake. Her head immediately exploded in staccato stabs of pain; she had moved far too quickly.

"Hangover?" Lisa waved at the empty red-wine bottle at the foot of the bed.

"Terrible," Hannah sighed, scratching her head.

"That's what comes of staying in and celebrating your birthday on your own. Your thirtieth, too!" Lisa leaned forward as if to whisper a secret. "That kind of thing only leads to trouble. And a headache."

"You could hardly call it 'celebrating,'" Hannah replied with a groan, putting a hand to her temple. "I fell more or less straight into a coma last night."

"Yes, that's what it sounded like."

Hannah looked at her in shock. "Did we speak on the phone?"

Lisa nodded. "Yes, we did. Three times."

"Really?"

"Yes, really."

"I can't remember a thing about it." Hannah felt her cheeks turn bright red.

"Nothing to worry about," Lisa said. "You only said the same thing you've been going on about for weeks. Well, it was actually more like mumbling than saying."

"What did I say?"

"That you don't know how you can go on without Simon, that nothing makes any sense, and on top of it all he's a self-centered bastard for killing himself without asking you first. Something along those lines."

"Shit!" Hannah fell back onto the bed with a loud sigh. "I really had hoped that was all a dream and I was just waking up from it."

Lisa sat down beside her on the bed and took her hand. "I'm sorry, my dear, it's all still true."

"Shit," Hannah said again as the tears sprang to her eyes. Every morning had been the same since Simon's death. She woke, a little confused and bewildered by her dreams at first, and then, as she gradually came to her senses, she was filled with this dreadful despair and hopelessness, which tightened like a band of iron around her chest so she could hardly breathe, and refused to let her go until she fell, completely exhausted, into bed late the following night.

Her days had followed the same pattern for two months, and things weren't getting any better. If time really did heal all wounds, it was doing it at a snail's pace that Hannah doubted would bring much relief in her lifetime. On the contrary, the more time went by since Simon's death, the deeper she seemed to sink into this black hole of sadness and rage, and the worse were the nightmares and fears that hounded her.

Her intention of returning to Little Rascals as soon as possible, to dispel all her gloomy thoughts and restore her everyday life, had been abandoned within the first ten minutes of setting foot in the place, when she was suddenly struck by such a massive panic attack that it had pulled the ground from beneath her feet.

She had stood there surrounded by noisy children, unable to move a muscle or utter a word. She'd been frozen by shock, incapable of a single clear thought apart from a few dreadful phrases that played over and over in an endless loop in her head: *We all have to die sometime. Even these children will die sometime; these sweet, innocent little children will be dead sometime. And their children, and theirs, and theirs, and theirs . . . It's all meaningless, meaningless, meaningless! We only live to move toward death. Each day brings us a little nearer to the end.*

Her mother, Sybille, had finally driven the crying and shaking Hannah home, bundled her daughter into bed, and called a doctor, who diagnosed posttraumatic stress disorder and prescribed complete rest. Hannah had followed these instructions—more than that, she had cut herself off completely. She now set foot outside her apartment only when it could no longer be avoided—and a variety of pizza-delivery services and the corner convenience store that delivered the essentials to her door meant this hadn't been for quite some time. She had dug herself in, wanting to be alone with her sadness and her pain.

The evening before had, of course, been particularly awful, for instead of celebrating her special birthday with Simon, she had curled up in her bed weeping, flipping aimlessly through the channels on her bedroom TV, and draining a bottle of wine all by herself.

It was only now, with Lisa sitting next to her, that Hannah could vaguely recall the telephone conversation during which Lisa had used all her powers of persuasion to invite herself over. Hannah declined straight out, saying she didn't want to see anyone, not even on her birthday—but, she now realized, Lisa had simply brushed her order aside.

"I think it's high time you got up, took a shower, and came out with me." Lisa's voice was gentle but firm. "Your parents think the same, if you're at all interested. Sybille's putting in an extra shift at Little Rascals to make sure I've got all the time I need for you."

"But I don't want to go out!"

"Of course you do! The sun's shining. It's a beautiful day."

"The day can't possibly be beautiful," Hannah retorted sulkily, challenging Lisa with her eyes. "Anyway, the doctor said I need complete rest."

"That may be. But I don't think he meant you should mope around the house getting drunk, and"—she leaned forward, reached under the bed, and pulled out two pizza boxes—"eating nothing but this crap." Lisa opened one of the boxes and made a face at the sight of the dried-up pizza remains.

"I'm not!" Hannah snapped, and tore the box from Lisa's hands. As her nostrils caught the scent of old pepperoni, even she had to suppress a shudder. She slid the pizza box back onto the floor to join the empty wine bottle.

"So?" Lisa wheedled. "Please will you get up and take a shower? You don't smell much better than that moldy pizza. I'll wait here until you're ready, then we're going out."

"But I really don't want to."

"I don't care."

"You can't force me."

"Watch me," Lisa replied. "I can."

"How?"

"Easy. I simply stay here and wait until you come with me."

"Good luck with that!" Hannah leaned forward and made to grasp her duvet. Lisa was faster. She tore it from her friend's hands and threw that on the floor too.

"And I'll sing!" She cleared her throat and began. *"Happy birthday to you . . ."*

"Lisa, *please!*" Hannah howled.

Unperturbed, her friend warbled on. *"Happy birthday to yooou!"*

"Stop!" Hannah snapped, putting her fingers in her ears.

*"Happy biiiiirthday, dear Hannah . . ."*

"Lisa, please! Don't torment me anymore!"

She fell silent, a guilty look on her face. "Sorry, I didn't mean to do that."

"It's okay." Hannah realized to her own amazement that she was suppressing a laugh. But she wasn't to be beaten so easily. "You know," she said, "it's not that I *want* to mope around like a recluse. I'm still grieving."

"I understand. But if you want my opinion, two months' grief, 24/7, is more than enough."

"Aren't people supposed to be in mourning for a *year?*"

"True," Lisa agreed. "But only a very few manage twelve whole months."

"Anyone who wants to can."

"Wrong! It's not only about you, you know."

"Oh, really?"

"No. It's high time you started thinking about other people. Your parents, for example. They're worried to death about you. And so am I."

"You've seen me; you know I'm okay," Hannah said in a last plaintive attempt to get her friend to go.

"Okay?" Lisa laughed. "Did you just say 'okay'?" She gestured expansively around the room. "You huddle here in your run-down den that smells like a big cats' cage, looking like you've just emerged from six months' solitary confinement." She shook her head, almost amused. "I'm sorry, but that is completely not okay."

"I'm still alive, aren't I?"

"I'd say in a vegetative state, actually. And as sorry as I am—"

"You're starting to repeat yourself."

"What?"

"You've said you're sorry at least five times."

Lisa grinned. "Well, well. There's still a tiny bit of Hannah lurking inside this stinky creature! Quite hard to find beneath the thick crust of filth, but I know she's somewhere in there."

"Ha ha."

"Yeah." She stood. "So get your hungover self out of this pit." She wagged her index finger. "Otherwise I'll have to start singing again."

"But what about the year's mourning?"

"Put something black on, by all means." Lisa nipped her objection in the bud.

"Okay." Hannah sighed. "I can see I haven't a hope in hell."

"Absolutely right," her friend agreed.

"Where are you dragging me off to?" she asked as she made a move to launch herself from the mattress.

"You should know."

"I haven't the slightest idea."

"You had something planned for today, didn't you?" Lisa reminded her. "We're going to the Lütt Café for coffee and cake."

Hannah stopped midmovement. "I don't think that's a good idea."

"Why not?"

322

"Because I . . . because I . . ." Tears filled her eyes again. "Because I'd planned that for me and Simon. It's our favorite café. And because—"

"Yes, because," Lisa said. "It's time to overcome your demons. That's why it's totally right for the two of us to go to the café."

"You think so?" Hannah sounded like a whiny little girl to her own ears.

"I do."

"But we could go somewhere else."

"We could," Lisa said, "but we're not going to."

# 51

*Jonathan*

"I gave you a bit of a shock, didn't I?" Grinning from ear to ear, Leopold was clearly enjoying the effect of his surprise visit. "You can close your mouth now. You're beginning to look a bit stupid."

"What . . . what are you doing here?"

"I've come to settle my debts."

"Debts? What debts?"

Leopold indicated a box at his feet that contained several bottles.

"Three bottles of red wine, a Riesling, whiskey, gin, and grappa," he said. He looked apologetic. "I'm not sure if they're all the correct brands. I went to the liquor store and asked for the best they had." He shrugged. "I'm afraid I can't remember exactly what I took last time I was here."

"You're crazy!" Jonathan exclaimed.

Leopold lowered his eyes. "Sorry," he muttered. "I know I was totally out of order."

"Don't be stupid!" Jonathan laughed. "I'm delighted to see you! But you didn't have to bring a massive supply of booze with you. There was really no need."

"There was." Leo looked at him again, a cautious smile on his lips. "There was," he repeated. "I had to. I actually owe you more than that, but I thought I'd make a start with the bottles."

The two of them said nothing but smiled at one another for a moment. Jonathan took a determined step toward Leo and hugged him with a hearty clap on the shoulder. He'd never hugged another grown man before, and was surprised how easy he found it.

"So," he said as he released his prodigal friend, "how are things with you? You're looking well." It was true: Leopold was wearing clean jeans, sweatshirt, and jacket; his beard was neatly trimmed, his hair tied back tightly, and he smelled distinctly of soap and Old Spice.

"Not here on the street," Leo said.

"Sorry," Jonathan said hastily. "Where are my manners? Please come in."

"I'm not disturbing you? Weren't you about to go out?"

"It wasn't important," Jonathan said, but corrected himself immediately. "I mean, yes, I was on my way to a café. And it would be lovely if you came with me. You can take all the time in the world to tell me what's been going on in your life since you up and left in the middle of the night."

"It's a deal!" Leopold laughed cheerfully. "You wouldn't believe all that's happened since then!"

# 52

## *Hannah*

"I'm finding it really difficult to go in."

They were standing outside the Lütt Café. Hannah looked doubtfully at the crowd of people sitting around tables behind the large window, chatting and enjoying coffee and cake.

"It's like removing a bandage," Lisa said. "The quicker the better. Just open the door and in we go!"

"I don't know . . ." Hannah indicated a group of laughing women. "When I look at these people I feel like an alien. As though I'd dropped in from another planet."

"Then don't look at the people," Lisa said with a shrug.

"That won't help," Hannah replied. "They'll all be looking at me! Or rather, *staring* at me."

"You're not that exciting."

"I feel like they can all sense a grieving widow from miles off."

"Don't be silly. You look wonderful!" Lisa opened the door and gave Hannah a gentle shove, forcing her friend to take an unwilling step inside.

She stood as if rooted to the spot on the mat.

"What is it now?" Lisa asked as she stumbled into her.

"I knew it," Hannah hissed over her shoulder, indicating with her chin a table on the right-hand side of the café. "Look—over there. He's staring right at me!"

Lisa followed her gaze. "Who?"

"Over there," Hannah whispered, nodding again toward the far-right corner, where two men were sitting at a round table over coffee and cake. One of the two, an older man with long white hair tied back in a ponytail, had his back to them. But the other, a man of around forty, dark haired, slim, good looking, was openly gawking at Hannah.

"Don't be ridiculous," Lisa said. "He's not staring at you."

"He certainly is," Hannah insisted. "He looks as though he's seen a ghost."

"Maybe he's very nearsighted." Lisa gave her another shove into the room.

Hannah turned to her, pleading with her eyes. "Please, let's go. I feel really uncomfortable."

"But—"

"Please!" she repeated. "It's not just that guy over there. I came here so often with Simon—the place is crammed with memories."

Her friend sighed. "If you're going to avoid all the places that are emotionally contaminated because you've been there with Simon, you'll need to move away from Hamburg."

"I know," Hannah replied unhappily. "I'll get my act together, I promise. Just not today! Let's just go for a little walk, okay? That's enough for a start."

"All right," Lisa agreed. "I don't want to torture you."

"Thank you!" With those words, Hannah swung the café door open and hurried out. She could still feel the gaze of the stranger boring into her back, but she didn't turn to look. She had no idea why the guy had stared at her so intently; she knew only that it felt really weird. Even over the several yards' distance between the door and his table, Hannah had noticed his eyes. Such a light, intense blue, out of the ordinary. It was as if with a single glance he had penetrated the depths of her soul. She shook herself as though emerging from some kind of hypnosis and took a deep breath as soon as they were out on the sidewalk.

"Are you okay?" Lisa asked.

"Yes. Fine."

"Excellent. So, where shall we go?"

Hannah thought for a moment. "We could pay a visit to Little Rascals," she suggested. "Maybe our mothers could use a little help."

Lisa looked at her in amazement. "Are you sure?"

Hannah thought again, then nodded. "Yes. Totally sure. I suddenly have a burning desire to be with some lively kids."

Lisa grinned happily. "That sounds more like the old you!"

# 53

*Jonathan*

"That can't be true! You're taking me for a ride, aren't you?"

"Not at all. It was just as I've told you." Leopold leaned back in his chair and stirred his coffee, clearly delighted to have rendered Jonathan speechless with his story.

"Yes, but who on earth would do such a thing?" Jonathan asked again, still unable to believe what he'd just heard. "Who, for God's sake, would park a car right there in the red-light district with the keys in the ignition? And the ownership papers on the seat?"

"I have no idea," Leopold replied. "And to be honest, I don't care. I've simply accepted this nice gift handed to me by fate, and I don't intend to concern myself with the whys and wherefores." He speared a piece of strawberry flan with his fork and pushed it into his mouth.

"What kind of car was it?"

"An old Ford Mustang," Leo replied through a mouthful of flan. "A classic, still in excellent shape."

"A Mustang?"

"Yes."

"Not a red one, by any chance?"

Leopold nodded in surprise. "Yes, a beautiful, gleaming dark red. What makes you ask that?"

"Well, I . . ." Jonathan tried to get his confused thoughts in order. "That's so weird." He tried again. "A few weeks ago, I saw a woman drive up the Reeperbahn in a red Ford Mustang."

"Uh-huh," Leopold said. "So maybe that was our good Lady Bountiful—who knows?"

"What did the documents say? The owner must have been named on them."

"I'm not sure," Leo said.

"How come you're not sure?"

"Well, it's not like I wrote it down. It was a man's name, I can remember that much. Blank, maybe?"

"Blank?"

"Something like that. Stefan Blank, I think."

"Hmm."

"But it doesn't matter in the slightest."

"Didn't you try to track down the owner?"

Leopold looked at him in incomprehension. "Why should I?"

"Well, I just think it would have been the right thing to do. You can't keep a stranger's car!" He couldn't help but think of the diary, which he had in his jacket pocket as he always did, guarding it like a precious treasure. But that was a completely different matter; there was no comparison between a Filofax and an expensive car. And Jonathan had started out by doing all he could to search for the owner.

"I didn't keep it, in any case," Leopold went on. He didn't look quite so casual as he had at the start of the cozy little chat; a deep crease had formed between his eyes.

"You can't just sell a stranger's car either."

"I think you can, if it's handed to you on a plate."

"But—"

"Listen, my friend," Leo interrupted brusquely. "I can understand someone like you having their qualms about it. But if you were in my shoes, you'd clutch at any straw that was handed to you. Wouldn't you?"

Jonathan lowered his eyes in shame and murmured, "I guess so."

"There you are. So that's what I did. If someone parks their car complete with keys and papers in full view of the world on the Reeperbahn, I take that as an invitation for whoever finds it to take it and do what they want with it. Don't you agree?"

"Yes," Jonathan said, looking back up at him.

"I should say so."

"Did you contact the police to check everything was aboveboard?"

Leopold laughed out loud, slapping his hands on his thighs. "The police? Are you crazy?" He snorted with mirth. "What do you think they'd have done with someone like me? They'd have immediately accused me of stealing the car and thrown me in jail." He shook his head with an indulgent smile. "No, of course I didn't go to the cops. I grabbed the car and made sure I got rid of it at the first possible opportunity."

"And how, if I may be so bold, does one get rid of a car like that?"

"Well, you don't take it to the Ford dealer," Leopold said helpfully. "I took it to the Billhorner Brückenstrasse in the Rothenburgsort district. It's a massive commercial strip, one dealer after the next."

"I don't know it."

"That doesn't surprise me. It's full of shady characters. You know— imports and exports, scrap yards that look more like car graveyards except for the colorful flags strung along the chain-link fences."

"Chain-link fences?"

"Let's just say this: someone like you would never go there to buy a car."

"So why did you take the car there?"

Leopold rolled his eyes in mock annoyance. "Because it's the place where I could most easily sell it. No questions asked, cash in hand . . ."

"How much did you get for it?"

Leopold grinned again. "Five thousand euros. And they paid for the two taxi drivers who took me there with the car and then ferried me back into town."

"Two taxi drivers?"

"Well, I haven't really been in a fit state to drive these last few weeks," Leopold said. "Anyway, I don't have a driver's license."

"No?"

"Not anymore. I should have retaken the test, but I've never had enough money." His grin broadened even more. "But I'm a rich man again now."

"I see."

"I can see you're not particularly impressed," Leopold said. "But it's more than enough for me." He ate another morsel of flan.

"Yes, yes," Jonathan hastened to assure him. "It's just that I'm still completely . . . It's such an unbelievable story."

"True enough. I couldn't believe it myself at first. But that's exactly how it was. And whatever you think, this unexpected gift saved my ass."

"What did you do with the money?"

"Invested it in shares."

"Really? Which ones?"

Leopold roared with laughter, so loudly that some people in the café turned and looked at him with disapproval. This was not the kind of behavior they expected in Eppendorf.

"Of course I didn't buy any shares!" Leo continued in a lower voice. "First of all, I headed back to the red-light district. I had no idea where I was going, really. I talked to a couple of buddies there, and they said we could use the cash to get totally tanked up." His face turned serious again. "But then, thank God, I saw the light. I told myself that fate was offering me a second chance, and I shouldn't mess it up again." He paused for another mouthful, although Jonathan suspected he was merely ramping up the suspense.

"And then?" he asked, to indulge Leopold.

"I rented a room in a cheap motel for five days and spent the time sobering up," he continued. "It wasn't much fun getting back on the rails by myself, but there was no way I wanted to return to the clinic. The last time, I left with a few choice words. 'You won't see me here again anytime soon,' or some such. So you can understand I didn't want to go crawling back."

"Did you manage it?"

"Just look at me." Leopold put a hand to the collar of his clean shirt. "I've never had it so good."

"I'm really glad to hear it. So you'll be retaking your driving test now?"

"No." Leopold gestured dismissively. "It's not important. I went to look at a little one-bedroom apartment in Barmbek, and because I could put down the first three months' rent on the spot, I got it." He sighed. "I was able to . . . What do they call it? 'Break the vicious circle of homelessness,' because once I've got a place to live, I can get social security. I even get my rent paid. And I've still got a bit left over from selling the Mustang."

"Freeloader!" Jonathan joked.

"Fat cat!" Leopold retorted. "Anyway, I just have to find a job now, and that should keep me off the streets once and for all."

"Are you looking?"

"Yes. But it's not so easy, even for a chef." He gave a crooked smile. "No one's actively searching for a fifty-four-year-old, and there are one or two unexplained gaps in my résumé. You wouldn't believe it, but having been on a board of directors isn't particularly helpful—no one believes I'm going to want to stand at a stove all day."

"Have you been to the employment office?"

"Of course," Leopold said. "If nothing else, to apply for my benefits. But they haven't found me anything yet." He laughed. "Well, they did offer me something."

"Not what you wanted?"

"It was a sports bar. It didn't seem quite the right thing for me to be serving alcohol."

"Hardly," Jonathan agreed and laughed too. "I wish I could help you," he added. "But we don't do catering at Grief & Son. And I'm afraid we deal in literature, not food."

"Selling things is the same, whatever the product," Leopold said.

"Well . . . um . . . ," Jonathan stammered, not knowing what to say. Did Leopold really mean it?

"Don't worry, I'm not asking you for work. I've realized that life in the fast lane isn't for me; I'm looking for something a bit more relaxed. I've got plenty of time to look—I'm doing nicely on my welfare payments and housing benefit."

"I'll let you know if I hear of anything."

"Please do," Leopold replied in a tone of voice that said, "And where do you think *you're* going to hear of anything?" He changed the subject. "I've rambled on enough. Tell me what's been going on in your life."

"Quite a lot," Jonathan said proudly. "I took your advice to heart: I've been running my life according to what the diary tells me."

"How's it going?"

"Wonderfully!" He began to count off on his fingers. "I've given up jogging and started playing tennis, I meditate every day, and every morning and evening I write down all the things I'm grateful for. During the last two months I've been to the coast more times than in the whole of the last five years, I've started singing again—even if it's only in the car and the shower—and I've been learning Italian."

"Wow! It sounds like you're keeping busy."

"It's fine. I'm doing most of it in my spare time."

"And how's the publishing industry?"

"Going well," Jonathan replied evasively.

"So everything's back in the black?"

"Not quite yet." It was Jonathan's turn to put a large piece of flan in his mouth.

"You haven't made any changes, then," Leopold said.

"I'm on the case."

"Hmm."

"What do you mean, 'hmm'?"

Leopold waved a hand. "Let's move on, before I step on your toes again. I think this calls for another slice."

"Excellent idea!" Jonathan was about to stand when his eyes fell on the door, and on the two women who had just come through it. One of them was tall and slim, with red hair; the other was a head shorter, with a curvaceous figure and a tousled short haircut.

Jonathan N. Grief felt as though someone had bashed him over the head.

Or like a firework had been lit inside him and was about to explode.

As if he were four years old again and was about to find the longed-for Carrera racetrack set beneath the Christmas tree.

Or his mother was about to take him in her arms and gently whisper "Nicolino" in his ear.

However absurd it sounded, he, Jonathan N. Grief, knew he was in love. And he had no idea who with.

For no sooner had this incredibly beautiful red-haired woman appeared in the café than she was gone again, sweeping out through the door and vanishing from view. In a reflexive action, Jonathan had risen a few inches from his chair and was about to push the table aside to run after the woman when Leopold's voice brought him back to reality.

"Hello? What's the matter?"

"I'm sorry?"

"You look like you've seen a ghost."

"Um," he stammered, "uh, no, um, it's nothing." He continued to stare at the door.

Leopold turned. "Who's there?"

"No one," Jonathan said quickly. "I just thought I recognized someone."

"And that's why you've gone as white as a sheet?"

"Have I?"

"Chalky white."

"Oh." Jonathan hesitated a moment longer, then pushed his way out from behind the table, almost knocking it over, and rushed to the door. He didn't care whether or not it was the right thing to do; if he'd learned anything in the past few weeks, it was to say yes. And that was why, even if it meant making a fool of himself, he simply had to find out who this woman was.

Under the astonished gazes of the café patrons, Jonathan tore open the door and stepped out onto the sidewalk. He looked left—nothing. And right—nothing. His heart racing, he ran to the nearest corner, but there was no sign of the red-haired woman. He hurried to the other end of the street. Also fruitless.

Slowly, he went back to the café but lingered outside for a few minutes in the wild hope that she might return.

She didn't.

The door opened behind him after a while, and he heard Leopold's voice.

"Are you coming back in? Or are you trying to make yourself scarce before the bill comes? There's no need—this is my treat."

Although he really didn't feel like it, Jonathan found himself laughing.

"What's up?" Leopold asked as they sat back down at the table and Jonathan stared into space. "I could do with a laugh."

"It's absurd," Jonathan said, breathing heavily.

"What is?"

"I've fallen in love."

"In love?"

"Yes." He nodded. "I've got it bad."

"I don't think I'm getting you. You've fallen in love? Just now, or what?"

"Yes. A woman came in here. I just looked at her and something went *boom*."

"Really?"

"Yes, really. Boom, bang-a-bang."

"Which woman?" Leopold turned, craned his neck, and looked around the café.

"That's the problem." Jonathan laughed again. "She went straight back out and disappeared from the face of the earth. I couldn't see her anywhere."

"Shit."

"Indeed."

"Does this happen to you often?"

"What?"

"You know, this love-at-first-sight thing."

Jonathan laughed. "No, never before! I don't even believe in it." He shook his head at himself. "But this woman . . . There was something about her. Oh, I don't know. It sounds completely crazy."

"I like crazy stories."

"I don't. At least, I didn't . . ." He paused and looked wide-eyed at Leopold.

"What's up now?"

"Sarasvati!"

"What does the psychic have to do with it?"

"Life adviser," Jonathan corrected.

"Whatever. What made you think of her?"

"She said that sometime this year I'd meet a woman I might even marry."

"And you seriously believe it? And that this was the one?"

"No idea." Jonathan shrugged. "I don't know what to believe anymore. But this much is clear: my life's been turned upside down since I found that diary." He brightened suddenly. "Wait. I have an idea!"

"And that would be?"

"The diary! That's it! It's all connected. The diary, this café, the woman I've just seen—it's all connected."

"I've no idea what you're talking about."

"Okay, slowly, from the top: Why are we sitting here?"

"Um . . ." Leopold looked at him in confusion. "Because we came here together?"

"Wrong!"

"Wrong?"

"We're here because it was set down in the Filofax. Whoever wrote that, it's his or her birthday and they wanted to celebrate it here."

"Sorry, but I'm still not getting it. What are you trying to tell me?"

"It's simple!" Jonathan jumped up from his chair. "I'll simply ask everyone here if it happens to be their birthday."

"How's that going to help you?"

"Process of elimination! If there's no one here whose birthday it is, then the woman I've just seen could be the one!"

"The one what?"

"For one thing, the one whose birthday it is—the *H* in the diary. And also, she could be the one who wrote the diary." Jonathan was delighted with his clever deduction.

"Jonathan?"

"Yes?"

"You're talking bullshit."

"I don't care," he replied with a laugh. "I don't give a damn."

"Just let me get this straight: so you're saying that if no one here is celebrating their birthday today, it could be that the woman you've just fallen head over heels in love with is also the author of the diary."

"You got it!"

"But even if it is her, it doesn't get you anywhere. You don't have any idea who the diary belongs to."

"Exactly."

Leopold sighed. "Then I don't understand how you think it will help you find the woman."

"Neither do I," Jonathan admitted, still smiling. "I'll cross that bridge when I come to it."

"I'm sure you will."

# 54

*Hannah*

"Hannah! Hannah! Hannah!" No sooner had Hannah entered Little Rascals than four little kids stormed up to her and wrapped themselves around her legs.

"Hey, careful! You're going to knock me over!" Hannah realized she was fighting back tears. Apart from that one attempt, when she'd abruptly left after only a few minutes, she hadn't been here for three months. That was an eternity for little children—at their age it must feel like ten years. Yet here she was getting such a warm welcome from her tiny charges, as though she were the most important person on earth.

Her wildly churning emotions included shame. She had simply abandoned these children, who'd become so attached to her in such a short space of time. Left them and hidden away in her apartment to wallow in self-pity, forgetting what really mattered in life. And what really mattered was the joy and happiness these children gave her on a daily basis—and which it seemed she had also given them in return! Yes, Simon had rejected such joys, but that didn't give her the right to do the same to the people who were important to her.

Before Hannah could lose herself in a sea of self-reproach, a pair of arms suddenly caught her from behind and held her tight. Now it was impossible to prevent a tear escaping. She knew who it was without turning.

"Mama!" She did turn, of course.

"Darling." Her mother's voice trembled as she gently touched her hand to her daughter's cheek. "I'm so pleased to see you here!"

"I know—you simply couldn't handle the little terrors without me." Hannah's attempt at a joke was swallowed by the cracks in her voice. It took a huge effort to prevent herself from breaking out in uncontrolled weeping in front of the children, who were watching the scene intently. Sybille, normally the embodiment of vitality and joie de vivre, looked as worn out as Hannah felt. Her red hair, which her daughter had inherited, looked lifeless and seemed to be threaded with far more gray than Hannah remembered. Her skin was pale and wan, her light-green eyes devoid of their usual shine. Hannah once again felt a pang of shame—was this her doing?

Her mother drew her close again. "It's all going to be better from now on," she whispered.

"Yes, it will," Hannah replied, her voice also a whisper. She drew back from her mother and smiled bravely. "After all, it's my birthday today!"

And at that moment, she decided that was exactly how it would be: Today was her birthday. Her second birthday. The start of her post-Simon life. She wouldn't allow it to be anything less.

# 55

*Jonathan*

"Well," Leopold said two hours later. "Looks like we've reached the bridge. How are we going to get to the other side?"

He and Jonathan had asked everyone in the Lütt Café whether they happened to be celebrating a birthday. They had even pestered the staff, asking if anyone had reserved a table in honor of a birthday coffee. They had then taken up a position by the door, pouncing on each person who entered and asking their date of birth. Negative, negative, always negative.

Now they were sitting outside on a bench by the Isebek Canal, having been asked by the café's owner—politely at first, then half an hour later somewhat more forcefully—to stop bothering the customers. He'd let them have their coffee and cakes on the house—anything to get them out of there. Jonathan had begun to protest and assert his citizen's rights, but Leopold had grabbed his sleeve and dragged him out with a hissed "The owner's rights are what count here, idiot!"

"At least we can be sure now that it's probably the red-haired woman who has her birthday today, and she's probably also the owner of the diary," Jonathan said.

"Great! As I said, we've reached the bridge now. All you have to do is tell me how we're going to cross it."

"No idea," Jonathan admitted. "But I just have to find her!"

"My God, you sound like Romeo."

"That's exactly how I feel."

"Then you should know what kind of an ending to expect. In case you don't know the play: it's not a happy one. So forget the redhead and find someone else to fall in love with."

"You don't understand!"

Leopold raised his hands. "Oh, I'm terribly sorry, Herr Grief! Of course, someone like me would have no idea what love is. I'm just a stupid old hobo."

"I didn't mean it like that. But only a few weeks ago I was firmly convinced that fate and destiny and all that stuff were complete nonsense, and now—"

"And now you believe that a woman you've seen from a distance for all of five seconds is the one for you?"

"Oh, I don't know." He sighed. "I'm all over the place. My thoughts are playing ping-pong in my head. I've never felt like this before in my life."

"You're lucky. I feel like that most of the time."

"Very funny."

"True, though."

"Hmm. When my mother disappeared, I felt something similar." He sighed again. "It seems like all the women who are important to me simply vanish into thin air."

"Come on, let's not get carried away. Okay, so you've fallen head over heels in love. But you can't start calling her 'important' to you just yet."

"I guess you're right." Jonathan stared at his shoes to avoid looking at Leopold. He felt like a twelve-year-old schoolboy after a disastrous math test.

"Why did your mother clear off into the sunset?"

"She never felt right in Hamburg and wanted to go back home to Italy."

"People don't leave their children for a reason like that!"

"'People' might not—my mother did."

"And you haven't seen or heard from her since?"

"During the first few years. She came to visit, and I stayed with her in Italy a few times. But then . . ."

"What?"

"Oh, when I was thirteen I sent her an idiotic card that took her from me once and for all. You could call it teenage angst."

"And there was nothing after that?"

"Total silence," Jonathan said. "I never heard a thing more from her."

"I'm sorry, but I can't imagine a stupid postcard from an even more stupid teenager could have such a catastrophic effect."

"Hmm." Jonathan shrugged. "I've often wondered about it. But eventually I stopped really caring."

"What did your father have to say?"

"My father?" Jonathan laughed derisively. "You don't know him. He said absolutely nothing, never even mentioned her name until recently. Now that he's suffering from dementia, he talks about her often. He even thinks his former assistant is my mother." He looked up and gave Leopold a crooked grin.

"Sounds like a classic dysfunctional family to me."

"You should know," Jonathan fired back. "What about your kids? Are you in contact with them?"

"I'm afraid not. Though not because I don't want to be."

"But?"

"Because I'm not allowed to."

"Oh."

"An injunction. Another consequence of my career as a drunk. I lost it once too often." He balled his fists. "But I swear to you, as soon as I have my feet back on firm ground, I'm going to fight for my rights, so I can be a proper papa to them again."

"Um, excuse me, but aren't they adults by now?"

"No," Leopold replied. "Tim's thirteen, Sarah fifteen. And before your eyebrows disappear from the top of your head, yes, I was a father late in life."

"At least you *are* a father," Jonathan replied grimly.

"You still could be."

"Hmph."

"It's true. There must be someone ready to snap up a filthy-rich eligible bachelor with a villa by Innocentia Park and his own publishing house."

"Let's leave the publishing house out of this."

"Okay. So, back to women. What happened with your ex-wife?"

"What do you mean, 'what happened'?"

"You just said that all the women who were important to you simply vanished into thin air. Did she disappear too?"

"Tina? No, she's still around, happy and in the best of health with her second husband and their daughter. She sends me a New Year's card every January first."

"How nice of her."

"Isn't it? If we forget the fact that her second husband, Thomas, used to be my best friend. Personally, I think her attentions are more the result of a guilty conscience."

"So what's Tina to you now?"

"What do you mean?"

"Well, seeing as you've only just mentioned her, and only after I asked, she hardly seems to be among your 'important' women."

"Of course she is!"

"You sure?"

"I was married to her, wasn't I?"

"You're the owner of a publishing house, but you're not really interested in that."

"Honestly!" Jonathan jumped up from the bench. "I think you're taking this all a bit far!"

Leopold smiled innocently. "If it's true, it hits home."

"I . . . I . . . I . . ." Words failed him.

"Come on, sit back down, idiot."

Jonathan N. Grief sat down, although he really couldn't explain why he didn't just leave without another word.

"Now, then, scout's honor," Leopold continued. "Did you love Tina? Really and truly, from the bottom of your heart?"

"Yes!"

Leopold looked at him wordlessly, that provocative innocent smile still on his lips.

"Well, I was very fond of her."

"Fond of her?" Leopold slapped his thighs. "You're telling me you were *fond* of your wife? And then you wonder why she ran off with another man?"

"Things were good between us."

"Obviously not as good as you thought."

Jonathan thought for a moment. "Maybe," he conceded eventually. His anger returned. "But regardless of that, to fool around with my best friend was the worst! It broke my heart."

"Oh? It wouldn't have hurt so much if it had been someone different?"

"Of course not!"

"Well, it's not so bad, then."

"What do you mean, 'it's not so bad'?"

"This whole business. You're suffering not from a broken heart but a bruised ego. That's much easier to deal with. All you need is willpower."

"Thank you for the psychoanalysis!"

"You're welcome, Herr Grief."

They sat in silence on the bench for a while longer, looking out over the water. Each stubbornly refused to say a word.

A paddle steamer full of day-trippers chugged down the Isebek Canal. Jonathan and Leopold watched it go by. Two rowboats, a kayak, and a paddleboat passed them; neither man commented. It was only when Jonathan saw a swan making its way along the bank that he cleared his throat.

"You're right," he said quietly. "I didn't really love her. And that's probably the reason she left. It seems that it's her leaving me for Thomas that pained me the most."

"You see!" Leopold clapped him on the shoulder. "It wasn't so hard, was it?"

"It was cheaper than my life coach, anyway."

"Your what?"

"Doesn't matter." Jonathan waved dismissively. "Anyway, if I compare how I felt earlier—when I saw that woman—with when I first met Tina, it's . . . it's the difference between day and night."

"Okay. Then we have to find her."

"That would be too good to be true."

"If you ask me, we have two options."

"Which are?"

"Either we hang around the Lütt Café for as long as it takes until she turns up there again. That is, provided the owner doesn't take out an injunction forbidding us from going within fifty yards of the place."

"Or?"

"Or we follow your theory, that it's all somehow related to the diary. We can search it for more clues."

"I far prefer the second option."

"Have you got it with you?"

"Of course." Jonathan reached into his pocket and took out the Filofax.

Leopold opened it. "Look, this is great!" he said enthusiastically. "*This evening, we're going for a crawl through the red-light district, having a night on the town until six in the morning. At dawn, we'll get ourselves a prawn sandwich at the fish market.* A wonderful idea, as ever!"

"Excellent. Staggering up and down the Reeperbahn along with a million other people is my ideal way of spending an evening. You'll have a blast with a mineral water and slice of lemon, and I'm bound to find the red-haired woman in the seething crowds at Hans Albers Square. Unfortunately, I won't be falling at her feet at the end, because there's nothing I hate more in this world than prawns." He peered at the open page. "Anyway, my friend, you're looking at the entry for September 22. That's hardly the day after tomorrow."

"Careful—sense of humor failure!"

"Have a look at a closer date."

"I'm on it."

Leopold leafed back to March 16, and they slowly worked their way forward, heads bent over the book. Every so often, Leopold laughed out loud at an entry that particularly appealed to him.

"Look here. This fits you like a glove: *Watch your thoughts; they become words. Watch your words; they become deeds. Watch your deeds; they become habits. Watch your habits; they become your character. Watch your character, for it becomes your destiny.* From the Talmud, or so it says here."

"And how is that relevant to me?"

"Think about it!"

"I have, and I can't say it's any clearer."

"Who said 'Hmph' when I suggested you could still become a father?"

"And who was the vagrant who ran off in the middle of the night a few weeks ago with a bunch of bottles?" Jonathan retorted indignantly.

"With the emphasis on 'was.'"

"Let's find something else," Jonathan said before they could descend into another argument.

They had now left April behind—including the particularly morbid instruction on April 1 to write their own funeral eulogy, which Jonathan took for an April Fool's joke, while Leopold thought it an excellent idea.

"Think about it," he said again, "All the things you'd especially want to hear at your own funeral! How do you want to have lived, what do you want to have done? What do you regret not having done?"

"Not throwing you into the Isebek Canal," Jonathan replied through gritted teeth. "Turn the page, will you?"

And then, at last! Finally, finally, finally, they came up with something useful. A specific instruction on May 11:

*"Go to the shop at Eppendorfer Landstrasse 28c,"* Jonathan read with excitement. *"Something will be waiting for you there. If you pick it up, you'll get something else as well."*

"I wonder what that means?"

"We'll soon find out! We're going there now. It's just around the corner."

"But it's not May 11 yet!" Leopold objected.

"You sound like the old Jonathan."

"Huh?"

"The new Jonathan doesn't care about such things anymore." He stood and strode off. Leopold followed, matching Jonathan's purposeful gait only with difficulty.

Ten minutes later, they reached Eppendorfer Landstrasse 28c. They saw with surprise that it was a small jewelry store. They also saw that the store had closed at six; they were seven minutes too late.

"What bad luck!" Jonathan said as he looked for a doorbell. Finding none, he knocked hard on the display window.

"What are you doing?"

"Someone might still be there."

"Yes," said Leopold. "The alarm system. And you'll set it off if you keep bashing at the window like that."

Jonathan lowered his hand. "You're right. Even the new Jonathan wouldn't want to risk that. Let's come back tomorrow."

"That wouldn't do any good." Leopold indicated the sign on the door. "They're closed on Saturdays, and won't be open again until Monday at ten."

"Damn!"

"Doesn't matter," Leopold said matter-of-factly. "If we're talking about the woman you want to spend the rest of your life with, a couple of days won't make any difference."

"Ha ha."

"I can't help wondering what's been left here for you. A pair of cuff links?"

"You're forgetting that it wasn't actually intended for me."

"True again. A pair of elegant diamanté earrings, perhaps? I imagine you'd look rather fetching in those."

"This doesn't seem like that kind of place."

They looked at the display, which consisted of a variety of hammered gold and silver pieces. Small signs stated that they were handmade, each one unique. Jonathan didn't have much idea about jewelry, but he liked them. They were tasteful and refined, not at all the kind of showy bling found in the expensive city-center shops. At the same time, he had to admit (through clenched teeth) that he had often bought such flashy trinkets for Tina in the past. Or sent Renate Krug to buy them.

Tina had given back the jewelry after their divorce, saying she'd never particularly liked the stuff anyway. Well, Jonathan thought cynically, she was saved from such tasteless impositions now, since Thomas probably showered her with plastic imitations from gumball machines.

*Get your act together!* he told himself. He thought he'd at last put all that behind him on the bench by the Isebek Canal, leaving himself well balanced and at peace as he considered his new life and the realization that his divorce was more a matter of wounded pride than a broken heart.

"So, what shall we do now?" Leopold asked.

"I'd say we should go home. And I'll be back here, waiting on the doorstep, at ten o'clock on the dot."

"Oh, rats!"

"Why rats?"

"I can't come with you then; I've got an appointment at the employment office."

"What a pity."

"No need to be sarcastic!"

"I don't do sarcasm."

# 56

## *Hannah*

Mondays are the best days on which to start something new. A diet, for example, or a fitness regimen. Clearing out the house and doing a really thorough declutter—that's what Mondays are good for. Even separations are easier to take on Mondays, when a fresh start to a pristine week lifts the spirits. Hannah certainly believed so, anyway. In the best of all possible worlds, the Monday would coincide with the first of a month, but as she didn't live in the best of all possible worlds, the nineteenth would have to do.

She unlocked the door to Simon's apartment and took a deep breath before going in. Hannah hadn't set foot in there since her outburst, and she was terrified of what she was going to see. If she had found it impossible to swallow a morsel of cake in the Lütt Café last Friday, it was hard to imagine how she would finish the task that now faced her. But she was at least going to try. She couldn't give in just yet.

Lisa, Hannah's parents, and Sören had repeated their offers to come help her, but she had declined each of them. For one thing, both her mother and Lisa were needed at Little Rascals, to allow Hannah this final day's absence. And even if they weren't, she needed to do this on her own—her own private catharsis for her and her alone.

In the hallway of the apartment, Hannah busied herself putting together the four moving boxes she'd brought. She had allocated three hours in which to pack up everything of Simon's she wanted to keep and store in her basement for the time being. She had booked a company to come at noon and remove all the furniture, clothes, books, CDs, and anything else that was still here, and to clean the apartment from top to bottom. The following day, Hannah would hand the keys back to the landlord, and the matter would be over and done with. Simon's life tied up once and for all.

She took another deep breath. She was about to take a difficult step, but it was an essential one if she was to continue with her own life. Close her eyes and leap—there was nothing else for it.

Before examining the contents of the drawers and cupboards, she started by cleaning up the aftermath of her wanton destruction. The kitchen was the worst hit. She swept up pasta, cornflakes, oats, loose-leaf tea, sugar, salt, and flour; wiped up the preserves from the floor; and piled it all in a large garbage bag. The espresso machine hadn't survived its ordeal; it went in the trash, together with the two broken tiles.

Hannah gathered up all the broken objects in the living room, noticing to her surprise that the TV was still unscathed. She took the photo of herself and Simon from its smashed frame and stowed it in her pocket. She wanted to keep that, if nothing else.

After thoroughly cleaning up, Hannah took the first packing box into the bedroom. She opened Simon's wardrobe and looked at his pants, T-shirts, sweaters, shirts, and suits. The familiar smell was almost too much, and she briefly closed her eyes before closing the closet doors with a determined thump. She didn't need any of it; she'd never wear a single T-shirt that would remind her of Simon. If she clutched it at night, weeping, like a child hugging her teddy bear, it would only open up the wounds again and again. And Simon's scent would soon be gone—she couldn't bear to think of that.

Hannah looked around the room. She didn't pack a thing, not even her own nightgown, which was tucked away in the top drawer of the narrow chest on the left, nor the large canvas print of Simon and her that hung over the bed. What did she want with that? She had the little photo of the two of them; a larger-than-life portrait at home would be too like a shrine to his memory. Maybe the canvas would be useful if she wanted to paint over it sometime. Or maybe not. She really didn't care.

Hannah found nothing she wanted in the bathroom, kitchen, or living room either. She had no need for a Bang & Olufsen stereo system, or Simon's extensive collection of British singer-songwriter CDs, from which he had often enjoyed playing her selected gems. No, Simon's music brought back such painful memories that a brief glance at the jewel cases was enough to reduce her to tears.

All that remained was the study. She took his laptop; maybe it contained files, photos, and emails she could use later. The recollection of Simon's password, which he had revealed to her in a not entirely sober but extremely sentimental moment, made her laugh, then immediately cry: IlHMu2099. *I love Hannah Marx until 2099.* "At least," he'd added with a wink. Well, that love hadn't lasted quite so long; his life, or rather his death, had got in the way.

Hannah searched around the desk. Like everything else of Simon's, it was neat as a new pin. The top was bare except for a hole punch, a small stapler, five pencils, and a pair of letter trays. Hannah gathered up the mail and put it in a box. She'd look through it later for anything important that needed dealing with. She opened the top drawer of the wheeled unit beneath the desk. It contained nothing but miscellaneous office supplies—staples, marker pens, Post-its, highlighters, a pair of scissors—nothing she wanted to keep.

In the next drawer, she found a thick binder in which Simon had filed away all his articles, neatly stowed in plastic sleeves. There were so many that they overflowed into the second binder beneath it. His life's work, neatly preserved. She hadn't the heart to throw it away, so she put it in the box with Simon's mail.

In the bottom drawer she discovered something that took her breath away. A white sheet of paper. On it was printed, in bold block letters:

## HANNAH'S LAUGH

Her hand shook as she reached for it. Only when she started to pick it up did she realize that it was the first page of a thick sheaf of paper. It took both hands to free the pile from the drawer. She set it on the desk and sat down to read it.

Another sob caught in her throat as she read the text on the second page:

*For my beloved Hannah, who has such belief in me.*

*Here it is, my first novel.*

A novel? Simon had written a novel? Why had he never told her? Why had he only talked about writing it someday, as though he hadn't even begun it—and now here was this thick manuscript?

A footnote, bottom right, caught her eye; next to the copyright note *by Simon Klamm* was a date. Four years ago! The book was almost four years old, so he must have written it shortly after they met, in a frenzy, since there were more than three hundred pages.

It made it all the more puzzling that he'd never said a word about it. Didn't he think it was any good? Was he embarrassed by it? Had he wanted to find a publisher first and then surprise her with it?

Whatever the reason for this well-kept secret, Hannah turned over to the next page and began to read.

*When couples are asked how they met, the stories are usually unspectacular. They sat next to one another on a bus. They reached for the last pepperoni pizza on the frozen-food shelf at the same time. They had shared an office for three whole years before they felt a spark, or they bumped into one another at a party, spilling a glass of red wine.*

*And if you go on to ask what attracted them to one another, you hear things like "He had such incredibly beautiful hands" or "She looked stunning in her summer dress" or "We kept discovering how much we had in common."*

*It was no different between me and Hannah. We met for the first time when I went to pick up my godson from the daycare where she worked. Not particularly spectacular—not to an outside observer, in any case. But for me, the moment I saw her, a whole new universe opened up before me. It wasn't her red hair, her wonderful green eyes, or her pretty face that changed my life so completely. No, it was none of those. It was her laugh.*

*A laugh I can hardly describe. If I were to try, the best I could do would be to ask you to imagine someone who radiates so much love, warmth, and happiness that they want to embrace the whole world—and are able to do so. There you have it. That is Hannah's laugh.*

Hannah read and read and read, flying through the pages. She couldn't comprehend why Simon had kept his book from her. And as she kept laughing or crying out loud at the novel's frequent surprising twists and turns (for although it started with their own story, Simon had soon departed from reality and written himself into a fantasy world), as her enjoyment occasionally turned to anger when he described Hannah as impertinent and egocentric, as she was once again moved at his thinly disguised portrayal of his mother's death—as all these emotions bubbled up inside her, she felt one thing above all others: pride. She was proud of Simon, of what he had created. Of the fact that he had achieved his dream of becoming a writer, regardless of whether the book was published. And at the same time, Hannah was incredibly sad that she had only found out about it now, after his death.

It was a little after five o'clock by the time she read the last page. She was now sitting on the floor in Simon's empty living room, because the movers had come and gone in the meantime.

Three young men had taken everything around her, throwing her one or two looks of irritation because Hannah didn't move from the corner where she was huddled up with two large boxes, completely absorbed in the manuscript. She didn't care what they thought of her; Simon's novel had her completely under its spell.

She thought it was good. She thought it was *really* good. Not only because Simon had written it and it was partly about him and her. But because . . . because she simply thought it was really good.

She read the last sentence, indignant and laughing through her tears. It read: *Yes, I will!* That damned suicide had finished his book with him asking her to marry him! So much for fiction and reality.

Lost in thought, she put the manuscript aside and wondered what to do with it. Tuck it away with the rest into one of the boxes, store it in her basement, and recall with a sigh every so often that Simon had written this lovely story? Burn it in a ritual bonfire? Or maybe she should submit it to a publisher? Would she be legally or morally entitled to do that? It seemed that Simon hadn't wanted to publish it, since he had simply shoved it into a drawer and not even mentioned it to Hannah.

She had no idea what to do.

But there was one thing she would do right away. She had now more or less been given her marriage proposal. It was only fair that she should release the rings she had reserved.

Hannah picked up her cell phone, Googled the number of the jeweler on Eppendorfer Landstrasse, and dialed. The jeweler answered promptly.

"Bernadette Carlsen."

"Hello, Bernadette. Hannah Marx here."

"Oh, hello!" the jeweler said in delight. "You've heard, then?"

"Um, heard what?"

"You know—that it all worked out." She laughed. "I'm so happy for you."

"I'm sorry, I'm not getting you at all. What do you mean?"

"What do you think I mean?" Bernadette Carlsen replied, sounding amused. "Your boyfriend came here this morning and bought the rings! He didn't hesitate for one second when I showed them to him, but simply went for it. I gave him the envelope as well."

"What?" Hannah's head was spinning. "It can't be!"

"I did wonder myself, since you'd said he'd be coming on May 11. But he said his curiosity had been so aroused that he just couldn't wait until then."

"But it can't be true!" Hannah said, more loudly than she'd intended.

"Um . . ." The voice on the other end was more hesitant now. "Did I do something wrong? Shouldn't I have given him the rings and the letter—should I have made him wait until May 11? I'm sorry, I didn't think—"

"It can't be true," Hannah interrupted, "because my boyfriend's dead."

Bernadette Carlsen said nothing.

"He died, you see?" Hannah continued, a little calmer now. "That's why it's impossible that he came to buy the rings."

"I don't understand."

"Neither do I," Hannah said. "I called to tell you that there was no need for you to reserve the rings anymore."

"Yes, but . . ." She paused. "So who was the man who came into my shop earlier?"

"That's what I'd like to know! Did you ask his name?"

"No, of course I didn't. I simply assumed he was your boyfriend. He had the diary with him and even showed me the entry. It all seemed so straightforward."

"What did he look like?"

"Hmm, good looking, if you ask me. Tall, dark hair, a touch of gray here and there, late thirties or early forties. And he had extremely blue eyes—they were striking."

"Okay," Hannah said. "That fits."

"Fits what?"

"Doesn't matter."

"So you don't mind that I sold him the rings?"

"No, not at all."

"I'm relieved to hear it." She took a deep breath. "And I'm so terribly sorry to hear about your boyfriend. I don't know what to say."

"Don't worry," Hannah said. "There's nothing anyone can say."

"Then, um . . ." Bernadette Carlsen's embarrassment was clear.

"Please don't worry about it. I mean it."

"Okay, then I hope you . . . well, that you're okay."

"Thank you very much."

They said goodbye and hung up. Hannah stayed slumped on the floor, staring into space. What was going on here? She had just discovered not only that Simon had written a novel ages ago and kept it secret from her, but also that some guy was wandering around with the Filofax, following the entries.

Bernadette Carlsen's description fit with that of the "customer" who had visited Sarasvati. And it also matched the description of the man in the Lütt Café last Friday—on a day and at a time that were also noted in the diary—who had stared at Hannah so intensely that it made her feel strange. It must have been him; she was sure of it.

It couldn't be merely a series of coincidences—that was impossible. Something was going on here! Even if it wouldn't bring Simon back, Hannah was determined to do everything she could to find out who it was.

Fine. This man was living Simon's "perfect year," and Hannah hadn't the slightest clue who he was. One thing she did know. Or two, to be precise. First, he had not only the diary but now also the engagement rings. Whatever he wanted with them. Second, he would show up at Da Riccardo on May 11 at eight o'clock.

He had it coming to him then!

# 57

*Jonathan*

**Monday, March 19, 6:23 p.m.**

Yes. Jonathan N. Grief had a guilty conscience. He had told a lie. And that just wasn't his way; it never had been. But he'd been given no choice, so he justified it to himself as a necessary white lie, to have led the jeweler to believe he was someone he was not. To have boldly claimed that he was the owner of the diary and therefore the legitimate recipient of whatever had been left for him there. He'd *had* to make that claim, hadn't he? After all, it was a matter of . . . of . . . of . . . Of what, exactly?

He didn't even know for certain that all this had anything to do with the woman in the café. It would have seemed more than peculiar if he had said to the jeweler, "I'm the one these engagement rings were intended for—but could you tell me who arranged for them to be here? A woman with red hair, perhaps? And while you're at it, do you know her name and telephone number? I'd like to call my future fiancée!"

Sitting in his reading chair, he wondered whether he was in his right mind to be chasing delusional dreams like this. He now owned two rings that clearly hadn't been meant for him. He had paid for them with his own money, although the moment the jeweler told him they cost five hundred euros precisely, it had suddenly struck him that this was what the money tucked away in the back of the diary was for. He'd been beset by scruples. Buying someone else's rings might almost be acceptable. But spending his or her money—that was where it went beyond mere fun.

Jonathan also now had scruples about opening the envelope the jeweler gave him along with the rings. Since that morning he had prowled restlessly through the house, going into his study again and again, sitting down in his armchair and picking up the envelope—but he still hadn't opened it. Which was a little strange, since he had now taken things so far that it really made no difference whether or not he looked inside. But privacy was privacy, and the flap of the envelope was sealed rather than just tucked in place. He remembered the trick of steaming a letter in order to open it without leaving a trace, which he had read about in his beloved boyhood comics—did it really work?

He shook his head. He had regressed to the age of twelve already; if this went much further, he'd be consulting a psychiatrist. A child psychiatrist, in fact—he allowed himself the little joke.

He was about to tear the envelope open with a loud "What difference does it make?" when the telephone rang. He pried himself from his armchair. He'd just steeled himself, and now this interruption!

"Jonathan Grief!" he barked into the receiver.

"Markus Bode here. Good evening."

"What is it?"

His CEO hesitated for a couple of seconds before asking, "Sorry, am I disturbing you?"

"No," Jonathan replied in a voice that probably suggested an emphatic *yes*. "What can I do for you?" he added by way of compensation.

"I just wanted to ask when you intended to come into the office again. The fiscal year is almost over, and I thought we intended—"

"Soon."

"I'm sorry?"

"As you said yourself, it's *almost* over. So not yet."

"But, Jonathan, I—"

"I'm sorry, Markus, but I don't have time right now."

"All right," Bode said uncertainly. "Then will you kindly get in touch when—"

"I will. Good evening!" Jonathan hung up.

He sniffed, his heart racing. He really should pick the phone right up again, call his CEO, and apologize for being so rude. It was completely insane. *He*, Jonathan N. Grief, was clearly completely insane. But he felt a huge, almost unbearable tension, so that he hardly knew himself anymore. What was the matter with him? What had happened, these last few weeks?

Before he could risk calling a psychiatrist instead of Bode and politely asking to be taken away—an urgent case—he grabbed the envelope and ripped it open.

The handwriting was the same as the entries in the Filofax.

*So you bought the rings. I'm so pleased! If you want to know just how pleased, come to Da Riccardo this evening. I've reserved "our" table for 8 p.m.*

*I love you!*

*H.*

H.! Just H. yet again! H., H., H. Haaaaaaaargh! But, more helpfully: Da Riccardo. A specific place. And a specific time. Aha! But . . . "today" wasn't actually today—it wasn't for another six weeks. May 11!

Jonathan would have to consult a psychiatrist after all; he couldn't hold out for that long.

But before getting drawn in to taking drastic action, he had a better idea: he would phone Da Riccardo. A reserved table was a reserved table—and a reservation was usually made under a name, wasn't it?

Five minutes later, Jonathan was very happy again. He had gone to his laptop, found the Italian restaurant with the help of a quick internet search, called it, and been informed by a very friendly and pleasingly indiscreet gentleman with an Italian accent (*A sign? A sign!*) that there was only one reservation so far for May 11. A table for two. In the name of Marks, which the friendly man had even spelled out for him. So, *H. Marks.*

Jonathan Googled again. *H. Marks.* In Hamburg. It couldn't be so difficult. *H.* could stand for . . . Helga, maybe? No, that sounded too old for the woman he had seen in the café—if indeed she turned out to be the same one, but hopefully, hopefully she was. Who knew what names parents might give their offspring, especially here in the elegant Harvestehude neighborhood. But he nevertheless ruled out Helga. Hannelore too. And Hedwig. What other women's names began with *H*?

He clicked on a names website. Hadburga? Hadelinde? Hadwine? Oh, for goodness' sake!

A quarter of an hour later he was down to a short list. Hanna, or Hannah. Heike. Helena. Henrike. Hilke—now, that was a real north German name.

Back to Google, this time an images search.

Five hours later, Jonathan N. Grief was not only unsatisfied but despairing. He had clicked through what felt like ten thousand photos and eighty thousand websites. But he hadn't found the woman he was looking for under Hanna(h), Heike, Helene, Henrike, Helga, Hedwig, Hannelore, Hadburga, Hadelinde, Hadwine—yes, he had even Googled that name from Absurdistan and even extended his parameters to include Helewidis, Heilgard, and other such car crashes—and the last name Marks. Maybe she simply wasn't online at all. At least not for the likes of him to find.

Exhausted, Jonathan sank his head down onto his desk next to the computer. A few seconds later he was fast asleep.

# 58

*Hannah*

"Do you really think that was a good idea?" Hannah looked doubtfully at Lisa, who was sitting in the passenger seat of her Twingo.

"We-e-ell," she said, laughing.

"What? Surely you're not doubting the idea now!"

"Only joking," Lisa replied remorsefully. "Sorry."

"For goodness' sake, don't sit there saying you're sorry. Just tell me whether or not it was a good idea!"

"Yes! It was good! It *is* good! Anyway, it's too late now. It's in the mailbox; we can't take it back now."

"Oh, shit! We should have thought about it longer. It was much too spur-of-the-moment."

"No, it wasn't. You're always saying you should follow your gut instinct—and now that's what you've done."

"That's certainly true."

"What's the worst that could happen?"

"Simon spins in his grave?"

"And so he should! I can't believe he kept it from you."

"Yes, well."

"Well—exactly. Get a move on, now, it's past my bedtime."

Hannah started the engine and steered the Twingo out of the broad driveway of the villa back toward the Falkensteiner Ufer. Lisa was right; she shouldn't think any more about whether or not she had done the right thing. It was done now.

She had driven straight from Simon's apartment to her friend's place, told her about the rings, and shown her Simon's secret manuscript. Lisa was as bewildered about both as Hannah had been herself—and agreed that she absolutely had to keep her rendezvous at Da Riccardo on May 11, if only to ask the guy who had the diary, and now probably the rings, too, whether he had a screw loose.

Together, they had cooked up the idea of what to do with the manuscript. They'd looked up the most renowned publisher in Hamburg and gone to Little Rascals, where Lisa had fed all 323 pages through their long-suffering copier while Hannah had composed a short but appropriately moving cover letter.

At Lisa's suggestion, she had marked the envelope containing the copy of the manuscript as strictly confidential, for the personal attention of the CEO. "To give it the necessary seriousness," as her friend had said.

And so the deed was done. Simon's novel, *Hannah's Laugh*, had now been lying in the Grief & Son Books mailbox for a full five minutes.

Hannah turned out onto Falkensteiner Ufer and stepped on it, before she could doubt herself enough to turn back and try to fish the manuscript out of the mailbox.

# 59

*Jonathan*

**Monday, April 30, 9:03 a.m.**

Somehow, Jonathan had managed it. He'd survived April without going entirely out of his mind. He had been helped by the Filofax (no, he hadn't written his own eulogy, but limited himself to a short-and-sweet entry on the "Notes" pages of the diary: *Jonathan N. Grief—a good man, may he rest in peace*) and by his conversations with Leopold, who had turned out to be a true friend over recent weeks. With such words of encouragement as "The idea of waiting for something makes it more exciting" (stolen from Andy Warhol, or so he said), the "hobo," as Jonathan called him in jest, was having more of a therapeutic effect than all the life coaches in the world combined could have done. Jonathan had become a master of composure. Kind of.

Apart from the fact that Markus Bode was *still* on his back with his constant requests to talk, and Jonathan *still* didn't know what to do.

Apart from trying to buy more time—for whatever reason—by telling Bode at the end of March that they should wait for another quarter to see how things progressed with the business. Just to make sure they didn't make any hasty decisions they would regret later. Or something like that.

Jonathan was beginning to feel rather stupid that he couldn't just pluck up the courage to tell his CEO, "Go ahead, my old man doesn't have a clue what's going on these days, but prefers to go for coffee and cake with his fake wife, and I'm just as clueless when it comes to business affairs, and I'm sure you'll manage admirably!"

It was absurd and incomprehensible. What on earth was getting him so hung up? What was making him so afraid, so hesitant, so . . . so incapable of making a decision? He was an intelligent adult, wasn't he?

He was sitting, as he did so often, at his dining table over coffee and a croissant, wondering what exactly his problem was. He didn't know. He knew only that there was something going on deep inside: something wrong, something lacking, something . . . something . . .

"You think too much." He could just imagine Leo's interruption. But the "hobo" wasn't here. They were both pleased that he had been working for two weeks now as a cook in a Hamburg café, and at that moment was probably whipping up the best scrambled eggs in the city.

With a sigh, Jonathan opened the Filofax to today's page. *Marvelous!* As though the creator of the diary were secretly peering over his shoulder, the entry was once again perfect for the situation in general—and for Leopold, specifically, who was currently cooking eggs:

*Make an internal inventory!*

*Do you know how Alcoholics Anonymous works? No? A pity, since their 12-step program for combating addiction is ideal for enabling anyone to be happy in life. The most important thing is to make an internal, and above all, fearless, inventory of yourself. This goes as follows: Sit down and think about the mistakes you have made in your life. Who you might have hurt, who you might have neglected, times when you didn't act particularly well— including times you let yourself down. What unfinished business do you have with other people? Be honest, however difficult it might be! And then set about making good those errors wherever you can. Set about ridding the world of any uncertainty. And from now on live your life with sincerity and honesty toward yourself and other people. What will this bring? Inner peace. Invulnerability. And above all, freedom. Freedom from fear.*

Jonathan read the entry over and over again. And once more. But however often he read it, the entry remained as clear and unequivocal as ever. However much he turned it around, it was there in black and white: a clear instruction to act.

Ever since his conversation with Leo by the Isebek Canal, Jonathan had feared that there might be a tiny little part of his life that he ought to put right or clarify, when the time was right. It was just that his inner stubbornness had prevented him from coming out of his sulk. Even though he knew that he was a little wide of the mark when it came to his personal sense of justice, to admit it—really admit it, to himself and *to another person*—was . . . was . . . necessary. The right thing to do.

He shoved his chair back, stood, and marched upstairs to his study to make a phone call. He picked up the receiver. Only then did he realize that he didn't know the number for the call in question, so he grabbed his cell phone, searched his address book for the contact, and dialed.

"Jonathan?" The woman's voice that answered sounded surprised.

He cleared his throat. "Yes. Hello, Tina!"

"Well, this *is* a surprise!"

"Yes, um, I know."

"Why are you calling me?"

"I wanted to apologize."

"Apologize?" She sounded a touch more surprised. "What for?"

"That I did wrong by you."

"Did you?"

"Yes."

"I didn't notice. Has something happened?"

"Yes," he said. Then corrected himself: "I mean, no. Nothing's happened."

"So what is it?" She laughed.

"I've realized something, is all."

"Sounds interesting!"

"I've realized," he began again, "that all the anger I felt against you and Thomas for years has been complete nonsense."

Silence. Then, even more surprised: "Really?"

"Yes. You didn't leave me for my best friend. You left because I never really loved you."

Another silence. Tina finally corrected him. "I left because we never really loved each other."

"'We'? 'Each other'?" Jonathan repeated in amazement.

"Yes, Jonathan. We were fooling ourselves and each other for a long time. We kept trying to play the perfect couple because it seemed good from the outside. And it was, but we weren't really in love. That was what I'd been looking for all that time—and when I realized it, I had to leave."

"Really?"

"Really."

"Why didn't you ever tell me?"

"I tried, but I just couldn't get through to you."

"No?"

"No, Jonathan." She laughed again—this time with a hint of sadness. "But I'm very, very glad you've told me about your realization." She sighed. "Because you're still a long way from being a lost cause."

"What do you mean by that?"

"I mean it in the nicest possible way, Jonathan."

"I get it," he said, though he didn't get a word.

"How are things with you, anyway?"

"Everything's fine," he said. "Okay, Papa's dementia is getting worse by the day, but that's more a blessing than a curse. Everything in the publishing world continues as ever, and besides . . ." He hesitated. No, he wasn't going to say it.

"And besides?" his ex insisted.

"And besides, I've met a lovely woman." Well, it wasn't a *complete* lie. He had met her. The redhead. In a way. Yes, he had. And if he was lucky, he'd be meeting her again soon.

"How nice!" Tina exclaimed. "I hope she's the right one for you this time."

"Yes. So do I."

"Listen, I've got to go. Tabea's whining. It's been great speaking to you. All the best!"

"To you too," he replied, adding, "And I'm sorry I never thanked you for your New Year's card." But she had already hung up.

Jonathan felt good nevertheless. He examined his innermost feelings. Yes, he felt very good. You could even call it a kind of "inner peace." It hadn't been so difficult after all, and certainly hadn't hurt. Crazy. He really was crazy!

On a roll, Jonathan reached for the telephone again, this time to call Renate Krug to ask her to make him an appointment with Markus Bode. The time had come for him to sit down with his CEO and exchange a few honest words. If it was half as easy as the conversation with Tina had been, what could go wrong?

"I'm glad to hear from you," Renate said as soon as she answered. "I was about to phone you. Markus Bode was here two minutes ago and—"

"What a coincidence," Jonathan said with a smile. Yes, it must be fate! "I was about to ask you to arrange an appointment with him."

". . . and he handed in his notice," his assistant said.

"I beg your pardon?"

"He's given his notice, Herr Grief. Markus Bode has just been to see me and handed me a letter of resignation."

# 60

## *Hannah*

Excited. Angry. Mixed up. Sad. Curious. Scared.

Hannah was all of these as she took her seat—almost ten minutes early—at the Da Riccardo table reserved for Marx.

The moment of truth had arrived. She was about to discover who the man was who, for almost six months, had been roaming the neighborhood with Simon's diary, walking in his footsteps. At least, Hannah was hoping he'd appear, because the question of his identity would no longer leave her in peace.

She and Lisa had repeatedly wondered what kind of person would find a Filofax and then, instead of simply handing it in (to the police, wherever), live according to the schedule of events it contained. Including buying someone else's *engagement rings*! They couldn't think of a single comprehensible reason, only that this certainly was not a normal person but a complete lunatic.

Lisa had begun by insisting that she go with Hannah to Da Riccardo that evening, as she didn't want her best friend to become the victim of a chain-saw-wielding murderer. But after much discussion, Hannah managed to persuade her that the probability of being bumped off was relatively low on a Friday evening in a popular restaurant under the eyes of numerous witnesses. She had nevertheless had to promise to contact Lisa on an hourly basis. "Otherwise I'm calling the police," her friend had threatened. "Or I'll come down there in person!"

In the meantime, Lisa had also read Simon's novel. She had been equally swept away, which meant it wasn't only Hannah's own opinion that it was a good book.

But to date, Hannah had heard nothing from Grief & Son Books, which she found a little disappointing. She had no idea how the publishing world worked, but she would have expected some kind of response in six weeks. Indeed, she had been secretly hoping for a euphoric phone call promising an on-the-spot contract.

It wasn't about the money—she didn't even know if she was entitled to any of it (and didn't want it, in any case). It was that she believed Simon's novel deserved to be published, even if posthumously.

As she so often did, Hannah thought of the story her boyfriend had laid out in the manuscript. Such a beautiful love story! Tears sprang to her eyes again. A wonderful story—and, sadly, not at all true.

She was about to reach in her purse for a tissue, when the curtain to her little booth was drawn aside by Riccardo.

Hannah looked up.

He was standing there. Before her eyes. The man with the blue eyes and the gray-streaked black hair. The guy who had stared at her in the café so weirdly that she couldn't really remember his face.

He was staring at her again now, a little uncertainly.

"Good evening," he said quietly. "My name is Jonathan Grief. Are you Frau Marx?"

She pushed her chair back a little, rose, and stepped toward him.

"Hannah," she said.

# 61

*Jonathan*

Jonathan's knees were weak as he got out of his car in front of the Italian restaurant called Da Riccardo at five to eight. His heart was fluttering in his chest, there was no other way to describe it, and he had no idea how he was going to get through the next five minutes—or, if things went well, the entire evening—in this state. Of course, that was if he was even going to meet the red-haired woman from the café in the next few minutes, for he was by no means certain that H. Marks was actually the red-haired woman from the café. Or, if she was, that she would be there.

He was more nervous than he'd ever been. But there was no question of pulling out now; he had feverishly awaited this moment for far too long.

He had been saved from thinking too much about May 11, that fateful day, because the days since Markus Bode's surprising resignation had turned out to be incredibly busy. Jonathan had been in the office every day since then. He wanted to make his presence felt by his staff, and he knew he should somehow start coming to grips with the work his CEO had performed. Some of it, at least.

After Renate Krug had told him of Markus Bode's resignation, Jonathan had raced to the press, tires screeching, and stormed into Bode's office. There, he had tried to sweet-talk him: offered him more money, a new company car, sole responsibility for the whole of the publishing house's output, if necessary a daily massage in his private office—but all in vain.

"I can't go on," Bode had replied. "And it has nothing to do with the fact that for years I've felt like a puppet on a string, dangling from your father's hands like you, with no real ability to make my own decisions—"

Jonathan had wanted to interrupt: "What do you mean by 'puppet on a string' and 'like me'?"

But Bode had continued, unperturbed, as he calmly cleared his desk. "My wife and I have realized that things can't go on like this."

"I'm sorry?" Jonathan asked in amazement. "You and your wife? I thought—"

"Ah. We've gotten back together."

"Really? How come?" Jonathan had intended to sound more pleased than horrified. He was pleased—very much so. But it would be nice if couples getting back together didn't mean Bode handing in his notice—*that* was more cause for horror than joy.

"Well," his CEO—ex-CEO—had replied, "as so often happens in life, and as you know yourself, a crisis is an opportunity. My wife and I had a long conversation yesterday, in which she told me that she still loved me, but that she'd given up feeling we were a family a long time ago, because my job had been grinding me down for years." He laughed. "As I've just said, a job that . . . But let's not go there."

"So what does that mean right now?"

"I'm taking a sabbatical. We're going on a round-the-world trip with the children."

"A round-the-world trip? With the *children*?"

"It's the ideal time for it. Our eldest starts school in two years, so it'll be impossible then."

"But you don't have to hand in your notice to do that!"

"I do. And I don't intend to come back here. I'm looking for something else. Something less stressful."

"You can stop right there! It's not so stressful here."

"Oh, Jonathan," Markus Bode said, giving him a friendly clap on the shoulder. "If you were in my shoes, you'd know what I was talking about." He winked. "As soon as I'm back from my travels, we could take up our tennis games again. I've really enjoyed beating you."

"Oh." Jonathan was speechless. "But . . . but . . . when do you leave? Grief & Son, I mean?"

"Effective immediately."

"Immediately?! How—"

"I've been here for a good fifteen years, so my notice period is six months. But I've also built up far more than six months of leave, so I think that more than covers it."

"Markus, I—"

"I wish you all the best, Jonathan," Markus Bode said as he shouldered the box containing his things. "You'll be fine! One more thing . . ." He pointed to some piles of paper on his desk. "There are some excellent manuscripts there. Maybe you could find the time to read through them?" No sooner had he spoken than he was gone.

So much for Bode and his sudden departure. But at that decisive, fateful moment, Jonathan didn't want to think any more about it. Okay, if he was honest, he hadn't wanted to think about it over the last few days either. In the office he had begun by pursuing a "business as usual" course, and beyond that prayed that everything would fall into place of its own accord. Somehow.

"It won't just happen," Leo had prophesied as soon as Jonathan told him of his plight, to which Jonathan had replied, "You just look after your scrambled eggs, pal!"

Now it was time to enter Da Riccardo. Behind the heavy front door, the restaurant turned out to be small and tastefully decorated in the Italian style. All the tables were occupied. Jonathan looked around nervously for the red-haired woman but couldn't see her anywhere. There were no single women at any of the tables, and he felt a wave of ice-cold disappointment sweep over him.

*"Buonasera."* A waiter approached him with a smile. "Do you have a reservation?"

"Yes," Jonathan replied despondently. "In the name of Marks."

"Follow me, please!" He gave an obliging nod and marched off. As Jonathan followed him through the restaurant, his heart began to beat wildly again. Was she there after all? *Could it be she is actually here?*

The waiter went up to a curtain and drew it aside. "Here you are, sir."

There she was. Sitting right in front of him. The woman with the green eyes and the wavy red hair. It really was the woman from the café. He remembered her face perfectly.

She looked at him without expression.

"Good evening," he said quietly. "My name is Jonathan Grief. Are you Frau Marks?"

She pushed her chair back a little, rose, and stepped toward him.

"Hannah," she said. Then she raised her hand and slapped him hard.

# 62

### *Hannah*

**Friday, May 11, 9:20 p.m.**

Another evening when Hannah was unable to appreciate the food at Da Riccardo, which had such an excellent reputation. After her frosty introduction, Riccardo had personally served them each a glass of Gavi and since then had not been seen on their side of the curtain. It didn't look like he was going to reappear—he probably thought Hannah a madwoman who only showed up here to make men cry in this private booth.

When she explained to Jonathan the reason for the slap—that he had swiped a gift intended for a dead man—he looked truly shocked.

"I had no idea!" he said. "I'm so sorry! I started out trying to find the owner of the diary, but over time I became fascinated by what you had written. And, well . . . after my visit to the psychic . . . At some point I started to believe that fate had given me a massive gift. It blinded me to reality, and I stupidly went too far, so that I even bought the rings. I admit that was completely over the top. Please forgive me. But as I said, I thought it was fate."

This little speech disarmed Hannah—how could she have argued with him, given all she believed?

She listened to Jonathan closely as he told her how he'd found the bag containing the diary hanging on the handlebars of his bike on New Year's Day. How the handwriting had reminded him of his mother, who had left him when he was still a child. And how he had met the rather bewildered-looking "Harry Potter" by the Alster. Only now did it dawn on him who it must have been.

They talked for a long time, Hannah pausing only now and then to text Lisa to say everything was fine and she shouldn't send the police or turn up herself. And it was true. Everything was fine, except that Hannah kept bursting into tears—so much so that on one occasion, Jonathan took her hand, but let go again as soon as she'd calmed down a little.

They clarified the situation with her name, that it was "Marx" and not "Marks." Had Jonathan searched the internet for "H. Marx," he would soon have come across a photo of her as proprietor of Little Rascals. Hannah told him about Simon's illness and his fear, on top of his existing despair at the loss of his job, to which Jonathan said that when he'd read the missing-person notice about Simon Klamm in the *Hamburg News*, the name had seemed somehow familiar, because he usually read the newspaper every morning. And that—another stroke of fate—the paper that day had been torn so that the photo of Hannah's boyfriend had been missing. Otherwise he would have identified him immediately as the man he'd seen by the Alster, and of course he would have notified the police.

They talked for hours, and although Hannah had originally intended to give the evil ring-and-diary thief a serious dressing down at Da Riccardo that night, she realized early on in their conversation that she actually liked Jonathan Grief. His rather old-fashioned, awkward manner appealed to her. He had charm, as her mother would say, albeit an unusual kind of charm.

"Well, we've talked a lot," Hannah said when she realized it was well past midnight. "And I still don't know what you do. Well, apart from leading your life according to someone else's diary. What's your profession?"

"I'm a publisher," Jonathan said.

"What do you publish?"

"Books."

"No!" Hannah said in amazement.

"Yes," he said slowly and uncertainly.

"Jonathan Grief?" she said. "You don't have anything to do with Grief & Son Books, by any chance?"

He grinned. "I do. It's my publishing house."

"That can't be true!" Hannah slapped her hand in a most unladylike manner on the table, making the glasses clink.

"I'm sorry, I don't understand . . ."

"Simon wrote a novel," she explained. "I didn't find the manuscript until after he died." She cleared her throat and had to pause to compose herself at the memory. "The book was called *Hannah's Laugh*, and a few weeks ago I left it in your company's mailbox."

"Oh," Jonathan said. He began to stammer. "I . . . You know . . . I haven't yet . . . Well, until recently I wasn't responsible . . ." He started again. "*Hannah's Laugh*, did you say?"

"Yes." She nodded.

"By Simon . . ."

"Klamm."

"I don't think I've seen it." He looked at her apologetically.

"I put it in the company's office mailbox. And marked it for the attention of the CEO."

"Aha!" Now Jonathan looked relieved. "I'm afraid my CEO gave his notice recently, so . . . Yes, that must be it. The manuscript is probably languishing somewhere on the slush pile. I'll look for it as soon as I'm back in the office."

"Really?" She smiled. "It would be wonderful if you could take a look at it."

"I'll be glad to!"

"Thank you very much."

There was a subtle cough and the curtain was drawn aside. Riccardo entered and politely asked whether they wanted to order anything else, since he would be closing soon; after all, it was nearly one o'clock . . .

"No, thank you," Hannah said. "We're just going."

She looked at Jonathan to confirm, and thought she saw a hint of disappointment on his face. Or maybe she was imagining it.

Fifteen minutes later, they were outside on the street. They stood facing each other, each uncertain how to say goodbye.

"Could I drive you home?" Jonathan asked, indicating his Saab parked across the road. "It's very late."

"That would be lovely."

They crossed the street to his car. He opened the passenger door gallantly for Hannah, and she got in. He took his place in the driver's seat.

"Where shall I take you?"

Hannah hesitated a moment. "Could you perhaps take me to the place by the Alster where you saw Simon?"

Jonathan started the engine. "Of course I can."

# 63

*Jonathan*

**Saturday, May 12, 8:30 a.m.**

The manuscript. Where was the damn manuscript? Panicked, Jonathan rummaged through the pile of papers on Markus Bode's desk, which until now he hadn't given a second glance to. He just hadn't gotten around to it. In truth, he hadn't felt like it.

But now, after yesterday evening with Hannah . . . after the evening he'd spent with this wonderful woman, he had to—he absolutely *had* to—find that damned manuscript! Because it was important to her, and so it was now important to him. He had therefore gone to the Grief & Son office first thing the following morning. He was anxious that none of his employees see him in such confusion.

Jonathan had hardly closed his eyes all night. He'd played through the evening with her again and again. It had been amazing, if dreadfully sad. She had lost the man in her life only recently. Not only was that horrible, but it also complicated the situation somewhat. He had wanted to tell Hannah Marx that ever since the moment he saw her in the café, he'd fallen hopelessly in love with her—yes, he had painted the scene with all its romantic details in glorious Technicolor. But he immediately took a mental step back when she began by explaining she'd slapped him because he had taken the diary intended for her now-dead boyfriend. Jonathan's spontaneous declaration of love no longer seemed such a good idea.

Hannah would never have accepted that. Not if she had anything like a heart. And she did have one; that much was clear. After that evening, Jonathan was smitten not only by Hannah's appearance but by her whole being—her warmheartedness and her irresistible laugh. She had an incredibly positive disposition, which shone through even despite the fact that she'd recently suffered such a blow. He could only tip his hat to her courage.

He thought of how he'd taken her to that spot by the Alster in the middle of the night and shown her the place where he and Simon had briefly talked about the swans as a symbol of transcendence. Hannah had burst into tears once again; Jonathan had taken her in his arms and held her tight—he couldn't have done anything else at that moment. She had clung to him, sobbing, like a little child, so close that he could feel her heart beating. He had closed his eyes and imagined that she was there in his arms not because she was grieving for another but because she wanted to be close to him, Jonathan N. Grief. It was almost too good to be possible, but maybe, one day . . . After all, so many incredible things had happened because of Hannah that he would otherwise never have believed possible.

So, now, where was the stupid manuscript? Addressed to the CEO in person and delivered by hand to the company's mailbox? Was it on Bode's desk at all? He had told Jonathan there were a few "excellent" manuscripts there. What if it wasn't excellent, wasn't even good? Had Markus Bode simply consigned it to the recycling bin?

But they didn't usually do that at Grief & Son Books; they usually archived all unsolicited manuscripts, even if they weren't interested in them. Although *archived* just meant they were packed into a box by an assistant reader and stored somewhere in the basement. He imagined himself sorting through endless piles of yellow mail cartons beneath a flickering fluorescent light . . .

*There!* There it was! Jonathan excitedly reached for a stack of papers, the top page marked in bold letters, *Hannah's Laugh: A Novel by Simon Klamm.*

He sat down impatiently at Markus Bode's desk, pushed the cover page aside, and began to read. He didn't get far. He stopped after the first paragraph.

He felt slightly queasy. *Simon Klamm.* Yes, the name was familiar. Unfortunately, not only as a journalist with the *Hamburg News.* No, Jonathan remembered something else that had come to him as he began reading *Hannah's Laugh.* A deeply unpleasant memory.

He jumped up from Bode's desk, so suddenly that the old swivel chair creaked and fell to the floor behind him. Jonathan took no notice but hurried across to his own office.

As his computer booted up, he drummed impatiently on his desk with his fingers. He hoped he was wrong. He hoped with all his might. Hoped beyond hope.

He wasn't wrong. His search for a document with "Klamm" in the file name produced a result. A rejection letter, which he had written himself four years ago, packed into an envelope himself, together with *Hannah's Laugh,* and returned to the sender.

Now Jonathan felt truly queasy. He felt dreadful as he once again read the letter he had typed with his own hands:

Dear Herr Klamm,

Yesterday, with increasing enthusiasm, I began to read the manuscript of your debut novel. I have to tell you that my enjoyment increased with every page I read—in fact I even took a printout home with me that evening, because I didn't want to stop. Your writing is sparkling, witty, and so entertaining that time simply flies by—and you have a talent for describing characters in such a way that one feels one is in the room with them.

I can only say *Keep it up*! I have discovered a major talent and I'm delighted! I can hardly wait to read the rest of the manuscript and look forward to meeting you in person before long.

Authors like you don't grow on trees.

So.

Period.

New paragraph.

New line.

My little joke. My dear Herr Klamm, I'll keep this mercifully short: I have never had such a poor manuscript (although I use the word *manuscript* loosely; let's call it a succession of superfluous words) land on my desk in all the years of my working life. To suggest that you even begin to write anything more would be a crime. In such situations, my advice is always to stick to what you know. I don't know what your profession is, but one thing is for certain, it's not that of author. I therefore recommend (I would like to say *beg*) you to move the manuscript to the Trash on your computer and *beg* (now I have said it) you to remember to empty it afterward.

I don't expect a reply to this letter (I would hate to have to read anything else by you).

Yours sincerely,

Jonathan N. Grief

Hot and cold. Jonathan turned hot and cold. Then hot again. Then cold again. Ice cold. Had he *really* written that? And then actually *sent* it?

Yes, he had. He couldn't really say what kind of mood he had been in to have composed such a hurtful letter—but now, with the rejection letter in front of him, he remembered it very well.

He hadn't read much of *Hannah's Laugh* then either. After only two or three sentences he had put it down as "dreadful kitsch." Something the world didn't need, let alone the literary world. And so he had composed and sent this very letter.

Why? Why had he? He asked himself honestly and candidly, as the diary's "internal inventory" instructed him to. Why had he done it?

He no longer knew. Jonathan N. Grief had absolutely no idea what his driving force had been. He knew only one thing: if he wanted the tiniest chance of spending any more time with Hannah, and maybe even winning her over, she must never, never, *never* find out about it.

# 64

"Don't you think it's a bit silly?"

"What's silly about walking barefoot through a meadow of wild-flowers? I think it's lovely!" Hannah replied.

"Of course the idea in itself isn't silly. But surely putting something like that down as a 'date' in a diary isn't necessary? You can just do that kind of thing whenever you want to!"

"You think so?" She looked at him defiantly. "When was the last time you did it?"

"Um . . ." Jonathan was caught out.

"You see?" she said with a look of satisfaction. "It's precisely because people never 'just' do it that I fixed a date for it."

"Fair enough," he murmured, a little ashamed, as he tramped barefoot through the grass beside Hannah. He hadn't intended to complain. On the contrary! Jonathan was glad she had wanted to see him again. And her suggestion of arranging their next meeting according to the diary made perfect sense to him in principle.

It was just that going barefoot made him feel so . . . well, naked. Vulnerable. Unmanly.

"Don't be such a wimp! Come on!" she called, laughing, as he picked his way carefully around a clump of nettles. "The first one down to the ice cream stand pays!" She shot off.

"The winner pays? What kind of logic is that?"

"Mine!" she shouted over her shoulder.

Oh, he liked her. He really did. So very much!

### Hannah—Monday, June 4

"I'm sorry, but I can't manage any more. Another tiny bite and I'll burst." Jonathan pushed his plate of half-eaten Lübeck nut torte aside with a pained expression.

"Bursting doesn't count," she replied. "The point was to eat until you feel sick."

"I've been feeling sick since two pieces ago."

"You should have said."

"I didn't want to disappoint you."

"But it's your birthday, not mine."

"How did you find out?" Jonathan asked.

The day before yesterday she had surprised him with a message inviting him to the Lütt Café on Monday afternoon for coffee and cake. That wasn't in the diary for June 4, and Jonathan had objected that he couldn't simply absent himself from the office during working hours on a weekday, but she had insisted. This was her plan for birthdays from now on.

"I called your office and asked," she said.

Jonathan spluttered on the mouthful of tea he had just drunk. "You called my office?"

"Yes, why not?" She grinned at him. "Your nice assistant was really helpful."

"Well, well." He was also grinning in a mischievous way. "I'll have to have a chat with our dear Frau Krug about data protection."

"Don't worry, she only told me the date, not the year."

"What's that supposed to mean?"

"Nothing." She laughed. Bantering with Jonathan was such fun. Like mental ping-pong. Ping and pong, pong and ping. "Speaking of your office, that reminds me. Have you found Simon's manuscript yet?"

He looked at her remorsefully. "I'm afraid not. I have no idea where Markus Bode put it before he left."

"I meant what I said, that I could copy it for you. It really isn't a problem."

"I'll take another look tomorrow, okay? If I don't find it, then please do."

### Jonathan—Sunday, July 15

"The sun doesn't affect me, actually," Jonathan said. "Italian genes, you know."

"Your back looks rather red, considering," Hannah said from where she was sitting behind him. "Are you sure you don't want me to rub some sunscreen on?"

"No, no need." He felt it was not only his back that was red, but also his face. Which had nothing to do with the sun that had been beating down on them for the whole hour they'd spent exploring the canals of the Alster by boat. Nor was the blood shooting to his cheeks due to the strenuous rowing or the fact that the heat and the sweaty exertion had forced Jonathan to remove his T-shirt ten minutes ago (whereupon he had noticed with delight that Hannah had stared at his body briefly but with apparent interest). It was the prospect of Hannah considerately applying the lotion, thereby touching his bare skin, and then . . . Yes, then even Jonathan N. Grief couldn't guarantee anything!

"Have you been given editorial notes on Simon's novel yet?" Hannah said, breaking the almost-erotic moment.

Jonathan winced with guilt. "Not yet."

*Damn!* She was asking about Simon's manuscript again. Jonathan had finally been forced to tell her that he had found it and sent it directly to one of the editors, "because they can give a much better evaluation of it than I can."

Now he was in a fix, since Hannah regularly asked him for a progress report. Which of course he could understand. She had a right to know whether or not the novel was any good. If only he had been honest with her and told her that he had read it and thought it was a fine thing for someone to sit down and write for their own personal satisfaction, but not everyone had the talent to write for the public. But he hadn't wanted to disappoint Hannah.

And if he were honest, he had not wanted to ruin his chances with her by giving a crushing verdict, as that would have . . . put a strain on her opinion of him. And, of course, he was still worried that she might somehow find out about his atrocious rejection letter, even though he had immediately and irrevocably deleted the file from his hard drive back in May.

Jonathan felt ill just thinking about it. The principle of living one's life in all honesty and openness was another matter when it came to peace of mind.

He resolved to tell Hannah as soon as possible that the acquisitions editor had unfortunately turned down Simon's novel. Even though the news was bound to disappoint her a lot. He had to do it, but not yet, not today. Not on this wonderful summer's day with her . . .

### Hannah—Saturday, August 25

"To be honest, I feel a bit stupid," Lisa whispered. "I'm not a chaperone!"

"Not so loud," Hannah hissed. "You'll wake him."

"Him?" Lisa indicated the snoring Jonathan. "He looks like a man in a coma to me."

Hannah laughed. "Rather a noisy coma."

"What was it I read?" Lisa asked. "Men snore because they need to keep wild animals at bay at night?"

"Glad to hear it. Who knows what wild animals would have attacked us here otherwise?"

"On the beach at St. Peter-Ording? Let me see . . . the evil North Sea shrimps?"

Hannah laughed again. Then she sighed, drew her sleeping bag more tightly around her, and looked up to the sky. "But seriously, now: Isn't it lovely to sleep out under the stars on a night like this? With the murmur of the sea as a soundtrack?"

"Yes, it is. But it would have been even nicer for you two if you hadn't brought me along."

"I can't spend a night alone with Jonathan!"

"First of all, we're in sleeping bags on the beach, and second, since when have you been such a prude?"

"I'm not a prude!"

"Oh yes you are."

"I'm not sure yet how much I like him."

"Believe me, you like him a lot. I've known you for a year or two."

Hannah said nothing for a moment, because she had no idea how to reply. Finally, she whispered, "Yes, I like him very much. But my head's all over the place. Simon hasn't been gone a year."

"And?" Lisa said. "In ten years, when you and Jonathan have three kids, no one's going to question whether you acted according to convention and waited twelve months from the passing of your first fiancé."

"Oh, get away!" Hannah scooped up a handful of sand and threw it at her friend.

"Hey, sand isn't fair!"

"Words aren't either!"

## *Jonathan—Saturday, September 22*

"I just can't believe you've never gone barhopping in the red-light district," Hannah said, shaking her head as they pushed their way through the crowds on the Reeperbahn. "Every guy in Hamburg's done that at some time in their lives!"

"Not me." Jonathan felt embarrassed, exposed somehow. He had thought the same thing himself often enough, but he hadn't wanted to lie about it to Hannah—and since the diary prescribed a night out in the red-light district, ending with breakfast at the fish market, he had immediately confessed to his Reeperbahn-free life.

"But what about your rebellious teenage years?" she asked.

"I was busy with other things then."

"What, for example? Sailing? Golf?"

"Yes, golf. For example."

"And you never staggered down the side streets off the Reeperbahn, drunk out of your skull, spewed somewhere, and made a real exhibition of yourself?"

Feeling annoyance bubbling up inside, he stopped and looked sternly at Hannah. "No. I've already told you! Can you stop it now, please? I don't need you making me feel more stupid than I already do."

She looked shocked. "I'm sorry," she said. "I certainly didn't mean to make you feel stupid."

"But I do," he sulked. "Like an innocent little schoolkid who hasn't lived."

"Well, now, come with me, little schoolkid!" She grabbed his hand and Jonathan felt as though an electric shock were passing through it. "We'll soon make up for lost time, so you never have to feel like that ever again." Laughing, she dragged him after her toward Hans Albers Square.

Four hours later, Jonathan had discovered that, despite his inexperience, he had the makings of a regular Reeperbahn cruiser. Swaying slightly, he stood by Hannah at the bar of La Paloma bellowing out ABBA hits along with about a hundred other drunken people.

An hour later they went to the Silbersack for more dancing, although *dancing* was hardly the right word for it given the crush—it was more like sardines in a tin trying to coordinate their movements as best they could with all the other sardines.

Another hour later, at Molly Malone, Jonathan was playing air guitar to U2's "With or Without You," while Hannah screamed like a wild groupie.

At a little before six, they were standing in the fish market. They didn't have prawn sandwiches, but they were arm in arm, watching the feverish activity of the night's revelers, somehow feeling a part of it all.

And at 5:34 precisely, Jonathan bent down to Hannah, kissed her on the lips, and whispered in her ear, "I love you."

### Hannah—Sunday, September 23

He had done it. Jonathan had kissed her. And she had returned his kiss. Very briefly, but nevertheless.

Hannah had been sitting in her apartment for hours now, looking through the two boxes of Simon's things that she had brought up from the basement on a nostalgic impulse. She was at a loss. Mixed up. Sad. Happy. She felt like laughing and crying at the same time.

Jonathan's kiss had been wonderful, and his declaration of love had made her weak in the knees.

A mere two seconds later she'd been overcome with such strong scruples that she had drawn away from him. Had told him she wasn't ready for that—it was too soon and she had to get home. She had dashed off and hailed a cab for herself, leaving Jonathan standing there in the fish market crowds. She wasn't even sure he'd understood her garbled words. But she couldn't have done anything else; her thoughts and her heart were so muddled that it had felt like self-preservation to get home as soon as possible.

Not that she was any less confused here at home than she had been at half past five that morning. On the contrary. She trawled through her feelings and came to no conclusion.

Jonathan had told her he loved her. Did she love him back? No. That is, she couldn't say. *Love.* It was such a big, powerful feeling. It had to be given time to grow. It required trust, which didn't materialize in just a few weeks. But there was no question that she had feelings for Jonathan. She liked him. Very much, even. She respected his seriousness, and the way he got his teeth into something. His unexpected humor, which could be as smart as it was sympathetic. And although it wasn't the most important thing, she hadn't failed to notice how other women looked at him; she had to admit to herself that she was attracted by his appearance. And maybe, just maybe, this "liking" and "attraction" could develop into love.

But only if she allowed it to. If she let herself get involved with him. Could she? Did she want to? Should she? So soon?

She opened one of the boxes. The photo of her and Simon lay on top. Hannah had packed it into the box because she couldn't bear to look at it. Now she gazed at it for a long time. At Simon, who had once been the man in her life, and herself.

"What should I do?" she asked softly, running her finger gently over Simon's face. "Can you tell me?"

The photo remained silent, of course.

Hannah thought of the diary she had put together for Simon, in which she had tried to advise him how to overcome his illness and enjoy the year ahead. After all the reproaches with which she had beaten herself up, all the "you can do it" delusions with which she had tortured herself after Simon's death, she had finally made her peace with the "fateful" gift to her boyfriend.

Because it was absurd to even *begin* to think that he had taken his life just because of that. And because everything she had written in the diary was exactly what she'd believed, and still did: that every day, every individual second of someone's life, was too precious to waste, to smother in care and worry. Life was for *living*, regardless of how long you had left. For ultimately, no one knew when their last moment would arrive, whether or not they were ill. That was why it was only *now*, only *today* that counted. Yesterday didn't matter, didn't count, and no one could change tomorrow.

Even if Simon hadn't had any use for her gift, her boyfriend had "bequeathed" it to Jonathan. Whether intentionally or by accident, for whatever reason, Simon had picked Jonathan's bicycle on which to hang the bag containing the Filofax. And last night, Jonathan had assured her that the diary had done for him exactly what she had intended: it had pushed him into the midst of life, the here and now. His boozy remark had been superfluous—she had eyes in her head. The joy, the sense of release that Jonathan radiated as soon as the talk turned to the Filofax, said more than the best-chosen words.

So, was everything that had happened since New Year's Eve meant to be? Should it have happened *exactly* as it had? *Must* it happen like it had? And did that mean it was right for her to give herself and Jonathan a chance? For her to follow her own advice and stop giving a damn about yesterday?

With a sigh she took from the box one of the binders containing samples of Simon's work. She leafed through the articles as though she'd find answers to all her questions in them, as though there was a secret message for her between the lines. She turned over page after page, sifting through Simon's life's work. She could remember one or two of the stories, as her boyfriend had sometimes been so excited by his work.

Except for his most important work, *Hannah's Laugh*. He had kept *that* from her.

Had the time come to really let go? Should she simply throw the boxes away? Put the binder in the recycling, throw away the few things of Simon's that she'd kept? Really free herself and start her life over again? She reached the last few pages in the binder. Right at the back,

Simon had stashed his important documents. His diploma. His master's degree. A confirmation of work experience. His certificate of completion of his vocational training. All placed neatly in plastic sleeves. A whole life. A whole damnably short life.

Hannah stopped abruptly at one of the last pages: a letter from a publisher.

*Dear Herr Klamm,* it said. *Thank you for sending your manuscript,* Hannah's Laugh, *to us. Unfortunately, the novel isn't suitable for our list. We are sorry that we can't give you any more positive news . . .*

So Simon had tried. He had sent his book to a publishing house and received a rejection. Not a pleasant experience, but probably not out of the ordinary. After all, she was personally . . . acquainted with the publisher himself and she still hadn't heard from the editor at Grief & Son Books, and was no longer hoping for an enthusiastically positive reply—it was all taking far too long for that. Good news traveled fast.

Hannah turned the page and found a rejection from another publisher. And another. And another. And on the last page in the binder, another. Was this why Simon had never told her about his novel? Was he ashamed of it? And had all these rejections robbed him of his courage to send the manuscript out again, or start another novel? Maybe. But . . . what did four or five rejections matter? There were so many publishers out there.

She was about to close the binder when she noticed she had missed another sheet right at the back. It was folded up tightly, so not immediately visible. Hannah smoothed it out.

She frowned when she saw the letterhead.

Grief & Son Books?

## Jonathan—Monday, September 24

"Get out of my way right now, or I won't be responsible for the consequences!"

Jonathan startled as he heard the loud, agitated voice coming through to him from Renate Krug's reception desk. It was Hannah!

"Got to go. I'll call you back," he said in a strangled voice to the agent he was on the phone with, and hung up.

At the same moment, his office door flew open and an angry—no, an *infuriated and enraged* Hannah stormed in. Renate Krug was at her heels, stammering out helplessly, "I'm sorry, Herr Grief, the lady just—"

"It's fine, Frau Krug," he said. "I know Hannah Marx, it's okay. Please will you leave us?"

Renate Krug hovered in the doorway for a few perplexed seconds, no doubt debating whether it was right to withdraw or whether she should call the police. He could understand it. Hannah's eyes sparked with murderous rage, and even Jonathan was afraid. He had no idea what had caused it. So he had kissed her. Maybe that had been a step too far for her, but this reaction was a little over the top!

"Hannah," he said in a soothing voice, rising from his chair as soon as his assistant had left the office. "What's the matter?"

"You!" she flung at him.

"Me?" he asked in confusion, moving to approach her.

She yelled at him at such a pitch that he froze to the spot.

"You asshole! You monster! You coward! You evil, evil man!" Her voice shook the frosted glass in his office door.

"Hannah," he said again. "I'm sorry, but I don't understand—"

"You don't?" In three strides she was by his desk, glaring at him in disgust. She slapped a sheet of paper down on the desk with a bang.

Jonathan glanced at it and began to shake. He wanted to say something, but he knew there was nothing he could say. He collapsed inside. It had happened. Hannah had found that dreadful letter.

"You really are the worst," she said, quietly but all too clearly. "Not only did you lie to me. You were probably laughing your head off the whole time at me and my dead boyfriend with his writing ambitions—"

"Hannah!"

"Shut up!" she yelled. "You destroyed someone's life. You took a man's hope away just for fun. You trampled all over him and left him broken, for no reason!"

"I—"

"I said shut up!" She hadn't said it, she'd yelled it. She lowered her voice again. "I never, ever want to see you again in my life. Never! Just to make it perfectly clear: I'm about to turn around and leave this office. I don't want to hear another word from you."

Jonathan swallowed hard but remained silent. What could he say? That he knew himself how horribly unacceptable his behavior had been? And yes, how unforgivable?

"If I can leave you with one last piece of advice, so you might have the tiniest chance of not going to hell: make your inner inventory. And do it right! I don't know anyone in the world who needs it more than you do."

Before he could react, she marched out of his office, tearing the door open with such force that it slammed against the wall and knocked off a chunk of plaster. Another bang told Jonathan that Hannah had left Renate Krug's reception area.

A second later, his assistant peeped fearfully around the corner.

"Is everything all right, Herr Grief?"

He didn't reply, but sank slowly back down into his chair.

No. Nothing was all right.

### Hannah—Monday, September 24

During the journey home, Hannah did nothing but cry and cry and cry. Interspersed with beating her steering wheel angrily. And refusing every one of the fifteen or so calls she received between Blankenese and Lokstedt.

She swore she would never speak to him again. Not ever. Jonathan Grief was dead to her.

# 65

*Jonathan*

*Tuesday, October 2, 11:08 a.m.*

When Jonathan landed at Amerigo Vespucci Airport in Florence, he was nervous. Very nervous. Very, very, very nervous.

To be precise, Jonathan N. Grief was so nervous that even as he entered the arrivals terminal, he wondered whether it wouldn't be better to make for the nearest free bench and wait with his carry-on bag until the next flight back to Hamburg that evening.

What did he expect to find here? Nothing but a mother who didn't even recognize him anymore. Sofia, who had ignored him for decades and, after a lukewarm cup of espresso, would wish him all the best for the future and a safe journey home.

If he was lucky. If not, he would see no one and come away frustrated. Why on earth was he doing this?

As he made his way reluctantly to the rental-car desk where he had reserved a vehicle, he recalled the answer to that question: Hannah.

This undertaking was the only connection he had left with her. Because the diary with the task she had set was the paltry remains of all that had once been. Of all that once could have been. And because

Hannah was right. Not only because he was a coward who, when making a second "fearless inventory," had been forced to acknowledge how fatally wrong it had been to lie to Hannah about his rejection letter to Simon. But more than that, because he had something else very important to work out as the first step toward finding his inner peace: he, Jonathan N. Grief, had to know why his mother had broken off contact with him.

Was it really because of a stupid postcard written by an angry teenager, whose hormones or whatever else had fogged his brain? Was that enough to cause a mother to turn her back on her only child?

That is, if he had remained Sofia's only child. Jonathan didn't know that with any certainty. Thirty years was a long time; maybe he had seven half brothers and five half sisters here in Florence; the Italians were known to be keen on reproduction.

The thought made him shudder and rejoice simultaneously (he had grown used to his new split personality). Could he be part of a Mediterranean tribe? Offspring of a major clan including some godfather who controlled the destinies of all Florentines? His imagination ran away with him, and he had to smile as he filled out the forms in the rental-car office.

Jonathan could all too happily have parried the questioning eyebrows of the young employee behind the counter with a breezy "Do you know who I am?"—except that his Italian wasn't yet good enough for that. And there was the fact that he didn't himself know who he was to the young man: simply Jonathan N. Grief from Hamburg, or an estranged descendant of Sofia the Great, wife of the famed Alfonso di Firenze, and therefore . . . No, even if that were the case, to express it would have taken quite a few more Italian lessons than the forty or so he'd completed to date on his language app. So he kept it to a simple *"Mille grazie"* when he was handed the keys to his car and given directions to the right parking space.

Ten minutes later, he was sitting behind the wheel of the Lancia he had been allocated. He sighed with relief. It had all gone smoothly so far. He was in Italy, and he had a car with a navigation system and even an address in the vicinity of Florence where he was now heading.

Tracking down the address had not been as easy as he'd expected. Renate Krug had been awkward about it when he first asked her. And she hadn't wanted to book his flight to Florence, saying that in her opinion it would be a waste of time and she was sure that after all these years his mother would definitely no longer be living there.

Jonathan had been taken aback. After their "family outing," Renate Krug had not been anywhere near as formal with him, but he had never experienced any argument from her or refusal to do what he asked.

And after he had tried to explain to her that the trip was extremely important to him for personal reasons and had asked her again for his mother's last known address; after he had assured her that, even if his mission failed, he wouldn't descend into a pit of depression, and, moreover, at over forty (!) he was more than capable of making his own decisions and accepting the consequences; after he had even confessed to her that, in a way, he owed it to the young lady Hannah Marx—whom she had recently had occasion to meet (although he kept quiet about the precise circumstances surrounding her memorable appearance, preferring to take the whole matter of his rejection letter to his grave with him rather than reveal it to another living soul)—to tidy up this loose end in the story of his life; and after none of this had borne fruit and Renate Krug continued to insist that the trip was something he should refrain from, Jonathan N. Grief had been compelled to remind his assistant that he was her boss and she was not his mother, so although he valued her opinion he was certainly not prepared to consider it when making this decision.

It was only after these tough negotiations that Renate Krug wrote down the address and booked the flight, scowling all the while and insisting that Jonathan would find nothing when he got there but an empty shack and a withered old cypress hedge.

Well, Jonathan would soon see. According to the navigation system it was a short half hour's drive from the airport to Via di Montececeri 20 in Fiesole, where his mother had last been known to live.

When he had entered the address into Google for the first time, back in his office, he hadn't known whether to laugh or cry. It turned out that Monte Ceceri (which meant "swan hill") was where Leonardo da Vinci had made his first attempts at flight in the sixteenth century.

On seeing this, it was not Leonardo that interested Jonathan, but the swans. He had immediately been tempted to pick up the phone to call Hannah and tell her about the extraordinary coincidence (swans . . . Alster . . . Simon . . . *capito?*) But of course he had thought better of it, as he had known what her reply would have been: nothing. Only the click of the phone being hung up, closely followed by a beeping on the line.

He would always be *persona non grata* to her—swans or no swans. Maybe the opposite. If he were to remind Hannah once again of the moment when he had last seen Simon alive . . . It didn't take much imagination to realize that her reaction would hardly be a tearful reconciliation, but more likely a full-on meltdown.

Nevertheless, it was right that he was here now. Regardless of the fact that Hannah would never forgive him, and his heart would remain broken until his very last breath—yes, yes, pathos was also something new to him, to go with the split personality—he nevertheless had to go through with this one to the very end. Because if he didn't, all that remained to him would be a return to his old life. And however things turned out here, that was something Jonathan N. Grief had no desire to countenance.

He started the engine and followed the instructions of the navigation device. He was far too agitated to appreciate the beauty of the landscape that passed on either side—the rolling hills, the cypresses and pines that certainly weren't old and withered, the olives and vineyards.

In order to get a grip on his nerves, he ran through the greetings he had planned for his reunion with his mother. If it happened as he hoped. *Ciao, Mamma! It's me, your son, Jonathan. Where have you been all this time?* He still hadn't quite decided whether to confront her right away with the question of her many years' absence. But what would be the point of beating about the bush? For one thing, his flight home was that evening, and in any case, after thirty years there was really no point in social niceties.

*Ciao, Mamma,* he repeated in his head like a mantra. *Ciao. Ciao, Mamma!* And once again: *Mamma!* With a swift gesture he switched on the roaring air-conditioning, as his eyes were streaming and his hands were wet with sweat on the steering wheel.

Twenty minutes later, he reached the outskirts of Fiesole and made his way through the narrow, winding streets. He knew he had been here a few times as a little boy, but his memories of this pretty little place were as deeply buried as his singing and tennis-playing ambitions had been. The street was lined with bright-yellow houses sporting green shutters and red pantiled roofs, and he passed a succession of evocative street names—Via Giuseppe Verdi, Via Santa Chiara, Piazza Mino da Fiesole—that suggested just why his mother had missed the joie de vivre of her hometown when she was stuck in the north. Hamburg street names, like Pepermölenbek and Brandstwiete, sounded dry as a crispbread in comparison.

And those views! When Jonathan reached Via di Montececeri, he stopped at the side of the road by a stone wall to allow himself a brief reprieve before the moment of truth, gazing out over the valley below. In the eyes of north German real-estate agents, his house right by Innocentia Park was the ultimate in *location, location, location!* But here and now, he realized that the view from his windows at home was only a few trees and three recycling containers. Swan Hill, on the other hand, lived up to the promise of its name; just looking at it filled him with elation. No wonder Leonardo da Vinci had been convinced that, if it were at all possible for people to fly, this would be the best place to do it.

Jonathan drove the Lancia a little farther, following the wall, then pulled over at his destination, turned off the ignition, and unclipped his seat belt. He took a few deep breaths before opening the driver's door to go look for number 20 on foot.

It was easy to find, and the yellow-painted building looked neither derelict nor neglected. Window boxes beneath the green wooden shutters were bright with . . . some kind of pretty flowers. One of the windows behind a wrought-metal grille was ajar, and the sounds of an Italian pop song reached his ears.

Jonathan N. Grief's heart leapt to his throat as he stopped by the front door. As he took another deep breath. And as he finally pressed the doorbell.

A few seconds later, the music was silenced. Jonathan heard footsteps. He saw the doorknob turn. And a moment later a stout woman of around sixty was standing before him, wearing a colorful apron. *"Sì?"* she said.

His heartbeat slowed.

This was not his mother; he saw that right away.

"Nicolò!" With a single step the woman was upon him, her arms thrown around him, covering his face with kisses.

No, she wasn't his mother. But Jonathan had a vague memory of her.

# 66

*Jonathan*

**Tuesday, October 2, 12:23 p.m.**

Francesca. His aunt's name was Francesca. Jonathan had no idea why his memory had thrown up *Nina* or *Gina*, since they were not even close to *Francesca*. But it didn't matter. What mattered was that he was sitting with his aunt in her rustic Tuscan kitchen, a plate of pasta steaming before him. If one of his authors had described a visit to Italian relatives in this way, he would have called it "cliché ridden" and directed the editor to strike it out mercilessly, but in real life, that was *exactly* how it was.

He was just getting over the euphoric greeting, with all the kisses and the stream of incomprehensible words, when Francesca dragged him into the house and served him food. So they were now sitting at the table, looking at one another, as Jonathan dutifully tucked into a mountain of pasta. He had no appetite whatsoever, but since his rudimentary knowledge of Italian had suddenly deserted him, it was a practical move to keep his mouth full.

After he emptied his plate, Francesca jumped up to refill it, but with the help of a barrage of gestures and a stuttering *"No, basta, grazie!"* he managed to prevent a second helping.

*"Allora,"* he finally added. And fell silent.

His aunt looked at him in anticipation.

"Hmm," he said. *Damn it!* There was so much he wanted to ask. Whether his mother still lived here. And whether she was at home, which he doubted, since his aunt would surely have fetched her. But it was hopeless; a few hours of learning Italian had hardly turned him into Umberto Eco. *"Parli tedesco?"* he asked, desperately hoping that Francesca knew a little German.

She shrugged.

*"Inglese?"* Maybe English was worth a try.

Another shrug.

He was about to suggest French or Spanish, when it occurred to him that he knew neither of those himself. What else could he try? Latin? After all, it was similar to Italian. But how far would he and his aunt get in conversation with *"Veni, vidi, vici"*?

"Nicolò," Francesca began. *"Sono molti anni che non ci vediamo."*

He nodded, although he hadn't a clue what it meant.

*"Come stai?"*

Ha! He understood that: she was asking how he was!

*"Sto abbastanza bene, grazie,"* he replied. It wasn't exactly true, but was the only reply his Italian app had given as a response to that question. A complex reply such as "Well, could be better—my company's going down the drain, Papa has dementia and thinks his secretary's your sister, my CEO's left, and I just lost the woman I've fallen head over heels in love with" was something for more advanced learners.

*Damn.* They weren't getting anywhere; it was pointless. But maybe there was no need for complicated words.

*"Mamma?"* he said, his voice a question.

His aunt raised her eyebrows and her hand flew to her mouth. She looked truly shocked. Did she think he took her for his mother?

*"Dov'è Sofia?"* He tried to be a bit more specific.

*"Che Dio la protegga!"* she cried. *"Non ne ha idea?"*

"Er, *scusi?"* What had she said?

*"Sua madre è morta. Da molto."*

*"Scusi?"* he repeated.

*"Aspetti un momento."* She stood and left the room. Jonathan stayed where he was, baffled. Where had she gone?

Francesca soon returned, a photo in her hand. She laid it on the table in front of him.

As he looked at it, tears sprang to his eyes.

It showed a white marble plaque by an urn grave, as was the Italian tradition.

*Sofia Monticello,* the inscription read. *July 18, 1952–August 22, 1988.*

# 67

*Jonathan*

**Tuesday, October 2, 9:34 p.m.**

When the plane touched down at Hamburg Airport at half past nine that evening, Jonathan was still so angry that he had to exercise extreme self-control to prevent himself from driving straight to the Sonnenhof, despite the late hour, and grabbing his old man as he sat in his armchair.

What a lie! What an incredible lie his father had deceived him with for most of his life! All those years that Wolfgang Grief had kept the truth from him! He only had to think about it and he was gripped with such fury that he was tempted to ignore the time, visit his father there and then, and take him to task. If it meant that the good Dr. Knesebeck had a heart attack or called the police, then so be it—he didn't care.

No, it wasn't because he was worried his father wouldn't survive a frenzy of rage from his son, oh no. It was because Jonathan wanted to confront him when Wolfgang's mind was as clear as possible, so that he understood at least part of what his son had to say to him. And the chances of that were far better by day than by night.

He paused for thought. The anger he was feeling at that moment threatened to tempt him into an act of violence, which could be exonerated with the defense of "crime of passion" if he drove to the old people's home now. On the other hand, if he slept on it overnight, he would certainly be accused of premeditation.

Jonathan balled his fists and waited impatiently for the safety-belt lights to go out as the aircraft reached its "final parking position," as they so beautifully put it. He had to get out of here; he needed fresh air! When he ran through the day's events in his mind, he wanted to cry out loud.

After he and Francesca had agreed that any communication beyond "Would you like anything more to eat?" and "It's a lovely day today" was bound to founder at the language barrier, Jonathan had unceremoniously led his aunt to his rented car and driven her through Florence to the German Institute, where they found a helpful employee. The young man had translated what Francesca had to say, his ears growing ever redder.

The story was as banal as it was sordid. So much for his mother being massively homesick for Italy. Ha! The truth was rather different. His father, that pillar of the community, Wolfgang Grief, had, it seemed, indulged in an affair. And when Sofia, a true-blooded Italian, got wind of it, she had demanded a divorce from her adulterous husband.

Of course, Jonathan's aunt had assured him, she would have preferred to take her son with her to Fiesole, but at the time she believed that he would have a better life in Germany. She wanted to make sure he had all the best chances—school, university, and ultimately, his family legacy, to take over the publishing house. She could've had no idea how things would turn out. On the day she received Jonathan's furious postcard, she had immediately booked a flight to Hamburg to tell him in person that she hadn't left "just like that." Until that moment, Sofia had believed that she shouldn't burden her son with her marital problems, but when she realized that he felt abandoned by her, she saw no other way than to tell him the truth.

Sofia must have been agitated and driven too fast on the way to the airport—and had skidded off the road while taking a corner.

His mother had been killed instantly.

"I'm sure she didn't feel a thing," his aunt assured him through her tears. Even the friendly interpreter had swallowed hard at these words and rummaged in his pocket for a handkerchief.

*Didn't feel a thing.* That certainly wasn't the case for Jonathan. At that moment he felt a whole range of things. For example, a monstrous, dreadful grief. All those years, he had felt a terrible knot in his heart whenever he thought of his mother, an impotent rage that grew from his firm conviction that she hadn't cared an iota for him. Or had cared less for him than for her *dolce vita* in Italy, at least.

How wrong he had been! What injustice he had, yet again, done to another person! And what had it done to *him* as a person? An emotional cripple, a lonely old divorcé, a self-righteous know-it-all, an unbearable pedant. And on top of that, a coward who couldn't even bring himself to stand up to his deranged father with his own point of view, to acknowledge that he had nothing at all against popular fiction. He had merely accepted his father's stupid attitude and even made it his own. If he were honest with himself once and for all, he admired authors who succeeded in truly moving their readers, touching them deep in their hearts and minds. Whether that was J. K. Rowling or Sebastian Fitzek—or Simon Klamm.

Yes, while he was waiting in the Florence airport, Jonathan had actually begun to read Simon Klamm's *Hannah's Laugh*, which he had asked Renate Krug to scan and send to him so he could load it on his iPad. And however much pain it caused him to read what this near stranger had written about his (albeit allegedly fictionalized) Hannah, he finally came to understand why he had always found it hard to bear books like that. Because they could also hurt. Hurt very much.

There was no way he could use it to justify his rejection letter to Simon Klamm; that was and would remain a singular, unforgivable *mistake*, but at least he could now admit to himself why he had done it. Not because the manuscript was bad—on the contrary. Because at the time, with all his self-pity and his unjustified anger after his divorce from Tina, his inability to come out from his own shadow and allow any feelings in, he had not been able to bear reading something like that, and had dismissed it as "dreadful kitsch."

What kind of a man had he, Jonathan N. Grief, become? Of course, it would be exaggerating to claim that his marriage to Tina had been a result of his emotional ineptitude. The fact that he had consciously chosen a woman who might have had things in common with him but whom he didn't really love. One who—how had she put it?—"couldn't get through to him." No, Jonathan didn't want to go that far; it would be mere kitchen psychology.

On the other hand, what was actually wrong with kitchen psychology? After all, sitting at his aunt's kitchen table (well, almost, with a slight detour from the table to the German Institute), he had learned a few things about himself that, looking back, made quite a lot of psychological sense.

Jonathan strode rapidly down the long corridor to baggage claim. He had still barely gotten himself under control, and the sight of people on the other side of the sliding glass door to the arrivals terminal cheerfully waving to loved ones did little to improve his mood. If he could be granted just one small wish, it would be to see Hannah there waiting for him.

Instead, he would be getting into a taxi alone and going back to his lonely house by Innocentia Park. There was no one to meet him. Not a single person who was interested in him. Well, apart from Leo. But he still didn't have a driver's license.

"Hello, Herr Grief."

Jonathan came to a halt midstride and turned in surprise. He saw Renate Krug smile uncertainly at him.

"What are you doing here?"

"I came to meet you, but you were in such a hurry that you swept right past me."

"Sorry, I never expected to see anyone here."

"Why would you?" She still looked hesitant.

"Yes, well, thank you!" Jonathan said, making an effort not to look so grim. Probably in vain.

"You know now, I suppose."

"Know what?"

"That your mother's dead."

"You know too?" he asked, perplexed.

Renate Krug nodded and lowered her eyes. "Yes," she replied quietly.

"But how . . . Why . . . ?" He stuttered to a silence.

His assistant looked back up at him. "Jonathan," she said, using his first name in a firm, determined tone. "I was afraid you'd have found it all out by now. Or almost all of it. That's why I'm here. To tell you the rest."

"What rest?"

"That I was the one. I was the reason your mother left your father."

Jonathan N. Grief sat in the taxi home from the airport, deep in thought. His assistant had offered to drive him, but he had declined. He wanted to be alone, so that he could think in peace. To mull over what Renate Krug had confessed at the table of a bistro in the airport, over coffee that neither of them had drunk.

How she and his father had an affair, many years ago. It wasn't a big, important affair, just a stupid fling, but it was damaging enough for Sofia Monticello, who had left her husband because of it. How they had all decided not to tell the boy, because that would be better for him. Not even after his mother died, since it would only have burdened him with guilt for the rest of his life if he believed he was somehow responsible for her accident because of his stupid postcard. Renate Krug had told him all that. Had asked him to forgive her for her behavior, explaining to him that there had been nothing between her and Jonathan's father for years (as if that made the slightest difference!) and that she was aware what an unforgivable mistake she had made, how much she had wronged Jonathan.

She had asked him not to confront his father with it, that it would be the end of him. Because, she assured Jonathan, Wolfgang Grief was only too aware, deep down, of his guilt. And he regretted it a hundredfold, even if he'd been unable to show it to his son. No one had ever taught him how to deal with emotions, just as he in turn had been unable to teach Jonathan. Ineptitude, indeed. But not malice.

Jonathan didn't know whether to believe any of it. Whether he could believe it. Whether he wanted to believe it. But ultimately, what difference did it make?

So he sat in the taxi and thought about it all. About what was to be done now. There was a lot—but one thing at a time. So much time had passed that a few weeks wouldn't make much difference. It all needed to be thought through and tackled calmly.

So calmly, that no sooner had Jonathan N. Grief arrived home than he was on the phone to Leopold.

"Jonathan?" his friend said sleepily. "What do you want? It's after midnight. I have to be up early tomorrow morning!"

"Listen to me, hobo," Jonathan said. "You're leaving your job at the café tomorrow."

"I'm doing what?"

"Leaving your job!"

"Why should I?"

"Because from now on you're my CEO at Grief & Son Books."

"Jonathan?"

"Yes?"

"Have you been drinking?"

"Not a drop. I've never seen more clearly in my life."

"But how's that going to work?"

"We'll see how. Don't worry, I'll make perfectly sure it's not too stressful for you. And that you have plenty of mineral water with lemon in your office."

"You're out of your mind! I can't."

"Selling things is the same, whatever the product. If you can do scrambled eggs, you can do books."

Jonathan hung up without giving Leopold the chance to argue further. *Fine. One thing done.* And on Thursday morning, as soon as the shops were open, he would go out and buy a diary.

A Filofax, a particularly nice one, leather-bound, for the following year.

# 68

*Hannah*

*Silent night, holy night . . .*

Hannah glanced surreptitiously at her watch. She and Lisa were running through one classic Christmas carol after another with the charges, who had been dropped off at Little Rascals at ten by stressed-out parents dashing off to do some last-minute shopping and put up Christmas trees.

The kids were having fun, but Hannah was having a day from hell. She only had to think of the "Christmas spirit" and she felt ill.

This was her first Christmas in five years without Simon. Granted, he had never been a big fan of all the fuss surrounding the holidays, considering Christmas to be a purely commercial invention of the retail trade (although they always gave each other a gift), and saying that Hannah's weakness for bratwurst hot dogs and mulled wine at the Hamburg Christmas markets was an incomprehensible departure from her otherwise excellent taste, an extravagance that simply wasn't necessary on top of all the stress people had at that time of year.

For that very reason, she had urged him in the diary to accompany her to one of the markets—at least after Christmas, since many of them were open until New Year's Eve. She'd wanted to try to convey to Simon the special, romantic atmosphere of the muted lighting and seasonal music.

Well, it was taking a lot of effort for Hannah to come to terms with the seasonal music. Another Christmas carol from a screeching child's lips, and she would probably lose it.

But it was almost one o'clock; she could survive the last half hour. That was when they were due to shut up shop, and she could leave all the hearty cheerfulness behind. At least until December 31. On New Year's Eve, they were due to open the whole day for parents who were, as ever, taken by surprise when the date came around, as if it didn't every year, and had to dash out to get nibbles for parties and a supply of fireworks. Hannah and Lisa planned a day off on January first, and then it would all take off again on the second. Yes, Little Rascals was going well, there was no denying it.

But once again, Hannah's tears were flowing freely. She hadn't noticed until Lisa gently brushed her cheek with her hand that she must have begun to cry sometime during "O Christmas Tree."

It was only natural that her waterworks were at the ready. The man who had effectively been her fiancé was dead, and to add insult to injury, she had a good dose of lovesickness. Well, not such a good dose; she hadn't known Jonathan long enough for that. And she was ashamed to even think the word *lovesick*, given that Simon hadn't been dead for a year yet. It was more like . . . a small but very concentrated, painful feeling of melancholy. A feeling of being abandoned. Betrayed by the man she had thought to be something special, if only for a brief time. Someone fate had delivered into her hands.

*Stupid fate!* Even the mail service was more reliable!

"Will you be all right?" Lisa asked shortly before two as they were tidying up after finally bundling the last little child into the arms of cheerful parents. "At Christmas, I mean?"

"Yes, of course," Hannah replied, sniffing and wiping her nose with her sleeve. "When the festivities are over, I'm going to lie down under my parents' Christmas tree and sleep until New Year's."

"Good plan." Lisa grinned.

"What about you?"

Lisa shrugged. "I think I'll do the same. But we can see each other during the holidays."

"I'd love to," Hannah said. "Provided we don't go anywhere near a Christmas market."

Lisa raised her hands. "No way! I know how much you hate them. All that bratwurst and mulled wine—yuck!"

They both laughed.

Ten minutes later, they were done and putting on their coats, ready to make their way to their respective parents' homes. Lisa opened the Little Rascals door, paused, and picked up a package that had been left on the doorstep.

"Look here," she said, holding it under Hannah's nose. "It's got your name on it."

It was true; someone had written *Hannah* on the parcel.

"Is it Christmas already?" Hannah said, trying to make light of it, although she felt the heat shoot to her cheeks. Because she recognized the handwriting—Jonathan's.

"Are you thinking what I'm thinking?" Lisa asked.

"Yes," Hannah said.

"Then open it!"

"You think I should?"

"Of course. What a question!"

"Okay." They closed the door and went back in. They sat down in the little kitchenette, where Hannah, hands trembling, slit open the thick packaging with scissors.

She found an envelope and a gift wrapped in Christmas paper.

"The present first!" Lisa said impatiently.

"No," Hannah said. "It's my package, and I want to open the envelope first."

She drew out the flap, since it wasn't sealed. She took out the folded letter and began to read.

> Dear Hannah,
>
> I really enjoyed reading the manuscript, *Hannah's Laugh*, by your sadly departed boyfriend, Simon Klamm. I would be delighted if Grief & Son Books could publish the novel, and I would like to make you an offer. Would you be interested in talking to me about it? I really think that *Hannah's Laugh* is an excellent book, and I believe that your fiancé's legacy will bring many people great joy.
>
> Yours sincerely,
>
> Jonathan N. Grief
>
> P.S.
>
> Dear Hannah,
>
> You were right, I was a coward. And an asshole. I really want to apologize for what I did, only I fear there is no adequate apology I could possibly give you. But I think I can at least explain. If you want me to.
>
> Jonathan
>
> P.P.S. Even if you don't want to hear my explanation and never want to speak to me again, the offer to publish *Hannah's Laugh* still stands!

"Shit!" Hannah sniffled.

"Shit indeed!" Lisa remarked. "And now the package, please! Right now!"

Hannah nodded and tore open the paper. She saw a Filofax. A diary bound in dark-blue leather, with white stitched seams.

"I don't believe it!" Lisa cried.

"Neither do I." Hannah opened the little book.

It was a diary for the following year. With handwritten entries for each day from January 1 to December 31. Again in Jonathan's handwriting. And for every date, a single repeated phrase:

*1.1. Forgive Jonathan.*

*1.2. Forgive Jonathan.*

*1.3. Forgive Jonathan.*

*1.4. Forgive Jonathan.*

*1.5. Forgive Jonathan . . .*

Hannah stared at the pages, stunned. Stunned and speechless. She breathed deeply, in and out. And then, slowly, she closed the Filofax.

"Come on, we're going to see our parents," she said.

"You can't just go to your parents' house as if nothing's happened!"

"Why not? Nothing has."

"Hannah, please! It's wonderful, what Jonathan sent you."

"True," Hannah conceded. "But what he did is totally unforgivable."

Lisa looked at her sharply. "Unforgivable? Who by?"

"Okay, by me. *I* can't forgive it."

"Really and truly?"

Hannah thought for a moment. Then she shook her head, slowly and sadly. "No. It hurt way too much. And . . ." She hesitated. "Jonathan did something really horrible to Simon with that letter. He hurt someone willfully and maliciously."

"Yes," Lisa agreed. "But I'm sure he didn't realize the damage he was doing. At least, I can't imagine he could have."

"But all of us have to live with the consequences of our actions. Whether or not we intended them."

Lisa sighed. "I guess you're right." She shrugged. "But I still think Jonathan's gift is sweet. Whether he's malicious or not."

"It's sweet, but it doesn't make things right."

"So will you consider his offer to publish?"

"Maybe. I don't know."

Outside Little Rascals, they said goodbye with a long, tight hug, and then Lisa strode off toward the subway station. Hannah got in her car and drove off.

Ten minutes later, she parked her Twingo again. But not outside her parents' house. She went up to the door of the building, looked for the right bell, and pressed it.

She almost cried out with relief when she heard the entry buzzer. Hannah ran up the stairs and was out of breath by the time she reached the top.

"I'm so glad you're in!" she said. "It's me, Hannah Marx. Can you spare me a little of your time? I know it's Christmas, but it's very important and I—"

"Of course I've got time. Do come in!"

Sarasvati smiled at Hannah and opened her apartment door wide.

# 69

*Jonathan*

Jonathan's cell phone rang, but he couldn't be bothered to rise from his chair and go over to his desk to see who was calling. It couldn't be Hannah—he'd allocated a special ringtone to her. He wasn't interested in any other caller; he was too busy.

He was totally immersed in the climax of a manuscript he was eager to publish as part of next autumn's list: *My Heart Is So Cold*, a debut by a gifted young author who had Jonathan totally under her spell.

A few months ago he wouldn't have picked up such a novel, let alone read it, on the basis of the title alone, but now he was swept away by the characters and the twists and turns the author had contrived. What a book! What a story! Epic! A story as . . . as . . . yes, as exciting as life itself.

For this was something Jonathan now knew: life produced the most amazing stories. He only had to think of himself. And of Hannah, who hadn't been in touch since he had left her his Christmas present, and he sadly acknowledged never would now. It broke his heart—and not because he would never acquire the rights to *Hannah's Laugh*. No, it broke his heart that he would probably never again be in the presence of Hannah's laugh.

He sighed and settled back into *My Heart Is So Cold*. A little later, his thoughts began to wander again, just as the story was building up to the grand finale, when the main character had to confront the shocking extent of her lover's betrayal.

This time he found himself thinking not of Hannah, but of his father. Just as Renate Krug had asked, he hadn't spoken to Wolfgang about what he'd discovered in Italy. He had decided to let it lie, that it was enough for him to know it himself. And so knowing, to explain his emotional failings and exorcise them. Which might not get him anywhere with Hannah, but maybe would help in the rest of his life. Or at least with the publishing business—the number of advance orders from the spring/summer list he had put together with Leopold was looking really promising.

Jonathan hardly felt any resentment toward his esteemed father now. No, what he felt for Wolfgang Grief was pity. After all, the old man had to live with himself—not to mention, in his more lucid moments, come to terms with the awareness of how his mind was deteriorating. It was moving to see how Renate Krug cared for him. Jonathan had suggested she take early retirement, so his former assistant was now free to play "Sofia" and visit the Sonnenhof every day if she chose.

His cell phone rang again. Sullenly, he put the manuscript aside and got up. Who could be so stubborn as to keep calling on a day like this during the holidays? It had better be important, or else . . .

"Hello, Jonathan. This is Lisa, Hannah's friend." Her voice was a whisper.

Oh. It *was* important.

"Um, yes?" he said, his heart thumping.

"We're on Marie-Jonas Square in Eppendorf," she said, so quietly that he could hardly hear.

"So?"

"At the Christmas market!"

"I'm not getting you."

424

"Look in the diary, you idiot!"

For a moment, Jonathan had no idea what Hannah's friend was implying, but then he grabbed the blue Filofax that lay on his desk. Opened it up to December 27.

*The best time for bratwurst at the Christmas market is AFTER Christmas. All the stress of the holidays is over, and you finally have time to reflect. That's why you should get down to Marie-Jonas Square in Eppendorf at five o'clock. If you refuse, I'm going to chain you to the children's carousel and leave you to spin around and around until you agree that Christmas markets are wonderful!*

"Are you saying I should come?" Jonathan asked, his voice shaking.

"Ah, so you're not as stupid as Hannah makes out. Yes, dummy!"

"But Hannah doesn't want to see me. I—"

"Nonsense! She even made a special trip to Sarasvati for a tarot reading because of you. I'm afraid the good lady only told her something like 'What will be, will be.' Huh! It looks like it's up to me to make sure that something will finally happen between you two!"

"Do you think that's what Hannah wants?"

An unladylike groan. "Yesterday, I went to the trouble of getting hold of Hannah's cell phone, looking up your number, and dragging her reluctantly out here so fate can finally have its way and I don't have to listen to her hideous whining a moment longer. So get your goddamn publisher's ass down here! And make it quick!"

"Okay, I'm on my way." Jonathan hung up.

And then he dashed off. Just as he was. He stumbled down the stairs in jeans, T-shirt, and slippers, tore open the door, and ran out into the early darkness of the December day.

Because right at that moment, Jonathan N. Grief cared nothing about the cold.

# EPILOGUE

## *Hannah*

**Monday, December 31, 6:28 p.m.**

"Well, great!" Lisa said as she upended the last child's seat on one of the little tables so that she and Hannah could sweep away the final traces of the devastation left behind after the day's Little Rascals session. They had put on a New Year's Eve party for the kids, including a wild streamer-and-confetti battle. "Only five and a half hours until the new year!"

"So?" Hannah said as she scraped the crumbling remains of the cakes into a trash bag.

"What do you mean, 'so'?" Lisa regarded her friend reproachfully.

"I'm sorry, but I don't understand what you're driving at."

"Of course you don't!" Lisa drew the pout on her lips into an even more exaggerated pout. "You're off for a wonderful dinner with Jonathan, then seeing in the New Year with him, while I'm left here alone!"

"Are you angling to come with us?"

"On your date?" Lisa looked horrified. "No way!"

"It's not a date," Hannah corrected her. "We're not on those terms yet. At least, I'm not. I like Jonathan, that's all. We'll see how it goes."

"I can imagine exactly how it'll turn out if you've got me hanging around at the table with the two of you," Lisa said, unable to suppress a grin. "You could wave goodbye to any romance."

"Don't be silly! I'd be completely okay with you coming along. And I'm sure Jonathan would too."

"I doubt Jonathan would agree with you, though he'd act the perfect gentleman. And I wouldn't be okay with it either. Anyway, I don't mind being on my own tonight. I hate all this New Year's hype; I'm usually in bed well before midnight."

"Then I don't understand what your problem is."

"Well, because the year's nearly over!"

"That's right. And then a new one begins. It happens every year, if you hadn't noticed."

"But I haven't met anyone!"

At last the penny dropped with Hannah. "Shit, I completely forgot. You mean because Sarasvati told you that you'd meet a man this year?"

"Precisely." Another gloomy pout.

"Oh, sweetie!" Hannah dropped the bag, went over to her friend, and took her arm. "Someone's bound to come along next year," she said as she stroked Lisa's back.

"I don't understand." Lisa buried her face in Hannah's shoulder. "Sarasvati's never been wrong before."

"Maybe she was having a bad day."

"Very funny."

"Or . . ." Hannah paused to think. "Or maybe she was talking about another kind of year."

"Huh?" Lisa looked up at Hannah in confusion.

"Yes, that could be it. The . . . the Chinese calendar, for example? Or the Indian one? Gregorian? I don't know—there's bound to be some calendar in which the new year comes around at the end of January, or even in February. Or whatever."

"So maybe I'm going to fall in love with a Chinese guy?"

"Or a Gregorian monk."

Lisa snorted with laughter. "It's kind of you to try and cheer me up." She sighed. "But if I'm going to meet someone, I'm beginning to think I should put my money into an online-dating app instead of any more tarot readings."

"Oh, don't! Just think of all the beer-bellied mother's boys on those sites! Anyway, you're being way too pessimistic. The year isn't over yet."

"You're right. I'll probably bump into the love of my life on the way home."

"It's possible."

A knock on the door caused Lisa and Hannah to turn. Through the frosted glass they could make out what looked like a man, wildly gesturing to be let in.

"We're closed for the day!" Lisa called.

The man put his gloved hands together as if in prayer and moved to bend his knees.

"Did one of the dads forget something?" Hannah went to answer the door.

"Or someone waiting to ambush us!" Lisa called after her.

"Oh, yeah. He's sure to have his eye on the remains of the mashed-up chocolate marshmallows," Hannah said as she opened the door.

"Thank you!" the man said. He walked in, desperation showing on his face, and removed his hat and scarf to reveal big ears and chin-length hair. Presumably the haircut was influenced by the ears. His tragic expression and brown eyes made him look like a dachshund who wants to jump up on a lady's knee but knows he's not allowed. Cute, somehow.

"What can we do for you?" Hannah asked.

He only had eyes for Lisa. No words passed his lips; it was as though someone had taped his mouth shut.

"Hello?" Hannah looked at him with a frown. First he insisted on coming in, now he was ignoring her? "What do you want?"

"What?" He turned to face her. "I'm sorry, I was . . . I mean, I'm . . ."

"Go on." Hannah glanced sidelong at Lisa, and her smile of amusement faded as she saw that her friend was in a similar state of shock.

"Um, yes, I wanted to ask . . . Please tell me you're open the first week in January! And that you have a place for a four-year-old girl!"

"You're in luck," Hannah said. "We're only closed tomorrow, back on the second, and we can take another child, yes."

"Thank goodness!" The man sighed. His eyes returned to Lisa. "You've saved my life!"

"Are things that serious?" Hannah asked.

Mr. Dachshund nodded. "Yes. I've got a really important project I need to have completed by the end of next week. My mother was going to take care of my daughter for me, because daycare isn't open until January sixth. But today, of all days, she slipped on a patch of ice and fell. Now she's in the hospital with both legs broken."

"Oh, that's really bad luck!" Lisa finally found her voice, although she didn't sound very regretful.

"You could say that!" the man replied, giving Lisa such a broad smile that it was hard to believe his poor, dear mother was lying in the orthopedic ward of the hospital. It would have been more fitting if she had run off to the Dutch Antilles with a lottery-winning millionaire.

"We're pleased to be able to help," Lisa said. The pout was back, but a supersweet one this time.

"You can't imagine how relieved I am." He lowered his gaze and his voice. "You see, I'm a single parent."

Oh. Hannah had to exercise every ounce of self-control not to break out in hysterical laughter at this twist of fate.

"Well, I'll just run across to the office and grab a registration form," she said, and left the two of them alone.

"What's your little girl's name?" she heard Lisa ask.

"Luzie," he replied.

"What a pretty name! That's what I'd call my daughter if I had one."

"Really?"

Hannah put a hand to her mouth to suppress a laugh. That was just . . . crazy!

As she looked for the registration form for new children, she corrected herself. No, it wasn't crazy. It was lovely.

Just as lovely as the fact that she was going to spend the evening with Jonathan—because the truth was, she was looking forward to it a lot. What luck that Lisa had turned down her invitation to accompany them. Hannah sent a short, silent thought out to Simon. Up to his cloud, or wherever he was sitting: *Don't take offense, my love. But I have an inkling that I might fall in love sometime during the coming year. It's what you wanted for me, after all. And you know what I always say: watch your thoughts!*

# ACKNOWLEDGMENTS

I would like to thank . . .

Bettina Steinhage, my editor at Lübbe. You once told me that you had always wanted to work with me. After this, our first project together, I can only say one thing: I would like to work with you again—OFTEN, please! Thank you, thank you, THANK YOU! You are AMAZING!

Wibke Bode. Not only a wonderful friend, but also an excellent doctor, who has been ready with her advice on all my medical questions.

My cousin Heike Lorenz, for the brainstorming session on my sofa. I'm so glad to have you in my life!

My friend Sybille Schrödter, for the discussion on the subject of happiness in life.

My friend and colleague Jana Voosen, for her valuable input and suggestions as beta reader.

Alexandra Heneka, my wonderful dramatic adviser—what would my stories be without your support?

Holger Vehren of the Hamburg Police press department for his constant readiness to offer useful information and advice.

Regine Weisbrod, a wonderful editor, who supported me in the development of the plot.

Dr. Petra Eggers, the best agent ever. There is nothing I can add to that.

Jutta Verständig for her expert advice on the tarot, and for the private readings.

The Laufwerk Hamburg team (www.laufwerk-hamburg.de), who were my sports experts, explaining all I needed to know about running speeds and heart rates for the opening scene with Jonathan.

My cousin Caroline Dimpker, Nicole Dolif, and Adriano Liotta of *Mamma* Leone on Eppendorfer Weg in Hamburg, for polishing up my rudimentary Italian.

The whole of the brilliant Lübbe team: Klaus Kluge, Claudia Müller, Torsten Gläser, Stefanie Folle, Marco Schneiders, and Christian Stüwe. It's lovely to know that you believe in me!

Production manager Anja Hauser for the fantastic design.

My daughter, Luzie. Whenever you laugh with me I know what life is all about. Mine, at least.

Matthias Willig. Thank you for everything. EVERYTHING! And in particular for drawing to my attention Erhard F. Freitag's quote: "If it hits home, it's usually true. And if it's true, it hits home."

I am particularly grateful to Sebastian Fitzek, who was kind enough to allow me to raise him to megastar status in this novel. Thank you, Sebastian! And it's true.

I'd like to say one more thing:

The rejection letter from an editor used in this novel is a REAL document. But I won't reveal the identity of the author who received it (only that he or she—who knows?—went on to become very successful), and not even that of the editor who sent it . . .

To nip any speculation in the bud, I was NOT the poor person whose mailbox it landed in.

*Last but not least: Thanks to Mama and Papa.*
*Without you, I wouldn't be here.*

# ABOUT THE AUTHOR

*Photo © Bertold Fabricius/pressebild.de*

Charlotte Lucas is the pseudonym of Wiebke Lorenz. Born and raised in Düsseldorf, she studied German, English, and media studies at Trier University and now lives in Hamburg. In collaboration with her sister, she has written more than a dozen bestselling novels under the pseudonym Anne Hertz. In *Your Perfect Year* Charlotte embarks on a search for the answers to the large and small questions of life.

# ABOUT THE TRANSLATOR

*Photo © 2019 Trina Layland*

Alison Layland is a novelist and translator of German, French, and Welsh into English. A member of the Institute of Translation and Interpreting and the Society of Authors, she has won a number of prizes for her fiction writing and translation. Her debut novel, the literary thriller *Someone Else's Conflict*, was published in 2014 by Honno Press, followed by *Riverflow* in 2019. She has also translated a number of successful novels from German and French into English. She lives and works in the beautiful and inspiring countryside of Wales, United Kingdom.